Secrets
at
Meadowbrook
Manor

Faith Bleasdale

avon.

Published by AVON
A division of HarperCollins*Publishers* Ltd
1 London Bridge Street
London SE1 9GF

www.harpercollins.co.uk

A Paperback Original 2018

2

A catalogue copy of this book is available from the British Library.

ISBN: 978-0-00-830696-0

This novel is entirely a work of fiction. The names, characters and incidents portrayed in it are the work of the author's imagination. Any resemblance to actual persons, living or dead, events or localities is entirely coincidental.

Typeset in Birka by Palimpsest Book Production Limited, Falkirk, Stirlingshire
Printed and bound in UK by CPI Group (UK) Ltd, Croydon CR0 4YY

MIX
Paper from
responsible sources
FSC C007454

This book is produced from independently certified FSC paper to ensure responsible forest management.
For more information visit: www.harpercollins.co.uk/green

For Jo and Keith, thanks for all your
support and inspiration.

Chapter 1

Gemma Matthews rang the buzzer, rubbing her gloved hands together and stomping her feet to try to ward off the cold. She had taken the bus, but still had a twenty-minute walk to get to the residential home. Despite the fact that she did the journey frequently, it was still a difficult one, in more ways than one.

The door was opened by Sarah, one of the carers at the home.

'Gemma, come in, come in,' she said, kindly, grimacing as a blast of cold air shot through the door. 'Blimey, it's freezing.'

'Hi,' Gemma said, still able to see her own breath. 'How is she today?' Gemma's voice wobbled, as it always did when she asked after her nan.

'Not too bad, love,' Sarah replied.

Gemma nodded and made her way in.

The warmth of the nursing home hit her as soon as she closed the door behind her. She wrinkled her nose at the familiar smell; the aroma she now associated with old age. Kenworth House was a residential home specialising in taking care of dementia sufferers. Unfortunately Gemma's nan was one of them, and she'd been here almost a year, ever since Gemma became unable to care for her at home. She signed

1

in at the big marble reception desk, her signature like a spidery mess across the page. If it wasn't for the smell, Gemma would think she had walked into a five-star hotel – the home was grand and expensive, which was reflected in its interior. Although Gemma knew they were struggling to afford to keep her nan here, she was determined. She had never been so determined about anything in her life, and now it seemed that determination had paid off.

She took the stairs up to her nan's room on the first floor. Out of habit, she knocked on the door before opening it straight away. She took a breath; every time she walked through this door, she had no idea what would greet her. Would her nan recognise her? Would she welcome her even? One thing she had learnt about dementia was that it was riddled with inconsistency.

'Hi, Nan,' she said as breezily as she could, going straight over to where her nan was sitting. She bent down to kiss her cheek, breathing in the familiar lavender scent that characterised Gemma's childhood, her family.

Her nan was staring out of the window, something Gemma often found her doing. She had a lovely view over the grounds of the home, which were vast with beautifully kept sweeping lawns, and flower beds ready to spring into colour. Her nan had always loved gardens, and Gemma was glad that she had this view.

'Gemma?' her nan asked uncertainly as she turned to her. Relief flooded through Gemma; it was a good day.

'Yes, Nan, and I've brought you some flowers.'

She took a bunch of wild flowers out of her bag, and put them under her nan's nose. Her nan smiled as she smelt them. One of her passions in life was gardening – her nan's not

Gemma's. Gemma remembered how weekends would be spent with her nan digging, planting or weeding while Gemma would read a book outside if the weather was good, watching her, being close to her.

'And of course your favourite wine gums.'

She handed them to her. Gemma liked bringing wine gums; when she was a kid, her nan would bring home packets from the post office on a Friday, and it would be a treat that Gemma looked forward to. After a fish and chip supper, they would share the wine gums. It was nostalgic but the only way Gemma felt she could cling to her past.

'Thank you, love,' her nan said with a slight smile.

'Let me put the flowers in water,' Gemma said quickly.

Her nan's room was large, with a plush beige carpet, a bed, with an old-fashioned eiderdown covering it, and two chairs arranged around a small table. When her nan first moved in, Gemma had brought her favourite pictures to put up, including her wedding photo and a photo of her and Gemma when they were on holiday. The rest of the room housed a few of her books, which sat on a small shelf, although they were largely unread.

Gemma picked up the vase with the flowers from her last visit, which she deposited in the bin before going to the sink to rinse the vase and fill it with fresh water. She arranged the flowers, put them on the table and then sat in the chair next to her nan. She was bursting to tell her her news, but she had learnt that in order not to startle her nan, she needed patience.

'So,' she asked slowly, 'how are you?'

'Oh I'm just grand, love,' her nan said with a smile. Her hands shook slightly as she gestured for Gemma to open the wine gums.

The door opened and Sarah came in.

'Can I get you ladies a nice cuppa?' she asked.

'Yes please,' Gemma replied. 'Tea, Nan?'

'That would be lovely, thank you,' her nan said.

As Sarah disappeared, Gemma took a wine gum and smiled.

'Nan, I have some news,' she started.

'Oh yes?'

Gemma saw the woman who had brought her up, the woman who was the rock in her life, until the cruel illness descended on their lives, ruining everything. Her face was the same, but her brain wasn't. When, like today, her nan recognised Gemma, she felt as if she'd won the lottery.

'You know I told you that I was going to apply for a new job?' Her nan shook her head, and Gemma felt angry with herself. She should never ask her if she remembered anything. 'Sorry. Anyway, I applied for a new job. As a hotel consultant to set up a new hotel in a gorgeous, gorgeous manor house.' Her words wanted to rush out of her mouth, and Gemma told herself to calm down. But she had never felt this excited before.

'Oh yes?' Her nan seemed to be following this.

'Meadowbrook Manor. It's in a small village in the Mendips. Anyway, the family are turning the house into a small hotel, or that's the intention, and they've offered me the job of helping them to open it.'

Technically, only one of the family had offered her the job, Pippa Singer; she hadn't met the others yet, which was a little strange. Or even seen the house in person, which was stranger still, but Pippa had insisted that she was perfect for the job without her even visiting and after only one interview. Gemma had jumped for joy when she phoned to tell her. No one had ever called her perfect before – no one apart from her nan.

'Well that sounds lovely, what good news.' Her nan's eyes shone. She gave Gemma's hand a squeeze. 'I'm very proud of you, you know.'

Gemma's eyes filled with tears. It was small, tiny, but it felt as if she had been handed the world.

'Yes, it's a dream job, and the best thing is that it comes with accommodation, so when the bungalow sale goes through I won't have to worry about where to live. And until then the salary means we will manage the fees more comfortably.'

Her nan's eyes flickered at that.

'The bungalow?' she asked. 'I don't quite . . .' She trailed off. She looked at the open packet of sweets in her hand as if she didn't know what they were. And Gemma knew she had lost her for today. It happened like that sometimes – one minute she was there, the next, she couldn't find her.

Sarah returned with tea and placed it down. Gemma picked up the mug and thanked her. Her nan was staring out of the window once again.

'Are you all right?' Sarah asked.

'Oh yes,' her nan replied. 'My daughter was just telling me about her new job.'

Sarah looked at Gemma, who had gone from elation to sorrow. In one easy move.

'You mean your granddaughter, love – it's Gemma,' Sarah said kindly. The staff at the home said that sometimes it helped to trigger memory if you corrected her, although Gemma could never bring herself to.

'Oh yes, of course, my granddaughter,' her nan said without a hint of recognition, and she popped another wine gum in her mouth.

Chapter 2

'Here we are, love,' the taxi driver said as he pulled up, got out of the car and held the door open for her.

Gemma eagerly stepped out, and an involuntary gasp escaped her lips as she could only stare, in awe, at the house in front of her. The house that she had craved so intensely to be inside was right here, in all its wonderful glory.

Despite the fact she had stared at the photograph of Meadowbrook daily, she still hadn't been prepared for its actual magnificence. Nothing could have prepared her for that. Like an old-fashioned doll's house that every little girl coveted. She had stared at the photo so many times it was tattooed on her brain. She had felt herself being drawn into it. She had studied the tall oblong windows as if she could see herself behind them. Peering out onto the circular drive, waiting for . . . well, she wasn't sure what the "her" behind the window was waiting for, although whatever it was, in this house, it would come. She knew that it would come.

She couldn't tear her eyes away, forgetting that the February drizzle was making her blonde shoulder-length hair frizzy and her best suit damp as she gaped, goldfish-like, at the place that would be her work and also her home for the next few months. How on earth had this happened? Part of her wanted to do a jig, another part to cower in the taxi forever.

'Impressive, isn't it?' the driver stated. Gemma could only nod as she pulled her purse from her bag and held some notes out to him. 'Best house in Parker's Hollow, probably in the Mendips,' he continued as they both stared at the Georgian manor house, which seemed, ridiculously, to be staring back at them.

In real life, the house was enormous. Grand, with impressive windows and an imposing front door. The drive and immediate entrance were immaculately kept, neat bushes lined up, and statues that looked genuinely aged, covered with moss, stood guard. The surrounding countryside, fields, trees, hedgerows complemented the house and even the air smelt different. A bird, or number of birds, squawked in the background as she gulped in the air; she was no longer in the city. She was in paradise.

'Right you are, love,' the driver said, bringing her back to the present as he handed over her change, and with a kindly wave he got back into the car.

Part of her wanted to run after the cab, part of her wanted to run up to the front door and burst into her new, albeit temporary, life.

Gemma tried to arrange her face into a smile, but the nerves that were jangling around meant she was unsure if it was a grimace. She gave herself a bit of a talking-to – something she had been doing a lot in the last few weeks – and she tried to smooth down her hair, which she now imagined was sticking up in all directions.

She was about to start her dream job. When she applied for it, back in December, she didn't for one moment believe she would get it. It seemed like such a golden opportunity, she rationalised that hundreds of people, at least, would apply, and she wouldn't stand a chance. But somehow, she was about to embark on a six-month contract, staying at Meadowbrook Manor, to act as their hotel consultant. Six months living at Meadowbrook, helping the family set up their new hotel, it was the opportunity of a lifetime. And it was her opportunity. She still couldn't believe it. She couldn't believe she deserved it. She didn't deserve it.

She took a breath as she watched the taxi disappear completely from view. Inside the impressively stunning house, waiting for her, were her future employers: the Singers. She was anxious about meeting them all. The speed between the application, her interview with Pippa and her being here now was less than two months; therefore, she had barely had the chance to process what was happening. Even when she had told her nan about it, it still didn't feel real. But, as she grabbed her suitcase and half wheeled, half hauled it up towards the front door, she knew what she'd been given was undeniably a gift. Now all she had to do was to do a good job and prove that Pippa was right to hire her. She hoped, prayed that she could do just that.

After all, there was no turning back.

Pippa Singer opened the door with a huge welcoming smile. Gemma couldn't help but be happy to see her new boss. She was beautiful, warm, kind and unlike anyone Gemma had ever met before.

When, knees literally knocking, Gemma had walked into the coffee shop in central Bristol and gazed around, she immediately recognised the stunning blonde woman, who was sitting at a table nursing a coffee, as Pippa. Meadowbrook and the Singer siblings had quite an online profile, mainly owing to the work they did at their animal sanctuary. Pippa was not only beautiful, but when Gemma tentatively approached her, she had also acted as if they were long-lost friends. For a minute, Gemma's nerves disintegrated, as she was mesmerised by this woman.

The interview flew by at an amazing speed. Pippa oozed warmth and kindness as she asked Gemma questions not just about her professional life, but her personal one as well. Pippa proved herself an open book, as she offered information about her family and Meadowbrook without Gemma having to ask a single question. She perhaps shared a bit too much information, Gemma thought. For her part, Gemma told Pippa how much she loved the house from the photo – now, she blushed slightly at the memory of how she had gushed about it having a personality and a soul. But Pippa had lapped all that up and said that she clearly "got" Meadowbrook.

Afterwards, back at the hotel where she worked in Bristol, she mulled it all over. It was the most unorthodox interview Gemma had ever attended – not that she had been to many – and when she got a phone call the following day saying the job was hers, she had to pinch herself a number of times. But Pippa had been adamant that she was perfect for the job, for Meadowbrook. She sent over an official offer, the start date being set for the first of February, which meant she had Christmas and January to sort everything out. She had been counting the minutes until she finally got to meet Meadowbrook in person, and she felt as if she spent the whole two months dazed and waiting for her phone to ring, only to hear Pippa say that she had made a terrible mistake, she meant to hire someone else. But that hadn't happened.

'Oh, Gemma, I'm so pleased you're finally here,' Pippa gushed, throwing her arms around her once again as if she were a long-lost friend. Gemma dropped her suitcase in surprise and then winced as it caught her foot. 'Sorry, sorry, do come in.' Pippa took the luggage and stood back to let her in. 'I insisted on my siblings not being here; I didn't want to scare you off before you even got to look at the place. But I have to warn you that once you've unpacked, they'll be waiting for you. Everyone's so excited to meet you.'

Pippa was breathless, and Gemma still hadn't spoken yet.

'It's lovely to see you again,' she finally managed, intimidation stabbing her, coupled with relief that she didn't have to step straight into the lion's – or Singer siblings' – den.

As she stepped into the grand hallway she felt herself shaking slightly – she was *in* the house! Just as she imagined herself being. The entrance hall seemed as big as her nan's bungalow, where she had lived all her life. With its polished parquet flooring, art dominating the walls, and the biggest vase of fresh flowers on an antique carved console table, it was unlike anything Gemma had ever seen. As Pippa grabbed her arm reassuringly, Gemma was rendered mute.

'So, where shall we start?' Pippa clapped her hands together. 'I know, I'll show you to your room. It was Harriet's room, but she doesn't live at the house anymore, so I thought I'd put you in there; it's such a lovely room. Also, it'll give you a feel for what the hotel might be like. God, can you imagine we are going to have paying guests here one day! I almost can't believe it's actually going to happen!' Pippa was hopping around, she was so animated and effervescent, the human equivalent of champagne, Gemma thought.

'I know, although of course there's a long way to go,' Gemma cautioned, trying to chase the blind panic away as it threatened to floor her. 'But it'll be lovely to see my room and get rid of my bags. Honestly, Pippa, I really want to thank you again – this is a great opportunity.' Gemma sounded like a stranger to herself as she spoke. She needed to collect herself, to stop acting so weirdly lest she lose the job before she even started.

'Oh no, thank you, I just knew that you were the one to help us from the moment I met you . . . no, before that, when I read your letter and CV, and I also know we are going to be the best of friends.'

Gemma was startled as Pippa engulfed her in a second embrace.

Settled into what was now her bedroom for the foreseeable future, she finally remembered to breathe. If Meadowbrook was to be her home for at least six months, while she helped the Singer family set up their hotel, she needed to think of it as such. She wasn't sure she would ever get used to the luxury she found herself in, but she was going to have to try. She needed to start embracing her good fortune rather than behaving like a rabbit caught in the headlights. After all, Pippa was so welcoming; she could only hope the rest of the Singers would be the same.

She unpacked her case; she hadn't brought too much with her, some work suits and a limited casual wardrobe. She didn't have far to go to the bungalow in Bristol if she needed anything else, but it felt presumptuous turning up with too much.

She went over to the floor-to-ceiling window of the

bedroom, which looked out onto the front of the house. With views over the Mendips, she was mesmerised. It was as she imagined when she looked at the photo, the woman in the window. That woman was her, it was actually her.

She pulled all her books out of her oversized bag and put them away in the bedside table. They were text books she'd used when she took her hotel management course, and she was praying they would help her now. Because it was a dream job, yes, but also a rather big job, and she had no idea how she was going to manage . . . She pushed the negative thoughts away and thought about how she had got to this. Throughout her life, people had put her down, not her nan, but almost everyone else. This job was supposed to end all that, give her a new start. She was not only doing this for her nan, but she was also doing it for herself.

She knew she was far too cautious, and always had been. Gemma took the safest option when she could, owing to her upbringing, owing to an ingrained fear that never left her. Her nan, who had brought her up, and was her only family, tried her best to bolster her confidence, but her vulnerability dominated her life.

And now her nan wasn't around, and Gemma felt alone. At first, the dementia wasn't too bad. Gemma could juggle her college course and taking care of her nan, but in time it got worse. Hence the residential home.

Missing her nan was something that would never go away. Watching someone you love slip away from you, however it happened, was the most painful thing. She wanted her nan, the woman who she knew, the one who tried to encourage her, who made her feel loved. But, unfortunately, after visiting her, she often ended up feeling lonelier than ever.

Now, though, in Meadowbrook she was being offered a fresh start, and God knew she needed it badly. It was a gift, she thought again, as she wiped tears off her cheeks, and she needed to make it work. Those were her new mantras, and she would keep repeating them, until she believed them.

Chapter 3

A knock on the door interrupted her myriad of thoughts. 'Hello,' she said, and after a beat, Pippa appeared.

'Is everything all right?' she asked. She had pulled her hair back, Gemma noticed, and although dressed casually – jeans, a sweater – she still looked elegant. Gemma glanced down at her suit and wondered if she was overdressed. But then she was starting work, and her nan always said first impressions were crucial.

'This room is stunning,' Gemma replied truthfully. From the king-size bed with the upholstered headboard and luxurious bed linen, which felt how she imagined lying on a cloud to be, to the en suite bathroom, this was better than she could ever have imagined. 'Honestly, if the rest of the house is like this, people will be beating your door down to stay here.' She smiled, trying to sound confident, to sound like the Gemma that Pippa had hired, not the scared little girl she was a minute ago.

'Oh! That's so lovely of you to say.' Pippa flushed pink. 'It's so important to me to make this work. You see, it's sort of the only real job I've ever had, and I haven't even really started yet! But I need to prove that I can do this, and I know you are the person to help me. Anyway, enough about that.'

Gemma was getting used to the idea that Pippa jumped from topic to topic. She had got an inkling of how much opening the hotel meant to her when they first met. Pippa explained how she had gone from living with her father – who had now passed away – to getting married in her early twenties to a man who had hurt her very badly. She didn't know the full story, but Pippa was so open she assumed she probably would at some stage. And Gemma felt a huge responsibility to help her. She was determined to do so.

Gemma stood up. She caught her reflection in the large, ornate full-length mirror and it took her by surprise, for a moment.

She'd undergone a bit of a makeover before her job interview; a long overdue image change. Her dark blonde hair had been lightened and cut into shoulder-length layers, giving it the illusion of thickness. She started wearing make-up, only a bit, but it did brighten her up. Gemma had never thought of herself as attractive, mainly because no one apart from her nan ever told her she was. But not anymore. New job, new Gemma, and now all she had to do was to meet Pippa's family and help them to open a hotel. How hard could it be?

She followed Pippa down the long, curved staircase, once again marvelling at the house and almost losing her footing. She couldn't begin to imagine how it would feel to live in it, or to have grown up here. A fantasy life.

'They're in here, the dining room,' Pippa said as she opened the door, stepping back to let Gemma go first.

Sitting around the most enormous dining table, she found herself looking at the rest of the family. She gulped and tried to find a smile.

The dining room was every bit as magnificent as she expected. She was so busy staring at a huge portrait of a handsome man, a beautiful woman with three small children and a baby, which she knew must be the Singer family, that she walked into the table.

'Ow,' she said, reddening and rubbing her hip.

'Are you all right?' Pippa asked as her family, all sat along one side of the table, looked at her with puzzled expressions.

'Sorry, I was looking at . . .' Words failed her.

Collecting herself, she concentrated on the siblings, who she felt she knew from her Internet research. Despite the fact that two of them had dark hair (Harriet and Gus) and one of them blonde like Pippa (Freddie), they shared familiar similarities. There was also an older woman, and another man with messy brown hair and a smile that almost put her at ease, who she assumed must be Gwen and Connor from details that Pippa had shared and she had committed to her memory.

Gwen was the family's housekeeper and second mum. She was semi-retired but she still pretty much ran the domestic side of Meadowbrook. Connor, her son, was Harriet's boyfriend, and they lived together in one of the cottages she'd passed on her way here. Gwen lived in the other. Gemma was piecing it all together in her mind, trying to keep track and concentrate. She needed to make sure she knew and remembered everything.

Freddie looked a bit like a male version of Pippa and was one of the most handsome men she had ever seen – he looked like a film star. The photo she had seen of him didn't quite do him justice; he was even more gorgeous in real life. As he smiled at her, her knees buckled, but she grabbed the table to steady herself.

Next to him sat Gus, who was handsome in a more

traditional way; hair flecked with grey, dark brown eyes and a serious expression. Harriet was undoubtedly attractive, well groomed and had an air of sophistication about her – they were a good-looking family. Intimidatingly so. Especially Harriet, whose demeanour was sharper and who was still eyeing Gemma with suspicion.

If Gemma were normal, she might have felt a stab of jealousy. Here she was, with no family except for a nan wasting away in a nursing home, and here were they, all attractive, living in luxury and having each other. But Gemma didn't do jealousy. Envy maybe, but not full-blown resentment. It wasn't in her nature.

'This is Gemma Matthews,' Pippa said with a flourish. 'Gemma, from left to right, that's Freddie, Gus, and Harriet.' She paused and smiled. 'And of course Gwen, who's lovely and the best cook ever; she'll help us to design all the menus for the hotel. And finally Connor, Harry's boyfriend who runs the animal sanctuary and is also a vet.'

'Hello,' Gemma said. She was gripping the table so tightly her knuckles turned white.

There was a woof and a shaggy Old English sheepdog rushed out from under the table and bounded up to Gemma.

'Oh, and not forgetting Hilda,' Pippa said as Gemma bent down to stroke her.

Well the dog was friendly at least and gave her a chance to try to compose herself. Whether she was nervous, intimidated, terrified or a combination of the three she was unsure, but she needed to pull herself together. She hadn't yet managed to get through an hour at Meadowbrook – how would she manage six months?

'Sit down,' Harriet commanded, sounding formal.

Gemma immediately did as she was told. She knew that Harriet used to work in investments in New York and had a reputation as quite a "ballbreaker".

'Right,' Harriet continued. 'Sorry to jump right in, but Pippa hired you before she actually told us she had even interviewed anyone.' She didn't sound delighted and Gemma felt uneasy at this piece of news.

'But, Harry, you said I could take the lead with the hotel,' Pippa objected.

'Well yes, and I know we've been through this a thousand times, but Gemma needs to understand that it's still a family business,' Gus pointed out, although he smiled reassuringly at Gemma. 'Pip, decisions this big should be shared.'

'Exactly,' Harriet added.

'I agree,' Freddie concurred. 'The thing is, Gemma, that this is our hotel, not just Pippa's, and I know my little sister is a little overenthusiastic about it but well, I also think that we should have met you before she offered you the job.'

Gemma felt her heart sink. They were going to sack her before she'd even had a chance to see the whole house at this rate. Perhaps she shouldn't have unpacked.

'Hang on,' Pippa said. 'Of course the hotel is a family business, which is why you are all here, but I am going to take charge, we agreed, so I think that I was perfectly within my rights to hire Gemma.'

As Gemma's head swung between the siblings, she wondered just what was going on.

'If you really believed that then why didn't you tell us before you actually offered her the job?' Harriet pushed. 'Instead of just having her turn up.' She smiled, slightly smugly, having made her point.

Gemma would not like to argue with Harriet.

'It was a surprise,' Pippa said, but she glanced down at the table a little shamefaced.

Gemma's heart sank. Pippa didn't have the blessing of the others to hire her, and she had done it without them because she didn't want them to disagree with her. Which she had a feeling they would have done. She couldn't imagine Harriet hiring her in a million years. Harriet would have hired someone more like herself, probably.

'Oh, great way to run a business.' Harriet's voice was laced with sarcasm. 'If only I'd managed to run a multimillion-pound trading desk by surprising everyone.'

'Now hang on, this isn't the same thing,' Pippa argued. 'And I know you wanted to be involved, but I thought as I would be working the most closely with the hotel consultant then I should have the final say.'

'Well it is almost the same, because it's our future,' Freddie countered. 'The future of our family home.'

'And therefore we need to agree on the big decisions,' Harriet persisted.

Gemma wondered if she should just leave. It was as if they had forgotten she was there.

'Hold on,' Gwen said. 'Before you all descend into a massive argument in front of Gemma, and let's face it, we've been through this enough times before she got here, perhaps we should give Pippa and Gemma a chance.' Her voice was calm and reasonable, and Gemma wanted to throw herself into her arms. 'After all, she's here now.'

'I agree,' Connor said, earning himself a scowl from his girlfriend. 'No, Harry, I mean I agree with you, Pippa shouldn't have gone behind your back, but . . . So how about you let

Gemma show you that she's the right person for the job?' He leant over and kissed Harriet's cheek as she pretended to pull away from him without actually doing so. They were clearly in love – it was written over both their faces.

'A probation period then,' Harriet said.

Gemma groaned inwardly. It was like being given sweets and then having most of them taken away again.

'That's a good compromise,' Gus reasoned.

'One month.' Harriet stared at Gemma, who looked at the table.

'I'm OK with that.' Freddie shrugged.

'I guess that's fair,' Gus added.

'Well, I suppose I don't have a choice.' Pippa didn't sound very keen.

Nor was Gemma. She thought about the fact that she had left her job for this, and the fact that her nan's bungalow would be sold soon and she would have nowhere to live. Not to mention the care home fees that needed paying. She needed this job. She had no choice but to do whatever it took to keep it. She decided to take a chance, to seize the day, something she had never done before, but something she vowed she would do from now on.

'Can I just say,' she started, trying to ignore the wobble in her voice, 'I have given up a full-time job to come here, and I was overjoyed at the idea that I would get a chance to help you to set up a brand-new hotel, but if you aren't able to agree with each other, I'm not sure how this is going to work.' She paused as she felt all eyes on her. 'I mean it is a family business as you've pointed out, and the future of your family home, so before we start, everyone needs to be on the same page.'

'Good point, Gemma,' Gwen said. 'Don't worry, love, they

bicker a lot. You'll get used to it, but when the chips are down they all support each other. Don't you?' Gwen glared at each of them in turn.

'Of course we do,' Pippa mumbled. 'Gemma, will you accept a trial period, just to keep the peace? After all, I knew as soon as I met you, you were right for Meadowbrook, so therefore I have every confidence in you, even if my siblings don't in me.' She folded her arms.

Gemma felt sick. She had to resist holding her hands up and saying she wasn't sure she could do it after all. But then again she thought of her nan, before she got ill, telling her that she was capable of so much, that she needed to aim for the stars and start taking risks. It was one of the last, most lucid conversations they'd had. She needed to take her words on board. She owed her that much.

'Of course. I'm confident in my abilities and am happy to prove it to you all,' she replied, feeling her leg shaking under the table and hoping she was a good liar, because she clearly needed to be.

'Right, well that's all decided.' Harriet finally smiled. 'So, welcome to Meadowbrook, Gemma, and perhaps we can now all go to the kitchen and have a nice cup of tea and some of Gwen's famous cake.'

'Great, thanks.' Gemma felt relief pumping through her veins, although she also felt a bit faint.

'Or I could make a cocktail?' Freddie suggested.

'Fred, it's only three o'clock,' Gus said.

'All right, all right, tea it is then.' He rolled his eyes.

Gemma felt as if she had jumped, or rather stumbled over the first hurdle. Hilda sat at her feet and thumped her tail against her leg. She had won over Pippa and Hilda, Gwen and Connor seemed supportive, so just the other three to go then.

The rest of the afternoon passed in a pleasant blur. Harriet was a little warmer towards her – slightly south of Siberia anyway, as they sat in the largest kitchen that Gemma had ever seen, apart from on *Downton Abbey*. Gwen put the most sumptuous-looking cake in the centre of the kitchen table, Connor and Gus made tea, and as they all sat around the less formal table, Hilda settled herself by the Aga and promptly fell asleep. It was such a family scene, Gemma thought, but one that drew tears to her eyes, as she had never had a family like this. Visions of Sunday afternoon tea with her nan and her, sat alone around the small Formica table, illustrated her childhood. Her granddad died before she was born. Her father left days after her birth, followed four years later by her mother. She hadn't seen either of them since. Her nan took over Gemma's care with a devotion that she knew she was lucky to have.

Gemma loved her nan and she couldn't have wished for more love in her childhood. She hated to sound as if she were ungrateful, but she often wondered what would have happened had her parents not left. When she was younger she fantasised that they hadn't, that they had stayed together and given Gemma siblings. Pure childish fantasy.

'Harry, I have to get back to the sanctuary,' Connor said, standing up, putting his hand on Harriet's shoulder and kissing her.

Gemma noticed the smile creep into Harriet's face, making her look so much prettier than she did when she was scowling.

'I'll be down later. Leave anything you need me to do in the office.'

'Gemma, you should think yourself lucky that you were interviewed by Pippa. When Harry had to hire an admin officer for the sanctuary she practically reduced every candidate to tears. All they have to do is make coffee and file and yet she acted as if she were hiring the next CEO of a multinational,' Freddie quipped.

'I am just thorough,' Harriet snapped, then smiled. 'But I did hire the only person who didn't burst into tears.'

Gemma didn't know why she was speechless but she couldn't find her voice.

'There's part of me who will always think I'm a woman on a trading floor having to show a bunch of sexist men who's boss,' Harriet continued. 'So I will apologise for that ahead of time.'

'Well, the hotel business is definitely competitive,' Gemma said, finally able to speak.

'We might get on just fine then, because I'm nothing if not competitive,' Harriet said, putting her hand out, palm flat towards Gemma.

Gemma ducked as if she were about to be hit, and Harriet rolled her eyes. Freddie laughed and even Gus looked amused. Gemma chastised herself – of course Harriet wasn't going to strike her. What was wrong with her?

'I was going for a high five, but never mind,' Harriet said, shaking her head.

'Gemma, tomorrow I'll give you a tour of the land – I've got a buggy,' Freddie offered.

'And he's not afraid to use it,' Gus quipped.

'I hope you're not too fainthearted,' was Harriet's parting shot.

Gemma *was* pretty fainthearted, but she had a feeling that she needed to change, and fast, to fit in here.

Chapter 4

A beeping interrupted her dreams and as she woke, Gemma wondered briefly where she was. She fully opened her eyes, feeling momentarily content as she looked around marvelling at her surroundings. She stretched and felt as if her whole body had been rested. It was definitely the most comfortable bed she had ever slept in, and there was no denying that the bedding was of the highest quality, nicer than that of the last hotel she worked in. She had learnt all about thread counts and Egyptian cotton bedding, and her guess was that this was pretty damn expensive. Meadowbrook was pure luxury already, so to turn it into a lovely boutique hotel didn't seem like much of a stretch. Although she had a long, long road ahead of her.

Last night she had eaten dinner with Pippa and Freddie in the kitchen. The others all had plans, but Gwen had prepared a meal – apparently she normally did – which they warmed up in the Aga. Gemma, having been too nervous to eat much in the days leading up to her arrival at Meadowbrook, devoured every delicious mouthful. Freddie had chatted about his ideas for a specialist cocktail bar as he kept the wine flowing.

Gemma had sipped the expensive-tasting wine cautiously.

'Don't you like wine?' Freddie asked, refilling his and Pippa's glasses but noting hers was still almost full.

'Yes, but I'm just not much of a drinker,' Gemma replied, taking a sip.

Freddie gaped at her in horror. Thankfully, Pippa had saved her by gushing about how much of a success the hotel was going to be now she was on board. The upside was that they didn't expect much from her; the downside was that filtering all the information being thrown at her was quite exhausting.

After they'd eaten, Gemma had pleaded exhaustion and had headed off to bed early. There she washed, changed into her pyjamas, set her alarm and then settled down with her text books, reading as much as she could before she must have fallen asleep.

There was so much going on, and she needed to process it, but she was feeling very overwhelmed. She told herself it was only day one, and she had, if she survived her probation, six months to get plans for Meadowbrook together, so there was no need to panic just yet. But Gemma was good at panicking.

She sat up in bed and wondered what they would need to do to the room she was in. It was pretty perfect. Expensive wallpaper on some walls, Farrow & Ball paint on the others, along with furniture of the highest quality. There was a pale pink chaise longue and a pale grey velvet armchair, a dressing table with a stool that matched the chaise and a walk-in wardrobe, bigger than Gemma had ever seen. It looked shamefully understocked with Gemma's clothes.

The en suite bathroom was also ridiculously luxurious, putting the beige suite in her nan's house to shame. When

Gemma thought about her daily routine there – the shower above the small bath that trickled rather than gushed and was never quite the right temperature – she couldn't compare it. This was a million miles from what she was used to. The huge bath was brass coloured and was almost big enough for a family of four. The shower had its own compartment with a glass wall along one side and the largest showerhead she'd ever seen. The basin and loo matched the bath; basically, the whole room looked as if it had stepped out of an interiors magazine – which she was pretty sure it had.

Gemma thought, briefly, how she wished people could see her now. Sat up in the huge bed, about to start the job of a lifetime. Firstly her nan, who would be so proud to see her doing so well. Then those who hadn't been quite so supportive. There was a long list, but at the top would be her ex-boyfriend, Chris, who had done his best to destroy what little self-esteem she had before dumping her when her nan took priority over his needs. And then her ex-boss, Clarissa, who took the tiny bit of self-esteem that she had escaped Chris with and tried to stamp all over that. They had nearly succeeded, but not quite, because she was here. She couldn't believe it. Boring, ordinary Gemma Matthews was at Meadowbrook Manor.

She told herself off for getting carried away. She wasn't here to gloat and of course, she needed to be vigilant; she had a huge task ahead of her. Being the sort of person who rarely got noticed throughout her life, Gemma noticed everything. That was one of her best skills, and she was sure that the key to the Meadowbrook Hotel was to find out what the house and the Singer siblings were really like, to unearth their personalities, to understand both the house and them fully. The hotel business was competitive and to stand out from the crowd wasn't going to be easy. But she believed the answers lay somewhere within Meadowbrook's walls.

Reluctantly getting out of bed, she opted for a quick shower – which didn't disappoint – before dressing. Her heart sunk as she realised that she really hadn't thought that latter part of it through. Not just because her clothes didn't in any way reflect the glamorous surroundings, but also because next to the stylish Singer sisters, she felt dowdy. She had brought work suits – all grey, navy and brown – and very few casual clothes. And compared to Pippa and Harriet in their expensive jeans and soft cashmere jumpers, her clothes were cheap and outdated. Looking at the few bits she'd brought, she realised she'd stand out, for the wrong reasons. God, even Gwen was more fashionable than she was. She tried to breathe and told herself that she wasn't going to cry or fall apart over her clothes. She would explain to Pippa that she hadn't been sure what to bring and she would ask advice. After all, she could always go shopping at the weekend, although she would have to watch what she spent.

Previously, Gemma hadn't the time, the money nor the energy to worry about what she looked like outside work. She had never been much of a girly girl. She didn't make friends easily and the few friends she had tended to be as uninterested in fashion as she was. At her last job the women she worked with had all been bitchy and seemed to look down on her, mainly because of Clarissa, who had taken an instant dislike to Gemma and ensured everyone who wanted to keep their jobs followed suit. Pushing her dark thoughts away again, she turned her attention to getting ready.

She opted for a pair of dark blue jeans and a red jumper, which had seen better days but weren't too bad, she supposed.

27

But she still didn't look like the Gemma she was trying to be and therefore she didn't feel like her. Confident, capable and attractive, that was who she needed to be. That was who she wanted to be, and she would strive to get there. She needed to take pride in herself, not just for shallow reasons, but also it was time she began to believe what her nan had been trying to tell her all her life – that she was good enough.

Feeling like a visitor – which of course she was – she tentatively made her way downstairs, taking her time, drinking in her surroundings. She studied each piece of art, wondering what the origins were. She took her phone out and took photos – they would inspire her when she was working in her room, hopefully. She made her way to the kitchen, to find Pippa already there looking both groomed and beautiful. She was making a pot of coffee and munching a piece of toast at the same time.

'Good morning, Gemma. I was going to bring you a drink, but then I realised I don't know if you prefer tea or coffee, or how you take it,' Pippa said, smiling warmly in greeting.

'Coffee please, just white please, no sugar.'

Gemma went to stand by the Aga, enjoying the warmth. She watched how Pippa glided about the kitchen, making everything look effortless. Gemma sighed inwardly – would she ever be able do that? She took a seat at the kitchen table and when Pippa handed her her coffee, she decided to try to claw back some control.

'Tell me about how the house runs at the moment,' she asked, pulling out her notebook. She was going to ensure she had it on her at all times. No detail was too small to miss.

'Of course, Gwen took care of everything really; we've only just convinced her into semi-retirement. She used to live here.

I'll show you her apartment; it's at the back of the house. But because only Freddie and I are here, she moved back into her cottage. Between you and me, she's got a sort of boyfriend, Gerry, and I think she wants her own space for their relationship.'

'So who takes care of the house now?' Gemma couldn't see Freddie with a pair of Marigolds, that was for sure.

'We have a cleaning company that comes in twice a week. Gwen manages them – we daren't mess with her when it comes to this house! We also have a local girl, Vicky, who comes up three times a week. She does a few bits, laundry and ironing. She also works for Harry and she cooks from time to time. The idea is that she will take on a bigger housekeeping role when the hotel opens. She's quite keen to do more cooking as well, and so we are sort of training her up, or Gwen is anyway. None of us can really cook – we were terribly spoilt by Gwen. We still are.'

'So the place is well looked after?' Gemma asked, making a note and adding Vicky's name to the back of the book with all the people she needed to remember.

'To be honest, at the moment Meadowbrook runs itself. I try to help tidy and clean sometimes, but it does take a lot to run the estate – Daddy taught us that. For example, Freddie and I organise the Meadowbrook events, which isn't profit-making but we hold them to raise money for the sanctuary, and we involve the whole community. Parker's Hollow is incredibly important to us, and with regards to the hotel we will have to keep that in mind.'

'Fair enough.' Gemma wondered just what the community was like – she hoped they wouldn't be against the hotel, but that was a worry for later. 'I can't wait to see the famous sanctuary.' Although she had heard a lot about the sanctuary, she hadn't quite got her head round it.

The Singers' father had set it up with Connor, because he was passionate about animals and wanted to make sure they were cared for. It started small but had grown and was quite well known nowadays, which Pippa explained was a double-edged sword. People came if they wanted to adopt a dog or a cat, but they also knew if they left animals here they'd be looked after. So it seemed when one was re-homed more would appear. They also had farm animals that were permanent residents and two alpacas. How this fitted in with a luxury hotel, Gemma had no idea.

'Well, of course it's at the heart of Meadowbrook now, and we have to raise money to keep it going, so that takes a lot of organisation. Our next big event will be the Easter party, so you can see how that works. But we also open our gardens every month, and we get coach trips booking to visit, even in winter. Anyone from the village can come in for free, but for outsiders we charge.'

Gemma was scribbling furiously. 'I did some research and saw the gardens were an attraction,' Gemma said. Although again, a luxury hotel break being interrupted by coachloads of people coming to admire the gardens; well that was another conundrum for her.

'Our roses won a big award at a national show last year and it's all gone berserk. It's Gus's baby, along with his partner, Amanda, now, so I'll let him tell you about them but yes, they are a growing attraction, and they generate a nice amount of income for the sanctuary.'

'So when the hotel is open you still intend on having all these events?' Gemma's brain was beginning to tick over.

'Well of course, the hotel will be a separate company and hopefully make money – or Harry will have my head – but we'll still need to raise money for the sanctuary. And well, that's as far as I've got really. I did think about us using here as a wedding venue too.'

'Pippa, if people want to stay somewhere quiet they might not want a coach full of people to appear suddenly, or to be part of the events.' She saw Pippa's beautiful face drop and immediately felt guilty. Why when she was only pointing something sensible out, she didn't know, but Pippa did look crestfallen. 'But that's OK, I will keep that in mind when I'm coming up with ideas.'

Gemma was even more unsure how it all would work, but she kept telling herself that it was early days and she didn't need all the answers right now. As long as she got them at some point . . .

'Oh! Thank goodness. I knew you were the right person. It's just, well, Meadowbrook is Meadowbrook and you'll soon see that, so the hotel has to reflect that. We have to keep our father's vision alive with whatever we do, you see. But of course you already understand that.'

'I do?' She did?

'The covering letter you sent in with your CV, about the soul of Meadowbrook.' Pippa tilted her head.

'Of course, Pippa, of course,' she reassured her. After all, that she did understand. The animal sanctuary, annual events and coachload of gardening enthusiasts she wasn't quite as sure about.

'Freddie, are you sure I'm not going to die?' Gemma's voice was carried into the wind, and if he heard her, Freddie didn't answer.

Gemma was holding on to the side of the buggy for dear life and trying to decide whether or not it was less scary with her eyes shut. On reflection, it was slightly less nauseating with them open. She snuck a glance at him – he was driving very intently and too fast across a bumpy field, up towards the lake. However, she couldn't help but think, again, that he was the best-looking man she had ever been this close to, or met. Even if he was also the worst driver.

Her ex-boyfriend, Chris, was nothing to rave about, although to be fair, neither was she. He was a couple of inches taller than Gemma who was five foot five, he had mousy brown hair, eyes that her nan always said were a bit too small and unremarkable features. She knew her nan didn't think much of him – in her pre-dementia days – but it was only now she could see that it was because he was constantly putting her down. At the time, she felt they were perfectly matched – two people who would pretty much go unnoticed through life. But Chris still thought he was too good for her, and he never tired of reminding her, until he left her, as most people in her life seemed to do.

Gemma's nan always told her that feeling sorry for yourself was unattractive and Gemma tried, tried really hard, to remember that, but sometimes she failed. It was as if she couldn't shake the expectation that everyone would leave her. And now, in many ways her nan had too, although she also knew that that wasn't her choice.

So, the new Gemma was trying even harder. Although she didn't have Pippa's ethereal beauty, or Harriet's striking looks, she wasn't unattractive. Since her makeover she was beginning to think she wasn't too bad at all. But a lifetime of feeling unremarkable wasn't just going to go away overnight. It was more inside than out. She was still a work-in-progress, especially at Meadowbrook where she was surrounded by beautiful, confident people, who reflected the house perfectly. Perhaps some of that would rub off on her if she were lucky. Or if she survived this buggy ride.

'You probably won't die. But at least you'll feel alive when we reach our destination in one piece,' he finally replied, screeching to a halt. '*Voilà*, the lake.'

They both climbed out of the buggy, and although her legs were still a bit jelly-like, she surveyed the horizon. It was a cold, crisp day, and the light bouncing off the lake reflected that. It was so peaceful, the winter sun shimmering on the surface as the water lay flat, and apart from the odd birdcall, it was blissfully silent.

'Do people fish?' she asked, finally.

'No, we swam in it as kids though, and I think Harriet still does sometimes. Not me – I prefer the indoor heated pool. There are public footpaths through the land, so we do get walkers, which is fine. Why, do you fish?' Freddie grinned.

'No.' Gemma wondered why he made her feel so awkward. 'I was just asking – you know, for the hotel.' She went closer to the lake, stumbling as she caught her foot on a large unseen stone.

'Bloody hell, don't fall in,' Freddie said, moving to help her as she righted herself. 'It'll be freezing. No, I wouldn't think we'd want to attract men in waders and suchlike anyway. No, my vision for the hotel is more *Bright Young Things*.'

'You want to attract bright young people?'

He turned to her, his lips curling up. 'No, well yes, but I mean like the film. Glamorous young people, having good old-fashioned fun and drinking cocktails made by *moi* – you know, I've done a cocktail-making course. Via the Internet, but still, they sent me a certificate.'

Gemma wondered if Freddie was joking, but for once he looked serious.

'You can learn via the Internet?' Gemma asked, trying not to sound as astounded as she felt.

'Yes, of course. They put loads of videos up, so I not only learnt recipes, but also technique. Even the whole throwing of the cocktail shaker, although I wasn't very good at that. But I perfected the mixing. I am officially a mixologist now. Well, I think I am. And tonight I will show you, and you can sample some of my signature drinks. I intend to be in charge of the bar at the hotel, and I'm going to design the drinks menu. It's my area of expertise after all.'

'Well, I'm not much of a drinker, remember.' Gemma was terrified. He was so sure of himself, although he didn't seem arrogant. She could only dream of a fraction of his confidence. She wondered if he would spare her any.

'Bloody shame.' He shook his head in disgust, and Gemma realised she might have to start drinking cocktails to keep the job.

'But I'll look forward to sampling some of your concoctions, of course.' She attempted a laugh.

'Oh brilliant, and if I were you I'd get good and hammered tonight.'

'Why's that?'

'You've got a meeting with Harriet tomorrow morning. She's much easier to deal with with a hangover, believe me. Right, come on, I'll show you where we host our main events and then take you to the animal sanctuary. Back in the buggy.'

'If I have to,' Gemma mumbled under her breath.

Just as she thought she was getting the hang of all this, she felt the ground being swept from under her again. Literally this time, as the buggy seemed to take off into the air.

She was so pleased to have her feet on the ground again, she almost threw herself down to kiss it. They had parked up at the animal sanctuary, and as Harriet had gone somewhere for supplies and Connor was working at the vets' practice, Freddie – with the help of Amy, one of the full-time workers – gave Gemma the tour. Amy clearly had a crush on Freddie, as she hung on his every word and practically ignored Gemma. Freddie was flirting with her masterfully, but then Amy was young and pretty, so why wouldn't he?

'So, how many animals do you have?' Gemma asked as they started by visiting the dogs.

'Loads,' Freddie replied. 'Would you say, Amy?'

'Oh yes,' Amy breathed. 'Loads.'

Gemma was sure it wasn't going to be the most informative tour ever.

She rubbed her temples. The dogs, who were incredibly excited and loud, had given her a headache, although she felt so sorry for them, all abandoned when they should have been in loving homes. She tried not to think that she could identify with them. They moved on to the cats, who were much more calming. The chickens were a surprise, as Freddie seemed very fond of them, and then she had been introduced to – yes, really – two alpacas, four pigs, three mini ponies, a donkey, a blind sheep, her "guide" lamb and three goats.

'So the alpacas, Sebastian and Samantha, are a bit stuck-up,' Freddie explained.

'Really?' Gemma noticed they seemed to be doing their best to ignore her.

'I think they think they're better than us, but anyway, come on, there's more to see.'

Gemma shook her head.

She tried to remember all the animal names, but there were so many, as Freddie told her the brief history and Amy showed how competent she was with each one – including the hoity alpacas, by petting them, or in the case of the pigs, giving them some food.

Gemma wasn't much of a country girl – in fact, she wasn't a country girl at all, so she was finding it quite intimidating. Even Cookie, Clover and Brian, the miniature ponies who were sweet and tiny, managed to scare her a bit.

'See over there . . .' Freddie pointed to the next field, where there were two cows, both with impressive horns, although one was much bigger than the other. They looked pretty aggressive. Freddie was standing very close to her, and Gemma could feel the heat radiating from him. Amy approached and wedged herself to Freddie's other side. Gemma nodded.

'That is David. You see, we had two gay cows.'

'Gay cows?' Just as Meadowbrook couldn't seem any more eccentric.

'Well bulls technically, as they're boys. David, who you see there, and Elton.'

'Elton and David?' Gemma wondered if she were dreaming.

'Yes, they weren't the friendliest to others, but they adored each other. Sadly, Elton died.'

'Oh no!' She felt sorry for David suddenly.

'Funny story, actually. Well not Elton dying, that was awful – we all cried that day – but I run the social media and I tweeted it and everyone thought that I meant Elton John had died, so it sort of went viral. Then I had to explain quickly that it was Elton, the gay cow, but it had already made a newspaper, and I got in a fair bit of trouble with Harriet, but it did get us a lot more Twitter followers, so it's not all bad.'

'So who's the cow, or bull with him now?'

'She's a cow, and after Elton died, David was pining badly, so Connor thought he would try to find him a companion. Well this poor cow who had been treated quite badly came up, and so Connor somehow got them together and they seemed to get on. Between you and me, I think she's a bit of a fag hag. She's called Madonna.'

'Of course she is.' Gemma couldn't help but laugh. This might be the maddest place she had ever been, but it was also the most entertaining. She realised how little she laughed in life, and with Freddie she felt like laughing a lot. This was a positive, and she was going to hold on tight.

Chapter 5

Gemma groaned when she opened her eyes. Her head felt fuzzy and heavy, not a sensation she was used to. In order to impress Freddie, she had made an effort last night to enjoy his cocktails, which he'd mixed for her and Pippa in the drawing room, and it hadn't taken much to get her drunk. Oh God, she was mortified.

She'd embarrassingly had to go to bed just as Freddie was getting into his (Martini) stride. She vaguely remembered Freddie making a cutting comment to Pippa about why on earth she had to hire such a lightweight. Oh God, she rubbed her temples. Pippa had said that she didn't make her applicants drink as part of the interview process. Freddie said she should have done, and Gemma tripped on the stairs, screamed, and they both had to help her up to bed.

She would have been offended if the stairs hadn't been moving. She was also too busy trying to see only one Pippa and one Freddie.

Gemma vaguely remembered saying to Pippa, as she helped her into her room, that she had no nice clothes, and she had an even fuzzier recollection of Pippa saying she would help. She wished the details were clearer. She wasn't quite sure, but she seemed to recall that Pippa said their father wouldn't let them spend much money for the year after he died – did that make sense? He'd given them a small allowance to live on, so they'd had to buy clothes in charity shops. She couldn't see Harriet Singer, or Freddie, wearing second-hand clothes. Maybe she dreamt it. Maybe she had a drunken reality that wasn't real at all. And this was why she stayed away from alcohol most of the time. Or actually it wasn't – staying away from alcohol was another way in which she wasn't normal.

Abandoning her failed attempts to go back to sleep, she shuffled out of bed and put on her gym clothes. It was only six o'clock, but she was going to use the gym, hoping that she might begin to feel better. It was such a privilege, having a gym on tap. In her last job she wasn't allowed to use the hotel gym – it was for guests only, and she couldn't afford expensive city gym membership prices, so she had joined a local running club. She wasn't very good at it, but she enjoyed the feeling exercise gave her, so she looked forward to the weekly group, when her nan's health allowed. She'd given it up for a while, but when her nan went into the home, she had started running more and more, and now she felt that she needed it – it seemed to help to keep her sane. It allowed her to breathe.

She was grateful not to bump into either Pippa or Freddie as she made her way down to the basement. Meadowbrook was a different world. Yesterday, she had been given a full tour of the house, and she'd been taken to the garden room, which hadn't been used for years, because apparently it reminded Andrew Singer, their father, of his late wife. It had been her favourite room, and when she died he shut it away; it hadn't even had the door opened until recently. Pippa said they sort of forgot about it, which seemed ridiculous.

Gemma couldn't imagine living in a house where you had enough rooms that you could shut one off and not notice, but that was Meadowbrook. The garden room did what the name said, and opened out onto the garden, which would make it wonderful for the hotel. Although the siblings were nervous about it, Pippa said they realised that it was time to lay the last of the ghosts to rest – especially as they all hoped their mum and dad had been reunited wherever they were now. It was quite moving as they surveyed the room, which was at least as large in size as the drawing room.

Although at the moment it was dusty and full of old furniture, one of the walls was practically made up of floor-to-ceiling French windows currently covered with heavy velvet drapes. She realised it must have been so painful for Andrew Singer to shut off such an amazing room. It would take a lot of work, but she could see it being Freddie's bar. In the day, guests could enjoy coffee, tea or light refreshments while enjoying the garden view, and in the evenings, it would be perfect for cocktails. In the summer, the doors could be opened, so that they could use the terrace for outside drinking and dining. Gemma began to get excited, as she could see it becoming a reality. Then the enormity of the task she had undertaken hit her once again, and she shrank back to uncertainty.

Trying to ignore the niggling doubts in her mind, she concentrated on the treadmill. She made a mental note when she went home for the weekend to pick up her swimming costume; the pool looked so inviting, perhaps she could add a daily swim to her routine. She knew she was already drawn into Meadowbrook, and she dreaded to think what would happen if she got fired after the probationary period.

She could only imagine what it was like growing up surrounded by this luxury, but at least the Singers were all trying to do something with Meadowbrook, which Gemma now understood. Because Pippa and Freddie were rattling around at home, and Meadowbrook felt as if it were a house that needed to be filled with people.

Yes, Gemma could see it being one of the most appealing hotels in the area. What with the beautiful house, set in the stunning grounds, you couldn't fail to have a luxurious, relaxing, perhaps even romantic break here. She still wasn't sure where the sanctuary would fit in with that, but she felt, instinctively, that somehow it would. Romance over the alpacas? She wished she felt confident enough to say what she thought sometimes; then she wouldn't come across as so uptight. She wished she were more like Freddie, or any of them actually.

Gemma headed into the kitchen after finishing her run, having showered and dressed in a simple pair of jeans and a white blouse.

'Oh hi, Gem,' Pippa said.

'I used the gym, I hope you don't mind,' Gemma mumbled.

Pippa looked so stylish in a plain black dress and tights with her hair pulled back from her beautiful face. She felt a stab of envy again. Where and at what point did life decide who would be pretty, rich and with a family who adored them? Or like her, unremarkable, worried about money, average in most ways and with parents who didn't like her enough, let alone love her, even to stay in her life? How was that even fair? She tried to push her thoughts to the back of her dusty mind. What was wrong with her?

'Of course not, you need to treat this place as if it's your home, honestly.'

In theory, Pippa was someone to dislike for literally having it all, but there was nothing about her that you could remotely take offence against.

'I'm so sorry about last night. I tried to warn Freddie I wasn't a drinker but, well, I don't think he realised how much I meant it.' Gemma flushed.

'Oh, don't worry. Fred is a terror. He feeds everyone his lethal cocktails. We have reined him in a bit. He was off the rails at one point – ten times worse than now. I mean he does like a drink, it's not a secret, but actually he can handle it now, and he can also go days without one. To be fair he doesn't often, but he can. Anyway plying you with cocktails, it's almost The Freddie Test.'

'Then I well and truly failed. He seemed very disappointed.'

'Oh don't worry about him, he'll be fine. Harriet's going to meet you in Dad's office in twenty minutes. She wants to explain everything; she doesn't think I've given you a thorough background to us and to Meadowbrook. She's probably right. I get so excited you see, I just get carried away.'

'I understand,' Gemma said carefully. 'And I guess Harriet is rightly protective of all of you, as well as the house.'

'Yes, that's exactly it! I knew you'd understand. I knew instantly when I met you, but I also knew if I let Harriet get involved she'd try to take over. I knew that this hotel didn't need a carbon copy of Harriet, which is exactly who she would hire; it needed someone like you.'

'Well I'll do my best for you,' she replied, feeling the pressure being loaded on top of the layer of flattery. Yes, she could see that Harriet would have taken over, and she saw Pippa in a bit of a new light. She was ballsy to go ahead and hire Gemma without the others knowing. She wasn't as meek as she sometimes came across.

'Oh, and when you've finished with Harriet, I'm going to help you with your wardrobe. I feel awful that I didn't tell you that you'd need more casual wear than suits, but we're about the same size and I've got loads of spare clothes. I've also got scruffier things, which you'll need when you get more involved.'

'What do you mean?' Gemma startled. Although, most of her clothes were tatty actually.

'Ah, perhaps I should have explained this before, but you see we all have our jobs at the animal sanctuary and, actually, it would be really good if you'd join us and help out – we think it'll give you more of a feel for the place.'

'You mean I have to work with the animals?' Gemma heard the horror in her voice and felt her heart sink.

Visiting the sanctuary had shown her how terrifying she found most of them. Surely they wouldn't make her muck out the pigs, or deal with that scary-looking bull? Or even Madonna. And the hostile alpacas. This was not in the job description. Although thinking about it, not much was in the job description.

'Oh, don't worry, it'll be fine. We all felt that way when Daddy said we had to in his will, but we all came to love working at the animal sanctuary and you will too.'

Pippa beamed and Gemma thought she must be mad. She would rather have a meeting with Harriet every day than do that.

Gemma sighed deeply, tried to remember her "calm" mantra and knocked on the office door.

'Come in,' a clear, well-spoken voice rang out.

Gemma said a silent prayer and pushed the door open. She stepped into the study, which still very much belonged to Andrew Singer. A huge mahogany desk dominated the room, with Harriet sat looking seriously terrifying behind it. There were some landscapes on the walls, very much in keeping with the rest of the house, a modern TV screen on another wall, and two leather sofas along with a drinks trolley, which looked pretty well stocked. The most dominating thing about the room, though, was a huge portrait of Andrew Singer. It was as if he were in the room with her.

'Sit down.' Harriet pointed at the sofa, facing the desk.

Gemma did as she was told and tried to look at Harriet rather than staring at the image of her father.

'We haven't changed a thing about our father's study,' she said, her voice softening as she spoke of him. 'Apart from putting the painting of him in here. It was upstairs – Dad was a little vain you see – but it seems right here, in his study.'

'I understand,' Gemma said carefully. 'I guess this is his personality right here too.'

'Yes, yes it is. I know when we open this hotel, if we do—' she narrowed her eyes at Gemma, who felt her cheeks flame '—then I suppose this will have to be changed, but it's so hard to eliminate him.'

'I don't see why you'd have to. This room isn't going to be used by guests, so as long as it's a functional office, you can have it as you want it. You might need to reorganise if more than one person needs to work in here. It might be nice actually, make you feel that your father has a place in the hotel.' Gemma hoped she hadn't overstepped the mark.

'I hadn't thought of it like that. Yes, you're right, I like that.'

Harriet almost smiled at her, and she sensed a little thawing. Gemma nodded. 'Right, well I suppose that's by the by. I wanted to speak to you because I doubt very much Pippa has given you the background.' The thaw had frozen over again.

'Perhaps only a potted history,' Gemma admitted.

'My sister is bright, beautiful and enthusiastic. She is committed to this project, more than any of us, but we have all decided to support her. Did she tell you about her divorce?'

'A bit, yes,' Gemma admitted.

'It knocked Pippa's confidence, so she needs this. She's never been a career woman but now she wants to be, and I for one want to make sure that happens. And of course, none of us want to see the house empty, and apart from Pip and Fred, none of us want to live here. Did you hear about last year?' Gemma shook her head, although she had. 'Right, well you know our father, Andrew, died suddenly, and it was a terrible shock to us all.'

'Yes and I'm sorry.' Gemma thought she could see a tear glistening in Harriet's eye. She liked the tiny human glimpses she got from her, but she wished there were more of them.

'Right, well yes, but anyway, that was when I came back from New York. My father, who had, shall we say, eccentric ideas, made a will, which meant all four of us had to live here, in this house, for a year. And we had to keep the animal sanctuary open, which is his great love – was, I mean – or we would forfeit our inheritance.'

'So you all lived together for a year?' Gemma knew all this, but was interested to hear about it from Harriet's perspective.

'Yes, and of course we hadn't lived together since childhood, so it was interesting to say the least. The year was tough for us all.'

'In what way?' Gemma asked, wanting to hear more.

'Oh many ways. But that's by the by. The upshot was that in the will, Dad stated that the house had to be kept in the family. So when Pip and Fred came up with the idea for opening the house as a hotel, Gus and I agreed, well eventually we did, because the house needs to be used and this seemed like a good way to ensure all the family could be involved.'

'I agree, and it will very much be a family hotel,' Gemma stated, trying to sound authoritative. She wanted to hear more about the year they'd spent together – it was intriguing – but Harriet was once more all business.

'Quite, although none of us agree exactly how at the moment, which is why your job isn't going to be easy. But enough of that. Right, well, I want to go through the details with you. The salary is fine. In fact, before Pippa hired you, I did the budget for set-up costs. I'll give you a copy, and if you do a good job then you'll be worth what we're paying you.'

Gemma felt more than relieved. Not only was she getting a good salary, much more than she used to earn, but also she was living rent-free, so in theory she should be able to ensure her nan's care was covered until the house sale went through. She almost wanted to hug Harriet, although she was far too scared to do so.

'I hope to prove to you that I am the person for the job,' Gemma said, her confidence increasing.

'Well if you're not, you'll be out. Sorry to be blunt, but this is our home, it's our passion, especially Pippa's, but it's also a business. Somehow we have to make money, or at least not lose any. You see, I have taken over the running of the animal sanctuary, which we are expanding, but I also look after my father's investment portfolio. I'm not going to pretend that any of us are in danger of poverty, I can't apologise for the fact that my father was awfully rich, but at the same time Meadowbrook is important for the animals, for the village, for the family and for our future generations, so I will do all I can to protect it. And besides, I like to succeed, so the hotel has to be a success.' She laughed, but she was obviously far from joking, and Gemma's new-found confidence fled as quickly as it arrived.

'So your role in the hotel?' Gemma asked, hoping her voice wasn't as shaky as she felt.

'Finances. I'll look after the money, which is what I do best. Gus isn't bad, but he prefers to look after the gardens, and he also paints, so I'm not sure how much use he'll be.'

'So, you're happy for me to carry on, trying to figure out how best to go about opening the hotel, for now I mean?' Gemma asked.

Harriet had shown her an almost human side. The way her features softened when she talked about her family was endearing. She was sure Harriet was ambitious and driven and even ruthless, but she seemed caring – she was hit with a wild notion they could be friends. But that was probably temporary insanity.

'For now. But you see, we all have different ideas, which might be a problem. I see a luxury hotel for professionals wanting to get away from their day-to-day lives – I almost think a kind of corporate retreat. Freddie thinks it should be full of beautiful people who want to spend time watching him make cocktails and getting drunk. Pippa wants to help those who have had their hearts broken – I don't know how on earth she thinks she'll manage to target them, by the way, unless we become the anti-Tinder, and Gus wants it to be a creative place where guests can explore their artistic side.'

'I see.' She really didn't.

'Well you probably don't.' Harriet stared at Gemma, who felt exposed under her gaze. 'And I'm not a tyrant, I do understand that this isn't going to be easy for you and honestly, I do want to support you. But I'm hoping you'll be able to see all that for yourself soon. I just want to reiterate: the house needs to maintain its personality. It also has to be beneficial for the village, Parker's Hollow, and the community as a whole. My father's memory needs keeping alive, and of course the animal sanctuary, the gardens, all have to be incorporated somehow.'

'Goodness,' Gemma started.

'Oh yes, and Pippa has to feel as if she's really achieved something. Fred as well to be honest.'

'Wow.' Gemma couldn't help but stare at Harriet. She really did expect a lot. What she described wasn't a hotel; it was a whole world.

'Yes, wow, but if you're as good as Pippa says you are then it shouldn't be a problem, should it?'

'Um, no. No, of course not.' She shook her head.

'Good, I'm glad we had this chat, and we've come to an understanding. Hopefully, we'll be friends in no time.'

'That would be lovely.' Gemma was surprised that Harriet would want to be friends with someone like her, but she also felt her heart lift a bit. It might be possible, after all.

'Right, what's your favourite animal? After all, we want you to get started at the sanctuary for the full Meadowbrook experience. The alpacas are quite fun.' Her lips twitched.

'Really?' Gemma's eyes filled with horror.

'No, not really, I'm teasing. The alpacas don't like anyone much, although they seem keenest on Connor. Do you have a preference?' Harriet spoke as if it were totally normal to be having this conversation.

'The cats.' She didn't hesitate – after her tour, the cats were definitely the easiest and the least scary. She had never had a pet, not even a hamster. Her nan offered to buy her a goldfish once, but it hadn't come to anything.

'Great, I'll put you on the feeding and petting roster. It's very sad that our domestic animals are waiting for loving homes. Really, I wish we could re-home them all, but it's a process, so we're always looking for people to come in and spend time with them – they need affection and love, as well as food.'

Again, Harriet took Gemma by surprise, she sounded so heartfelt.

'I'd be delighted.' She was delighted, because it wasn't the alpacas.

'Right, so tonight we're all having dinner here at the house – we try to have a family meal once a week at least – so you'll meet Connor, Gwen and Gus properly. Unfortunately Amanda can't make it, but you'll meet her soon. Tomorrow, in fact. The gardening club are due, so it would be great to spend time with them and Gus, getting to know the gardens.'

'It all sounds great.'

It did, Gemma thought, feeling a little cowed still, but she also felt a stirring of hope. Harriet was scary, she was confident, and she clearly knew what the purse strings needed to be doing, but at the same time, she seemed fair and reasonable. And if she needed to cuddle a few cats to keep her dream job then she would be happy to do so. She might feel a bit browbeaten and out of her depth, but she also would do anything to keep the job here at Meadowbrook and make it a success. She needed it. But more than that, she realised that she really, really wanted it.

'This is fabulous, Gwen,' Harriet said as they sat around the formal dining-room table. Gemma was overwhelmed by family mealtime at Meadowbrook. Her family meals consisted of herself and her nan and whatever was on special in the supermarket that day. Her nan wasn't a bad cook, but she made traditional things, lots of mashed potatoes, vegetables and meat and nothing considered "foreign". Tonight they were eating a pasta dish, which was made from scratch, even the pasta. Gwen always cooked the food for family night; she wouldn't have it any other way. The sauce, which was tomato-based, was the nicest Gemma had ever tasted, and all the vegetables were grown at Meadowbrook. There was also home-made garlic bread, and a fresh salad – again from the Meadowbrook garden.

'If you serve food like this, you'll have people flocking to the hotel,' Gemma said.

There was an easy chatter around the room. Everyone, even Harriet, was relaxed as she and Connor shared some affectionate looks and touches. Gemma still had her guard up, but sitting here, seeing how the family operated, she almost wanted to let her barriers down. Almost but not quite, hence why she tried to stick to comments only relating to the hotel.

'Thank you, that's what we're hoping,' Gwen said. 'We thought it would be a feature that we serve as much food that we grow here as we can, and if we don't grow it here, then we buy local products.'

'What about meat?' Gemma asked, noting there wasn't any and nor had she had any since being here.

'Well,' Connor started, looking around the table, 'we're pretty much vegetarian, you know with the animal sanctuary and everything. Well I am anyway, as is Harry, but Pippa, Gus and Freddie eat some meat.'

'Was your dad vegetarian?'

'No, that was the irony of Andrew Singer: he rescued animals but he did eat them, well none from the sanctuary, of course, but from the local farm, and well, he justified it by not justifying it, really,' Gwen explained. 'Andrew made up his rules as he went along.'

'Fred's inherited that from him,' Gus said.

Freddie scowled but didn't argue.

'When I got involved with the animals, I just couldn't eat meat anymore. I have to admit, I do eat fish sometimes,' Harriet added. 'So I have put a ban on rescuing fish in the sanctuary.' She laughed again.

'I'm the same,' Pippa said. 'Actually, I'm trying to be vegan, but it's not easy because I really like cheese.'

'I've learnt how to cook more vegetarian food,' Gwen said. 'And I'm starting to look into vegan baking – we need to get ahead of the times, I always think. It's becoming ever so fashionable, after all.'

'You're right, it is,' Gemma said. Her nan wouldn't have coped well with her being vegetarian. Especially as when she was a kid, they ate a lot of meat from tins, which thinking about it might not have actually been meat. 'It could be a great angle for the hotel too.' Her mind started whirring. 'You know, a vegan hotel. I'll do some research, but I'm sure they're not very common.'

'We don't want to scare guests off, though,' Harriet pointed out. 'I think perhaps we should offer a fabulous vegan and vegetarian menu, but we should cater for the carnivores too.'

'And it will create goodwill locally if we buy meat, like Dad did from the farmers,' Gus pointed out. 'My daughter Fleur's a vegetarian and she called me a murderer the other day.' Gus shook his head. 'But then sometimes any excuse to attack me . . .' He focused on his plate.

'And I'm largely vegetarian, although I am partial to the occasional steak,' Freddie offered.

'So not really veggie at all, mate.' Connor grinned. 'More like a flexitarian.'

Connor was so lovely, Gemma thought, very different to Harriet, mainly because he wasn't at all frightening. He was incredibly good-looking in a non-groomed, natural way, but he clearly only had eyes for Harriet, which actually made him even more appealing. He wasn't quite Freddie-gorgeous, though, but then Gemma didn't think anyone was.

'OK, but we can definitely say we specialise in good, local, home-grown vegan food, it'll be a good angle. I'll put it down on my notes and do some research.' Gemma continued to sound professional.

'More wine, anyone?' Freddie said, reaching for a new bottle and pouring it.

Gemma had barely touched hers, and she noticed him glare at her before moving on past her glass.

'The wine is lovely,' she said, trying to placate him.

'How would you know, you've barely touched it?' he pointed out.

'I've had some and it's delicious.' She felt herself colour.

'Never trust a woman who doesn't drink – that's my motto,' Freddie said.

'Don't we know it,' Harriet joked. 'Although after your last girlfriend, you shouldn't trust a woman who does drink, either.'

They all laughed, including Freddie.

'Oi,' Freddie objected. 'But yes, you do have a point. Loretta drank like a bloody fish and was as untrustworthy as they come. Maybe I shall trust you after all, Gemma,' he conceded.

She shook her head. This family was mad.

'Well, I'd like to propose a toast,' Pippa said, raising her glass. 'Welcome to Gemma, and here's to the Meadowbrook Hotel.'

Chapter 6

'**M**y God! It's spectacular,' Gemma breathed.

She was wearing a pair of Pippa's skinny jeans, which she felt and looked good in, an oversized black jumper, wellington boots that were in the boot room and were Gemma's size, and a stylish Barbour jacket. Gemma had been transformed into "country". Even Freddie had done a double take as he passed her in the kitchen.

'Thank you.' Gus looked delighted. He had the family nose, like Freddie, and his hair, greying slightly, was the same colour as Harriet's. Increasingly she saw similarities between the Singers – looks-wise. Personalities were an entirely different matter.

It was still intriguing how four children could be born into the same house, brought up largely the same way and yet be so different. As an only child, she would never have that experience. She often fantasised when she was younger about having a brother or sister. She would have loved to have someone, especially now, with her nan in such a bad way, but she didn't, and she was cross with herself for dwelling on something that had never happened and never could.

Gus was taking her on a walk in Meadowbrook Manor's "back garden". Which, unlike any back garden she had ever seen, seemed to stretch for miles and was surrounded by perfectly trimmed hedges, all the same height.

'Do you measure the hedges?' she asked with a smile.

'No, Gemma, but they are all pretty much the same height – our hedge guy is a perfectionist.' He smiled.

The garden was dotted with beds full of different flowers and plants, leading to the award-winning rose garden, which was not in full bloom now but she couldn't wait to see it when it was. There were a number of water features, which commanded attention, and a large fountain in the centre of the garden. At the very top, separated, were the vegetable gardens, fruit cages and a huge greenhouse. Gemma thought all it was missing was a maze. She wrote that down. But then, where would they put a maze and would they spend their time rescuing a drunk Freddie? She crossed it out.

Gus showed her the benches next, which were recently added so that visitors could sit and enjoy the gardens from every vantage point. He also explained why they had chosen various flowers. It was obviously a lot of work, but it was so worth it.

'But wow, I mean I have never seen gardens this beautiful in real life. Only on TV,' Gemma gushed.

She was struck, suddenly, by how much her nan would love to be here. This was the first part of her life that her nan wasn't part of, that she couldn't be part of, and whatever happened from here on in, it was just Gemma now. Oh, how she would have loved these gardens though.

'What's wrong?' Gus asked, his voice full of concern.

'Nothing, sorry.' She tried to brush a tear off her cheek. What the hell was she doing? This was beyond unprofessional.

'Gemma, are you crying?' His voice, so full of warmth, set

her off and before she could help it, she was properly crying.

'No,' she sobbed.

Gus led her to a bench, where he guided her to sit down.

'Sorry,' she said again.

'Hey, I might be flattered that the gardens reduced you to tears, if they're the right kind of tears, of course.' He laughed.

'Oh, but it *is* just the most beautiful garden I've ever seen. You see, my nan loved gardening. We had a good-sized garden, of course nothing like this . . .' She gestured with her arm. She had told herself to hold back personally at Meadowbrook, but she had to explain her behaviour. 'As I told Pippa, my nan is in a home, she's got dementia, and I miss her.'

Gus gave her a brief but warm hug. 'Hey, I miss my dad, you know. Especially out here, as he loved gardening too. I talk to him while I work. I know your nan's not dead but, well, it must be terribly difficult.'

'It is, but you know, life goes on as they say.' Gemma tried a feeble attempt at a laugh, which sounded more like a gurgle.

'Yes, but you're human and that's what Meadowbrook needs, so if you ever need to talk, I'm quite a good listener, as are the roses I always find.' Gus grinned.

'That's kind of you to say.' He was possibly the kindest man she'd ever met, although that perhaps wasn't difficult.

'I mean it, and you live here as well as work here, so I hope we will all be friends.'

'Even Harriet?' Gemma said, before quickly slapping her hand over her mouth. 'Sorry.'

'Don't be.' Gus laughed. 'Yes, I have a feeling, even Harry.'

'But anyway, back to the gardens. How on earth do you get them this amazing?' Gemma shook her head; she needed to steer herself back onto more stable ground.

'It takes a lot of work, more than I ever imagined when I started working on them. Dad, well he loved the gardens and put his heart into getting them into shape, and we feel that it's a tribute to him to continue his work. My partner, Amanda, who you'll meet soon, deserves most of the credit, as well as our wonderful gardening club. But to be honest, I'm not sure how it will fit in with our guests, which is one thing I wanted to talk to you about.'

'What do you mean?' Gemma detected some concern in Gus's voice.

'Well this hotel, we all have our doubts, apart from Pippa. But even Fred questions it sometimes. You see, who will want to stay here while there's a bunch of old – by the way, don't let them know I called them that – ladies in the gardens at least once a week, sometimes more. Our gardening club are very funny, they're loud and well, perhaps not what you'd want if you're looking for peace and quiet.'

'I see.'

'But at the same time they are crucial to our gardens and more than that, the gardens are important to them. It gets them out, it gives them so much, and we would never take that away from them.'

'It's going to be difficult to characterise this hotel, isn't it?'

Gus had a point. If you're paying a large sum of money to stay in a boutique hotel in the country, did you want squealing old ladies wielding trowels? Oh, goodness, how on earth was she going to pull this off?

'The thing is . . .' Gus said, showing her to a beautifully ornate garden bench and gesturing her to sit, 'Meadowbrook is our father. But now we're all trying to put our stamp on it too. Harriet loves the house and wants it to be successful – in

Harry's mind, being successful means making money. She's not greedy, but still the hotel needs to be profitable because she doesn't do anything that isn't. Fred, as I'm sure you've gathered, wants a party hotel. He used to organise parties and club nights for a living, and was very successful for a while, although of course he drank most of his profits. And although he's calmed down a lot, well a bit . . .' Gus paused to scratch his head '. . . he wants the house to be full of fun. Pippa wants it to be a place to heal people, which as it's not a hospital or rehab, we're all a bit sceptical about. I know what she means, this place does make you better, it made us all better, and it's a very special house for that, but as I said, you can't suddenly open a hotel for broken hearts – everyone would think you were mad.'

'Of course they would.' Gemma smiled. 'And you?'

'I want Meadowbrook to be full of creativity. I worked in insurance before my father died – can you believe that?' Gemma shook her head, although she knew this already. 'Well, I did, and I was boring, miserable and grey. I looked grey, I thought grey, but then I started working on these gardens, and I felt something I hadn't since childhood. I also started painting again – I loved art as a child and wasn't bad at it, but Dad didn't approve – that's another story. So anyway, I kind of want to offer people the chance to garden, paint, bake with Gwen even, work with the animals, get the whole Meadowbrook experience. But then of course that's not an easy thing to put into a package, is it?'

'No, it really isn't.' Gemma felt her heart sinking. After conversations with each of the Singers she was feeling increasingly confused, baffled and totally at sea about what the hotel model could actually be.

'Right, well you've got your work cut out for you. Oh look, there's Amanda and the ladies – come on and I'll introduce you.'

Gemma was crying again, but this time with laughter. The gardening club were the best bunch of women she had ever met, and they also sort of reminded her of her nan, before she got ill. Edie was immediately her favourite, as she took her to show her how she cultivated the amazing roses.

'I've managed to grow some from scratch, and also some hybrids. See, I think of this one as the Singer rose.' She showed Gemma a peach-and-red coloured rose, which was just starting to bud.

'I am impressed, Edie,' Gemma said. 'This is incredible.'

'Well I have loved these gardens for years, and I put my heart into it. It's a real treat for me to get to work on them as well. I mean, who normally gets the chance? Andrew Singer let us all share these gardens, God bless his soul, and I'll always love him for that. Oh, and I had a hip replacement last year too. I'm like a new person now!' Edie gave a jump to demonstrate her fitness, then she grabbed hold of Gemma as she landed, almost taking them both down.

'One day, do you think you'll show me how to look after the roses?'

'Of course I will, love, but now come on, meet the others.'

Gemma tried to remember names – she didn't want to write them down as that seemed rude – but she started forgetting after she was introduced to Margaret, Rose and Dawn. There were ten of them altogether, including Edie, and each was as welcoming as Edie had been. She managed to enjoy hugs and excitement as the women vied with each other to show Gemma their part of the garden. And Gemma lapped them all up.

Amanda, an attractive woman with long red hair, tied back, wearing overalls, which she somehow managed to look good in, stood back and let the women enjoy their time, boasting about their work to someone new. Pride radiated from each and every one of them, and Gemma could see how magic Meadowbrook was yet again. These women largely lived alone in small homes and some lived in a retirement complex in the village. In Meadowbrook's garden, they were given a new lease of life, and they worked hard in return. She also discovered many of them got involved in the Meadowbrook events. She could feel the community spirit radiating from everyone around her, and it made it feel as if Meadowbrook were wrapping around them all like a blanket. She tried not to blink back tears. This felt like family; she missed her nan more than she ever thought possible.

'Hi,' a voice said.

Gemma turned, hoping her eyes weren't too misty, and found herself looking at Amanda.

'I didn't want to interrupt the ladies, but now they've turned their attention to tea and biscuits, I can say hello properly.'

She was attractive, her face a little weathered, which made sense as she worked outside. Although Gemma didn't know Gus well yet, she could already see them as a good fit.

'It's so nice to meet you. I've heard so much about you. And the wonderful job you do with the gardens,' Gemma said, tears fully pushed back.

'We're all lucky to have this to work with . . .' Amanda gestured around. 'Anyway, welcome to Meadowbrook. As someone else outside the family, see me as an ally. They are all wonderful, of course I'm biased with Gus, but they are just so passionately wrapped up in life here, in the memory of their father, that they can seem a little . . .'

'Tricky?' Gemma offered.

'Good way to describe them. Anyway, just so you know, if you ever need to chat, just give me a shout.'

'That's really nice of you.' Gemma felt shy, a bit like being the new girl at school.

'Not at all. Have they got you working at the animal shelter?'

'I'm starting after the weekend – cats.'

'Oh, good call. We have Fleur's two kittens living with us now. They were here, but since Gus moved in with me and Fleur stays every weekend, it made sense. They're pretty naughty though; although my daughter, Hayley, loves them too.'

'It seems you've got a lovely family,' Gemma said.

'It's been a lot of work but yes, we are all figuring it out. The girls get on really well, although Fleur is a bit older, fourteen, which can be a difficult age. Gus is wonderful and I couldn't be luckier to have him.'

'It sounds great.'

Gemma didn't know what it felt like to love someone so much that your eyes actually lit up when you talked about them. She certainly didn't feel that with Chris, did she? Her nan, yes, but then that was different. Chris, well, she wasn't sure how she had let him dominate her for so long. And even then, he was the one who ended the relationship. She never saw it, did she? Now she was beginning to. She was learning that men weren't all like Chris, who cared only about himself and treated Gemma like she was his own shabby doormat. Oh God, it was dawning on her more and more what a fool she had been.

'Oh, there's a downside, Gus's ex-wife is a total bitch. She ran off with his friend, yet she continues to try to make his life hell. And poor Fleur, now she's older, is caught in the middle. I can't really say too much as it upsets him, but I don't think his ex liked it when he inherited from his father, and she doesn't like him being with me. But most of all, she hates that Fleur seems to prefer to spend her time over here at the moment. So, you know, nothing's perfect.'

'Meadowbrook seems as near to it as you can get, though,' Gemma breathed.

'Yes, yes, it really is. Come on, let's go and get tea and you'll hear all the village gossip.'

Amanda gave her arm a squeeze and led the way, and Gemma was more than happy to follow.

Chapter 7

Gemma sat cross-legged on her bed with her books and notes spread out in front of her. She had been at Meadowbrook just under a week, but she was already fretting that her focus wasn't what it should be. Not least because she was going home tomorrow. She had toyed with the idea of splashing money she barely had on a second-hand car, but when she broached the subject with Pippa, she insisted that she borrow her car. Pippa said to think of it like a company car, yet another perk of the job.

She had to go to the bungalow, where she was reluctantly going to stay until Sunday evening to start sorting through some of her nan's belongings. The process from her nan going into the home to her putting the bungalow on the market and now it being under offer seemed to have taken ages, but with the sale going through, she needed to be on top of it all.

Gemma wasn't looking forward to going back. It was as if she had slightly lost herself in her new life, during the past few days at Meadowbrook, and now she was going to be reminded of her reality.

She was also cross about the way she was conducting herself. The way she was with Gus, showing him her vulnerable side. And Amanda had been so open and lovely that

Gemma had told her more than she intended to. Nothing bad, just about her nan, but that was personal, and she was trying to be purely professional. She was terrified of being too open, of crossing the line, and in order to keep the lines clear she had to hold herself back. If she started letting them see her, too much of her, who knew where it would end? She couldn't take that risk, although already she feared she was.

She was here to do a job, not make friends, but with Pippa's insistence on them becoming "great pals", Freddie's attempts to loosen her up, and her fondness for Amanda and Gus, it was already proving difficult. Even Harriet seemed to be blurring the lines, by asking her questions about herself that Gemma didn't really want to answer. Nothing awful, just about her upbringing and her schooling, friends, that sort of thing. But although to most people that would seem normal, Gemma wanted to keep all that to herself. She needed to keep her professional head on; she needed to keep her barriers up. She couldn't afford to forget why she was here.

She was reading about hotel management, hoping her text books, whilst factual, would help her to put some of the nuts and bolts in place, when there was a knock at the door. She scooped the books up and shoved them under the bed.

'Come in,' she trilled.

The door opened and Pippa appeared. As usual, she looked effortlessly gorgeous, even in jogging bottoms and a sweat-shirt, and she always seemed to be smiling. Although she had been warned that Pippa had a temper, and could be stubborn, Gemma had never seen any evidence of this. She hoped she never would.

'We missed you at dinner tonight,' Pippa said, striding into the room and sitting cross-legged on Gemma's bed.

Earlier, Gemma told Freddie – or rather mumbled to him – that she wouldn't make dinner as she had work to catch up on and she'd grab a sandwich later. The reality was that she couldn't face it. She was feeling emotional, so it felt safer to be alone. And she was used to being on her own every evening, since her nan had gone into the home, so being with people, anyone, was taking some getting used to. She knew she was too hard on herself. She expected to know what to do, how to handle the family, but she didn't and that frightened her.

'Sorry, but I really wanted to get stuck into work as I'm off for the weekend.'

'We're going to make such a winning team, I just know it.' Pippa looked at Gemma expectantly.

'Oh yes,' Gemma said, trying to muster up some enthusiasm. 'I totally agree.'

'And we're going to be the best of friends,' Pippa continued, grabbing one of the pillows and hugging it to her chest. 'I mean, I haven't had a proper girlfriend for years. Mark, my ex-husband, didn't like me having friends, so I lost touch with all of them, and then I did get back in touch with one, Bella, but she went out with Connor. And he broke up with her because he was in love with Harriet, and she was so upset she couldn't see me anymore, so I lost her. And of course I have Harry, I suppose, but she's my bossy older sister, so you can be my first post-divorce, real non-family friend.'

Gemma was a little taken aback, although she had come to expect these outbursts from Pippa, which could sometimes be hard to follow.

'Well, of course, but you are also my boss,' she pointed out. Arm's-length, she warned herself.

'I hate to think of myself like that, as a boss. I'd rather think we're partners, and in the spirit of partners we can of course be friends. I really enjoy our chats, don't you?'

'Um, yes.' They were a bit one-sided though, Gemma thought wryly.

'And I am so glad that I divorced Mark. It's taken a while, but I am so much happier now. I didn't realise how unhappy I was until it was over, and I've got Harriet to thank for it really, although we almost fell out over it. We did fall out for a while, actually. The thing is, Mark wanted to get his hands on Daddy's money, and he was plotting with Freddie's ex-girlfriend.' A sad look passed over Pippa's face, and her eyes filled with tears.

'My God, that's terrible.' Gemma instinctively reached out to give Pippa's arm a squeeze. And poor Freddie – he didn't come across as the sort who would let anyone mess him around, but then it just went to show . . .

'He was controlling and pompous, and he put me down a lot actually.' Pippa had tears in her eyes.

'Pippa, my ex-boyfriend was a bit similar,' Gemma said without thinking. 'I mean, he put me down all the time. Chris liked to tell me what to do. In the end he finished with me, because he thought that we'd move into my nan's house when she went into the home. When I told him I had to sell it to pay the fees, he dumped me.'

OK, so much for arm's-length, but she found she couldn't help herself. She was not only angry, but also feeling something akin to relief. She'd never told anyone about Chris, apart from her nan, but her nan hadn't seemed to understand.

'Oh my God, I knew we had so much in common. Although, of course, you didn't have Harry to save you. You see, Harriet found out about the plotting, but Fred and I refused to believe her, which caused a rift between us. Poor Gus was stuck in the middle. It all worked out in the end, though. Gwen videoed them together and proved it to us, but it was a pretty horrible time, I can tell you.'

'It must have been. Imagine losing your father then having your husband turn on you too,' Gemma said, feeling bad for Pippa, Freddie and herself. 'I do understand. I lost my nan and then Chris – well, not exactly the same but similar.'

Gemma felt tears pricking her eyes as she looked at Pippa. She had felt so browbeaten, so hurt, so many things. It felt that only now, at Meadowbrook, was she beginning to process them.

'It's so weird how similar, really! And poor Fred was upset too. Well, actually, his ego was bruised mainly. He didn't love Loretta, that's his ex, as much as I thought I loved Mark, but actually I let Mark control me for so long I didn't know myself anymore.'

Gemma nodded. God, it sounded so much like Chris, but without the big house, the inheritance or the brother.

'Thank you for being so understanding. I guess I'll let you get on.'

Pippa looked as if she would like an invitation to stay, but Gemma suddenly felt exhausted and needed to sleep.

'I really need to pack. I know I'm only off for the weekend, but I need to make sure I have the essentials.' She tried to sound light-hearted. 'And thanks again for lending me the car.'

'Well, we'll see you for dinner Sunday evening? We usually all go to the local pub, so I hope you'll join us. About seven?'

'I'll be back before then, so that will be lovely.'

Gemma knew better than to try to get out of it – it seemed

that being with the family was part of the job description. It really was a wonderful job, good pay, great living conditions, but it was also the strangest job she'd ever had, and one she really didn't know if she understood. No, she definitely didn't understand.

After Pippa finally left her room, Gemma started to pack. She threw some of her clothes into a holdall; she didn't worry about looking good back home, so she took her old clothes rather than the nice ones Pippa had lent her.

She thought that when she got her first paycheque she might go and treat herself to some new clothes. Having worn those that Pippa had passed to her, she was beginning to enjoy looking better than she usually did. Surely, it was better late than never? She was twenty-eight, not twelve, but so what? She did feel a bit of a new lease of life coursing through her veins. Was that the Meadowbrook effect?

She left early and the house was quiet. She walked quietly to the front door, where a bunch of flowers caught her eye. They were just the sort her nan loved, wild garden flowers, and there was a note attached. She picked it up.

Gemma, Amanda and I remembered you saying your nan loved her garden flowers, so we picked these for her. I do hope she likes them.

Love,

Gus and Amanda

Bloody hell, she thought as she wiped the tears from her eyes. She felt as if she were being drowned in kindness, and she didn't quite know how to handle this alien feeling.

Driving Pippa's shiny Mini Countryman was also a new experience, she thought as she pulled herself together. If she didn't stop being so emotional then Harriet would definitely fire her. She was pretty sure of that. She felt a rush of freedom as she drove away from Meadowbrook and also some relief, as she didn't have to worry about what she did or said for a while. She programmed the sat nav as she wasn't sure of the best way to get home and as it'd been a while since she'd driven, she felt nervous as she negotiated the traffic.

When she told Pippa she was going home for the weekend, Pippa made it clear that she was more than welcome to stay at Meadowbrook at the weekends. In fact, she said she'd rather have her there as the house felt less empty. And Gemma would be grateful not to go back to the bungalow. It reminded her too much of the past. It had been her home, but now it belonged to no one. Her nan was never coming back to live there, and although she used to wonder if her mum would come back and find her, she never had. She used to worry that if they moved or even went on holiday – which was a week in a caravan every summer – her parents wouldn't know how to find her.

But of course she finally had to accept that they never had and never would. Who knew if they were even still alive? Gemma often wondered what happened to them. Had her dad met someone else and got a new family? Likely. Had her mum recovered from what her nan referred to as her "troubles" and also gone on to find happiness? Probably. Did they ever think about Gemma? Doubtful.

When Gemma told her the whole story, one of her college friends Jane had suggested that they try to find out what happened to them, using the Internet, but after initial attempts hadn't yielded any results, Gemma got cold feet. She suddenly realised that having been rejected when she was a child was bad enough. She wasn't sure if she could cope with being rejected again.

Over the years, she had also asked her nan if she knew, but her nan was as much at a loss as she was, or so she said, and Gemma had never had any reason to doubt her. She said that her father had panicked, he was young and he felt trapped, so he fled just after she was born. Her mother, Sandie, nan's daughter, had to be a mum to Gemma, apparently, but she was sad all the time and one day she left too, when Gemma was only four. She hadn't been in touch since. Her nan was upset about it, she missed her only child, and was happy to talk to Gemma about her, but as far as she knew, she'd never tried to find her, either.

It was funny, well not funny but strange – when Pippa talked to Gemma about growing up without a mum, Gemma wanted to relate to her. But she held herself back, because she also spoke about her wonderful father, with a love and respect that sparkled in her eyes, and Gemma couldn't understand that at all.

She'd been away less than a week, but the bungalow felt cold and unlived-in as she walked through the front door. She flicked on all the hall lights and made her way to the kitchen. She sighed as she looked at it through fresh eyes. There was such a stark contrast with Meadowbrook. She was angry with herself for thinking that; she might not have grown up with the luxury of Meadowbrook, but she was always comfortable and fed, and she never thought of the bungalow as lacking until now. She was a grown-up; she had always been grateful for what she had, and she needed to remember that. This was her home, and she had been lucky to grow up here with love and warmth.

However, this would be someone else's home soon and she wouldn't belong anywhere. Trying to stave off self-pity, she went through the mail, putting the bills in one pile to deal with and junk mail straight in the recycling. There was nothing personal, except an envelope from her last employer with her final payslip – it was higher than she'd expected as she hadn't taken all her holiday, but it still wasn't anything near what she was earning at Meadowbrook.

She made herself a cup of tea, glad she had stopped at the petrol station to get some milk, and studied the kitchen, making mental notes as she waited for the kettle to boil. She decided she would keep the appliances for now, because she wasn't yet sure how often she would be coming back, but she could pack any personal items she wanted to keep and then the rest would go to charity, or be thrown away. She set to work and for a while, lost in the task at hand, she forgot to think about anything. She blanked all feelings of sadness, of worry, of loneliness out of her mind as she put things in boxes and tried to think about nothing.

After making progress in the kitchen and living room, she headed upstairs. She stopped briefly by her nan's bedroom. The door was ajar and the emptiness of it winded her. The bed stripped, the bedside table devoid of its usual glass of water, reading glasses and book. Even the wardrobe and the chest of drawers were empty. Gemma had packed her nan off with as much as was familiar that she could fit into her new room at the home. The rest she had taken to the local charity shop – there was no point in having it hanging around. But it made her feel empty; there was no sign of her nan in her room anymore.

She hurried to the bathroom, where all that remained was

an old bar of soap. Sighing, she made her way to the spare room, which had been her mum's room when her father left and her mum came back here to live with Gemma. But there were no traces of her now. The walls were an old cream, the curtains red, and the small queen-size bed was devoid of bedding. It had been a dumping ground for ages, and there were piles of boxes and bags that Gemma would have to go through at some point; but she couldn't face it yet.

Her room was the last room. The smallest room in the house. At one point, when she was about eleven or twelve and it was clear her mum wasn't coming back, her nan tentatively suggested she move into the bigger room and Gemma could decorate it as she liked as her birthday present. But Gemma couldn't bring herself to do so. It was as if she still believed her mum would come home one day, so she had stayed in her small boxroom with the single bed. It was a nice room though – it faced the back garden and was light. She had painted it a pale blue colour, duck egg it was called, and she had a white wardrobe and bedside table that she'd got from IKEA. Before Meadowbrook, Gemma thought it was all she needed, but now, well, now she wasn't quite so sure.

She had never been ambitious – she was too afraid to be so. She knew that she needed hours of counselling to unravel her feelings, but she was too scared to take chances. She just wanted to be safe. Her nan made her feel safe, or as safe as she could feel having been abandoned by her parents. This bungalow made her feel safe. Doing her hotel course was the biggest move she had made, but then she'd had to give it up to look after her nan, so she almost felt she was being punished for having tried to change things. And even working in a job she hated was what she thought she needed, deserved. But now her nan was gone, she didn't have the safety net anymore, which is why she had taken the huge risk of the job at Meadowbrook. And yes, it was wonderful, but it was also more terrifying than she ever imagined.

She lay on the bed, trying to contain her fears, trying to hear her nan's voice tell her that she could do this, and the tears that came were welcome, because she needed to feel something, even if it was sadness.

Gemma slept fitfully in her small bed, mainly because she had got used, in such a short time, to Harriet's king-size bed, and she woke herself up a number of times by almost falling out. She put the hot water on, made a cup of tea and then when she was confident the water would be hot enough, took a wash in the over-the-bath shower. She felt as if she were betraying her nan somehow by comparing everything to Meadowbrook, but she couldn't help it.

The thought hit her: what if this didn't work out? What if after the month they asked her to leave? Then she would have to get another job, and she knew any job she got wouldn't pay anything near what the Singers were paying her. She might be able to rent a small bedsit and all luxury of Meadowbrook would be forgotten. Even the comfort and space of the bungalow would be out of reach. The idea was absolutely horrifying.

She needed to make a success of this – her future, and her nan's immediate future, depended on it. And that was why she had never taken risks before. They were bloody, bloody terrifying.

Pushing her fears firmly away, she got dressed and left the house. She drove the twenty minutes to Kenworth House, for her weekly visit, basking for once in a warm car rather than the usual bus and the walk.

As she made her way up the tree-lined drive to the Victorian building, she marvelled, again, at how you would never know on appearance that this was full of old people. The grounds were well kept, the house itself impressive. A little smaller than Meadowbrook and filled with lost lives, which is how she thought of it. Most of its residents had problems remembering who they were, or who their loved ones were. It was so incredibly sad for everyone concerned. Gemma had researched as much about dementia as she could, and her only conclusion was that it was cruel. Horrible and cruel.

Gemma waited for the door to be opened, then she chatted with staff who were now familiar, checking that all was OK, or as all right as it ever would be. As she made her way to her nan's room, she was comforted in the fact that she knew she was well looked after. Although it was expensive, the fact that her nan's bungalow was in a good location and had bags of potential meant that they'd been offered the asking price, and she would be able to stay here at Kenworth for years if necessary.

Gemma didn't want to think about her nan dying, because when she did, she would be all alone.

She held her bony hand as her nan sat on the high-backed chair, which had been positioned so she could look out of the window. Gemma sat next to her, gazing at the trees and the grounds through the rain-splattered windows. The wild flowers had been arranged on the table in front of them, and they looked far more beautiful than Gemma's normal offerings, sparking a smile in her nan, which was priceless.

'The job's interesting,' Gemma said.

Filling her nan in on the Meadowbrook saga was cathartic.

Speaking aloud, voicing her fears and hopes, seemed to be helping her more than getting tangled in her own thoughts. And although her nan was largely unresponsive – almost completely today – she felt as if she were being listened to. And, at least they were together.

'The family are so kind to me, Nan, but I wished I felt that I deserved it. I know you always told me I did, but well, you are the only person who ever knew me properly, and I always struggled to believe in myself, didn't I?' Tears glistened in her eyes and she wanted to keep them in check.

Suddenly, and without warning, her nan grabbed her hand and squeezed it. She didn't speak, but the intensity in her eyes did, and Gemma felt safe again. It was brief but it was there.

Sarah put her head round the door and said it was time for her nan to go to the communal room for the afternoon's entertainments. Her nan responded to Sarah more than she had Gemma, by giving her a smile and a nod, which cut to the quick, although she knew she wasn't supposed to take it so personally. Gemma reluctantly stood. She bent down and kissed her nan's leathery cheek.

'I love you, and I'll make you proud of me, you'll see,' she said, feeling her emotions on the verge of failing her.

'Oh, love, I'm already proud of you.'

Her nan's voice took her by surprise. For a minute she wondered if she'd imagined it, as she looked at her nan to see the same unreadable expression on her face.

Gemma kissed her cheek again, leant down to hug her, breathing in the smell of her perfume – lavender – and enjoying the warmth of her frail body. Then Gemma left the home, walking into the cold air, basking in the warmth of those words as if it were a beautiful summer's day.

Chapter 8

Gemma pulled off the wellington boots she was becoming accustomed to and adjusted the socks that nearly came off with them. She let herself in the back door, having taken a hike up to the lake to clear her head. She'd been here for almost three weeks, and although it was still overwhelming, the place was becoming familiar. As was the family. In very different ways.

Pippa was still on a mission to make Gemma her best friend. They were spending practically all their evenings together, and Pippa was undoubtedly lovely: warm, open, friendly and interested. She told Gemma all about their upbringing at Meadowbrook, the tragedy of losing their mother when Pippa was barely a toddler, how Harriet had stepped up to the role of matriarch of the family, and how awful it had been when she had to go to boarding school. Gemma had been filled in on the history of the Singers, and it gave her a clearer picture of who she was working with; although she wasn't sure that Harriet would be pleased at quite how much Pippa was sharing with her.

At the same time, Gemma still wasn't as forthcoming in return. She chose carefully what she said to Pippa – it was necessary to hold part of herself back for so many reasons.

She was honest, though, as she talked her about her nan's dementia, about Chris and also, without meaning to, she'd said a bit about her parents leaving her. Pippa liked to ask about Chris, in the way that it bonded them with his similarities to Mark. Gemma couldn't help but be more open than she had ever intended, and she enjoyed Pippa's friendship in a way she never had with anyone else.

Her relationships with the rest of the Singers varied from person to person. Gus was her favourite after Pippa, but then he was the least demanding on her time. As well as the gardens and his paintings, he had Amanda and the two girls to keep him busy, so he left the details of the running of Meadowbrook largely to the others. But Gus was funnier than he appeared, and he was easy to be around. When she thanked him and Amanda for the flowers, they brushed it off as if it were nothing, rather than one of the nicest things anyone had ever done for her.

Gemma saw him at the animal sanctuary and, of course, in the gardens with Amanda, where they always tried to involve her. Increasingly, Gemma was beginning to appreciate the gardens as a way to make her feel relaxed, so she was trying to get more involved, letting them teach her a little about plants and flowers.

In the sanctuary, Gus liked to work with the pigs, and he explained how fond he was of them as he introduced her to them. They had five pigs now: Napoleon, Cleopatra, Geoffrey and Bubble and Squeak. They were enormous and Gemma found them quite intimidating; four were from homes where they were supposed to be domestic micropigs who turned out to be fully grown. How could so many people be duped like that? Probably served them right for trying to be fashionable with their pets; although, of course, it was the animals who suffered in the long run.

Not that the Meadowbrook pigs exactly suffered. They had lots of room, a lovely shelter, plenty to eat – as Gus explained, it was all organic, which meant they probably ate better than she did. They were very content and well looked after, so at least they had happy endings, even if they were anything but micro. The final pig, Gus had told her, was his favourite – although out of earshot of the others; apparently, pigs were sensitive. This was Geoffrey, a pig who was used for breeding and had been retired to Meadowbrook. According to Gus, Geoffrey was the warmest, most loving pig he had ever met. Gemma didn't get too close; she just took his word for it. But Geoffrey did seem to be enjoying his new retirement home.

She was getting used to being with the cats, and was happy to feed them, pet them, talk to them and get to know them. Connor had introduced her to each of them, showing how caring he really was, as they patiently went to each one, making sure they spent time petting them all.

There were fifteen cats at the moment, and an old man called Albert was her favourite. He wasn't the friendliest – in fact, he hissed at her quite a bit – but he was a big tabby who looked as if he had a permanent scowl. For some reason, Gemma was spending her time trying to win him over. She felt as if he needed a friend, even if he didn't know it. She also had a ridiculous notion that if she could win him over, she might be able to do the same with Harriet.

She realised that at Meadowbrook they were all a little potty about the animals – they all had names, personalities and were talked about as if they were people – but she also found that she was quickly doing the same. Albert, her grumpy old man, was now one of her favourite things about the place.

Harriet was perfectly polite to her, but she definitely hadn't thawed totally, and still treated her with suspicion. Harriet asked a lot of questions and although Pippa did the same, Gemma always felt Harriet wanted to trip her up. She knew she might be paranoid, but it was just how she felt.

And Freddie clearly thought she was an idiot. It didn't help that she turned into a klutz around him, always banging into things, or stammering, unable to get her words out. It wasn't the image she wanted to project, but she found him so intimidating, in a different way to Harriet. She was getting used to drinking more now, although it still wasn't enough to impress Freddie. The problem was that she wished she could be more like him, and deep down she knew she also wished that he liked her a bit more.

The house was eerily quiet as she made her way into the kitchen to make a cup of tea. She did so and then went to take it upstairs. She wondered if anyone was home. Meadowbrook felt wrong when it was empty – too big, too quiet – and she could see that the house needed filling with people. She understood more why they thought a boutique hotel would be perfect.

She heard voices coming from the study and although she knew she shouldn't, she paused. Hoping that whoever was in there wouldn't suddenly come out, she put her ear to the door.

She heard Freddie's voice. 'Look, Harry, she might come home anytime, so perhaps we shouldn't be talking about her here.'

'We're not doing anything wrong,' Harriet countered. 'I'm just saying that she's been here for a few weeks, and I'm not sure what she's done in that time.'

Gemma felt her heart sink into her thick woollen socks.

'Well I think she's done loads,' Pippa said loyally. 'She's getting a real feel for the place, and she's great with the cats.'

'That's all well and good, Pip, but she's meant to be helping us come up with a model for the hotel, and as far as I can see she barely even mentions it,' Harriet continued.

'I'm not sure that's fair, Harry. I think she's getting a feel for the place,' Gus mumbled. 'She is interested in the gardens, and as Pippa said, the sanctuary. I think you're being a little harsh, Harry.'

'And she hasn't even tried to talk to me about the cocktail bar,' Freddie huffed.

'But—' Pippa started.

'No, Pip, I know you think she's your friend, but she is here to do a job. Right, my proposal is that her month's trial is up end of next week, so we ask her to present her ideas to us in a professional way. We need something concrete, so if they've got substance, if she's got substance, we'll know then.'

'But that's so not fair,' Pippa argued.

'Why not?' Freddie asked.

'Because I really like her,' Pippa said weakly.

'You really liked your husband and look where that got you,' Freddie pointed out.

'Fred, that's unnecessary,' Gus said.

'Sorry,' Freddie mumbled.

'Anyway, I didn't like him that much.'

Everyone laughed.

Once again, Gemma marvelled at their relationship. They bickered, yes, but they were so close, and they loved each other. They were all so different but they supported each other. And Gemma was reminded, starkly, that she was an outsider. Literally, as she couldn't pull herself away from the door.

'So we're agreed then,' Harriet said.

'Not exactly,' Pippa huffed.

'Look, Pip, I hope she works out, I really do, and I'm glad you two get on so well, I'm just saying that perhaps if we get her to do a presentation for us, then we'll have a clearer idea about her proposals for Meadowbrook and if she even has any. I'm not doing this to be horrible, but it is business at the end of the day.' Harriet sounded kinder.

'We *are* paying her a decent salary, after all,' Gus concurred.

Gemma liked him a little bit less.

'Yes, and if we're ever going to open this hotel, we need to get plans underway,' Freddie stated. 'Sooner rather than later.'

Gemma balked – it wasn't as if he seemed to do any work, after all.

'Well, I suppose asking her to present her ideas isn't too bad. After all, I am confident she has loads of them,' Pippa conceded. 'But let me tell her. You guys – well not you, Gus – but you two will probably scare her off if you do it.'

Gemma scurried away before she got caught.

Her heart pounded as she shut the door. She had known she wouldn't be able to pull it off. But then she had to – she had no choice. They were going to ask her to present her ideas. She didn't have any, well she did, but she didn't have anything like a clear plan yet. She'd have to get one done and quickly.

She propped herself up on the bed, the bed that might not be hers for much longer, and sipped her cold tea. Then she pulled her books out from under the bed and opened one entitled *A Practical Guide to Opening a Hotel*, and began to read.

Chapter 9

'Ow, Fred, you kicked me,' Pippa shouted.

Freddie glared from across the table. Gemma let herself glance, briefly, at him. She had a good idea of what was coming but, of course, she kept quiet. They were having breakfast, and Gemma couldn't shake the conversations she'd overheard yesterday. This always happened to her, didn't it? No one thought she was ever good enough. Gemma tried to breathe – drowning in self-pity doesn't do anyone any good, she heard her nan's voice saying.

'Sorry,' Freddie mumbled, 'it was an accident.'

'Gemma, the thing is that Harry and the others, well me too, of course, but not me as much as the others—'

'Pip, spit it out,' Freddie interrupted.

'Sorry.' Poor Pippa looked both uncomfortable and distraught. 'The thing is that well, of course, you have your month's trial, which I didn't want, but anyway, we were wondering if you'd be able to give us a presentation at the end of it, so we can all sort of see where we are with the hotel planning so far.' Pippa looked down, unable to meet Gemma's gaze.

For selfish reasons, Gemma might not be thrilled about it, but of course they were perfectly within their rights, actually sensible, to do this. She just needed to pull the presentation off in order to keep her job. And at the moment, she was still pretty unsure if she could.

'Of course, I was going to do that anyway,' Gemma fibbed. 'At the moment, I have so many ideas that they all need putting in some kind of order, which was my next step, so no problem.' She smiled broadly. 'But also, Pippa, I've made a list of five of the nearest small hotels in Somerset, and I thought we could visit them all – research purposes. I want to show you what's already out there. Mostly so we make sure we do something different, stand out.

'And, Freddie, we need to have a proper chat about the bar you're planning. I have already started looking into the licences and legalities, but it would be good if we could start talking through the details.' She felt her leg shaking under the table, but she hoped she sounded professional.

'Of course,' Freddie replied, surprise lacing his voice.

'Great.' Gemma smiled. 'So, Pippa, how about today for the hotel visits? No time like the present.'

'Oh, I'd love that,' Pippa squealed in delight. 'And we get to spend the day together!' She really needed to take "boss" lessons from Harriet.

'And I'll start putting down my bar ideas today as well,' Freddie said. 'Then we can have a meeting.' He seemed to have a found little bit of respect in his voice too, as he gave her one of his gorgeous smiles, which almost made her melt.

But, it seemed as if she had dodged a bullet. For now anyway.

Gemma felt relaxed as they visited the last hotel on her list; it had been a really good day. The idea had come to her when she read a chapter in her book about hotel identity. One of the many problems she faced with the Meadowbrook Hotel was that the family didn't share the same vision. But, she reasoned, Pippa was the driving force, so if Gemma and Pippa could come up with a model together, then that would be a huge step forwards.

The first hotel, The Swan, was popular with golfers. Situated very near to a major golf course, the main building was Georgian, a bit like Meadowbrook; however, it had been built on and added to through the years to make it bigger, so it looked a bit mismatched. Inside was smart, but what soon became apparent as they sat in the bar and had a coffee was that the clientele were older, mainly middle-aged, and mainly wearing golf attire.

The next hotel, Somers House, was part of a swanky London chain, and was small and boutiquey. It was so painfully trendy and modern inside that Gemma thought they might actually be in London. It was very strange, obviously aimed at Londoners who wanted to get out of London but not actually get out of London. And pay exorbitant amounts for it. And the people staying there were young, too cool for their own good, all paying more attention to their screens than to anyone else. The art on the wall was unfathomable, and the prices were eye-watering, even for a cup of coffee, which came served in something resembling a tiny bucket rather than a cup. She could see that this might appeal to Freddie, but she didn't voice that particular thought.

The next two were more like guesthouses, trying to masquerade as boutique hotels. They were nice, certainly, but there was nothing unique about them, and they didn't hold a candle to Meadowbrook with their loud patterned carpets and oversized furniture.

The final hotel was the one closest, in distance, to Meadowbrook. The Darnley billed itself as "an exclusive, luxury, sophisticated yet cosy home from home". It seemed a big shout.

As Pippa parked in the car park, she looked at Gemma. 'I have a feeling that I'm going to like this one best,' she said.

The Darnley was in the middle of a small town high street, the front entrance opened to the road, and the car park was around the back. It was a townhouse, really, and quite pretty, but of course, being on a busy high street, again Gemma was relieved to find there would again be no comparison to their hotel.

'It's bigger than Meadowbrook will be, more rooms I mean; although it doesn't have much in the way of grounds, and the impression I got from the website is it's a little bit pretentious,' Gemma replied.

'But I like it so far,' Pippa said as they got out of the car and stared at the ivy-covered building.

Gemma nodded. She and Pippa had worked well together today. They had both chatted throughout viewing each hotel, and Pippa had pretty much managed to keep on topic; although they did veer off into Mark territory in the golf hotel – it was one of his favourite courses. But apart from that she had been impressively focused. Maybe Pippa was almost as worried about Gemma getting fired as Gemma was herself.

They mounted the steps up to the tall building and found themselves in the reception area, where a number of sofas were scattered and a modern, dark wooden desk ran along one side of the entrance hall. A tall, fairly good-looking man glanced up and smiled warmly at them.

'Hi, we were wondering if we could get a coffee,' Gemma asked. Although she and Pippa had drunk so much coffee already, they would soon start bouncing off the hotel walls.

'You're not saying here?' the man asked, who on closer inspection had a name badge on – Edward Farquhar.

He was in his early forties, Gemma presumed, well spoken, wearing a dark navy suit and tie. His formal attire matched the hotel.

'Well no, we were just in the village and popped in for a drink.' Pippa smiled.

'Well, you are most welcome at The Darnley,' Edward said charmingly. 'But I recognise you – aren't you Pippa Singer?'

'Yes, I am. Have we met?' Pippa asked, eyes crinkled in question.

'No, I saw your picture in the local paper to do with your animal rescue.' He was suddenly charm personified as he smiled at Pippa as if he were going to devour her.

'Our sanctuary,' Pippa said.

'Yes, of course.' His eyes seemed to light up. 'I'm Edward. I own this hotel, and I would be delighted if you would join me for that coffee,' he said. 'And you are?'

'Gemma Matthews,' Gemma mumbled, already feeling like an unwanted guest.

Edward picked up a phone, ordered coffee to be served in the residents' lounge and then gestured to them to follow him.

He led them through to a room similar in size to the Meadowbrook drawing room, although it had far more furniture crowded in. The carpet was deep and cream, it was almost scary to walk on it, and there were clusters of tables with small sofas set around them.

Pippa admired the room, which Gemma thought was too full. The windows faced the front of the building and looked out onto the village road where shoppers passed by. The coffee arrived on a silver tray, in a silver pot with bone china cups. Gemma's head was whirring. What she was trying to do was not only ensure that Meadowbrook was different to what was on offer in the area, but also come up with its unique selling point and a clear strategy of who their target market was. So far, every hotel she'd visited had given her plenty of ideas as to what Meadowbrook shouldn't be, rather than what it should be.

'So,' Edward said once coffees had been poured, 'are you living at Meadowbrook?'

'Yes,' Pippa said, unusually quiet.

Gemma snuck a glance, and she seemed to have become a little pink in the cheeks.

'Ah, yes, your father was a fine man,' Edward gushed.

'Did you know him?' Pippa asked, her eyes lighting up.

'Well, no, not exactly, but I knew *of* him and admired him greatly. I've seen the house, and Parker's Hollow is a lovely village. But the house is magnificent. Who exactly lives there?'

'Well, funny you should ask that,' Pippa started, 'we're opening a hotel.'

Gemma noticed the smile freeze on Edward's face for a moment. Gemma was hoping that that piece of information wouldn't be made public yet, but it was too late. She was cross with herself for not telling Pippa to keep it to herself.

'Really? A hotel?' His eyes filled with suspicion.

'Well, yes, perhaps.' Gemma took over, trying to contain

the conversation. 'You see, it really depends on a lot of things. But I don't want you to think that we're here checking out the competition.'

'Oh no.' Pippa sounded horrified, as if she'd just realised how that sounded. 'No, we're here to try to make sure that our ideas for Meadowbrook don't tread on the toes of any other local hotels,' she explained.

'So I don't have to throw you in our dungeon for industrial espionage?' Edward arched an eyebrow.

'You have a dungeon?' Gemma asked.

'No, but we do have a very dusty wine cellar.' He laughed, as did Pippa.

She put her hand on his arm, in what seemed like a flirtatious gesture. 'Oh, honestly, trust me, our hotel won't be anything like this. It's really lovely here though.'

'It's been in our family for years, a bit like Meadowbrook, I guess, but it only became a hotel twenty years ago with my parents,' Edward explained. 'I took over five years ago when they decided to retire to the South of France.'

'How lovely. And how are you finding it?' Pippa asked.

Gemma felt invisible once again, as Pippa and Edward seemed engrossed in each other. But she didn't mind – it gave her time to take in the details.

'Oh! Wonderful. I wanted to put my own stamp on it, so I revamped the restaurant, and we're getting quite a reputation for our food now,' he said.

'Well that's fantastic,' Pippa replied.

'You know, if you ever want any advice or help, just call me.'

'Thank you. Sorry, I should have explained that Gemma's our hotel consultant,' Pippa said.

Gemma groaned inwardly as the spotlight turned to her.

'Oh, well you could probably teach me a thing or two,' Edward said, eyeing her with suspicion. 'But I won't pick your brains now, not when you're working for the lovely Pippa.'

Goodness, he was definitely on a charm offensive, Gemma thought as Pippa seemed to preen at his words.

'We ought to go, Edward. Lovely to meet you and thank you for the coffee,' Gemma stated after a few more compliments were thrown around.

Edward stood.

'Lovely to meet you too, and, Pippa?' She nodded. 'Take my card; if you call me, perhaps we could have dinner? I'll even let you pick my brains,' he joshed.

'That would be lovely.'

He held on to Pippa's hand a second too long as he placed the card into her palm. Gemma smiled to herself; it had almost been a constructive day, and it looked as if Pippa had got herself a date out of it. Edward wouldn't be her cup of tea, far too posh, confident and a bit too charming, but Pippa seemed quite taken with him, as she raved about him the whole drive home.

Her happiness was short-lived. She and Pippa were still giggling as they walked through the door at Meadowbrook and headed for the kitchen.

'Please, no more coffee,' Gemma said.

'No, but I thought a glass of wine might be nice.' Pippa sounded hopeful.

'Lovely.'

For once, Gemma actually did fancy a glass of wine. Perhaps Meadowbrook was turning her into a lush; although she still couldn't handle more than a few glasses, so she was still a fair few bottles away from both Freddie's league or his approval.

They burst into the kitchen and stopped short. Harriet was sitting at the kitchen table and she looked furious. Gemma automatically panicked that she was about to be fired; she almost cowered in the doorway.

'Harry, what's up?' Pippa asked.

'Where have you been?' Harriet asked.

'Oh, visiting hotels. We've had a great afternoon, actually. Very constructive.'

'Right, well glad someone did. Bloody Connor,' she fumed. Gemma began to breathe again. 'I can't stand it anymore,' Harriet shouted.

'Wine, definitely.' Pippa appeared unruffled as she went to get a bottle out of the wine fridge, grabbed three glasses and poured.

'Should I leave you?' Gemma asked uncertainly.

'Yes,' Harriet said.

'No,' Pippa said at the same time.

Gemma looked anxiously between them.

'Oh stay, for goodness' sake,' Harry said, draining her glass in a way Freddie would be proud of.

Gemma wasn't sure it was the warmest invitation, but she stayed put.

'Why are men so annoying?' she whined as she grabbed the bottle and refilled her glass.

'What's he done now?' Pippa asked in a way that suggested that this wasn't a one-off.

'He's just so bloody messy. We had all that work done, knocking the two cottages together, and everything was shiny and new. Don't get me wrong, the house is lovely, but I feel

91

like I'm constantly tidying up after him, or tripping over his mess. And then I sound like a nagging wife, which makes me hate myself. I'm not supposed to nag or act like a wife. Why is it so hard?' Harriet took another big gulp of wine.

'Harry, I keep telling you, it's because you haven't lived with a man before, and Connor is good in so many other ways; after all, he always brings you coffee in bed in the morning.'

'Yes, he does do that.'

'And he clearly loves you so much. We all see the way he looks at you, right, Gemma?'

'What, oh yes, he really does. And the other day when he was showing me the cats' routine, he was saying what an amazing job you were doing with the sanctuary and how fantastic you are. His eyes lit up when he spoke about you, and about how lucky he is to have you.'

Gemma remembered how his eyes crinkled at the edges as he spoke of Harriet, and she had felt a stab of sorrow that she had never had that effect on anyone. She probably never would.

'Was he?' Harriet narrowed her eyes.

Gemma nodded.

'Harry, you are just going through what any couple goes through when they start living together: teething troubles. And it's worse for you because you lived on your own for so long,' Pippa said. 'You both need to learn to compromise, if you ask me.'

'And don't forget that although your cottage is big compared to many places—' Gemma was thinking of the bungalow '—you were used to the space here, which is very different.'

'Oh, I'm sure you're both right. My apartment at New York was so tidy because I was never there, and when we lived here it was immaculate, mainly because of Gwen and the cleaners.'

'That's your answer.' Gemma had finished her glass of wine and felt emboldened. 'I know Pippa said that you have a cleaner once a week – just increase that.'

Harriet turned her head to Gemma. 'You mean get Vicky to come in more often to pick up his mess?'

'Why not? You'll pay her to do it, after all. Say, Vicky comes to your house for one hour every morning, on her way here. She gets a bit of extra cash, and you have a tidy house.'

'You make it sound so simple,' Harriet said. 'Why does she make it sound so simple?' She turned to Pippa.

'Because it is. Why didn't we think of it?' Pippa asked.

'God knows, but thanks, Gemma, yes, that's what I'll do. But I am still going to tell Connor to try to be tidier.'

'I'm sure he will be. You tell him you're hiring a housekeeper and as his mum was a housekeeper, I expect it might actually make him think,' Gemma pointed out.

'Bloody hell, you're right,' Harriet said grudgingly. 'OK, so maybe I got you wrong,' she conceded.

'I told you that she's good.' Pippa was hopping around like an excited kitten as she reached for another bottle of wine.

'OK, Gemma, thank you, that's almost brilliant. But Connor needs to stew a bit more. What we need is a girls' night.' Harriet took a large swig of wine.

'I'm in, shall I unearth some pizza and put it in the oven?' Pippa asked.

'Yes, God, I'm so hungry now I'm not upset,' Harriet said. 'Gemma, you're in?' It sounded more like a command than a question, but quite a nice command.

'I absolutely am,' Gemma said, raising her wine glass. She could do this, she told herself. Today she had leapt over hurdles, in work, and now with Harriet. She was almost not scared of Harriet at all really, well only a bit. 'Where's Freddie though?' she asked.

'Pub with Gus. Connor might be there too, for all I know. But anyway, boys, even brothers, are a banned topic tonight.'

'Oh, I will definitely drink to that,' Pippa said, giggling. 'Although can I just tell you about Edward Farquhar?'

'Who the hell is he?' Harriet asked, and Gemma sat back and relaxed as Pippa explained.

'And, Gemma, what did you think of him?' she asked as Pippa finished.

'He seemed charming.' Gemma chose her words carefully.

Harriet seemed as if she were going to ask more, but she just nodded.

'What about you, Gemma, have you got a boyfriend?' Harriet asked. Her voice was softening with the wine, as was Gemma.

'No, I had one, Chris. It didn't go well – he was after a free home really,' she said.

'Like Mark. No wonder you two get on so well.' Harriet grinned. 'But you know before Connor, I had terrible taste in men too.' She leant in conspiratorially. 'I am ashamed to admit, but I had an affair with a married man, who turned out to be a total dick.'

'Wow.' Gemma was stunned. She wasn't sure what the appropriate response was.

'But you know, I was a dick too, as I should never have done that. We women, we need to stick together.'

'I'll drink to that.' Pippa grinned.

They clinked glasses and Gemma forgot to feel intimidated as she actually began to have fun.

Chapter 10

'My God, are you hungover?' Freddie asked as Gemma walked into the kitchen.

Gemma tried to move her head to look at him, but pain ripped through it, and she bashed her elbow on the doorframe. God, that hurt. Her eyes were bloodshot, and she had barely slept last night because the room wouldn't stop spinning. Her mouth was thick and furry, and she was also feeling pretty nauseous.

'Ow,' she answered, rubbing her elbow and trying to stem the threatened tears.

'And you look like you've just woken up in a hedge. Well done.'

She would have glared at him if she could.

'Now, tell me, Gemma – who doesn't drink – how did this happen?'

'Harriet had a row with Connor.'

'Oh yes, he came to the pub with me and Gus; those two argue a lot. Harry's bossy, Connor's too laid-back, but they do really love each other, have done since they were kids, really. A match made in heaven, but when they row then maybe hell? Anyway, he was pretty miserable.'

'Harriet wanted us to have a girls' night and there seemed to be a lot of wine.'

'And yet when I try to get you to drink you never do.' Freddie shook his head.

'This might be why.'

'Yes, I see your point.' Freddie grinned. 'Right, drink this tea. I know you don't want to but honestly, you'll start to feel better. And here . . .' He reached into a drawer and handed her some paracetamol. 'I won't try to get you to eat, but we can have our meeting outside – fresh air will definitely help.'

Gemma was startled – he was being nice.

'Our meeting?' She rubbed her head. Bang went the idea of going back to bed.

'Yes, we were going to talk about the cocktail bar this morning and what we can do, because obviously my time is precious.'

'I can see that,' Gemma replied, thinking that Freddie didn't seem to do an awful lot as far as she could see. He did go to the sanctuary for a bit every day, and he played with social media, but apart from that, he seemed to swan around in his buggy most of the time.

'As I was saying, what we can do is to go for a walk around the estate. I'll tell you what I am thinking about with the bar and you can listen, and ask questions if you're up to it. What do you think?'

'Sounds great.' It really didn't.

Half an hour later, she met Freddie by the back door. There was no sign of Pippa, but Gemma had left them singing to Eighties songs in the snug at some point last night. It must have been late, she was sure, as she literally crawled up to bed.

She looked in the wall mirror trying not to recoil in horror at what she saw. Gosh, she looked terrible. Her hair seemed to have taken on a life of its own and was sticking out in all directions. She wished it was summer; she could have done with hiding behind sunglasses.

'Hangovers suck, don't they?' Freddie said.

'How come you're never hungover?' Gemma asked as they set off. Freddie seemed to drink like a fish yet always look amazing.

'Oh, I'm hardened. I don't really get hangovers. And actually, I don't go as mad as I used to. Maybe compared to you, but not compared to the old me.' A serious look crossed his face before he wiped it away with a smile. 'We just had a few pints in the pub then we had a couple of brandies back at Connor and Harriet's – it wasn't exactly wild. Especially as Gus was talking about Amanda and how much he loved her, and Connor the same about Harriet, so basically it was more like a bloody coffee morning.'

Gemma raised her eyebrows. 'I see.'

'But anyway,' he said as they headed out through the garden and towards the public footpath, 'I have been giving the bar a lot of thought. Serious thought.'

'Well that's good.'

The fresh air was beginning to help with the headache, Gemma decided. Although she still felt rough, so her plan was to try to let Freddie speak and merely listen. It was pretty much her plan in life, in actual fact. And she was impressed – it was practically the first time he had been serious around her.

'I was thinking that the garden room would be the best room for the bar.'

'I agree, not least because it opens up, so in the summer you could have outdoor drinking.' Gemma wondered why she hadn't already told him she thought this. She really needed to be more vocal about the hotel.

'And a smoking area, because let's face it, people still smoke,' he pointed out.

'There's a decision to make, and that's whether you open the bar to the public or if it's just for residents.' Gemma felt herself clicking into work mode.

'Residents only. For one, Parker's Hollow is a very small village, and the pub should benefit from us having a hotel, not worry about losing customers. Also, it's only going to be a small bar, so I would rather keep it to residents, unless we are hosting a private party, but surely that's the same, because we're still not open to the public.'

That made things easier, Gemma knew, as she had been looking into this. A small residents-only bar in the garden room would be much simpler to set up and get authorisation for. And as Freddie talked, Gemma was impressed. No joking, he had really thought this through, and his passion was clear in his ideas. Gemma thought she must have misjudged him a bit; there was nothing lazy or entitled about the man she was with right now.

'Which brings me to the practicalities,' she said, determined to support him. 'We need to draw up a proposal for the bar, and we also need to look at the legalities and get a licence.'

'A licence?'

'Yes, you'll need an on-premises licence, and it shouldn't be a problem but there's a lot of admin involved. Basically, the licence has to be held by a person, not the hotel as such, and there's an exam involved, legal checks, that sort of thing. And we obviously have to hope that no one objects to it. We can go through the process together, but I think we could easily do it ourselves.'

'What do you mean?' He stopped walking and turned to face her.

'You can pay companies who specialise in licences. Obviously you still have to sit the exam, but I think we can handle the application ourselves. And save some money.' As far as Gemma could tell, it seemed fairly straightforward.

'Great, if you say so. Harry'll be pleased if we save money, but I am definitely one hundred per cent going to be the licensee. It's my baby, the bar I mean.'

'So you don't have criminal history then?'

'Of course I bloody don't – what kind of question is that?' he asked, his voice incredulous.

'A very sensible question,' she replied, forgetting to be nervous. 'You might have been drunk and disorderly, or caught with drugs or anything really.'

'Well I definitely have not,' he huffed. 'You can do all the checks and I'll come out squeaky clean.'

'Well that's great, glad to hear it. It's good to know you are a law-abiding citizen,' she said, trying to pacify him.

'Oh no, I've just been lucky. You see, I never got caught.' His grin returned. 'Oh look, there's Gus,' Freddie said, waving frantically.

Gus was heading towards the summer house, a beautiful building, full of light, not far from the main house. When Gemma had had her tour, Freddie had explained it used to be their mother's studio, then it became the Singers' den when they were teenagers, and now it was mainly Gus's studio. Freddie hadn't wanted to take her inside then, as it was full of Gus's work and he wasn't there. But she was dying to see his paintings.

'Hey,' Gus said as he unlocked the door, a big canvas under his arm.

Freddie gestured for Gemma to follow him in.

'Welcome to my studio. Would you like to see my etchings?' Gus laughed, and Gemma joined in.

'Gus has all the lines,' Freddie joked. 'Lucky he's spoken for, otherwise we'd be beating the women off,' he said sarcastically.

'Right, Gemma, would you like a grand tour?'

'I really would, Gus.'

'You look different, what is it?' Gus turned and stared at her.

'She's hungover.'

'Oh yes, right. So, there is the small kitchen area, mainly used for cleaning brushes now and making the odd cup of tea.'

Gemma was still getting used to their idea of "small". It was bigger than the kitchen in the bungalow, with a coffee machine, kettle, small oven and even a slim dishwasher. The summer house was really only one big, light airy room, but Gus showed her there was a small wet room, and a storage cupboard behind two doors. She could have happily lived here, although of course Gus and his paintings would probably object.

'So the main space, which used to be stuffed with furniture, is now just a painting space.' He gestured to the room where a couple of easels were set up.

She sneaked a look and on one was a picture of some flowers, quite traditional but with a bit of a twist, not that

Gemma knew much about art. On the other was the beginnings of a painting of a pig: Geoffrey. Along the wall were some finished paintings – again, traditional in style but with a bit of a different perspective to the normal landscapes and portraits. They were good, Gemma thought. Bold, attractive, she could imagine them hanging on the walls at Meadowbrook . . .

'Have you thought about using Gus's art in the house when it's a hotel?' she asked.

They both shook their heads.

'I do have some pictures up there, actually, but only in the attic rooms,' Gus said.

Gemma nodded; she'd seen them but hadn't realised he had painted them. Her head was buzzing with ideas, pushing the headache away.

'Think about it, they could be for sale; it could be a character of the hotel. Maybe just in the bar to start with, or in the bar and the hallways. I mean, I know the art in the house is gorgeous and, for example, I wouldn't change the drawing room, but give it some thought. Especially if Gus also offers painting classes to the guests.'

'What? Why would I do that?'

'Well, people could come here and do a day or two painting course. I mean there's no reason why not, and if you also sold your paintings then they would have something special to take away from their stay here.'

'But I only paint for fun and I'm not a teacher. I've never taught anything, and I'm not even that good.' The colour drained from his face.

'You are incredibly good,' Freddie argued, giving him an affectionate pat on the back. 'And if it makes you happier, we

101

can call them workshops, which sounds a bit more casual, doesn't it?' Freddie suggested. 'Harry would like that; it fits in with her idea of corporate retreats.'

'Yes.' Gemma could suddenly see ideas gelling. 'Imagine, you could set them up in here, and people would love it,' Gemma added. 'You said you wanted the Meadowbrook Hotel to have a creative element, so there you go.'

'Well I suppose it's an idea,' Gus said uncertainly.

'God, sometimes I almost think you know what you're talking about,' Freddie said, patting Gemma on her shoulder. She immediately turned as pink as one of Gus's pigs. 'Perhaps you should be hungover more often.'

'Fred, leave her alone.' Gus grinned. 'But yes, those are definitely things to think about.'

Gemma felt so pleased with herself that she spun round, lost her balance and knocked into one of Gus's easels. Luckily it was empty, as it crashed to the ground with her on top of it.

'God, I'm so sorry,' Gemma said as she tried and failed to get up, tangled as she was in the wooden frame, but both Freddie and Gus were too busy laughing to help her up.

Chapter 11

'Hello, Albert, how are you today?' Gemma asked in a voice that sounded as if she were talking to a baby.

She'd never even spoken to a baby, so why she'd suddenly developed this ridiculous voice she had no idea. She was growing fond of all of the cats, and Albert and she had quite a bond. He reminded her of herself. Not the most attractive, a bit scared of people, unloved, alone, living in a cage. Of course that wasn't quite her, and she didn't live in a cage . . . yet.

'You're pretty great with the cats,' Connor said as he came up behind her. 'Did you have a cat?'

'No, I didn't have any pets, which is why I thought this would be terrifying, but I love being around them – they are quite calming for some reason.' Gemma realised she meant the words as soon as they were spoken. The cats could be loud, demanding, but when they let her pet them and rewarded her with a purr or two she felt content. 'It makes me sad to think they've been abandoned.'

'I know, it's tough working here; even Harriet finds it hard.' He laughed. 'But you have a way with the cats, and they are the best judge of character.'

'Thanks. You and Harriet seem so different,' she said carefully.

She was intrigued by each of the Singers, even more so than when she first arrived at Meadowbrook. They were all different, yet alike. They bickered but were fiercely loyal. They were all manner of contradictions and contrasts, and she found them all fascinating. She worried she was growing a bit too fond of life with them; after all, the end of her first month was almost upon her and it could all be over soon enough. Hence her bravery in talking about them. She wanted to drink in every detail while she still could.

'We are. We grew up together though, so we know each other inside out. She was my first best friend really, so I guess although we are different, we are the same person in many ways too. If that makes sense?'

'That sounds romantic.' Gemma stroked Albert and wondered if anyone would ever think that about her. Doubtful.

'I'm the romantic one, she certainly isn't.' He laughed again. 'But she's got a soft centre has H, a heart of gold, and when she cares about you, well let's just say no one will get away with hurting you.'

Gemma continued to stroke Albert. Connor's eyes were full of love, and she couldn't help but wish someone would look like that when they spoke about her, but why would they? Harriet was attractive, clever, funny (when she wasn't scary) and successful. She might not be like Connor, who seemed softer, calmer, more laid-back, but she was certainly nothing like Gemma, either.

'Next you'll be telling me her bark's worse than her bite,' she said.

'Oh God no, her bite is actually worse than her bark.' Connor grinned.

The door swung open and in walked Harriet.

'My ears are burning,' she said simply, and Gemma stared very intently at the cat as she willed herself not to blush.

'Oh God, H, we were talking about you, but only good things.' He kissed the top of her head and she smiled.

'I was joking, but anyway, what else would you talk about, Con?' She arched a perfectly shaped eyebrow.

'Where's Hilda?' he asked, wrapping his arms around her.

'With the dog group – she likes hanging out with her pals,' she explained to Gemma.

'Was Hilda from here?' Gemma asked, slightly embarrassed by their affection, but not wanting to let on she was uncomfortable.

'Of course!' Harriet said.

'We would never buy a pet when we could rescue one, but actually it was Harry really, she and Hilda fell in love.'

'We were kindred spirits, both felt abandoned, but had lots of love to give,' Harriet laughed.

Gemma opened her mouth to say that was how she felt about Albert, but she closed it again. She wasn't ready to give them that much of herself.

'And now we are a family, and although Harry thinks I'm messy, actually it's mainly Hilda.'

'Oh don't be ridiculous, Hilda is perfect.'

'You see, Gemma, I stand no chance when it comes to Hilda. Which reminds me the other night . . .'

'I did have a bit of a hangover,' Gemma admitted, feeling her face colour. No one had said she had made a fool of herself, but the idea that she might have done had been burning inside her ever since.

'I felt terrible too, but thanks, Gemma, I really needed it, and it was me pushing it, not Fred for once,' Harriet said, smiling warmly at Gemma. 'Although Fred is incredibly angry we drank his good tequila.' She laughed again.

'We drank tequila?' Gemma's brow furrowed.

'Oh, Gemma, yes, you said you'd never tried it, so we had shots. But you didn't like it, your face was a picture, so you only had one. Pip and I carried on though.' She grimaced. 'Which was not my best idea.'

'No wonder I was so ill the next day.'

'Sorry, but if it's any consolation, when I got home I tripped up the stairs, couldn't be bothered to move and when Connor found me I was asleep.' Harriet chuckled.

'She was snoring.' Connor reached over and gave Harriet a hug.

'At least you remembered,' Gemma pointed out.

'Well yes, unfortunately I always seem to remember when I get drunk; it's not always a good thing. Right, anyway, Gemma, we'd better go.' She was back to her usual business-like self.

'Go where?' Gemma asked.

'We've got a meeting with the Easter event committee up at the house. Didn't Pippa tell you?'

'She said there was a meeting, but she didn't tell me she wanted me there.'

'Oh, didn't she? Well, I think it'll make sense for you to join us. These people are the most important locals when it comes to Meadowbrook, along with the gardening club of course, and I for one think it's a good idea to for you to understand them.'

'Harriet, no one understands them,' Connor pointed out.

Harriet quickly filled Gemma in on who she was about to meet as they walked up to the house. It transpired that the

Meadowbrook events always involved the villagers. Not only was each event a Parker's Hollow community occasion, but they also raised funds for the animal sanctuary. Gemma tried to keep up both with the fast pace Harriet was walking at, and also with the speed at which she spoke.

John, the vicar was prominent, and he was also in charge of the morris dancers.

'I didn't think they existed anymore,' Gemma said, having never actually seen real morris dancing, apart from in *Midsomer Murders*, her nan's favourite television programme.

'Tip: don't let John hear you say that,' Harriet replied.

Gemma took mental notes as Harriet continued to talk. The vicar/morris dancer's wife, Hilary, was famous for her quiches, which she sold alongside Gwen's cakes at most events. Then there was Edie and Rose, who Gemma had met from the gardening club. Gerry, Gwen's "friend", liked to build things and was also happy to dress up as anything, which they didn't like to think about. Samuel was the oldest member but still came along to every meeting, despite being deaf as a post and always forgetting to wear his hearing aid . . .

There were others too, but Gemma was sure she would never remember them all. However, as Harriet talked about them with fondness in her voice, she was intrigued. It was funny how these spoilt siblings, growing up with all this privilege, seemed so committed not just to getting their hands dirty with the animals, but also involving the community. It showed they were good people, but actually, Gemma already knew that. She wasn't working for a corporation after all but a family, a family with a big heart it seemed, and she really needed to remember that. Even Harriet.

The Easter event committee were already gathered around

the dining table. Gemma suddenly had the idea that when the hotel opened, they would keep this as the dining room and guests would all dine together; if they didn't want to mix, they could arrange to dine privately in their rooms, perhaps. But, instead of turning the room into yet another hotel dining room, they would get an experience eating here, a bit like in the grand houses of the old days. She was both surprised and delighted with her brainwave. It felt as if it would work. Meadowbrook brought people together, and one way perfect for that was for them to dine together.

'Hello, everyone,' Harriet said confidently as they stopped chattering and all stared at Gemma. For some reason she immediately felt herself blush.

'Oh, hello, Harriet, and Gemma – this is Gemma.' Edie took over the introductions. 'I told you about her – she's going to set up a hotel here. And she's a lovely girl.'

Gemma felt herself turning red from her toes to her ears.

'Ah yes.' John looked at Gemma over the top of his glasses. Next to him was a woman who looked very much like him; she could have been his sister, but Gemma already knew from Harriet that she was his wife. 'We do need to talk about this hotel. I mean, what will it mean?'

'What do you mean, what will it mean?' a man, who Gemma assumed was Gerry as he was sitting very close to Gwen, asked.

'For the village, for our events, that's what he means,' Hilary explained in a calm, quiet voice.

'*Can everybody speak up? I can't hear a bloody thing,*' Samuel shouted.

'Oh, love, I thought you were asleep,' said Rose, who was sitting next to him.

'*What?*'

'*We were trying to get Gemma,*' Hilary shouted, '*to tell us about this hotel.*'

Gemma gazed at everyone; they were all looking expectantly at her. Harriet and Freddie both wore the same amused expressions, whereas Gus and Pippa were a little more concerned.

'It's very early days,' Gemma explained, 'but as far as I am aware, it won't mean any changes for your events.' Although she didn't add that the meetings would probably have to be held elsewhere. 'And, of course, it will only benefit the village. You know, like bringing new job opportunities.' Gemma's cheeks were so hot she could fry eggs on them. She hadn't been prepared for this at all.

'What kind of jobs?' Edie asked.

'We haven't worked that out exactly, but cleaning, waitressing, work in the kitchen, the bar, guest relations, that sort of thing. And as this will be a small hotel, there won't be large groups staying here, you can rest assured.'

'Gemma, I'm Doris – we haven't met. I do the raffles along with Mary here.' She gestured to another lady who sat next to her, who Gemma had seen at the gardening club. 'We really do enjoy a good raffle, don't we, Mary?'

'Oh yes, selling tickets is something of a skill of ours, if we do say so ourselves,' Mary added.

'Anyway, we don't mind the coach trips that come to see the gardens, very civilised they are too, but you see we are concerned,' Doris continued.

'About what?' Gemma asked, trying very hard to follow.

'Oh, what do they call them, you know, the chicken thing and the male deer. They come to get drunk and have sex.'

'What on earth?' Gemma said, baffled, as Samuel spluttered.

'*Who's having sex?*'

'What she means, Gemma,' John said, taking over, 'is these stag and hen parties. We don't want our village invaded by people wearing penises on their heads.'

Gemma was aghast. Did the morris-dancing vicar really say "penis"? Freddie choked. Harriet looked as if she were going to fall off her chair trying to contain her laughter. All eyes were on her.

'We won't have any stag or hen do's here,' Gemma said. 'Absolutely not. And definitely not any who want to be tacky.'

She thought about her last hotel. They did have some hen and stag parties there, and they could get rowdy – other guests had made some complaints – but no, that wouldn't ever be a feature of Meadowbrook.

'Really?' Freddie sounded disappointed.

'Absolutely not. If a bride-to-be wants to come and relax with a couple of her best friends, that's one thing, but we are going to be a lovely boutique hotel, which will reflect the character of both Meadowbrook and Parker's Hollow. There won't be any inflatable penises or it is peni?' Gemma finished.

'Peni? Are you kidding?' Freddie laughed.

'Well said, Gemma,' Pippa finally interjected. 'And we will keep you informed of all and any progress, of course. There's a long way to go, but this village will always be at the forefront of our plans.'

'I might like a little job here,' Edie said.

'Doing what?' Margaret asked. 'It's not like you're young anymore.'

'Since my new hip I'm like a spring chicken. Or hen.' Edie

110

laughed mischievously. 'I like the sound of guest relations, does that involve—'

'No, Edie,' Harriet said quickly. 'Now, can we get back to the task at hand, the Easter event?'

'*Can you all speak up?*' Samuel shouted again and then promptly started snoring.

Gemma had never been so grateful to hear the meeting being wound up. The Meadowbrook Easter Committee had defeated her. She had never seen anything like it, and how she was supposed to design a luxury hotel, where it seemed these people would be involved, she had no idea. Goodness, if guests were spending hundreds of pounds a night, they didn't want to encounter Edie's flirting, the uncertainty of whether Samuel was dead or not – she swore he stopped breathing at one point. Or John, the vicar, extolling the virtues of morris dancing; there had been a monologue they felt lasted for almost half an hour.

The Singer siblings all seemed so comfortable with them – no, more than that, fond of them. Gus was his usual kind self, helping all the ladies up from their seats when they – eventually – got ready to leave. Pippa thanked them all effusively; although they hadn't really done anything. Harriet said how much she was looking forward to seeing them next week for a follow-up meeting, as nothing had been decided in this one. And Freddie helped Samuel get out to the waiting minibus, which they used for the gardening club and committee meetings.

'I haven't seen you in church,' John pointed out to Gemma as they both stood by the front door.

Freddie came back just at the same time, and he grinned like a naughty schoolboy.

'Well, you see, I've been going back home at the weekends.' She had, although this weekend she was going to stay at Meadowbrook and drive to see her nan on Sunday afternoon.

'Ah, well, if you stay here on a Sunday, our service is at ten o'clock.'

'You can go this Sunday, can't you? You did say you were here this weekend.' Freddie smirked.

'Well—' Gemma hadn't been to church since she was at junior school.

'Fantastic, and perhaps you'll bring this reprobate with you.' John patted Freddie on the back. It was Freddie's turn to look horrified.

'I'd love to but . . . but I have my chickens to look after, in the mornings,' he stuttered.

'Well, if I help you we can be finished before church,' Gemma offered with a smirk.

'You couldn't—' Freddie started.

'Splendid, it's a date.' John the vicar beamed with pleasure.

'It really isn't,' both Freddie and Gemma said at the same time.

Chapter 12

'You are doing it wrong,' Freddie stormed.

Gemma turned and glared at him. He was earning his position as most annoying Singer ever.

'How on earth can you feed chickens wrong?' she asked tetchily.

It was early Sunday morning, pouring with rain, and she should be having a nice relaxing morning at home, but instead, she was out in the horrific weather feeding chickens and being shouted at by Freddie.

'You offered, if you remember, and look, you have to scatter the feed in the right way.' He took the bucket off her and demonstrated by doing exactly what she had been doing.

'If you hadn't told John, the vicar, I was around for church, we wouldn't be in this position,' Gemma pointed out, too wet, frizzy and cold to remember to be intimidated by him. Besides, in his huge raincoat, wellies and a hat that made him look like a fisherman, she couldn't really find him so today.

'You were the one who roped me in and offered to help with the chickens,' he shot back.

'It wasn't my idea, it was John, the vicar's.' She felt like stamping her feet. She never got angry but she felt it now. As well as tired, cold and wet.

'Humph, it's still all your bloody fault.'

Gemma was about to respond, but as she turned to do so, she tripped over a chicken and went flying, landing on her bum. At least that cheered Freddie up, as he laughed heartily.

'Oh, Elizabeth Bennet, I know she's annoying, but you shouldn't have tripped her up,' he chastised the chicken, while actually picking her up and petting her. 'I hope she didn't hurt you.' He clearly meant the chicken, not Gemma, as he examined her and then, when satisfied, he put her back down, where she clucked as she walked away.

Gemma was dumbfounded. 'Aren't you going to help me up?' she asked.

'No. Now, we better get back to the house and cleaned up if we're going to make the bloody church service, and let this be a lesson to you.'

Gemma opened her mouth to shout at Freddie's departing back, then closed it again. She struggled up and then huffed back to the house after him.

What did people wear to church? She had cleaned herself up with a quick shower, and now she was staring at her wardrobe. She opted for a pair of fitted black trousers – courtesy of Pippa – and a soft grey jumper that she had bought from Zara last weekend when she had allowed herself a small shopping spree. Just as she had finished dressing, there was a knock on the door and Pippa's head appeared.

'Are you all right?' she asked.

'Yes, fine, although my bum might be a bit bruised.'

'Freddie told me what happened – he's a terror.' But Pippa's eyes sparkled with mirth.

'He's angry because he thinks it's my fault he has to go to church.'

'Oh, it'll do him good.'

'Come with us, Pippa, please?' Gemma asked.

'Oh, I'd love to, but Harriet and I have to walk the dogs. The weather's awful and we're short of volunteers today, so sorry.' She looked anything but sorry. 'I'm sure you'll have a lovely time. John's sermons are interesting to say the least.'

'Judas,' Gemma said, then worried she had overstepped the mark.

'There, see, you know this Bible stuff already, you'll fit right in.'

Gemma could hear Pippa chuckling as she walked off.

Gemma stood in the large hall waiting for Freddie. She was studying a portrait of an old lady, who she'd assumed when she first came here was a family member. However, when she asked Pippa, she laughed and told her that her father was poor growing up, and didn't have portraits and suchlike, so he had bought some old paintings, which he said he liked, despite not knowing the subject from Adam. For some reason this made Gemma feel closer to the Singer patriarch; he didn't always fit in, either.

It was going to be painful, not just going to church, but also the fact that she and Freddie had to spend time together. She was unsure how he felt about her. At times, he seemed to dislike her, and who could blame him? She was awkward and clumsy around him. At other times, he made her laugh and made her feel more carefree than ever. He was a conundrum. More than any of the other Singers, she couldn't figure him out. Or perhaps she couldn't figure out their relationship together.

When he appeared, looking impossibly handsome in smart trousers, a shirt, top buttons undone, poking out from a V-neck jumper, she bristled, ready for the attack. But to her surprise, he smiled.

'I guess we'd better get going. If we're late, John, the vicar, will make our life hell, come on.'

'OK.' Gemma put her coat on and as Freddie opened the door, she followed him out. 'You've cheered up,' she said carefully as they made their way down the drive.

'Oh, probably the vision of you splayed in the chicken coop. Sorry, but it was funny.'

'Well, actually, it was quite painful,' Gemma retorted.

'Oh, for God's sake, Gemma, you really need to get a sense of humour.'

'I have one, thank you very much.' She could feel this descending into another argument, and she had no idea why.

'Sometimes you do, but other times you are so serious. Anyway, I guess that will come in handy at church. I shall be trying not to laugh at John's sermon, and you won't find it funny, anyway.' He winked at her to show he was teasing.

'Want some?' Freddie whispered, passing a small silver hip flask to Gemma.

She was shocked. As she looked around, no one seemed to notice, and she was glad they were sat near the back. The church was lovely; incredibly pretty, not too big and, thankfully, quite full. Although Gemma and Freddie were the youngest there by about twenty years. Gwen and Gerry were at the front – luckily, they hadn't seen Freddie and Gemma sneak in a bit late – as well as some of the gardening club and events committee.

'What's in there?' she hissed back. She couldn't believe he had brought a hip flask to church – well actually, thinking about it, she could.

'Whisky, it's good for shock.'

'What shock?'

'And now if you will all be upstanding, some of our ladies will sing "Amazing Grace" for you.'

As Gemma saw Edie, Rose, Margaret and Doris get to their feet with three other women she hadn't yet met, and the organist started playing, she soon understood exactly what Freddie meant.

'I didn't know people clapped in church,' Gemma said as they waited outside, for what she was unsure, but everyone else seemed to congregate there, huddled under umbrellas.

Gwen and Gerry stood with them.

'Oh, in this church pretty much anything goes,' Gerry explained. 'And the ladies, bless them, they do like a bit of praise.'

'John likes to involve as many people as possible. Next week is family service, where it's more focused on the children, so many of the younger families in the village come,' Gwen explained.

'I do some puppetry,' Gerry said proudly.

'The "Amazing Grace" rendition is something I can never un-hear.' Freddie shuddered.

It had been, at best, an interesting interpretation, as they all sang different words at different times. The poor organist got totally confused, and it was clear that none of it was planned.

'Oh they enjoyed it though, Fred, which is the main thing.' Gwen smiled.

'Well, as interesting as that was, I'm not sure I'll be making it a regular thing,' Freddie added.

'John will be disappointed – he loves it when any of you guys come,' Gwen said.

'Why?' Gemma asked.

'Andrew and I used to go to church every week, and I think John felt as if it validated him somehow having someone from the big house – you know, like in the olden days.'

'Was he a vicar then?' Freddie asked.

'Of course not.' Gwen rolled her eyes. 'But he's very traditional. He misses your father being there, and I guess he was hoping with four of you that at least one of you would take up the mantle.'

'You should,' Gemma said suddenly. 'Maybe do a rota, so that one of you goes every week, and if you don't want to go alone, then Harriet could take Connor, and Gus, Amanda. But well, if it means that much to the village . . .'

Gemma knew by the way that Freddie was staring at her she had overstepped the mark yet again.

'My siblings won't be happy with that idea,' he scoffed.

'No, Freddie, Gemma's right, it will make the village happy. You all go there at Christmas and Easter, so if you could at least all try to put in an appearance a bit more . . .'

Gwen sounded like a parent, Gemma thought.

'Think of the goodwill it will create for the hotel. When we apply for licences and permits, you will need a lot of local support,' Gemma added, quite enjoying herself. 'The more they feel you are part of them, the less they'll want to object to anything.'

'Fine, we'll ask the others tonight, but if I have to go, then you are coming with me,' Freddie stated.

'If I can I would love to,' Gemma replied, with a big smile.

Actually, she meant it. She had found a kind of peace there in the church. Apart from when Edie and co were singing, of course.

Chapter 13

It was the day of the presentation – the end of Gemma's first month at Meadowbrook – and she was draped in exhaustion as she dragged herself out of bed. She hadn't slept well and when she did, her dreams were filled with anxiety, namely Freddie laughing at all her ideas and Harriet physically throwing her out of Meadowbrook. Thinking about it, she was probably awake at the time.

It was March and it seemed to have been raining constantly. However, today, as she glanced out of the window she saw it was dry for once, so she decided to go outside for a run, to try to wake herself up, clear her mind and try to calm her nerves. She felt as if she would never be calm again.

The last week had flown by. Sunday she'd had to go to church again, but this time with Pippa. Gemma didn't mind, but post-church the day had been difficult. She had gone off to see her nan almost straight after, not stopping to eat anything. By the time she got to the home her stomach was rumbling, but she had to content herself with a couple of custard cream biscuits with her tepid, milky tea. The room seemed to be smaller as Gemma underwent her weekly rituals of changing the flowers. She had also brought some room fragrance, as every time she visited, the room seemed to smell a bit staler. She would have taken a scented candle, but they were banned for obvious fire hazard reasons.

Her nan herself had looked brighter than she had done in a while. Her eyes shone, and she was animated as she chatted about other people in the home. But she seemed to have no idea who Gemma was, and she kept asking if she was in charge of the bingo. Gemma had wanted to tell her about Meadowbrook, pour out her feelings about the upcoming presentation, the Singers and the fear that threatened to engulf her, but her nan wasn't in a listening mood. When she left, she missed her nan, the nan she had grown up with. Even more than that, it threatened to eat her alive.

Gemma had stopped at a service station on the way back. Wiping the tears, she'd picked up a sandwich, which tasted of nothing, but at least took the edge off her hunger. Still she felt heartbroken after leaving her nan; she also felt confused. She felt as if she had two totally different worlds – Meadowbrook and her nan – and she didn't know how she could reconcile them. If she ever would.

Pulling herself together, she spent the rest of the week working on the presentation. But despite devoting her every waking hour to it, she still didn't feel as if she had a firm grip on it all. She was terrified that she was going to lose this dream job. She veered from confidence in her ideas, to insecurity, to a reasonable conclusion that they would feel that progress had been made, to the ultimate one that she felt she hadn't made enough progress. Thus, they would fire her. She was stuck on a wheel of misfortune.

She had pages and pages of notes, and yellow Post-its were sticking out from all her text books, but putting it into some kind of logical order, to demonstrate that she was right for the job, was proving more difficult than she hoped. And she also needed to convince herself first.

She pulled on her "seen better days" gym kit, resolving that if she did get to keep the job, she would treat herself – nothing too expensive, though. She was trying to incentivise herself to take control of the day. She kept trying to come up with motivational phrases, thinking of her nan and what she would have said before the evil dementia set in. If she could do this, if she could pull it off, it would show that she really was as worthy as her nan used to tell her she was. She also knew she would be practically homeless and destitute without the job, which should have been enough of a threat. But more than that, she felt she needed to do it for her nan. She might not always know who Gemma was these days, but even so her nan was the only person who had ever known the real her.

She ran downstairs and the familiarity of the house startled her. It felt as if she had been here forever, and she constantly had to remind herself that this wasn't *her* house, it wasn't *her* home. And after today, she might be banished from it forever. She tried not to think about how much she would miss about Meadowbrook, and how she would miss the Singers, especially Pippa – it was too much, and it loomed over her like a nasty thug.

She set out through the hidden gates in the garden, running past the summer house, where she could see Gus's paintings inside, following the public footpath, waving to a couple of people walking their dogs. She lost herself in her thoughts; the cold, crisp day was invigorating, although she was beginning to sweat from the run. She also breathed in the fresh air and really did feel that the county had a different effect on her, not quite calming but something akin to it.

As she ran, she went through the presentation she had prepared in her head, reciting it, committing it to memory. Deep down she felt she had got it right, but then she wasn't the judge, and Harriet made Simon Cowell look like a sweet old lady.

'Hello.'

Gemma turned, and Harriet jogged up beside her with Hilda at her heels. Gemma stopped.

'Hi,' she said unsurely. This was all she needed, when she was trying stop feeling like a basket case.

'Keep jogging, we can talk at the same time,' Harriet commanded.

'Speak for yourself,' Gemma mumbled, but she started jogging again.

Hilda barked and then settled down, following them.

'I'm glad I ran into you, literally!' Harriet laughed. 'Ready for the presentation?'

She sounded jovial and looked immaculate in her smart running gear, her dark hair pulled back off her face, which was slightly red but devoid of sweat. How did she manage to look this good on a run? Gemma was pretty sure she looked like a scarecrow next to her.

'I will be, but you know, sometimes I think I have more questions than answers,' Gemma said truthfully. There was no point in false bravado, especially as it felt as if Harriet could see right inside her.

'That makes sense,' Harriet said, sounding almost kind.

Gemma tripped over a stone and stumbled but quickly righted herself.

'Oh, OK.' Gemma was confused. Was Harriet doing this to unnerve her?

'Look, Gemma, I am going to be honest. When you first arrived I was pretty sure you weren't up to the job, and I am quite a good judge of character.'

'I kind of got that.'

'I felt there was something about you that I couldn't figure out, as if you were hiding something. But, after initially feeling that way, I want you to do well. You've sort of fitted in with the family without me noticing, and the community. I heard Edie talking about you, and she's a fan. Well, anyway, you've ingratiated yourself already which, by the way, is no mean feat, so I really hope you do well today.'

'Really?' Gemma felt breathless – whether from the run or from Harriet's presence she had no idea. But she was totally confused.

'Yes, I really do hope you don't mess it up.' Harriet jogged off in the opposite direction, with Hilda wagging her tail by her side.

And as Gemma started walking, slowly, back to Meadowbrook she felt a little better, with Harriet's good wishes still ringing in her ears but the fear of messing it up very, very real.

'So, in conclusion, I've typed up an action plan for the next month.' Gemma sounded confident; she felt in control. Her conversation with Harriet had given her a little boost, after she'd stopped feeling as if her nerves would eat her alive. 'My priority,' she continued, handing a piece of paper to each of them, 'is to decide who you are going to be aiming the hotel at. Who are your guests? Because we need to start thinking about PR and marketing, and until we know who our market is then we can't do that.'

'What do you think?' Gus asked.

'I think Meadowbrook has a unique personality. I think that needs to be reflected in the hotel, but also you don't have many rooms – I think if we rented them all out there are nine?'

'There are ten, but Freddie and I haven't decided about our living arrangements yet. One of us will move into Gwen's rooms, but well, we might need a room here too.'

'Just a point, I think ten rooms would work better,' Gemma replied. 'It allows up to twenty guests, and of course some people might come on their own, so you need to maximise available profit,' she said pointedly to Harriet. 'Then I think even one room will make a difference, but of course it's a while before the hotel will open its doors, so that is something for you to discuss.'

'Good point,' Harriet said. 'Also, as someone will be on hand in Gwen's old rooms then perhaps it would be strange to have a family member in one of the rooms.'

'Great, so I'm getting kicked out,' Freddie moaned. 'Thanks, Gemma, for making me homeless.'

'Shut up, Fred, nothing is set in stone,' Gus retorted.

Gemma was surprised but she was almost enjoying herself, as she firmly felt in her stride. 'In order to make it worthwhile you need to charge for what people are getting – luxury, which you already have, peace and quiet, but also a creative space. I haven't quite tallied up the room rates yet, Harriet. I think we'll do that down the line, but you do need to charge five-star prices.'

'So only wealthy people?' Freddie asked.

'They don't have to be wealthy, but you can't make it too cheap. You won't make money and you'll also potentially attract the wrong people. You don't want the young and rowdy, even if Freddie thinks you do.' Freddie scowled at her. 'But in keeping with the house and the village, you want classy, well-behaved people who want a luxury break. Either for romance, or with a best friend, small groups of friends even, and of course we are putting together a corporate package too, but I want that to be separate.' Gemma almost wondered who was talking – who was this confident woman? She could barely believe it was her; although of course her knees were knocking together under the table; luckily no one noticed.

'But we can offer gardening, baking, painting, or spending time with the animals as well?' Pippa asked eagerly.

'Well there's a great marketing angle – take some time out from the rat race, or your usual everyday lives, and enjoy a creative pursuit. We can put together different packages – that's the beauty of Meadowbrook. I think we need to pitch it as a break in the beautiful Mendip countryside in one of the finest, unspoilt manor houses in England, where you will be pampered, taken care of and given the opportunity to indulge in creative pursuits, if you so choose. Long, beautiful walks, award-winning gardens, to either sit or work in, baking work-shops with a master cake-maker, or painting workshops with a talented local artist.'

She paused, satisfied to see they were hanging on her every word. 'And if you want to you can visit the local animal sanctuary and meet, play or feed the animals. With wonderful home-cooked, locally sourced food and a creative cocktail bar, indulge, pamper and enjoy yourself in a unique, exclusive boutique hotel.' Gemma surprised herself with how carried away she was getting. She could see it now – all of a sudden she could see the reality. It would be a hotel, and she was sure it would be a successful one. And she, little Gemma Matthews, was going to be a part of that.

'Wow,' Pippa said. 'That's amazing, Gemma, I can see it now.'

'Actually, me too,' Freddie said grudgingly. 'Not bad at all.'

'I think it sounds great,' Gus added.

'Good job,' Harriet said simply. Coming from Harriet, this seemed like the highest praise of all.

'Thank you.' Gemma was experiencing a new sensation – praise heaped on her and not from her nan! It felt good . . . no, it felt amazing. She was almost floating on the air, she was so, so happy.

'So, as far as I'm concerned, we're ready to go ahead,' Harriet said.

'Do you mean I've passed the probation?' Gemma asked.

'Of course you have, as if there was any doubt.' Pippa launched herself at Gemma, nearly knocking her off her feet with her hug. Harriet nodded.

'Gemma, you need to see our solicitor to get all the legal side of it underway. We would prefer you to use the family solicitors, as they look after Dad's estate.'

'Of course,' Gemma agreed. 'I've spoken to Freddie about the licence, and we can talk about any other legalities and permits we need to sort out.'

Gemma knew they might need permits to change the house into a hotel, but it varied from local authority to local authority. There was much to be done on the practical side, of course. The kitchen would need to be changed to commercial, there were all sorts of health and safety issues, rooms would have to be set up properly for visitors, but at the moment none of them seemed insurmountable.

'Well, you can't do it single-handedly, and your job was to help us get this place open,' Pippa said; she was glowing as well. 'So, now we have the green light, we need to involve other people. Oh, I am so excited, Gemma. You have done such a marvellous job so far, I'm so thrilled.' Pippa hugged her again.

Gemma was so happy she even hugged her back, warmly. She forgot herself for a minute and let herself bask in the moment.

'Right, Fred, go and get some champagne. Gus, go with him and get glasses,' Harriet ordered.

'Yes, boss,' Fred quipped.

'Bugger off, Fred. We have something to celebrate,' Harriet snapped, but she had a big grin on her face, and she looked at Gemma and winked.

Gemma fleetingly wondered if a wink could kill you, but it seemed that Harriet might actually be beginning to like her.

They all sat in Andrew Singer's study.

'What do you think Daddy would think of the hotel?' Pippa asked.

'I think he'd be proud of you, well all of us, but particularly you, Pip,' Gus replied.

'I agree,' Harriet added, slinging her arm around her sister's shoulders.

'Me too, although of course I am involved as well.' Freddie opened the champagne and poured everyone a glass. 'I'm full of ideas for the bar,' he puffed.

'We all are – it's a family business, and Daddy would love that,' Pippa pointed out. 'Imagine how proud he would be to see the four of us working together.'

'God, who would have imagined that when we came back for his funeral, we would all end up working together and as close as we used to be as kids!' Gus marvelled. 'When we had tried to live together for a year it was almost as if we were strangers, Gemma.'

'And we definitely had our moments; it wasn't plain sailing, was it?' Freddie added.

'But look at us now, we are thick as thieves once again,' Pippa trilled.

Gemma was struck, again, at how she was an outsider here, and she couldn't help but envy them, for the millionth time, for having each other.

'Here's to the Meadowbrook Hotel.' Harriet raised her glass and they all clinked glasses.

'To the Meadowbrook Hotel,' they all echoed.

And Gemma vowed that she might not be one of them, and she never would be, but she would do all she could to make sure they did open a hotel that all of them, including her, could be proud of.

Chapter 14

'Wow, you look lovely,' Gemma said. She was just heading downstairs for dinner, when she bumped into Pippa coming out of her bedroom, dressed in a black trouser suit, full make-up and high heels.

'Thank you. Did I forget to tell you I was going out?' Pippa said.

'You didn't mention it, no. Where are you off to?'

In the five weeks Gemma had been here, Pippa didn't go out, apart from the local pub, or to Harriet's, and occasionally to see Gus and Amanda.

'Oh well, I don't want to make a fuss, but I've got a date.'

'A date? Who with?'

They started walking down the stairs together.

'Edward, from the hotel, you know.' She blushed. 'He's taking me for dinner in Bath, which will make a lovely change. I'm actually quite excited. I haven't had a date since the divorce, well, before that, unless you count the odd date night with my ex-husband.' She laughed.

And Gemma did have to admit, she seemed to radiate happiness.

'Well, I hope you have a lovely evening.' Gemma gave her

an impulsive hug. She'd never initiated a hug before, and Gemma had no idea why she'd done so.

Freddie was in the drawing room, making drinks.

'Ah, just the people. I think I've perfected the Meadowbrook signature cocktail,' he said, brandishing a glass. 'Come and have a taste.'

Pippa strode in and took a sip.

'You know, Fred, that's not bad. Try it, Gem.'

Gemma did as she was told. It was nice, fruity, not too strong, either.

'Oh wow, that is good,' she said.

'You know, I've used blueberries from our fruit cage, and I'm going to do a raspberry version. I can't tell you what else is in it, because I'd have to kill you,' he joked.

'Freddie, you might have to tell someone, otherwise you'll have to be at the bar at all times,' Gemma pointed out, taking another sip. It was delicious as the cool liquid slid down her throat.

'Good point. I will tell someone but not yet. Oh, and I am not having Edie be my cocktail waitress, by the way; she seems to think the job's hers. Anyway, shall I make us all some more, just to make sure that I can repeat the success?'

They all heard the doorbell.

'Who's that?' Freddie asked. Any of the family always came round the back entrance.

'Oh, I have a date, didn't I tell you?' Pippa said. 'Anyway, Gemma will explain.' She dashed off before anyone had a chance to speak.

'Right, well,' Freddie said, looking around the room. Gemma shuffled from foot to foot. Awkwardness filled the enormous drawing room. 'So, who's the bloke?'

'A guy we met from a neighbouring hotel.'

'I hope she isn't dating the enemy,' Freddie said.

Gemma hadn't thought of that.

'No, I don't think so. His hotel is totally different, nothing like Meadowbrook.' Gemma chewed her lip. Should she have worried about Pippa going off with Edward?

'Yes, but Pippa doesn't have the best taste in men.'

'Who does?' Gemma said without thinking. Freddie looked at her in surprise. 'Anyway, I'll just go and get something to eat and leave you to it,' Gemma said, wanting to run away.

'Or we could go to the pub for dinner,' Freddie suggested. 'I mean, I'm famished after all this genius cocktail-making and I don't feel like cooking.'

'Really?' Gemma asked.

'Why not?' He shrugged.

'OK.' Gemma smiled.

Part of her felt terrified at the thought of them being alone for an evening, especially as she would be expected to make conversation; she was glad she'd had that cocktail now. Another part liked being around him. It was so confusing. She went to get her coat and shoes, while Freddie waited by the front door, which he held open for her.

'Are you all right to walk? It's just that I'm not sure how much alcohol I've had.'

'Sure, at least it's not raining,' Gemma said. Way to go, talk about the weather, she chastised herself.

They made their way down the drive and she had a brainwave.

'Shall we see if Harriet and Connor want to come?' Even Harriet would be better than being alone with Freddie.

'Oh no, Harriet's dragged him to see some play. Poor guy was dreading it, but he likes to keep my sister happy.'

'That's sweet.'

'Yeah, but four hours of some dreadful modern play aimed at the middle classes who think they're intellectual would test any relationship.' He laughed. 'But she went with him to some godawful vets' convention where they talked about fleas for hours, so he owes her.'

'You see, that's how relationships should work, isn't it? Couples should be able to do things they might not want to do for each other,' Gemma mused, thinking of Chris again. 'You know, compromise.'

'Well, maybe. When I dated Loretta, my last ex, we liked the same things, so that never came up. Although, we both liked fast living, so we were probably both too pissed to think about anything else.'

'Well, they do say opposites attract, don't they?' Gemma persisted.

'I guess, which means I should be with a woman who doesn't drink, has no sense of humour and hates parties,' Freddie quipped. 'God, sounds like I should be dating . . .' He stopped suddenly and looked intently at his feet. Gemma felt herself turning red, from her toes to the tips of her ears. 'Well, maybe not everyone should date their opposite,' he added quickly.

'No,' she agreed, suddenly feeling miserable.

Freddie held the door open and greeted some of the regulars, who Gemma now recognised. They went to the bar, where the landlady, Issy, greeted them warmly.

'What are you drinking?' Freddie asked.

133

'White wine, please,' Gemma said.

Since being at Meadowbrook, she was definitely getting a taste for wine, and maybe now cocktails. Hah, perhaps she wasn't so opposite to Freddie, after all. After six months here, she might even be able to drink more than him. No, now she was being silly.

'You go and find a table, and I'll grab the drinks and a menu.'

Gemma found a table near the bar and drummed her fingers on the table nervously. How was she supposed to cope being on her own with Freddie? Why had she agreed to come? The whole thing unsettled her.

'Right, Gemma, I'm going to have a steak, which I always have when I'm not with my judgemental family. What would you like?' Freddie asked as Gemma glanced at the menu.

She had lost her appetite, so she picked the first thing she saw.

'Fish pie, please.'

'Right you are, I'll order. And I'll get more drinks, just in case.'

He was gone a short time and came back with two more glasses of wine, white for her and red for him.

'So, Gemma, why don't you tell me about you,' Freddie asked, not sounding as if he were teasing her for once.

'What do you want to know?'

Gemma dreaded opening up, but she also almost couldn't help herself when she was here. Despite her determination to keep herself closed off, she had let them all know more about her than she wanted to; it was the Meadowbrook effect.

'Look, I know nothing, apart from you live in Bristol, work in hotels and, according to Pippa, are like that woman on telly.'

'What woman?'

'The Hotel Inspector, I think she's called. Anyway, I mean about your life before you came here.'

'There's not much to tell, really. I'm not really like the Hotel Inspector.' Gemma paused, she did watch the show though, and she'd probably learnt quite a lot from her. 'I do love the hotel business, though,' she admitted. 'I've always wanted to open a hotel from scratch, so this is a dream job.'

'Do you have a boyfriend? I mean, I presume not, as we've not seen hide nor hair of one since you've been here, but you do disappear at times, so maybe . . .'

'No, I visit my nan, in the home.' Gemma felt her cheeks colour. This was why she didn't want to do this – she didn't want to have to talk about herself. In fact, she needed to put a stop to it now. 'I'm pretty boring, which I'm sure you already know.' She almost challenged him with her eyes.

'No, Gemma, I'm sure you're not boring.' He cleared his throat and sounded serious. 'It's sad about your nan. I miss my dad so much and, well, I barely remember my mum, so I sort of understand. What about your parents?'

'I don't have any. My dad left when I was born practically, and my mum went off four years later. My nan brought me up.'

'God, that's hard, I had no idea. Have you not seen either of them since?'

'No, nor heard from them. I always thought it must be my fault, that they left because I was so awful. My nan always tried to make me feel otherwise, she really did, but you can't help . . .'

'The same with us, only having dad around growing up – I mean he loved us very much, and he was wonderful, but

135

you always think there's something missing. You know, not having a mum.' He looked so sad, she wanted to reach out to him.

'Oh God, I know exactly what you mean.'

They held each other's eyes and Gemma felt something changing between them.

'But you know, we were luckier than most. But anyway.' Freddie looked so serious, Gemma had never seen this side to him, and she felt tears threatening her but she didn't want to cry.

'Hey, Freddie, I'm interested to hear about your club nights. Pippa said you used to run the best ever.' She felt the need to change the subject for both of them.

As Freddie flushed with pleasure, she thought she'd probably dodged a bullet. They were both on safer ground now.

'Well, we did have quite a reputation. Mind you, it was fun, but goodness knows how we survived it. I mean night after night, party after party . . .'

He launched into an explanation of what he did and every time he paused, Gemma asked him another question. The spotlight was well and truly off her, and she was determined to keep it that way.

After a third, or maybe fourth glass of wine, which was enough to make her just a little bit tipsy, and a delicious fish pie, Gemma and Freddie made their way back. It was warmer and lighter now, being March, and Gemma felt a little excited about spring at Meadowbrook.

'Freddie?' she said.

'Um.'

'Thanks for dinner tonight, I really enjoyed it,' she said, giggling. She felt herself trip, so she reached out to lean against a wall.

'Oh, you're quite welcome. Gemma, where are you?'

'Arghhh,' Gemma screamed. It was a hedge, not a wall, and she was now in it.

'Very welcome.' Freddie laughed as he grabbed her and pulled her out. 'Bloody hell, Gemma, I have never met anyone as klutzy as you.'

As she tried to brush leaves out of her hair she didn't answer him – she was too busy feeling like a total fool.

Gemma got herself into bed. She had said an awkward goodnight to Freddie at the door; she wanted to be alone with her humiliation. It seemed every time she thought she was making progress, or at least managing to behave like a normal human being around him, she would do something stupid, and as he said, she was so clumsy. But why? They'd had a great conversation today, she felt a barrier coming down between them, but then she had to go and make a fool of herself. If only she hadn't lost her footing and fallen into a hedge, or walked into furniture every time she saw him, or tripped over his favourite chicken . . .

She had to remember why she was here, why she'd applied for the job, why she'd thanked every single one of her lucky stars when she got the job. It was time to remember who Gemma Matthews really was and to put all this nonsense to bed. She couldn't let them get to her; she couldn't afford to be distracted. There would be no more drinking, falling over, worrying about being liked – no, from now on it would be all about the job.

She was about to turn the light off and settle down to sleep, when there was a knock on the door. Pippa put her head round.

'Oh good, you're still awake.' She came in and settled on Gemma's bed.

'How was your date?' Despite her tiredness, she did want to know.

'Ah, it was lovely. Oh, Edward is so charming and funny. And you know, he told me all about the hotel business. He was so helpful. Anyway, I had a fun night and we're going out again next week.' She giggled like a schoolgirl and Gemma couldn't help but join in.

'I'm so happy you had a nice time.' Gemma meant every word.

'And now maybe we can find someone for you. I'll ask Edward if he's got any dashing single friends.'

'Honestly, Pippa, I've got enough going on with this hotel. I can't even think about men.' She meant it; if only she could get the image of Freddie out of her mind, that is.

Chapter 15

'So, all the legal issues are being handled, and there are no problems as far as we can see. Freddie is studying for his licence, Gwen is looking at menus, and Pippa is looking into getting each of the rooms ready.' Gemma looked up at the room.

Almost another month had passed, and she had managed to keep her head down a bit as they fully welcomed spring. She told Pippa she had so much work to do, which she did, but also she was worried about being drawn into a world where she didn't belong. She needed to be careful. And she was amazed at how much work she was getting done.

'I thought we'd start with the attic rooms, which need the most work,' Pippa said. 'They are all doubles, but we need to sort out the bathrooms. There are only two bathrooms for five rooms. Those two can be joined to two of the rooms, which leave three that are in need of an en suite. I've got Roger coming over later to have a look.'

'Who's Roger?' Gemma asked.

She had been delighted to hand over the actual building and design to Pippa, who said it was her forte. It certainly wasn't Gemma's.

'A local builder who specialises in older properties. He's

worked here before, and so he knows it pretty well,' Harriet explained. 'And he also knows what restrictions there are. He did mine and Connor's cottage, so he's pretty much part of the family.'

Gemma nodded. Of course he was.

'Right, well, it's really happening,' Gemma said. 'Well, we still have a long way to go, but at least we are seeing progress.'

'And as well as studying for my licensing exam, I'm also getting the garden room cleared out and opened up,' Freddie added. 'Then Pippa and I are going to design a bar.'

'I can see it now,' Harriet said. 'It'll be a lovely bar.'

'And we are only opening to residents?' Gus asked, frowning.

'Don't worry, Gus, we'll let you and Amanda in,' Freddie joked.

'Yes,' Harriet replied, ignoring Freddie. 'I think that if we open it up we might get all sorts of people who our residents might not want to mix with.'

'Are you talking about Edie?' Freddie laughed.

'We love Edie, she's family to us, but if she moved into the bar – which, let's face it, she would – then it might hinder our business,' Harriet replied with a smile.

Gemma laughed. She was trying so hard to keep at arm's-length but at the same time, she felt so drawn to their lives.

'And also it keeps goodwill with the pub if we don't take any of their customers,' Gus pointed out.

'Exactly, and perhaps it might be quiet at times, but that's where we try to operate the other side of the business – private functions. That's something that Freddie is going to look into as well,' Gemma said.

'I just worry that we're aiming at people with money and the house will lose its soul,' Pippa sighed.

'But that won't happen, because Meadowbrook will attract lovely people. It's not just about money,' Gemma explained. 'It's about people coming here because they want to, because they'll hear great things about it, because they feel that they want a creative break, but you can't just open the doors to anyone, sadly.'

Gemma knew that, for example, she would never in a million years be able to afford to stay here, but as Harriet kept reminding her, it needed to turn a profit. And of course she knew how it worked: if you didn't price high then it wouldn't seem exclusive enough – people had to aspire to stay.

'Edward says that we'll have to offer huge discounts in the beginning to attract people.'

They all turned to Pippa. Since her first date, they had heard a lot of "Edward says", but they hadn't met him, apart from Gemma. Harriet tried to get Pippa to bring him to a dinner, but she said he was too busy. She was enjoying his company, though, and telling Gemma all about it, but she was, sensibly, Gemma thought, taking things slowly this time.

'We'll cross that bridge when we come to it,' Harriet said.

'Oh damn, is that the time?' Freddie said, glancing at his watch. 'We've got the Easter event committee turning up any minute.'

'Right, well, we're finished here for now,' Gemma said, trying to sound professional. 'While you guys have your meeting, I'll type up the minutes.'

'You don't want to join us?' Pippa asked.

'I think my time is best spent doing this,' Gemma said. 'Anyway, I've been to the other five meetings.'

The implication was clear. Gus and Freddie chuckled.

'God, Gemma, was that a joke?' Freddie teased.

They were taking a long time, far too long, to get the event sorted, although the theme had been decided on: Peter Rabbit. There was a film out and it was on TV again. Gemma wondered how Beatrix Potter would feel about that, but it would prove popular with the children and hopefully make a lot of money.

They were recreating Mr McGregor's garden – Gus was going to play him – and have lots of games based around the children helping Peter Rabbit to steal carrots and dodge the grumpy man. This would include the traditional Easter egg hunt, a game of hide-and-seek with the Easter bunny – Gerry – and a big picnic at the end. It all sounded so idyllic, so like a childhood should be, and Gemma was almost looking forward to it. Especially as it transpired that she wasn't expected to don a costume, but to sell raffle tickets with some of the ladies. At the moment there was a debate about who would be Peter Rabbit, but it looked as if it would end up being Freddie; although he objected on the grounds that he was far too tall.

Gemma loved hearing these ideas, loved seeing how it brought the village together, loved being a part of it, it was all so endearingly mad, but it wasn't part of her job. She would help, yes, she would even try to enjoy it, but did she need to be in every meeting?

Although she was slightly disappointed by not going, they were a lot of fun, after all. Crazy but more entertaining than television.

She sat cross-legged on her bed, surrounded by paper-work. She typed all her notes up and lost herself in ideas for the hotel. She didn't hear the knock on the door and when it opened, Harriet's face appeared and she jumped.

'Sorry,' Harriet said. 'I took the gamble you weren't prancing around naked.'

'No, luckily I don't prance very often.'

'Working hard?' Harriet, for the first time ever, sounded uncertain.

'Yes, come in,' Gemma said.

Harriet carefully moved a sheet of paper and perched on the edge of the bed.

'What can I do for you?' Gemma asked.

'Well, it's Pippa. You know, for someone I adore and am related to, she's a bloody idiot when it comes to men.'

'Aren't we all?' Gemma said.

'Well, actually, until Connor, yes, I wasn't blessed by making the best decisions. But Pippa seems to put every man she's in a relationship with on a pedestal. First Mark and now this Edward guy. And I wondered what you thought about him.'

'Well, when I met him, which was only brief, actually, he seemed OK. A bit older than I would go for, but Pippa seemed to like him, and he was quite charming.' Gemma decided to tread carefully; this was one of the lines she tried so hard not to cross.

'I just wish she'd let us meet him, so I can get a bit of an idea about him.'

'Maybe you should insist on it?' Gemma suggested.

'Not that anyone ever listens to me, but I might.' Harriet smiled.

'Harriet, one thing I have learnt is that everyone listens to you.' Gemma pointed her pencil at her, then blushed. Bloody line-crossing again. 'But I don't think you should worry

143

– Pippa talks about him a lot to me and it seems that she is taking it slowly. I don't think they've even had a sleepover yet. Maybe you need to learn to trust her a bit more?'

'I tell you what, if you get him to come to dinner, then I'll back off.' Harriet raised her eyebrows.

'OK, but let me figure out the best time to do it. I don't want to upset either of them.'

'Honestly, Gemma, I think I'm almost getting used to having you around.' She squeezed her shoulder, and for once Gemma didn't flinch as if she were going to be hit.

Chapter 16

Gemma was trying hard not to laugh. She had definitely found her sense of humour. They were all collected in the hallway waiting to head out. It was the day of the Easter event and Gemma's first taste of a Meadowbrook event. It was a bright spring day, but still fairly nippy. Gemma was wearing her smartest jeans, a blouse and jacket – she looked and felt good; she wasn't even nervous about selling raffle tickets. Poor Freddie was huffing and moaning. His Peter Rabbit costume was undoubtedly cute, with a blue jacket, a bag slung across his back and the big rabbit head in his arms, but of course it was anything but "Freddie". It at least gave Gemma a first taste of seeing Freddie anything but self-confident.

'I don't think I can breathe in this head,' he said.

'Oh, Fred, you'll be fine – there are holes for the eyes and mouth,' Pippa pointed out. 'And I haven't complained about my costume.'

They both turned to look at her. She was dressed in a red dress and jacket, as Peter Rabbit's friend, and she managed to pull it off; somehow managing to be both cute and gorgeous. Although she only had rabbit ears, not a full head, to be fair to Freddie.

'Why couldn't I do what you did and just have a bit of the outfit?' he huffed.

'Because you're the star, Fred. Now stop complaining and let's get moving.'

They reached the field, where an incredible job, transforming a sizeable chunk into Mr McGregor's garden, had been done. Gemma was impressed at how much work had gone into it; the family and the committee had gone to town. Everyone pitched in, and Gemma had been drawn into the Meadowbrook community. She could see it working *for* the hotel for the first time, rather than against it.

Connor and Harriet were both waiting for them. They had brought Agnes, the blind sheep, and her lamb, Abigail, into the field, where they were both munching the grass. They were tame and the children loved to pet them both. The tiny ponies – Cookie, Clover and Brian – had been given bunny ears, which they didn't seem to mind, as they chomped at the carrots they'd been bribed with. However, Gerald, the donkey, stood at the back of the field, looking longingly at the huge fake carrots that Gerry had made out of papier-mâché. According to Gwen, Gerry had spent hours making them, and he was proudly showing them off to anyone he could.

The goats, Piper, Flo, Romeo and baby Kayne, were in the next field; they were friendly enough but didn't like crowds. Although Freddie said the goats were in some kind of *ménage à trois*, it was Piper who'd given birth, and Romeo was the proud father. Poor Flo was a third wheel, Gemma thought.

The alpacas were busy ignoring everyone, safely tucked in their paddock. The cows were a safe distance away, as always, and the pigs were doing what they usually did, either lying down or eating. Apart from Geoffrey – who was now not only Gus's favourite, but everyone's. He was so friendly, and Gus said he might bring the children over to meet him later if they wanted. Apparently, Geoffrey was very fond of children and didn't even try to eat them.

While everyone busied themselves with their particular tasks, Gemma took a tour. In the tea tent, Gwen presided over some gorgeous cakes, which made Gemma's mouth water. Hilary had a stand for her quiches, which looked delicious. There were tables set with cloths around, and drinks were tea and coffee with a small bar serving Pimm's and cider. Fraught parents were often grateful to pay a lot of money for a drink, Freddie had explained to her.

'Gosh, must practice being grumpy,' Gus, aka Mr McGregor, said.

He was wearing brown trousers, a blue shirt, beige waistcoat and a hat. Amanda came up behind him.

'Don't forget your rake,' she said, handing it over to him. 'Gemma, how are you?' Amanda asked.

'Good, thanks. What are you up to today?' Gemma regretted that she didn't see as much of Amanda as she would have liked, but she seemed to be really busy with her business and her daughter, Hayley, who seemed to do a lot of out-of-school activities.

'I'm with you on raffle tickets and on standby if the refreshment tent gets busy, so hopefully we can have a good gossip.'

A couple of teenage girls came up – one was tall with dark hair and was striking, the other looked like a mini version of Amanda.

'This is Fleur and Hayley,' Gus said. 'And this is Gemma, who is helping with the hotel.'

'Oh, Gemma, I've been dying to meet you. Aunt Pip talks about you all the time,' Fleur said.

She definitely had something of the Singer look. And the Singer confidence, Gemma decided.

'Well, it's lovely to meet you. I was hoping to see you at the house sometime,' Gemma said warmly.

Fleur had Gus's colouring, but she must have had her mother's features; it was clear she was going to be a heart-breaker. Gus cleared his throat uncomfortably.

'God, don't say that in front of Dad,' Fleur said, rolling her eyes and sounding like a teenager. 'I'm busy, I've got school-work and you know, a social life, which Dad doesn't seem to understand.'

'Oh I'm sure, but hopefully you'll come up when you can and see what plans we have for the hotel,' Gemma said quickly.

'You used to love going up to Meadowbrook,' Gus said sadly.

'Oh, for God's sake, Dad, how many more times? I'm busy. And you don't live there anymore. I have your house, the sanctuary to visit, not to mention Mum nagging me that I'm not home enough. God, I'm only one person! Come on, Hayley, let's go and look after the ponies.'

Hayley trotted off after Fleur, also rolling her eyes. Gus put his arm around Amanda.

'I'm so sorry about her,' he said to Gemma.

'Oh, she was very polite to me, really.'

'She's fourteen; all hormones and hating her parents,' Gus explained.

'She's a bit harsh to both Gus and her mother – thankfully, I seem to be exempt. Honestly, Hayley's a year younger, but she's learning teenage behaviour fast.' Amanda laughed.

'Oh God, now I feel so guilty – my daughter is ruining your daughter,' Gus said, and Amanda shook her head.

'You know, I was a horrible teenager, so I am guessing this is karma. What were you like, Gemma?' Amanda asked.

'Oh, you know, pretty typical. Boy bands, crushes, nothing too bad.'

Gemma felt desperate to change the subject. She had been such a serious teenager, she didn't behave badly; in fact, she'd never behaved badly in all her years. She had a couple of friends, but they didn't spend time together out of school. They didn't smoke, drink or even kiss boys. They did talk about boys a bit, they weren't totally atypical, but they didn't expect any boy to ever notice them. And they didn't.

'Hopefully, we'll survive the next few years then.' Gus grinned. 'And at least Fleur loves animals. She might not go up to the house much these days, but when she stays with us she does come to the sanctuary to see the animals. She says she wants to be a vet like Connor, which we are encouraging.'

'Oh there you are, Gemma.'

Gemma turned to see Edie, Rose, Doris and Margaret approach, all wearing bunny ears. They did look quite comical, but sweet.

'Are you going to show Amanda and me the ropes with the raffle tickets?' Gemma asked, somehow feeling relieved to get away from talk about her past.

'Oh yes, we're the bunny girls,' Edie said, handing a pair of bunny ears to Amanda and her.

'Hugh Hefner would be turning in his grave.' Freddie suddenly appeared behind them, draping his arms around the older ladies.

'Oh, young man, I'll have you know I could have been a Playboy Bunny in my day,' Doris said, waggling a finger at Freddie.

Gemma didn't know whether to laugh or cry.

'I'm sure you could.' Freddie looked a little scared as he backed away.

'Right, we've got ten minutes to gates open, let's get this show on the road.' Gus clapped his hands together, and they all went off to their various posts.

Amanda and Gemma were a little bit busy gossiping, so when Edie came over to tell them off for not selling enough tickets, they both promised to try harder.

'We don't really need to, though,' Amanda said as Edie walked away. 'Look at her.' They both glanced over to where Edie was press-ganging people into buying tickets. 'But I guess we should try.'

'How about we try the refreshment tent?' Gemma suggested.

She was enjoying herself. In the outdoors, with Amanda for company, watching everyone enjoying Freddie's impression of Peter Rabbit wasn't a bad way to spend a day. She'd almost forgotten she was wearing rabbit ears.

The refreshment tent seemed to be a good idea. Not only did they get a glass of Pimm's, but Amanda also introduced her to more of the villagers and especially younger residents – under sixty anyway – she hadn't met before. There were quite a few families, and she soon discovered that the Meadowbrook events had such a good reputation now that people came from further afield. They even managed to shift most of their tickets.

'Shall we go and watch Gus and co?' Amanda suggested, both with a second Pimm's in their hands.

'Sure.' Gemma followed her out.

It was a huge success, she could already tell as she watched Freddie/Peter Rabbit with Pippa by his side lead a number of children around the garden, with Gus/Mr McGregor trying to chase them. She couldn't help but feel impressed, and as Amanda went to check on Fleur and Hayley, she watched them, totally absorbed.

'He's surprisingly good with kids.'

Gemma turned to see Harriet at her shoulder.

'Who?' Gemma felt her face flush.

'Fred, of course. He's doing a great job.'

'Oh yes, they seem to be having a great time, the children I mean.'

'Oh really.' A smile curled at Harriet's lips. 'I thought you were staring at Fred – did you even notice the children?'

Gemma was shocked. What on earth? 'I was watching all of them,' Gemma objected, feeling as if she were the same colour as her drink.

'Oh come on, Gemma, I'm pretty sure that you have a little crush on my younger brother,' Harriet teased.

'I certainly do not.' Gemma tried to sound as indignant as she could as she burnt with embarrassment. What the hell?

'Right, course not.' Harriet laughed, and she put her arm around her.

Gemma felt angry, then she felt scared. Did she have a crush on Freddie? Was that what this was? All the clumsiness, all the awkwardness, how tongue-tied he made her feel. And then the other night when they had dinner together she had been irrationally happy. Until she'd fallen in the bush. Perhaps that was why she was so scared of the effect Meadowbrook was having on her.

'I don't. Harriet, I am here to do a job, and I'm not thinking about anything else.'

Although Gemma was terrified of Harriet, she was more terrified of having feelings for Freddie. For so many reasons. Not least that he wouldn't, didn't, give her a second glance unless he was either insulting her or laughing at her.

'Oh lighten up, Gemma, I'm not accusing you of anything. My brother is a good-looking man; if you did have a little crush it wouldn't be the end of the world.' She shrugged.

'Well I don't,' Gemma snapped. 'Anyway, he wouldn't like someone like me,' Gemma pointed out.

'That doesn't mean you don't fancy him.' Harriet laughed; then, seeing the frown on Gemma's face, she stopped. 'Oh, for goodness' sake, I'm only teasing. Sorry, please don't get upset. Anyway, what do you think of the event?'

'It's really amazing. You've all done a great job.' Gemma began to calm down.

'It's so great – I mean look at the effort that's gone into it – and we're making loads of money for the sanctuary. We're so lucky to have such a great community, you know.'

'It's funny, but I wouldn't have put you down as a "community person",' Gemma said, still annoyed by her earlier comments.

'Me neither. I didn't have a community in New York, but here, well I love being part of one. I've changed a lot since being back at Meadowbrook.' She sounded a little wistful. 'You might not think so, but I'm even softer now.' Harriet grinned and then she broke into a broad smile. 'I might not have mastered warm, but by next year . . .'

'You're softer when you talk about your family, Connor and the animals, even the village,' Gemma conceded.

'I know we must seem a bit intimidating, I get that,

especially me, but you seem to be doing a good job, so maybe you can soften up a bit too.' Harriet arched her perfect eyebrow.

'You don't think I'm soft?' Gemma was surprised.

'No, you aren't hard either, but it's not that simple. I think you're very guarded and formal most of the time, actually. I still haven't fully figured you out, by the way.'

'Oh—' Gemma was intrigued by this view of her, when Pippa interrupted them.

'What are you two doing huddled over here?' Pippa asked.

'Just having a chat,' Harriet said. 'Pip, you've done another fabulous job, by the way,' she added.

'Oh it's been great, really enjoyed it. Goodness knows how we'll top it next year but anyway, I came to say the morris dancers are about to do their closing performance, and John will never forgive you if you don't both come and watch it.'

'Freddie, the idea was to let the kids find the Easter eggs, not you,' Harriet said as later they were all collapsed on sofas and chairs in the drawing room.

Freddie was making his way through a mountain of chocolate, and Harriet was on the sofa, snuggled up to Connor. Gus and Amanda were also cuddled up, and Pippa sat next to Gemma. Gwen and Gerry had brought tea and leftover cake; they were all exhausted. Although Gemma didn't feel as if she'd done much, she was as well. She had helped put all the animals away, as well as lending a hand to clear up the catering tent, and she'd got involved in another long conversation with John, the vicar, about the history of morris dancing. Which still left her feeling none the wiser.

'Right, I vote we get a pizza delivery tonight,' Connor suggested.

'We've just eaten a mountain of cake, Freddie has worked his way through goodness knows how many chocolate eggs, and you want pizza?' Harriet asked.

'I really do, it's been hungry work today.'

'Where are Fleur and Hayley?' Gwen asked.

'In the snug watching TV,' Gus said. 'I'll go and ask them what they want. They'll definitely want pizza,' he said.

A phone buzzed, and Pippa reached and took it out of her pocket.

'Oh it's Edward – he wants to know if I fancy a drink, so count me out,' she said. Pippa stood up. 'I'll see you later, don't wait up.'

'More pizza for us then.' Connor smiled as he waved her off.

'Honestly, I'm not sure I can eat another thing,' Gemma said, feeling full of chocolate, cake and happiness.

'Me neither. Gemma, do you fancy a long run tomorrow around the estate?' Harriet asked.

Being alone with Harriet, having to try to keep up with her superior pace, looking dowdy next to her high-fashion workout clothes?

'I'd love to,' she heard herself saying. Look how far she'd come, Gemma thought.

Chapter 17

'Happy birthday,' Pippa shouted, making Gemma jump as she walked into the kitchen.

She rubbed her eyes, Was she still dreaming?

'Wh-what?' she mumbled, her brows furrowed.

'Oh, don't think you can get away with it. Remember, I've seen your CV. I know that today, the sixth of April, is your thirty-first birthday, and we're going to spoil you.'

Gemma's eyes almost popped out of her head. How had this happened? How had she . . . As the colour threatened to drain from her face, she blinked and then composed herself. It was a stupid mistake, a really stupid bloody mistake, but one she would have to live with.

Pippa led Gemma over to the kitchen table, which was laid out with a pot of coffee, croissants and condiments, and Freddie was already sat there, although he looked as if he were still half-asleep. His hair was tousled and Gemma had a strong urge to touch it . . . Oh God, where had that come from? She pinched herself, and it hurt. Damn, she definitely wasn't dreaming.

'Happy birthday, Gemma,' he said, smiling impishly. 'Sit down.'

Gemma did as she was told, still in a state of shock.

'Right, well, coffee first then breakfast.' Pippa clapped her hands together. 'And I know today is a work day, but I'm taking you to Bath to a spa for a well-deserved pampering. That's my gift to you.'

'Wow.' Gemma was lost for words.

'That sounds like a treat for you as well, Pip,' Freddie pointed out.

'Well, Gem can't go on her own. And tonight we're having a big family meal, everyone's coming, Harry, Con, Gwen, well she's cooking too, Gerry, Gus, Amanda, even the teenagers. It's going to be a proper celebration for you, for all the hard work you've done so far and because well, because I think we've become such great friends and you're a big part of Meadowbrook.'

Gemma's eyes darted towards Freddie, who was pouring milk into his coffee. She literally had no idea what to say as emotion welled up inside her.

'Wow.'

'Oh for goodness' sake, say something else.' Freddie looked up. 'How does it feel to be properly in your thirties now?'

'It feels exactly the same.' She wasn't even actually thirty yet. 'But, you know, I haven't had a fuss made on my birthday for a while, so I'm sorry but I'm just a bit overwhelmed.'

She tried to keep her emotions in check. Her nan always used to make a big deal of her birthday, but for the last three years she had forgotten, nor did Gemma remind her. This was the first birthday she'd had for years. And it wasn't even her birthday.

'Oh you poor thing.' Pippa put her arms around Gemma and gave her a hug. 'I know, with your nan's situation, we really wanted to spoil you.'

'Well I'm touched. Thank you.' Gemma tried to steady her

hand as she took a sip of coffee. She thought about what must have happened, and she wanted to kick herself for her mistake, but she tried to stay calm – no, not calm but excited. She needed to be excited. 'And as for dinner, that sounds so perfect, I just, well, it was just so unexpected. I didn't really think about celebrating my birthday at all. In fact, I all but forgot about it,' she trilled.

'Oh but we must celebrate,' Pippa said. 'I love birthdays.'

'Absolutely and, Gemma, tonight I am going to serve my new, improved Meadowbrook cocktail in your honour,' Freddie announced with a flourish.

Pippa giggled. She was so giddy, it was like it were her birthday. In the midst of her idiocy, Gemma had a slight brainwave.

'What I would love is if Edward could join us for dinner.'

'Edward?' Freddie looked up from his croissant.

'Yes, you've been seeing him for a few weeks now, so you should make sure he comes. I'd love to meet him properly.'

'So would I,' Freddie added.

'Oh I don't know, I mean the whole family . . .' Pippa looked mildly horrified.

'Thanks, Pip, we're not monsters and Gemma's right: bring him tonight, best get us all over with in one dinner than drag it out.'

'Oh go on, I'm dying to meet him properly,' Gemma pushed. 'It would make my birthday,' she said.

'He might be busy,' Pippa said.

'Well tell him to be un-busy,' Freddie said, and Gemma was grateful for his support, especially as he didn't know Harriet had put her up to it.

Gemma was overjoyed suddenly – she was going to get

Edward Farquhar served up to Harriet on a silver plate. It was turning out to be the best birthday ever.

Even if it actually wasn't her birthday.

The spa was more fun than relaxing, because Pippa didn't stop talking. Gemma stretched her legs out and enjoyed the feel of the fluffy bathrobe and slippers she'd been given. This was what friends did, have girly time together, and she had never, ever done this before. It was wonderful. After all, she'd never had a friendship like this before.

Edward had agreed to dinner and all through the massage, which they had on tables that were side by side, Pippa gushed about Edward; he was wonderful and good-looking and he was teaching her about running a hotel. Gemma made all the right noises, but she was almost drifting off, so she didn't catch it all.

'Before we go home, I'm taking you to my hairdresser for a wash and blow-dry,' Pippa said.

'But I've been totally spoilt already.' Gemma was incredulous. This was all so, so much. She had never done this before in her life, been pampered like this, and she felt as if she were walking on air. She hugged Pippa impulsively, something she was doing increasingly.

'And you deserve it.'

'Thank you,' Gemma replied, feeling emotional.

No one apart from her nan made her feel like this. Damn remaining professional and focusing only on the job – how could she when she had people like this around her?

Gemma felt like a million, trillion pounds. She couldn't stop looking at herself in the mirror. Who was this woman? Her hair framed her face, which was changed by the application of make-up that Pippa had also booked her for. Keri, the girl doing her make-up, made it look so easy and she talked her through every step, so Gemma thought she might be able to do something similar – if not quite as good – herself. Growing up, she had always been slightly dismissive of the girls she knew who troweled on make-up and were obsessed with clothes, but mainly because they all seemed to dislike her. But what she was learning was that putting more time into her appearance was increasing her confidence. If she had known the power of a good haircut, some make-up and nice clothes, she might have done it years ago. She might have avoided being bullied.

Perhaps that was one downside of growing up with her nan – not that she would ever criticise her. Her nan was old-fashioned, and she tended to dress Gemma in a way that didn't really fit in with everyone else. She made a lot of her clothes – which did lead to bullying – and even her school uniform was always slightly too big for her, but then money was tight and it needed to last. God, growing up was hard, but then now she was an adult and it was time she took responsibility for choosing how she looked rather than trying to fade into the background. Meadowbrook wouldn't countenance that. After all, she had started making an effort in her last job at the hotel after Clarissa told her she expected her to look her best to reflect the hotel, although she was never quite good enough. Now, it was time to step it up.

She pulled on her only black dress; she'd bought it in a sale. It fell a little above her knees and hugged her figure without being too tight. She teamed it with black tights and a pair of high-heeled black shoes that Pippa, who thankfully had the same-sized feet as her, lent her. She twirled around, stumbled and realised she best not run before she could – literally – walk as she made her way downstairs.

Pippa and Freddie were waiting in the drawing room when Gemma, walking carefully, joined them.

'I've made a jug of cocktails,' Freddie said. 'But Pip seems to think we should wait for the others.'

'Of course we should; anyway, they'll be here any minute.'

'God, you look different.' Freddie did a double take. 'What have you done to yourself?' he asked. Confusion flashed in his eyes.

'I had my hair and make-up done,' Gemma stammered. She felt warm inside at his noticing her.

'Well you look lovely,' Freddie said.

Gemma nearly fell over, from shock rather than clumsiness – it was the first compliment he'd paid her.

'Doesn't she just. Gorgeous,' Pippa gushed, giving Gemma a squeeze. 'You know I always thought you were really pretty, but you didn't seem to think so. Hopefully now you can see what we see.'

Pippa really was the most generous person she had ever met.

'Thanks to you, Pippa,' Gemma said. She didn't know how she would ever thank her for such a wonderful day. Work, that was how, working at this hotel and helping Pippa realise her dreams – that was how she would thank her.

There was a lot of activity from outside as Harriet, Connor, Gus, Amanda, Fleur and Hayley burst in.

'Happy birthday!' Harriet said, thrusting a present at Gemma.

'Oh! And we got you something too,' Gus said, handing her another package.

'Oh yes, I almost forgot.' Freddie handed over a small gift too.

'Well open them,' Fleur commanded.

'Of course,' Gemma said carefully, shocked and touched. 'Where's Gwen and Gerry?' she asked as Freddie started pouring cocktails.

'Oh, Mum's been in the kitchen for hours and Gerry's helping her,' Connor explained. 'Don't wait for them, honestly,' he added, eyes twinkling.

Gemma opened her presents and felt her eyes fill with tears. Harriet and Connor had given her a beautiful blue sweater, and she immediately loved it. It was so soft, possibly the nicest item of clothing she'd ever had.

'I thought the colour would suit you,' Harriet explained. 'What with your colouring, your eyes.'

Gemma was surprised. 'It's gorgeous, thank you,' she said genuinely.

Gus had painted a small watercolour of Meadowbrook Manor and had it framed.

'Oh! That's so beautiful, amazing, thanks.' Gemma wasn't going to be able to contain her tears for much longer as her eyes filled.

'Dad always gives the best gifts because he's such a great painter,' Fleur said proudly.

Gus glanced at her as if he wasn't sure he'd heard correctly.

'Open mine,' Freddie said. 'It's nothing exciting but I got it in Bristol the other day.'

There was a small box and inside was a silver "G" on a chain. Gemma was taken aback.

'It's gorgeous. I love it!' She pulled it out and put it on.

'Wow, I don't know how to thank you,' she said. She had never, in her whole life, received such wonderful gifts.

'Right, drinks.' Freddie started handing them out.

Gemma's eyes sparkled as she took a glass with happiness as well as tears.

'Uncle Fred, can we have one?' Fleur asked.

'No,' Gus said.

'Oh Dad, I'm fourteen.' Fleur pouted.

Gus looked angry but Amanda put a hand on his arm.

'If you guys have non-alcoholic cocktails now we'll let you have half a glass of champagne later,' Amanda said.

'Oh yes, that would be better,' Fleur said.

'I love champagne,' Hayley, who was a year younger than Fleur, said as if she drank it all the time.

Amanda shook her head, grinning.

'Of course, you know drinking responsibly is important, girls, so if you are going to drink I'd rather it was when you were with us,' Gus said, sounding like the father he was.

'Oh for God's sake, Dad, it's not like I go down the park with a bottle of meths,' Fleur said. 'Who do you think I am? Uncle Fred?'

No one could help themselves as they all burst out laughing. When the doorbell rang to announce Edward's arrival, Gwen and Gerry had joined them in the living room. They'd given Gemma a huge bouquet of flowers, nothing like the ones from the service station that Chris used to give her for her birthday, and Gwen said she would put them in a vase after dinner so she could enjoy them in her bedroom.

As Pippa led Edward into the drawing room, Gemma did her best to regain her composure and focus. But she couldn't stop fingering the necklace, feeling warm and fuzzy. This must be what it felt like to be part of a family, to have more than one person who cared about her, to have people actually think about her. She wished, more than anything, she could tell her nan about this. She wished, more than anything, that her nan could be here to celebrate with her.

'Everyone, this is Edward,' Pippa said.

Edward smiled broadly as he greeted everyone.

'Lovely to see you again, and happy birthday,' he said to Gemma charmingly.

'Thank you,' she replied politely.

Perhaps Harriet was being paranoid. Edward sounded sincere and genuinely pleased to meet them all.

'Nice to meet you,' Freddie said, handing him a cocktail. 'Gosh, Pip, he looks like a blonde version of Mark.'

Fleur burst out laughing, but was then silenced with a small shove from her father.

'Who's Mark?' Edward asked, a smile still plastered to his face.

'Her ex-husband,' Fleur said before anyone could stop her.

The silence filled the room.

'Shall we go through to the dining room? Dinner is just about ready.' Gwen, as usual, saved the day.

Pippa organised the seating arrangements, and Gemma was mortified to find herself sitting next to Freddie with Connor the other side. Harriet was next to him and along with Edward, made up one side of the table. Fleur and Hayley were tucked away at one end, and Gwen at the other with Pippa, Gus, Amanda and Gerry on the other side of the table. The table was dressed beautifully: crystal glasses for every type of wine and water, heavy silver cutlery, a decanter of expensive red wine and two antique candelabras.

'So I'm guessing that if this is going to be your main dining room, when you open the hotel, you'll have smaller tables in the here?' Edward asked, surveying the room. 'My guess is you could get at least ten tables in here.'

'No—' Pippa started.

'Yes,' Gemma interrupted. 'Although the details haven't been finalised.'

Harriet nodded approvingly at her, but Pippa gave her a questioning glance.

'You know I really would be happy to help you with anything,' he said.

'Isn't that great?' Pippa said.

'It certainly is,' Harriet replied. 'And I'm sure that Gemma would appreciate hearing any of your thoughts, and we all bow down to your expertise, of course.'

'I'd be happy to help, but I can already see that Meadowbrook is special,' Edward stated, sounding humble.

'The Darnley is lovely too.' Gemma smiled sweetly.

'Can we change the subject? It's Gemma's birthday, so let's not talk hotels. Although, I bet you don't have a signature cocktail as good as mine,' Freddie boasted.

'Or any alpacas. Do you have alpacas?' Connor added with a chuckle.

'Or an in-house master painter and master baker.' Gemma was enjoying herself.

'Or a gay cow,' Fleur threw in.

'Don't forget the gardening club, I bet you don't have a gardening club,' Gwen added.

'I'm not sure I understand.' Edward still had a smile on his face but was bemused, as anyone listening to them would be.

Gemma marvelled at how quickly she had got used to the Meadowbrook ways. Not that long ago she was permanently wearing the same puzzled expression that Edward currently wore.

'Oh stop teasing him,' Pippa snapped. 'For God's sake.'

Freddie went round the table refilling everyone's wine.

'Here's to Gemma, happy birthday.' Gus led the toast.

'And to Gwen, thank you for cooking such a lovely meal,' Harriet added.

'To Edward, thank you for joining us,' Pippa gushed.

'And to all of you, for making this the best birthday I've ever had,' Gemma said, and she let the tears fill her eyes and genuine emotion fill her voice as she clinked glasses with them all.

Chapter 18

Gemma couldn't believe it when she looked at the clock on her bedside table. It was gone eleven, and she hadn't slept this late since she was ill with the flu a few years ago. She groaned. For someone who didn't drink, who didn't get hangovers, she was becoming almost used to them. But then it had been her fake birthday, after all. Dinner had gone well – after the initial awkwardness Edward had been the perfect guest. He had been attentive to Pippa, asking polite, non-hotel questions, he'd complimented the cooking, the house, and Gemma thought that at least Harriet's mind would be put at rest now. After dinner he had cried off, saying that he needed to be at work early the following morning, and Pippa, after a long, lingering farewell, had come back to join them.

Gwen and Gerry retired home after clearing up, but Freddie was on a mission to get everyone drunk. Fleur and Hayley sneaked off to the snug. Later it was found they had smuggled half a bottle of champagne, not enough to do any damage, but Gus hadn't been pleased. Fleur called her dad "a boring old fart", and in the end they had left under a bit of a cloud. Freddie seemed to find it funny, and Pippa said it reminded her of when they were teenagers.

They regaled Gemma with stories from their past, how

Harriet and Connor had been caught sneaking alcohol to the summer house, and how the others tried to join in but were sent away. How Freddie tried making vodka at school once, which nearly exploded, and their father'd had to make a hefty donation to prevent him from being expelled. How Pippa, who did nothing wrong ever, once had a date with a boy who her father didn't approve of, because he smoked and swore a lot, and was grounded almost for the rest of her life. But she wasn't, because she managed to twist Andrew Singer around her little finger, unlike anyone else. They talked of their past with such fondness that Gemma couldn't help but feel little stabs of envy.

Her teenage years couldn't have been more different. At school, she tried so hard not to be noticed. She was so average, in all ways, but that didn't deter the bullies. She didn't get invited to parties, of course. Her best friend was studious and as boring as she was, they didn't spend time together outside school, and they were probably only friends as they were both so unpopular. Gemma would never have dreamed of doing anything against the rules; she wasn't built that way. She didn't ever engage in sport, as she was hopelessly uncoordinated, and she dreaded gym class. She was also too scared of other girls to join any clubs. She didn't feel she belonged. Not having parents made her feel different, for as long as she could remember. She never fully fitted in anywhere.

She listened with envy, longing but also with guilt. She loved her nan, and she hated having negative thoughts about her childhood. She grew up so terrified about losing the one person who loved her, she thought being as invisible as she could be was the best way forwards. Had she missed out on living? She was beginning to feel now as if she had, and despite her determination she was being drawn into the web that was the Singers – they were intoxicating, addictive, and she couldn't help herself. She wanted to be a part of them. For the first time in her life, she actually wanted to try to fit in.

After they had emptied more bottles of wine, and Connor had dragged a reluctant Harriet home – he had to get up at the crack of dawn to see to the animals, after all – the party had finally broken up. Freddie started snoring on the sofa, and Gemma was yawning and having trouble keeping her eyes open, so Pippa chivied them both up to bed. It was the first time that Gemma had been reluctant to do so.

Today she was due to go to the sanctuary to see the cats, as she did every day, then she was driving to the bungalow. The sale was still going through, not exactly at breakneck speed but she needed to continue emptying and sorting the furniture and belongings out. She had so much to do that she had decided, reluctantly, to stay there for the night and visit her nan the following day before heading back. She was finding she missed Meadowbrook when she wasn't there and as her job had an expiration date, that was dangerous. Making herself stay away for the odd night was a good reality check for her.

She pulled on some old clothes and made her way downstairs. There was no sign of anyone, although the dining room had been cleared as if last night's dinner hadn't happened. She wandered into the kitchen, which was again empty, and made a coffee, drinking it quickly before heading out.

When she opened the door to the cats' home, Jenni, one of the sanctuary workers, greeted her with a big smile.

'Hi,' Gemma said.

'Hi, Gemma, thank goodness you're here.'

'Why?' She didn't normally get such a warm welcome.

'I need to give all the cats their flea treatments, and I can't find anyone to help. Amy isn't in until this afternoon, Connor is at the surgery, and I don't know where Harriet is.'

'Right.' Gemma's heart dropped.

Not only was she horribly hungover, but she'd also gone from five-class luxury treatments yesterday to holding squirming cats while Jenni gave them their anti-flea stuff. Not great with her hammering head. Nor were the scratches she endured, nor the shrieking yelps of the cats – although they weren't being hurt, they obviously didn't like being handled in this way. Only her Albert stayed still and purred.

Just as they finished, Harriet appeared.

'Jenni, I've just got your text,' she said.

Despite the late night and the drink, Harriet looked impeccable.

'Ha, I've finished now,' Jenni said. 'Gemma helped.' Jenni smiled again and left.

'Sorry, I got caught up.' Harriet looked guilty; Gemma thought she had probably ignored the text on purpose. 'Are you all right, Gemma?' she asked kindly.

'I'm not sure. Some of those cats have really sharp claws.' Gemma rubbed her arm.

'Hungover?'

'Yes, a bit.' Gemma followed Harriet out. 'You?'

'Yes, and Connor's not happy. I kicked off at him last night for dragging me home and I wasn't very nice to him, which means I feel dreadfully guilty today.'

'It was the drink talking, surely?'

'Yes, of course it was, but I'm not sure what's wrong with me. I love Connor, I really do, but it's as if I, oh I don't know,

I sabotage it at times. When I told Connor how I felt about him, he said that we could never be together because he wasn't enough for me and that I needed the big career and the bright city lights. And I don't, I know I don't, but I think I've changed my life so drastically to be here, to be with him that sometimes I feel as if I should be doing more than I am. It's frustration with myself I guess, but I take it out on him, which isn't fair.'

Gemma was slightly taken aback by this unexpected confession; although Harriet had been more open with her lately, this was another step.

'Once the hotel's up and running, don't you think you'll have far more to do then?' Gemma said uncertainly.

'Yes, of course, but I need to stop stuffing up with Connor. He won't put up with me if I turn into a harridan at regular intervals. Anyway, I'm not sure why I'm telling you this . . .'

'Because I'm here.'

'Yes, you are here, and so that makes sense. Yes, you seem to be becoming the unofficial Meadowbrook agony aunt.' Her phone beeped as Gemma felt startled at her words. 'Right, I'm needed in the office. See you Sunday night – dinner in the pub as usual?'

Gemma nodded. It cheered her up that for the first time as an adult she had a usual.

'Oh, by the way, thanks for getting Edward here last night. He seemed all right.'

'I thought so.'

'I mean, a bit old for her, but then she does like the older man, but not like Mark so, well, fingers crossed . . .'

She was just about to leave to drive back to Bristol, when the door opened and Fleur appeared.

'Ah, Gemma, you're here,' Fleur said happily.

She was such a pretty girl, Gemma thought, and confident. If Gemma ever had a child, she would want her to have Fleur's confidence rather than Gemma's lack of it.

'Hi, Fleur. I was just about to go. I've got to go home for a bit.'

'Oh, I'm staying all weekend, so I thought I would spend a bit of time with the cats. I do love cats.'

'Me too.'

'Dad says the pigs are the best listeners but I think cats are.'

'I agree, and I also find them quite calming.'

'You know I get lonely here sometimes and the cats make me feel less so,' Fleur almost whispered.

Gemma glanced at her; her eyes were downcast.

'What do you mean? You've got your family, Hayley, everyone.'

'I know, but here's the thing,' she sighed. 'I love being here, more than at home really. My stepdad is so strict, and he always moans about me making a mess, even though I think I'm normal, and Mum always fusses around him, so I prefer it here but then I miss my friends. I wish I knew people my own age here and then I could spend more time here. Does that make sense?'

Gemma nodded. She remembered being a teenager, lonely, insecure. She found it hard to make friends everywhere, so she knew Fleur was nothing like her, but she also knew how much of a struggle being a teenager could be.

'You know, I reckon if you just went to the village, you'd soon find some people your own age. I mean where do teenagers hang out?' Gemma asked.

'Parks, bus stops probably! Parker's Hollow isn't exactly full of stuff to do.'

'Well, not that I'm recommending hanging out at bus stops, but you know if you spend a bit of time in Parker's Hollow, you might be surprised by how many people your age are in the village.'

'You know I might just do that. I hardly ever go into the village. Thanks, Gemma, thanks for listening and not telling me I'm being silly.'

'I don't think you are.'

As Fleur hugged her, Gemma grinned. Maybe Harriet was right: she was the unofficial agony aunt of Meadowbrook.

Being at home, which she no longer thought of as home, was becoming increasingly depressing – from the moment she pulled up in Pippa's car and saw the "Sale agreed" sign, to when she opened the front door to a blast of cold, empty air and beyond. She picked up the post, which had piled on the threadbare doormat, and took it through to the kitchen. Although the weather was spring-like, the bungalow was cold and she indulged herself by flicking the heating on for an hour. It was good for the place, anyway, to air it, even if it wasn't her home anymore.

She sorted the post into piles. Bills, junk mail and a letter from an old friend of her nan's who wrote occasionally and, Gemma realised with a pang, didn't know her nan was in a home now. She ought to reply to her explaining, so she placed that with the bills. She would also read the letter to her nan, which might give her some comfort.

She searched on the Internet for a local firm who would remove all the furniture and dispose of it however they saw fit. Sadly, most of their furniture had seen better days. The sofa was sunken with age, a bit like her nan. The upright chair was OK but dated, the coffee table scratched and old-fashioned, and the sideboard, which was from the Fifties, was possibly the only thing of interest.

Gemma emptied it of old books, photo albums, and other bits and pieces, boxing them up accordingly. She wouldn't give the photo albums away, of course; they were all she had left of her childhood, her mum's childhood and her nan. There were her nan's wedding photos – when she got married, her nan looked a lot like Gemma – and then her mum's baby photos. She was a cute blonde child, and Gemma wondered how she managed to turn into an adult who would abandon her only child. She wiped tears away, furiously. That was the problem with coming back – emotion got the better of her. She put the albums with the pile of things she was keeping. It was still a very small pile.

She went up to the loft and dusted off some old suitcases. Thankfully her nan wasn't much of a hoarder, so the loft was pretty empty, and she packed the things she was keeping. She would take them back to Meadowbrook, she decided; then she could get the rest of the house cleared. She needed to say goodbye to it once and for all. She didn't want to keep coming back and revisiting the emptiness of her life now, without Nan in it.

Her poor nan, she thought as she sat down in the chair, hugging an old patterned cushion to her chest. It wasn't much to show for a lifetime, was it? She always worried that her nan, who had been in her late forties when Gemma was born, had given up her life to bring Gemma up, and she'd settled for taking care of her grandchild rather than following her dreams. She never remarried after her grandfather died, and when her mum skipped off into the sunset when Gemma was four, her nan devoted her life to her.

Gemma had asked her once if she had prevented her from doing things with her life, and her nan had laughed and said no. She said she loved her grandfather and when he died she didn't need to meet anyone else. She said that she was happy working part-time in the local post office so she could take care of Gemma, and she said that she missed her daughter but she didn't know what had gone wrong with her. She put it down to a broken heart and said that one day Gemma might understand that her mum couldn't cope without him, but that was as far as their discussion ever went. It was painful for them both, in different ways, Gemma guessed, but she never shook the guilt that she had somehow ruined her nan's life, although she knew they loved each other very much.

It had, in many ways, taken going to Meadowbrook and seeing the Singer family interact for her to see how families worked. And hers, although very different, far too small, too insular, too isolated, was at least full of love. And when she felt jealous about the siblings, about the house, about the life they had, she remembered how much her nan loved her, and she realised she was so, so lucky to have had that. But now it was gone.

She took an afternoon nap in her old bed; her emotions, as well as her hangover, getting the better of her, and when she woke it was dusk. She felt lonely, she was alone, and she missed her nan even more keenly when she was at the bungalow. She wondered if she always would, but the problem was that in some way she was still here, although in others she wasn't. Dementia was cruel not only to the sufferer, but also to those who loved them.

She was alone. She always thought she would be all right on her own. When Chris dumped her, when friendships slid away because she was too afraid to let anyone fully into her world, she thought she would be OK, but now she wasn't so sure. Because she didn't feel very OK and she didn't know what the hell to do about it. Was it time to let people in? Or had she, in fact, already done so? If, or when, her job at Meadowbrook ended, she knew she would still like to have the Singers in her life. She had come to rely on their friendship, and she had a suspicion that they, especially Pippa, may feel the same about her. At her – real – age of twenty-eight, had she finally realised the value of friendship?

Chapter 19

'That colour really suits you,' Pippa said as they made their way down to the pub for their Sunday evening supper.

Gemma basked a little in the compliment. She had felt emotionally drained when she left her nan that afternoon. It had been one of her quiet visits; she wasn't confused, just not really there. It was as if someone had turned the lights out inside her. The flowers, roses that Edie had cut for her, didn't even provoke a reaction, the wine gums went unopened and the letter that Gemma read to her nan didn't even warrant a flicker of recognition in her eyes.

She didn't speak, she seemed to look right through Gemma, and it had been like talking to a shell as she read the letter and told her all about Meadowbrook and the mix-up with her birthday. She had held her hand, but it was cold to the touch, and as she said to one of the home's many staff, it was as if her nan had left her body. The carer explained, kindly, that that happened sometimes, that patients would recess into the deepest parts of themselves. Apparently, her nan had been like this for a couple of days. She was relatively healthy, in body but not in mind, and it was heartbreaking to see someone you loved, or even anyone for that matter, this way.

But the minute she got back to Meadowbrook, changed

her clothes, put on the lovely new sweater that Harriet had given her, straightened her hair and applied make-up, she became a different person. She was full of grief for her nan, that wasn't going to go away, but she had learnt to push it into the background – she had to, otherwise she would go insane. She was actually excited to be back at Meadowbrook, relief intermingled with happiness.

'Thanks, I love it,' Gemma replied as Pippa linked arms with her. She had long since given up trying to keep her at arm's-length, of course.

'Keep up, you two,' Freddie shouted from where he, Harriet and Connor were striding ahead. 'I'm so hungry.'

'Oh for God's sake, Fred,' Pippa complained, but they picked up their pace.

They reached The Parker's Arms just as Gus was parking his car. He and Amanda got out.

'My nieces?' Freddie asked.

'No, simply had to watch something on TV – *Game of something*.' Gus looked perplexed.

'Thrones, Gus, *Game of Thrones*,' Amanda said, sounding a bit exasperated. 'Honey, you're going to have to stop being an old man, and come to terms with the fact that Fleur is growing up and this is just a horrible teenage, hormonal phase.'

'Oh boy, don't mention the word hormones around me.' Freddie shuddered.

'She's full of bloody hormones,' Amanda said pointedly.

'I'm sorry.' Gus held his hands up. 'I don't understand teenage girls, and I was just getting really close to my daughter and then suddenly she's replaced by a monster who doesn't want to talk to me, answers questions with not even one word but abbreviations, and certainly doesn't want to be seen with me.'

Gemma's heart went out to him; he looked so lost. But then, she knew, after her conversation, so was Fleur.

'It'll pass,' Harriet said, and Amanda gave her a grateful smile. 'We went through it and we came out the other side. Just be as understanding as you can. Being a hormonal teenage girl sucks in many ways.'

'Please stop saying that word,' Freddie shouted. 'You're nearly putting me off my food.' He opened the door to the pub and they all followed him inside.

The pub was half-full, as it was normally on a Sunday evening, but as their group walked in, it seemed to go quiet. Everyone turned to stare at them, no one greeted them and, Gemma noticed, as they went to find a seat, all the tables had reserved signs on them.

'What's this?' Connor asked. 'Don't tell me that we need to book now?'

Steve and Issy behind the bar looked uncomfortable as they refused to look directly at Connor. Or at any of them.

'We're full tonight,' Steve said, concentrating really hard on a glass he was polishing.

'You don't look full,' Freddie objected.

'Well we are,' Issy snapped. She didn't seem her usual happy self.

Suddenly, the other customers in the pub became very interested in their own drinks.

'Hold on—' Freddie started.

'No, Fred, if they say they're full, they're full.' Connor took hold of his arm. 'Come on, let's go.'

Both Freddie and Harriet looked as if they were going to

object, but Connor managed to steer them both out through the door by practically pushing them.

'What the hell?' Freddie asked.

'I don't know, but arguing wasn't going to help, I could feel it,' Connor said sensibly. 'Whatever is wrong with Steve and Issy, we don't want to push them.'

'But I'm hungry,' Freddie reiterated.

'There's a vegetable lasagne in the fridge at the house. Come on, we'll heat that up and perhaps sort out what on earth is going on,' Pippa said.

'Who wants a lift?' Gus asked as he and Amanda made for the car.

Everyone apart from Gemma ran to get in, but Freddie and Harriet won.

'Of course we'll walk, then,' Connor said. He held out his arms for both Pippa and Gemma to take.

'Harry, make a salad and dig out some garlic bread too,' Pippa instructed as they drove off.

'What do you think that was all about?' Pippa mused as they started walking back.

'No idea – it was as if they were angry with us, but why?' Connor said. 'And for them not to say, but to keep insisting they were full when they clearly weren't . . . that was just weird.'

'Maybe I'm being naive here, but couldn't they just have been full, I mean with bookings for later?' Gemma said.

'Have you ever seen the pub full on a Sunday? Yes, quiz night is standing-room only, and sometimes Friday and Saturday, but Sunday is always quiet. And we go there every Sunday night, don't forget.'

'Look, let's get to the house, see what the others think and then come up with a way of finding out what the problem is,' Gemma suggested as they all picked up the pace. It was certainly a puzzle.

'Hang on a minute, why me?' Gemma asked after dinner had been eaten and the plates cleared away.

'You're sort of impartial. Well, you're not, but you don't know them as well as the rest of us,' Freddie pointed out. 'If they didn't want to tell us the reason that they're clearly trying to bar us from our local pub, a pub we support very well, by the way, then maybe they'll tell you.'

'And I do agree with Fred. Gemma, you are the most level-headed. Well, after Connor,' Harriet added.

'Am I not level-headed?' Gus asked.

'Not at the moment, not when you are all upset about Fleur,' Amanda pointed out. 'And I'd do it, but they know Connor and I are totally entrenched in this family, so you're probably the best bet.'

'Here, I've dialled the number.' Harriet passed the phone to Gemma when it was already ringing.

'But—' Gemma began to object but then Issy answered.

'Parker's Arms, good evening.'

'Oh hi, Issy, it's Gemma Matthews, you know, the Singers' hotel consultant?'

'Gemma,' Issy said. Her voice immediately turned cold.

Gemma got up from the table, as she could feel eyes all boring into her and she felt uncomfortable enough already. She sneaked off into the utility room so she could talk, although she could sense they were trying to listen in.

'Issy, we got the feeling tonight, or the Singers did, that they weren't welcome at the pub, and well we, I mean I, was wondering what was wrong.' There was a pause. 'Have they

180

done something to upset you? Because if they have, I really would like to know.'

'Look, we've always had a great relationship with the Singers, but to hear that they are opening a bar at Meadowbrook and that they didn't even have the guts to tell us themselves but let us hear about it from someone else. And if you think that the whole village won't be objecting to the licence application then you've got another thing coming,' Issy stormed, warming up.

'Issy, who told you this?' Gemma remained calm but her heart sank into her feet.

'It was Heather, who works in the village shop, she heard it from Stacey, who is on the PTA at the local school, and her husband is one of the governors – he's something to do with luxury bathrooms, I believe.'

Gemma tried to follow, but she was already lost.

'And I guess they must have heard it from . . .?'

'No idea, but that's not the point, the point is the whole village is talking about it – how you are going to put in a bar and restaurant, which you plan to attract all our customers to? We even heard you're planning on undercutting us with price and that you don't care about the fact that we'll probably go bust because you've taken all our customers.' Her voice was quite shrill.

'Issy, we haven't spoken to the village about the hotel, beyond the initial conversation, because most details haven't been pinned down. What I can tell you is that one, it has a bar, but it will be open for residents only, as will the restaurant. We aren't opening to the public at all, and the main reason for this is that there's absolutely no way the Singers would contemplate trying to take your customers. If anything we're hoping to encourage our guests to visit your pub, because it's the heart of the village and we'd definitely recommend it to them.'

'What? What are you saying?' she asked, her voice emotional.

'Only people staying at the hotel will be able to use the bar, and of course we may host some private events, but honestly, it's not going to be anything like your pub. There won't be any non-residents drinking here, and we are definitely, categorically, not after your customers. We would never do that to you, I mean the Singers wouldn't.'

'Well that's not what we've heard.'

'Clearly, but listen, I think you've been given the wrong information. If only you'd said something when we were there, we could have cleared this up then.' Gemma tried not to sound irritated, but she hated gossip and it seemed villages like this ran on gossip. 'I'm guessing that someone, somewhere has got the wrong end of the stick.'

'Right, well I'll need more than your word. I'll need assurances, Gemma. Perhaps this *is* just gossip, but if you are sure you're not going to try to ruin us then you won't mind putting it in writing.' She was still a little frosty.

'And you'll get them. Issy, please don't think for one minute the Singers would dream of doing anything to harm your business. And if you want it in writing, then that won't be a problem.'

'I didn't want to think they would do anything to hurt us, nor did Steve.' She sounded a little contrite, finally. 'But you see when we were told, well we couldn't ignore it. And I'm sorry that we didn't let you have dinner tonight, or speak to you about it, but well, as you can imagine, we were very upset.

We were told you were going behind our backs, so we thought we'd teach you a lesson about that – you know, by pretending the pub was full.'

'Of course, I totally understand.' She didn't, she thought it was ridiculous for them not to have confronted them all, but then villages could be strange things, she was learning. 'Look, I promise I will sort out the gossip, not sure how, but please bear with us, and if anything else comes up, just come to us directly and we'll sort it all out.'

Gemma felt quite pleased with herself for clearing that up. When she explained it they were all a little open-mouthed.

'But we haven't said anything like that to anyone,' Harriet said.

'Someone must just be spreading rumours,' Amanda said.

'Well whatever's been said, it's become a victim of Chinese whispers, and we need to put a stop to it right now,' Harriet slammed. 'By the way, good job, Gemma.'

'I agree,' Freddie added. 'We purposefully said we wouldn't do anything to harm the village. They need to know that.'

'Not least because otherwise we'll get all manner of objections to the licence and the permits we need,' Gemma pointed out. 'And thank you, Harriet.' She was still a little startled at the compliment.

'So what do we do?' Gus asked.

'Gemma?' Harriet said.

'What?' Gemma's eyes darted around the table.

'You're in charge here, well sort of, so I propose you call a village meeting, where you do a presentation to everyone and reassure them about the hotel.' Harriet smiled. 'The whole of Parker's Hollow, we need to get them onside.'

'Oh that's a good idea, I'll help of course,' Pippa added.

Gemma felt herself turn ashen. Speak in front of the village? She wasn't capable of that . . .

'And we'll get Gwen to bake – they always love her cakes,' Pippa continued.

'Well don't you think it would be better coming from one of you?' Gemma asked. 'After all, you are part of the community here, so perhaps one of you should give the presentation.' The idea was fuelling her dread.

'Yes, but you are our hotel consultant and so they should hear it from you. My suggestion is that you do the presentation to the village and we'll all be there to support you.'

'Also, don't forget we've seen your CV,' Pippa added. 'You've got loads more experience at giving presentations than we have. Well, apart from Harriet, but hers were all numbers – no, you are definitely the woman for this job.'

Everyone else raised their hands as if they were taking a vote.

'Well—' Gemma could think of a million reasons why this wasn't a good idea. None of them she could voice, however.

'That's decided then,' Freddie said, moving on to discussing what they were going to have for dessert.

Chapter 20

'So, John, I thought that I'd ask you for your support,' Gemma began, chewing her lip anxiously.

She had been well and truly thrown into organising the village meeting. Pippa was smitten with Edward and was spending more time with him, Freddie was busy studying for his licensee exam; although they were a long way off from him having to take it. Gus was supportive and said he would ensure the gardening club were all on side but that, between the gardens, painting – he was holding an exhibition to raise money for the sanctuary – and having to try to keep Fleur away from drugs, he really had no time. Harriet said she was up to her eyes as she had survived year end, accounts wise, but she had to come up with business plans, budgets and projections for the coming year. And of course Connor was genuinely busy looking after the animals.

Her best support had come from Gwen, who advised Gemma to speak to John, the vicar, told her to invite all of Parker's Hollow to the village hall, and offered to bake loads of cakes for the meeting to soften everyone up. But Gemma still had not only to organise the meeting, but also to host it, speak at it and face the hostile villagers, who she could only hope didn't turn up baying for her blood. Freddie had painted a picture of them brandishing pitchforks when upset; she could only hope that he was joking.

'Do you want me to get my morris-dancing troupe there?' John asked.

'Um, well actually I want the whole village there,' Gemma replied.

'No, I mean we could come and do a dance for you. I mean we wouldn't do it for just anyone, but now you've explained the problem I think it would be great for morale to have a jolly dance from us.'

'Right.' Gemma didn't know how to react; really? Morris dancers at a meeting about the hotel? It made no sense, but then much of Parker's Hollow seemed make little sense. It was definitely a unique village. And John was looking at her so hopefully. 'That's really kind of you. I am sure it will put the whole village in a very good mood.'

'Exactly. And I shall make an announcement at our next church service.'

'Thanks, John, you're a star. I don't know where all these rumours have come from. They really are untrue, you do know that?'

'Of course, don't worry, I know the Singers and I trust them. And we will get through this, but also, I will personally try to find out who started these awful rumours. My men have experience in security.'

'Really?' Gemma was yet again confused.

'We saved the animal sanctuary from attack last year, so this should be easy for experienced men like us.' John puffed his chest out proudly.

'Well if you could find out if someone did start them deliberately, I would be so grateful,' Gemma said unsurely.

'Let's arrange the meeting for a week's time. Friday is always a good day, in the evening after work, of course. Hilary can book the hall out for you, and we'll both spread the word. Then we'll get our investigations started ASAP.' He saluted.

Gemma didn't like to think about John and his troupe being all Parker's Hollow had to offer in terms of security, but still, she was over the moon that she had him on board. Edie and the gardening club were engaged, and Steve and Issy from the pub were also now onside, after a lot of grovelling and a promise that they would put anything in writing. Vicky, who helped with housekeeping, was also spreading the word, and she would get everyone on the Meadowbrook events committee to do the same. Although she didn't hold out much hope for Samuel, she felt as if the situation were coming under control.

If only she could say the same for her nerves at the idea of having to speak publicly.

Freddie was in the garden as she made her way back.

'Everything OK?' he asked. He gave her shoulder a squeeze, which was both unexpected and more welcome than she would ever have imagined.

'I think so. John's on board, although he's insisting on dancing at the meeting.'

'That man will dance at every given opportunity. Honestly, he really is the most committed morris dancer I've ever met,' Freddie said.

'Have you met many?' Gemma raised an eyebrow.

'Well no, not really, but out of the whole group of them, he's the most fanatical. I think he likes the outfit. Oh God, imagine if he wears it in bed with Hilary—'

'Stop right there!' Gemma held her hand up. 'Far too scary to think about, although now I can't think about anything else!'

'Sorry, come and have a coffee with me, and we can chat through what you are going to say at the meeting, if you like.'

Gemma was surprised. He was being genuinely kind, and serious, which wasn't quite like Freddie.

'Oh! I would love that, I'm so worried about it,' she said as he led her inside; although of course she stumbled on the doorstep, but thankfully Freddie didn't seem to notice.

She and Freddie were making a list of points to make and he was proving helpful. Once again, Freddie surprised her by how seriously he was taking it. He was making intelligent, well-thought-out suggestions, and Gemma wrote them down and tried not to let the shock show on her face.

Harriet burst into the study. Freddie jumped as the door banged open and Gemma, who'd been very aware of his close proximity to her, felt her cheeks burn.

'What are you two up to?' Harriet demanded. She looked angry, which made Gemma feel as if she'd done something wrong. Which was ridiculous, of course.

'We were going through points for the meeting,' Freddie said. 'Why the tantrum?'

Gemma had noticed that Freddie was the only one who would confront Harriet in this way, Pippa and Gus were far gentler, but then that applied in most areas of life.

'Connor, of course. We've had such a lot going on at the animal sanctuary, and although we've had a good month for re-homes, we're always getting more. I'm overseeing the building of two more shelters in the field, and expanding the pig pen because Connor has agreed to take two more, who have outgrown their current homes—'

'What's this got to do with anything?' Freddie interrupted.

'My point is that we've been so busy and I know with the hotel it's only going to get busier, so I asked Connor if we could book a weekend away. I really fancy a change of scene and it would do us both good to spend two or three days somewhere lovely, just the two of us – goodness knows our relationship could do with it – but he's said it's out of the question.' She finally took a breath.

'Why, why is it out of the question?' Freddie asked.

'Because of the damn sanctuary and the practice. He said that we are needed here, but to be honest, once the animals are settled in, surely we can leave it for a few days?'

'Perhaps if you organise a rota for care when you're away then he won't have that argument,' Gemma suggested.

'What do you mean?'

'Well, pick the date, make sure there is a vet to cover at the practice, then between the rest of us draw up a rota to make sure that someone or two of us is on hand for the sanctuary at all times. Gerry and Gwen are in the cottage, and he's pretty good with anything practical.'

'That's not bad. And although Jenni doesn't normally work weekends, I can pay her to stay at mine and dog-sit Hilda, so she'll be right on hand, and of course Amy is pretty good. Gemma, you might be a genius, yet again.'

Gemma flushed; it was pathetic the way she lapped up any compliment.

'She isn't just a pretty face, you know,' Freddie said, and Gemma nearly fell off her chair.

'Right, I am going to google a really nice hotel in London,'

Harriet said, beaming. 'Oh! And I can tell Connor it's research. I wish I'd spoken to you before trying to get him to agree this morning and causing a huge row. Oh well, I guess I'll have to grovel to him once again.' With that, she skipped off.

'No one in my family, I mean no one, has a functional relationship.'

'Gus seems to,' Gemma pointed out.

'Yes, but only because Amanda is a saint. She is so good for him. She calms him down and stops him from being a complete misery. OK, no one apart from Gus in this family has a functional relationship.'

'But Harriet and Connor will be all right?' Gemma was more concerned than she thought she would be.

'Oh yes, those two are mad but they're made for each other.' Freddie lapsed into silence and as a wistful look appeared in his eyes, Gemma wondered if he was thinking the same as her. How nice it would be to be made for someone and have them made for you.

Chapter 21

'Are you all right? You look very pale,' Pippa said.

Gemma felt bile rising up. She gave a small nod – it was all she could do. She had been trying and failing to keep her nerves under control all day. She had almost drunk a whole bottle of Rescue Remedy, and she'd even tried to meditate, but that hadn't worked out.

Gemma and Pippa got to the village hall early to set up. Freddie said he would join them as soon as he could, as did Harriet, Gus, Connor and Amanda. Gwen was due any minute to lay out the cakes, which Gemma hoped would serve as enough of a bribe. If the smells coming from the Meadowbrook kitchen were anything to go by, then it should work.

They started putting out chairs. Gemma's hands shook slightly as she and Pippa lined them up.

'How many people do you think will come?' Gemma asked, hoping her voice wasn't shaking as much as she thought it probably was.

'Loads, everyone wants to know what's going on at Meadowbrook,' Pippa said, oblivious to Gemma's discomfort.

'You know, I still think maybe you should say a few words.' Gemma tried a last-ditch attempt.

'Oh I'm going to. After John and his gang have done their dance, I'm going to introduce you.'

That wasn't what Gemma had in mind.

Gwen and Gerry arrived with a mountain of cakes. Gemma felt physically sick.

Freddie gave her a reassuring pat on the shoulder when he arrived with the rest of the family.

'Are you OK?' Freddie asked, surprising her with his kindness.

'I'm just nervous,' she said, trying to sound dismissive. 'You know it's really important to us that we clear up any negativity – a lot rests on this.' She wasn't making herself feel any better.

'Oh just imagine the audience naked,' Freddie suggested.

'Not a good idea, that might send her over the edge – Samuel, eww!' Harriet looked horrified as she laughed. 'Connor will be here a bit late, unfortunately,' Harriet said. 'He had a last-minute emergency at the vets'.'

'Amanda should be here any minute,' Gus said, glancing at his watch.

Just then, Amanda burst in, all fresh-faced and wearing a nice dress, which was unusual. After everyone cheek-kissed in greeting, they all settled in chairs near the stage at the front of the hall. A PA system with a wireless microphone had already been set up, chairs lined each side of the room, and Gemma, once again, tried to suppress the need to throw up.

'You look lovely,' Harriet said as she hugged Amanda.

'Well, my lovely partner is taking me out to dinner at the Ivy Bistro in Bath tonight, so I thought I'd make an effort.'

'Yes, I know the timing isn't great, but I booked it ages ago.' Gus looked slightly bashful. 'And anyway, hopefully we won't miss much of the meeting.'

'Hey, if you need to leave then you leave, we can handle this,' Freddie said kindly.

Gemma took a second to check if she'd heard right. Freddie was being nice to everyone and he hadn't taken the mickey out of anyone yet, which must be some kind of record.

Edie, Rose and Doris were first to arrive, and they took their spots in the front row, where they also saved a seat for Hilary, and Samuel, as his hearing dictated he would need to be near the action. Gemma was slightly relieved that she would have some allies up front. Edie reached into her pocket, pulled out a paper bag and offered everyone a sherbet lemon.

'I always like a sweet when I go to the cinema,' she announced.

'But, Edie,' Harriet said, lips twisting in amusement, 'this is a village meeting.'

'Yes, well I am sure it'll be just as entertaining.'

That was what Gemma was afraid of.

'So, in conclusion, we are still very much in the planning stages of opening Meadowbrook as a small boutique and, most importantly, family hotel. We have a long way to go, which is why we haven't spoken to you all in the village about it before.'

Gemma paused and wondered for a moment if she were having an out-of-body experience. She could hear herself talking but it didn't sound like her. Who was this confident woman who had managed to orate to a hall full of people without stumbling more than a couple of times? She had even held the microphone without hitting herself in the face with it. To her ears, her voice sounded clear. She'd remembered everything she rehearsed, and the speech she had prepared had been seamless. She could hardly believe it, it was as if someone else had inhabited her body.

'And as I have said, you have our assurance that nothing will be done to the detriment of the village. Parker's Hollow is such a special place and Meadowbrook is part of that; the Singers are proud to be part of it, and I promise you that the hotel will reflect that. In fact, the reason they have chosen to open a hotel is to ensure that Meadowbrook Manor can very much be a part of Parker's Hollow for many years to come.'

'Can we have that in writing?' a younger man who Gemma didn't know said, but he was sat next to Steve, the pub landlord, and Steve and Issy were nodding their heads vigorously.

'I don't see a problem with that, um . . .?' Gemma glanced behind her to where Harriet was sat with the others; Harriet gave a nod of her head.

'Gavin, I'm Gavin.' He smiled. 'I'm a teacher at Parker's Hollow Primary.' He then stood up. 'My wife and I are fairly new to the village, well we've only been here five years, and we've got two little ones now, so for us, we want to keep the village as it is.'

'Well it will be, honestly. We will put anything in writing if it helps.' Gemma looked back at Harriet, who nodded. 'And Meadowbrook will only work as a hotel if Parker's Hollow stays the same, if that makes sense.'

'OK, well then I'm happy,' Gavin said.

'Great, thanks, Gavin. Right, are there any other questions?' She was feeling so pumped – she had got through her talk in one piece and not only that, but the audience in the hall also looked enraptured. No one was baying for her blood. Yet.

'Hi.' A grey-haired woman stood up. 'I'm Derry, and I work at the local store, well, I manage it, actually.'

'Hi, Derry,' Gemma said. 'And what's your question?' she prompted.

'Yes, well, it's a bit embarrassing, but I just have to say it. What about the sex parties?'

The room went quiet. Gemma glanced back at the Singers. Freddie coughed to disguise his laughter, and Harriet looked startled. Pippa and Gwen were both blushing.

'What sex parties?' Gemma asked, sounding as calm as she could.

'We were told that you were going to be holding sex parties at the hotel. You know, where people pay money to have orgies.'

The hall was totally silent. Gemma didn't know whether to laugh or cry.

'There will absolutely be no sex parties,' she stated. A sea of hands went up. 'And yes, you can have that in writing.' The hands went down again. 'Not only are they illegal—' she paused, not actually sure if they were '—or they should be, but Meadowbrook is not going to countenance anything like that. Where did you hear that?'

'Pat who delivers the papers heard it from someone and he told—'

'Yes, OK, I understand,' Harriet interrupted impatiently. She had come to join Gemma on stage.

'These rumours are ridiculous, and we can assure you that they are totally false,' Gemma added. 'Right, so any other questions?' Surely that was enough?

Edie put her hand up.

'Is there any more entertainment?' Edie asked.

'Um, no, Edie, I'm afraid not.'

'But the morris dancing was so good,' Doris added.

Half the hall started clapping.

'Thank you.' John and his troupe who were standing at the back of the hall took a bow and flushed with pleasure.

'Yes, they were, but there's no more, I'm afraid,' Gemma said.

'Can you sing?' a man, who identified himself as Jack, the church organist, asked. 'Because I'm happy to play the piano if you can.' He gestured to an upright that was against the back wall.

'Um, no.' Gemma was horrified.

'Oh that's a shame, it would be nice to have a sing-song, wouldn't it?' Margaret said, and the hall all mumbled in agreement.

Even the younger members seemed keen. What was it with Parker's Hollow?

'I'm tone-deaf, I'm afraid,' Gemma explained.

'What about rapping?' Edie suggested. 'You're a youngster, surely you can rap? I have to say I do like a bit of that Jay-Z man, he's really quite good and doesn't swear too much, either, not like that Eminem man.'

Harriet finally took the microphone from Gemma, whose mouth gaped open, goldfish-like.

'Sorry, ladies and gentlemen, but there won't be any rapping tonight. However, there is cake at the back of the hall, baked by our very own Gwen, and you are all invited to stay for a drink and something to eat, and to ask us any other questions you can think of.' Edie put her hand up. 'As long as they are to do with the hotel,' Harriet said sternly, and Edie's hand went back down again.

'Ah, Gemma, if I might have a word,' John said as he tried to move her away from the crowd without knocking his cymbals together. It wasn't proving easy.

'John, thank you for this evening, it was a really lovely way to open the meeting,' Gemma said.

Although she wasn't an expert in morris dancing, and she was pretty sure they weren't the most coordinated dancers ever, they made up for it with their enthusiasm. Handkerchiefs flying everywhere.

'You are most welcome. I will do anything for the family, you know that. Which brings me to the next order of business. Myself and my men, David, Ian and Malcolm especially, have been asking around about how this rumour started. So, Steve from the pub was told by Rachel, who delivers vegetables, who heard it from Pete in the butcher's, who heard it from Seth, the farmer, who heard it from Claire, the hairdresser, who heard it from Louise, one of the teachers at the primary school – she works with Gavin who you just met – and she heard it from her boyfriend, Wayne, who works in a garage in the next village, and he heard it from Pat who delivers his *Sun* newspaper every day, and he got it from Rita in the post office, and she heard it from this man who bought one first-class stamp.' He looked satisfied and Gemma was speechless. 'I, I mean we, are pretty sure that although it spread around like wild flower, the man with the stamp was the one who initiated it.'

'And does anyone know who this man is?'

'Unfortunately not. He's not from Parker's Hollow, we are sure of that. But we questioned her at length, and although Rita gets a bit carried away, she remembered him as she thought it was odd that he only wanted one stamp when he didn't even have a letter with him, so she was a bit suspicious, but only after, when she thought about it. At the time, she was happy to sell him a stamp and listen when he said that

Meadowbrook was going to be a rowdy hotel.' John turned very red at the mention of the parties. 'He said all sorts, from what I can gather. All while buying a single stamp! Anyway, he didn't give a name, but we have managed to get a description and do a Photofit drawing of him for you.' John proudly produced a piece of paper.

On it, Gemma found herself staring at a man with what seemed to be a triangular head, little hair, a very large nose and a pair of round glasses. It reminded Gemma of a character in the game Guess Who, which she loved as a kid. She bit her lip as she felt the irrational urge to giggle. She was pretty sure this wasn't going to lead her to whoever started these rumours.

'John, you've been very helpful, really amazing job you've all done. Can I keep the picture?' Gemma asked, trying to sound polite but knowing they would never identify the culprit from this.

She felt her heart sink. If someone was trying to scupper the plans for the hotel, they needed to know. They needed to make sure that the hotel wasn't sunk before it opened. OK, she might be being a bit dramatic, but that was how it was when you cared about things. Apart from taking care of her nan, this was the first thing she had ever been truly passionate about.

'Of course, and anything else you want us to do, you only have to ask.'

'Thank you.'

Gemma was genuinely fond of John and his wife, Hilary, who came up and handed her husband a piece of cake.

'Aww, how lovely,' John said, clashing his cymbals together joyfully.

'So, well done this evening, Gemma,' Harriet said when they were all back at the house, exhausted.

It felt as if they'd been in that hall for hours. No one would leave until the last piece of cake had been eaten, and there was a bit of a scuffle between Samuel and Jack as to who would get said last piece. Gwen had split it and the worst fight in the world had been averted. Gwen really should work for the United Nations, Gemma thought.

'I'm sorry I missed most of it.' Connor looked genuinely disappointed. 'But the morris dancing was good.'

'They were on fine form. They only dropped their sticks five times, and I think one of the handkerchiefs is still on someone's head.' Freddie laughed.

'Well on a more serious note,' Gemma said, pulling the drawing out of her pocket, 'John gave me this, after much questioning of everyone in the village, and I can't even begin to recount the people the gossip went through. Anyway, he has come up with a drawing of the man who they think started the rumour. But I warn you, it's highly unlikely that anyone actually looks like this.' She handed it to Harriet. 'In fact, I didn't like to say this to John, but it's quite ridiculous.'

Gemma stood back as they crowded around Harriet.

'Blimey, does anyone look like this?' Freddie said.

'I hope not,' Harriet said.

'I have never seen anyone like that in the village,' Pippa said.

'Or anywhere,' Freddie added.

'Right, well we might have averted this crisis but, unfortunately, despite John and the morris dancers' best efforts, we're no further forwards,' Gemma finished.

Chapter 22

Gemma was frustrated. It was a week after the presentation and things had been, as usual, full-on at Meadowbrook. She was drowning in paperwork, and her head was close to exploding. She went for a walk in the garden.

'Hey, pet.' Edie stood up from where she was tending the roses and smiled broadly.

'Edie, how are you?' Gemma asked as the older woman grabbed and hugged her. 'It's not gardening club today, is it?'

'No, but my roses need a bit more work this time of year, so Gus brought me up. By the way, love, I'm not sure I told you how well you did the other day, you know, the presentation – well it was very good.' She went back to the roses.

'Thanks, Edie.' Gemma knelt down next to her. 'To be honest I was so nervous, and well, I'm glad it was OK.'

'Oh you must be used to doing presentations to people much fancier than us; Harriet told us you did, anyway. But you did a great job, and I for one am glad the family are all on track with the village again.'

'Yes, it's such a relief. This hotel means a lot.'

'You know, Andrew Singer would approve. Of the hotel and of you,' Edie said as she pruned.

'Wow, that's lovely to know, Edie. I find the work quite

overwhelming at times, well I do at the moment, actually.'

'I know, and you've got your nan to worry about. You know I don't have family, either. Meadowbrook, Parker's Hollow, that's become my family, so I understand. And if you want to become a member, well I'm very welcoming.' She clipped a bright pink rose and handed it to Gemma.

Gemma inhaled the scent. It smelt of summer, and she found she had tears in her eyes.

'I would love that, Edie, thank you.'

They hugged again.

Once she pulled herself together from that encounter, Gemma knew she needed to be away from the sanctuary, from Meadowbrook, from the Singers, just for a few hours to go through the paperwork with a clear head. She reasoned that she just needed a change of scene.

She found herself in the small town where Edward's hotel was and selected an old-fashioned tearoom on the high street. She found a seat tucked right at the back, pulled out her laptop and ordered a pot of tea. This was quite a treat, actually. She started reading the latest email from the solicitor and lost herself a bit in the document.

'Mrs Farquhar,' a voice said loudly. 'What are you doing back?'

Gemma turned around, startled at the sound of the name. A very tall, smartly dressed woman stood at the counter – she was clearly Edward's mother. Gemma felt relieved – for a minute she thought perhaps it was Edward's wife. The woman serving behind the counter seemed very excited to see her.

'We're back from France for a bit. You know, to keep that son of ours in check and look in on the hotel,' Mrs Farquhar said, smiling warmly. Gemma tried not to stare, but she did resemble her son in a way.

'I hope it's all good,' the tearoom lady said.

'Of course, it's all going swimmingly.' There was an impatience in her voice. 'Now, Christine, dear, could you do me a takeaway Earl Grey? Edward seems to have run out, and as soon as I get hold of him, we'll be having words.' She laughed, unconvincingly.

As she passed over the tea and waved away any offer of payment, Gemma turned back to her screen. Pippa didn't mention anything about Edward's parents being here. Oh well, she didn't have time to dwell on it; she had a load of legal jargon to decipher.

'What's going on?' Gemma said as she walked into Meadowbrook and straight into Harriet, who was fuming.

'Oh! Thank goodness, where were you?' Harriet snapped.

'I was working off site. What's wrong?' Gemma thought about telling Harriet about Edward's mum, but Harriet looked thunderous, so she decided against it.

'We've had a health and safety person turning up, saying that there were reports we were serving food to the public here, which of course we're not. Pip opened the door to them. Of course she welcomed them in and told them all about the hotel. Thankfully, Freddie called me and I rushed up here.'

'But how? We are nowhere near open.'

'Exactly, I did explain that, and they were fine, but apparently someone called them and reported us for not having a commercial kitchen.'

'We know that – it's on my list, but not yet.'

'You weren't here,' Harriet pointed out.

'I know, Harriet, but I wasn't to know this would happen. I didn't call them. Now, did you ask who did?'

'Of course, I'm not an idiot.'

Gemma kept quiet. Harriet was back to being scary although, actually, Gemma didn't feel as scared of her as she used to. She was all bluster.

'And?' Gemma asked calmly.

'Anonymous tip. What if it's the same as whoever started the rumours?' Harriet responded a little more calmly.

'Um, maybe it is more serious than I first thought. Right, are they still here?' Gemma asked decisively.

'Yes, Pippa is serving tea and cake in the kitchen.' Harriet rolled her eyes.

Gemma went with her.

'He was very nice,' Pippa said later after the health and safety guy had left, assured that they weren't open to the public.

It had actually turned out quite well, bizarrely, as Gemma explained their plans, gave him a very rough idea of timescale and got some tips from him. Pippa, of course, had utterly charmed him, and he was pretty much putty in her hands by the time Gemma even met him.

'Pippa, first the rumours and now this. I think we need to find out who seems to have it in for us,' Gemma said.

'Oh, I don't think it's anyone, I think it's just a village misunderstanding. Someone could have reported us before your presentation, and now everyone's happy, on board with things, I'm sure that'll be the end of it.' She smiled.

Typical Pippa. Gemma wished she had some of her optimism, but maybe not all of it – Gemma thought the perfect balance was somewhere between Harriet and Pippa. Gemma was virtually their middle ground. Yet again, she was feeling herself being pulled into Meadowbrook a bit too much. But she couldn't stop herself.

'Anyway, I should get ready, Edward is going to be here any minute.'

'Oh, you're going out?'

'Early supper. He's taking me for dinner on Saturday night too. Honestly, I think we're stepping up our relationship quite a lot now.'

'Oh, are you meeting his parents?' Gemma asked.

'No.' Pippa looked confused. 'Remember, they live overseas; we might not be quite at the holiday point just yet.' She grinned.

Perhaps Edward was going to surprise Pippa, she thought, as her friend skipped off to get ready.

Gemma was sat at the kitchen table looking at the picture John the vicar gave her when Edward walked in.

'Pippa said to come and keep you company while she finishes getting ready,' he said.

'Oh, hi,' she said, quickly hiding the picture.

'What have you got there, a love letter?' Edward joked.

'Something like that. How are you?'

'Good, nice to see you, Gemma. I trust everything's going well with the hotel?' He sat down opposite her and smiled warmly.

Gemma could almost see what Pippa saw in him, although he definitely wasn't her type.

'Yes, although there's a long way to go. But you know all about that. Please tell me it gets easier.' She laughed.

'I'm afraid it really doesn't. But you know, it's the best business in the world, and I think Pippa and her siblings really seem to have a good grip on it, and you. From what I hear you're doing an amazing job and, Gemma, don't be surprised if you get headhunted.' He smiled again.

'Please tell me you're not offering me a job.' Gemma was only half-joking.

'Of course not.' He laughed. 'My lovely Pippa would kill me. I wouldn't do anything to risk losing her.'

A phone buzzed, and Edward pulled it out of his jacket pocket.

'Sorry, I've got to take this.' He answered the phone as he walked out of the room.

Gemma couldn't help but move to the door to try to listen.

'Mum,' he said, his voice barely above a whisper. 'I'm just out at a meeting. I'll be back later . . .'

Gemma couldn't hear anything else as he must have moved away. What the hell was going on with him? But she couldn't worry about him and Pippa; she had a hotel to focus on.

She needed to think, so she went to see the cats. She nearly turned and went out again, as she opened the door to see Connor attending to one of them.

'Hi, Gemma.'

'Hey, are you all right?' She had to go in, although she'd been hoping for some peace and quiet.

'Yup, pretty good. Don't tell anyone, especially Harry, but I'm taking her away as a surprise this weekend, so I'm feeling a bit pleased with myself.'

'Well Harriet will be happy; although I'm not sure she seems as if she likes surprises.'

'Oh, she'll love it. You know she badgers me to go away all the time, so I told her that I'm on call this weekend, so not to make plans, but really I've got it all in place to whisk her off.'

'She's a lucky girl.'

'No, I'm lucky. Anyway, sorry, whenever I see you I always talk about myself. I don't know why – I never thought I was self-obsessed.'

'You're not, but I guess when I'm here you talk to me, when I'm not you talk to the animals!'

'Yes, you're right, I tell the animals everything. Anyway, how are things with you?'

'Well I have to admit, and I didn't want to tell any of the family, but I'm a bit worried about this attempt at hotel sabotage. Someone reported us for running a commercial kitchen when we're not.'

'What does Harry think?'

'I'm not sure. Pip thinks it might be someone from the village, before the meeting, you know.'

'That makes sense. But how about you?'

'I don't know. Connor, I was near Edward's hotel earlier, in a teashop, and Edward's mum came in.'

'And?' Connor looked amused.

'Well I mentioned his parents to Pippa, but she thinks they're overseas. Edward was here and his phone rang. Although he left the room, I heard him tell his mum he'd see her later but after his date with Pippa, it sounded like. As I said, I couldn't hear the rest of the conversation, but I've got a bad feeling. For Pippa.'

'What do you think it is?'

'I don't know, but it makes no sense that if he's serious about her, which, by the way, she thinks he is, he wouldn't tell her his parents were visiting. I'm worried he's messing Pippa around.'

'God, don't tell Harry, she'll never agree to come away with

206

me. But if you've got a bad feeling, then you should do something about it.'

'Like what?' Gemma asked, confused.

'OK, I might regret asking this, but I always ask myself, when something seems wrong, what would Harriet do?'

'Oh crap,' Gemma said.

'Exactly. Right, better go.' Connor patted her on the shoulder and he left her.

As she watched him depart, she thought she would seek Albert's advice in the hope that he gave her a more straightforward answer. But he just nestled into her and purred.

Gemma was in her pyjamas reading, when there was a knock on her bedroom door. She glanced at her phone – it was just before nine. Pippa opened the door before Gemma could speak.

'You're back early,' Gemma said.

'Ah, well it was an early dinner. Edward had hotel business. Poor thing is so busy, and I guess that will be us soon. He was saying this evening how hard it'll be for me to run a hotel and have a relationship, which to be fair I am getting a sense of.'

'But the hotel comes first, right?' Gemma asked, narrowing her eyes. What was this guy playing at?

'Course.' Pippa chewed her lip uncertainly. 'And I've got the family to help out, but you know, I will have to make sure I can have a relationship too. I think Edward might be the one, you know.'

'But you've only known him for a short time.' Gemma had a sinking feeling.

'Oh, you sound like Harry. But, Gemma—' she stood up

and twirled around the room, laughing '—when you know, you know. And after Mark I'd never go out with a man who was that arrogant again. Edward is almost the opposite.'

Gemma knew what she had to do. She had to find out all she could about this guy and make sure that his intentions towards Pippa were honourable. And who better to ask than his mother?

Chapter 23

'Right, well you'll do,' Gemma said to her reflection.

When she was offered the job at Meadowbrook she worried about setting up a hotel, about whether she was capable of doing the job, but she had no idea it would entail looking after cats, dealing with morris-dancing vicars, going to church, learning how to drink, public speaking, and now going on a fake date. None of this was in the job description.

After Pippa left her she had been stewing about the Edward situation, and it was threatening to distract her from the hotel. This was why she wanted to keep her professional life separate from her personal, but she had failed miserably. So she thought about what Harriet would do. The plan she came up with surprised even herself.

'Hang on,' Freddie had said. 'You are suggesting we go to The Darnley when Pippa is out with Edward on Saturday to act as spies?'

'I wouldn't put it quite like that but, Freddie. We need to suss things out. If his parents are here, then there's probably a reason why he hasn't told Pippa, and I just want to make sure there's nothing dodgy about him. I even thought we could talk to his mother if we can.'

'I'm sure there is,' Freddie said. 'Anyone whose surname is almost the same as a swearword—'

'Freddie!' Gemma grinned.

Freddie really did bring out the lighter side of her, when she wasn't falling over, of course. Their relationship, so to speak, was more complicated than it was with the other Singers. At times they seemed to get on – when she was quizzing him for his licensing exam, which he was taking seriously, or talking about the bar, he impressed her – but then there were other times when he still teased her and she felt like an awkward schoolgirl around him.

'OK, so we are going to go for dinner, pretending to be a couple, and seeing what we can find out?'

'I didn't want to worry everyone, and I certainly didn't want to bring it up with Pippa, but, Freddie, will you help me?'

'God knows this is crazy – even Harriet would hire someone to do this for her. Actually, she'd probably hire you, so OK, let's do it, but I'm pretty sure you'll find it's all something and nothing. But if the food and wine isn't good then you'll be in trouble,' he finished.

So here she was, about to go on a fake date with Freddie to check out Edward, on behalf of Pippa, who would kill her if she even had any idea. She hadn't told anyone but Freddie; Harriet needed her weekend away and Gus would fret. She looked in the mirror and had to admit that she looked nothing like her old self. The dress she'd chosen was more fitted than she was used to but it seemed to suit her; she had a slim figure, she just wasn't used to showing it off.

'You know this isn't a real date, don't you?' Gemma mumbled to herself as she sprayed a cloud of perfume over her, its overpowering scent causing her to choke.

'Oh, you look nice,' he said, not disguising the surprise in his voice, as she found him mixing cocktails.

Gemma just stared at him, suddenly unable to speak. Freddie was wearing a jacket, shirt and a pair of jeans, and he did look good. But then he always did. Gemma felt her nerves building up. She wasn't sure she would feel this terrified even if it were a real date; actually, she'd probably have fainted by now.

'Aren't you driving?' Gemma asked, trying to distract herself from said nerves as Freddie drained his glass.

'No, I called a cab; I think I might need to drink to get through this,' he replied dryly.

Gemma bit back a retort. He was basically saying he had to be drunk to spend time with her! Although, of course, Freddie did seem to use most occasions as an excuse to drink.

'Here, hand me one of those cocktails,' Gemma demanded, and Freddie seemed both surprised and impressed as she downed it almost in one.

'So, Gemma, what is our plan tonight?'

'I don't know exactly.' She actually had no idea. 'But we need to see the place in action, maybe try to talk to members of staff, find out if his mum is there . . .'

'Right, so that's nice and vague. Sorry, Gem, but I'm not sure this is going to bear any fruit. Hopefully the food will be good though.'

Their cab ride consisted of Freddie sat in the front, chatting to Malcolm, their driver, who was from the village and in the morris-dancing group, while Gemma sat in the back, fretting. It was awful, she thought – they were on a fake date, sure, but just as she thought Freddie and she might get on, he made her feel as if he resented spending time with her. He was the most confusing, infuriating man she had ever met, but tonight wasn't about that – she had to try to focus on digging out the truth about Edward. But since Harriet had accused her of having a crush on her brother, Gemma's feelings had been even more confusing. And Gemma didn't like having feelings.

They pulled up in front of the hotel, and Freddie opened the door for her. She heard him arrange for Malcolm to collect them.

'My lady,' he said with a smile, offering her his arm.

Nice Freddie was back. She stumbled in surprise.

'Gemma, try not to fall over until after dinner.' He laughed as he took her arm and led her inside.

'Table in the name of Rivers,' Freddie said to the woman who greeted them at the entrance to the restaurant. He had made the booking online and said they best use a pretend name. Where he got Rivers from, she had no idea. 'Busy tonight?'

'It's a bit quiet, but then it's the time of year,' the woman said. 'I'm Davina Farquhar, owner of this hotel.'

Gemma was taken aback. This wasn't Edward's mum, not the woman she'd seen the other day. Was she Edward's sister?

'Oh.' Gemma smiled. 'Are you Edward's sister?'

Freddie looked at her with something akin to pride.

'No.' Her brows wrinkled in confusion. 'I'm his wife.'

Gemma almost felt her knees buckle as Freddie quickly steered her in the direction of the restaurant.

The restaurant was only half-full and when they were handed menus, Gemma could see why. It was fine dining at its worst, and the prices made her eyes water. Full of weird ingredients, things she had barely heard of, and for a village in the heart of Somerset, she was sure it was a bit too much. Even in London, they'd struggle with this.

'So, married.'

'It seems so.' Gemma tried to relax. Without even trying, their work was done, but she wasn't feeling victorious; Pippa would be devastated.

'Bloody hell, who would eat eels wrapped in prosciutto with a fig dressing?' Freddie changed the subject. 'And are eels local?'

'No idea, my knowledge of fish stuff isn't great. Shouldn't we talk about Pippa?'

'No, not here. Let's try to have a nice dinner and we'll chat about it on our way home. OK?' he said reasonably.

Gemma nodded. Walls might have ears or something – he was right. And it made sense why Edward didn't tell Pippa his parents were here.

'So I guess we're both going for the steak?' Gemma said.

It was the only safe thing on the menu, and as she had been mainly vegetarian since arriving at Meadowbrook, she was ashamed to admit she was salivating.

'Absolutely. Don't tell Pippa or Connor, or they'll make you hang out with the cows so that you feel guilty. And the cows don't take kindly to most people.' Freddie laughed, and Gemma giggled, although then she immediately felt guilty. 'They chased me once, well that was back when Elton was alive, but I survived to tell the tale, just.'

'Really?'

Gemma was at a loss for words; she wished she could think of something witty to say. Actually, just something to say, full stop. And she wished she could stop thinking about poor Pippa.

Halfway through the starters – which was something that claimed to be foraged from a nearby forest – a man appeared, and Gemma choked on the green thing she was trying to chew. She blinked in case her eyes were deceiving her. Unbelievably, he looked pretty much like John's drawing, apart from his head, which was not quite as triangular. The evening was getting even more bizarre. She gestured to Freddie, who turned round.

'Freddie, I think it's him, the man from John's drawing,' she hissed, her eyes as wide as dinner plates.

'Bloody hell.'

They both took a large swig of wine and studied the man again. No, there was no mistaking the bald head, the round face, the oversized nose, the glasses and the odd tufts of hair around the ears. She took back everything she said about John's detective skills.

He was going from table to table, speaking to the diners, and as there weren't that many, it wasn't long before he was upon them.

'Charles Hudson,' he said. 'As in Rock.'

'What?' Gemma asked, trying not to stare.

'Rock Hudson.'

'Are you related?' Freddie sounded more astonished than Gemma was feeling.

'Oh no.' He laughed. 'I just . . . Well anyway, I'm the deputy to the manager here at The Darnley, and I'd like to welcome you here this evening.' He extended his hand to Freddie, who shook it.

'How nice, please sit down and join us for a glass of wine.' Freddie gestured as he summoned a surly waitress and asked her for an extra glass.

'Well that is kind.'

Charles seemed keen enough to sit down and have a drink, and Gemma hid her surprise; she would never expect staff to drink when they were working, but then she remembered Freddie would be running the bar, so that policy was pointless. If the Meadowbrook bar ever made a profit, it would be a miracle.

'So how are you finding your Darnley experience?' he asked.

'Oh, actually, we're not staying here,' Gemma stammered.

She felt out of her depth now. She could barely string a sentence together.

'More's the pity,' Freddie boomed. 'But actually we're fairly local, and we heard about this, um, this amazingly cosmopolitan food, so we just had to check it out.' He waved his arm expansively around the dining room.

Gemma hid her mouth behind the napkin; Freddie had suddenly become rather dramatic.

'We do pride ourselves on our fine-dining experience, and we offer five-star luxury in all areas. To be honest, we are the best hotel in the Mendips, and that is not something to take lightly.' He puffed out his chest.

'Well we certainly don't have anything like this in Parker's Hollow where we live,' Freddie continued as if he were on stage, re-creating Shakespeare.

Gemma was wide-eyed with something between horror and amusement.

'Although we have heard that they are trying to open Meadowbrook Manor as a hotel,' he added.

Gemma wasn't sure she would have rushed in with that, but hey.

'Oh, you've heard about that?' Charles asked.

'Yes,' Gemma said. 'It sounds awful,' she managed.

'Yes, we've heard there are going to be sex parties and all sorts going on. The village won't stand for it.' Freddie puffed. He was really in character.

'Yes, I'm pleased that you know all about what they're up to. Do you know the Singers?' Charles asked, but carried on before waiting for an answer. 'Well between you, me and the kitchen sink, the family are clueless. They think they can just open a hotel, but we've got the whole village behind us, so it's not going to happen.'

'Us, who's us?' Gemma asked.

'Oh, well you know, it's just a figure of speech.' He looked shifty.

'Why does it matter to you if they do open a hotel?' Gemma pushed, but Charles stood up to leave.

'I really must get back to work. Right, well lovely to meet you . . .?'

'Spencer and Joan Rivers,' Freddie said with a smile.

Gemma choked on her wine as Charles got up.

'Why does every man my sister falls for want to ruin us?' Freddie asked when they were alone again. 'And not only that, but he's also bloody married.' He shook his head.

'Do you think it's conclusive that it was them?'

Just as she felt confident, she was now riddled with doubts – it was hardly a confession, after all.

'He was so shifty and his face lit up when I mentioned the fact the village wouldn't stand for it. I'm pretty sure he must be involved in some way and that means Edward too. Ah good, dinner.'

A waitress delivered two steaks, which looked so charred that Gemma couldn't even face trying to eat.

'And, Gemma, you said they couldn't ruin a steak. Right, there's a pub down the road, I think – let's go and get a drink, and a packet of crisps,' Freddie suggested as he called for the bill, hiding the uneaten steaks in a napkin.

'Can't we just go home?'

'No, Malcolm has morris-dancing practice, so he can't pick us up until the allotted time.'

'Course he can't.' Gemma shook her head.

Having a drink turned out to be a good idea. Gemma, terrified about how poor Pippa would feel when they told her, needed some Dutch courage, and Freddie kept her entertained with Meadowbrook stories. She found his company easy, after the initial awkwardness, but that was probably the double vodkas on a mainly empty stomach. He made her laugh the way no one else had ever done before. When he wasn't being mean to her, that is.

The evening flew by and when Freddie took her arm to go and meet the cab, she found herself feeling oddly disappointed. They made their way up the high street back to the front of the hotel, when Gemma suddenly saw Edward getting out of his car, whistling and swinging his car keys.

'Freddie, Edward's there, he might see us!' she panicked.

Freddie looked around for something to hide behind, but there was nothing. Just as Edward was almost upon them, Freddie grabbed her, pushed her against the wall and kissed her, ensuring both their faces were obscured.

'That was close,' he said as he pulled away.

Gemma put her hand out to steady herself against the wall. Her knees buckled, and she felt sensations that she had no idea how to identify. She had never been kissed like that before. She tried to slow her breathing; she could barely stand.

'Gemma, are you all right?' Freddie asked.

'A little too much vodka,' Gemma mumbled, barely able to get the words out. Her head was spinning, her heart beating out of her chest, and her legs were still like jelly.

She was saved by Malcolm's arrival.

Gemma was glad that Freddie sat in the front of the car, so she could try to collect herself in the back. As the two men chattered easily, Gemma slowed her breath, feeling her body heat return to somewhere near normal temperature.

As they got back to Meadowbrook, Freddie once again held the car door open for her.

'Only one thing left to do now,' he said, looking at her with his deep blue eyes.

'What?' she asked.

Part of her wondered if he was going to kiss her again. She was horrified to find that she wanted him to.

He grinned impishly. 'Decide which one of us is going to tell Pippa the bad news.'

Chapter 24

Gemma almost felt sorry for Edward. A week after her and Freddie's "date" at The Darnley, he had been summoned to Meadowbrook. Somehow, Gemma had got the short straw – not a huge surprise – and Freddie had happily let her break the news to Pippa. First, she addressed her concerns regarding Edward's parents visiting, then before Pippa could throw any objections, she brought up the wife, and finally the man from John's picture. All in all, it seemed inarguable, and Pippa hadn't even tried. But she had been upset and Gemma felt awful.

Pippa and Harriet had spent quite a lot of time holed up together, Harriet clearly worried about the effect this would have on Pippa's confidence. Although Harriet told Gemma she had done a good job, she clearly felt it was her job to pick up the pieces. Pippa was fine with Gemma, but she did feel irrationally excluded, and if she was honest, jealous. When Pippa explained how wonderful Harriet was being, Gemma felt a pang. She didn't know why, but the more she was trying to stay on the outskirts, the more she wanted in. And she was slightly worried that Pippa blamed her somewhat. Their relationship hadn't soured, but she was spending more time with her sister.

Also, since the "date", her relationship with Freddie had become infuriatingly confusing. He treated her exactly the same as he always did, with a mixture of disdain, amusement, warmth and teasing, but she couldn't help but remember the feeling of his lips on hers at the most inappropriate times. She would feel her head heat up and the emotions that it conjured up were new to her; she went to bed thinking of him and woke up annoyed with herself for still thinking about him.

She was in the office which, although still very much Andrew Singer's study, had become more of a working office now. Another desk had been moved in, a computer set up and as she was often, at the moment, in there alone, Gemma had grown to love the room.

Gemma was drawn to the painting of Andrew Singer and to him. She could almost see how he could have had such influence over the family, the village and everyone he met. Apparently, even the alpacas liked him. He had a kind face but a strong one. He was a mix of all his children and at certain times, with the change in light, she saw parts of them all in his face. She found herself talking to him quite a lot – asking his advice and telling him her ideas for the hotel. If that was madness, then it wouldn't come as any great surprise to her. She was clearly mad. Meadowbrook had made her so.

Pippa popped her head round – she looked nervous. Gemma had learnt the tells: she was chewing her bottom lip, her face was devoid of its usual glint, and she was fidgety.

'Hi.' Gemma looked up from the desk and smiled.

'He's due any minute. Everyone's in the drawing room. I know it might seem a bit ridiculous to have nearly everyone here but, after all, it's about the hotel, not just me, which affects the whole family,' she said quickly.

'That's fine, Pippa, there's strength in numbers, and he's bound to deny it, so the more people there are, the more likely to get the truth out of him.' Gemma tried to sound calm. 'And Harriet is possibly worse than the Gestapo for that.' She laughed, and Pippa almost smiled.

'Exactly, and as Harry said, if he's intent on ruining our hotel before it opens, he might try other things, so we need to threaten him and show that he can't push us around.' She jutted her chin out, trying to sound more angry than sad, but she failed. 'But then, we did draw the line at putting him on the rack,' she managed to joke.

'Ha! Right, well good luck.' Gemma smiled.

'Oh no, I want you there. As my friend.'

Gemma raised an eyebrow. She was flattered. 'Really?'

'Of course, come on then.' Pippa took her hand and gave it a squeeze as they left the office.

Gemma squeezed back reassuringly. Perhaps they were all going to be OK, after all.

Harriet, Freddie and Gus were lined up on one sofa. Gemma resisted the urge to laugh – they were all wearing black, a bit like a good-looking mafia family. Gwen was sat in the biggest armchair, looking every inch the matriarch, and Gemma stood behind it – she hadn't got the wearing black memo, unfortunately – as Pippa led Edward in.

He was wearing a pair of chinos, and a shirt with a jumper tied around his shoulders. He wore a broad smile, and if he was surprised to see himself facing the Singer family en masse, he didn't show it. He was composed and totally unaware of the firing squad he was about to face, it seemed.

'Sit down,' Harriet barked.

He did so. His even features rearranged themselves into questioning ones. Pippa went over to her siblings and perched on the arm of the sofa. Gus gave her hand a squeeze.

'Edward,' Pippa started, her voice a little unsteady. 'I asked you here today because we received some disturbing information.' She glanced at Harriet for reassurance; she nodded. 'Firstly, it seems you have a wife called Davina.'

The colour drained from Edward's face. 'Can we talk about this alone?' he asked Pippa.

She shook her head.

'Not only that, but it also seems that rumours have been spread throughout the village about our hotel – and those rumours, which have caused us problems, were started by your assistant, Charles someone.'

'Hudson,' Freddie added helpfully. 'As in Rock.'

'What?' Gus asked.

Pippa shook her head.

'That's impossible,' Edward countered.

He didn't seem rattled, and Gemma wondered, briefly, if they had got it wrong.

'No, it's not impossible,' Harriet interjected. Her voice was as harsh as Pippa's was gentle. 'We traced the source of the ludicrous rumours back to your assistant manager, and we can only draw the conclusion that your assistant was in cahoots with you, acting on your authority to try to ruin our hotel before we even got close to opening. And did your wife know your plan was to date Pippa as part of this whole thing?'

'Now hang on—' Edward finally coloured, but then Harriet's voice had been as sharp as glass.

222

'No, we won't hang on, actually,' Freddie interjected. 'Why can't you just admit it?'

'I think there must have been a huge misunderstanding,' Edward maintained. 'Charles might have mentioned the hotel to someone, but that's all. I shall have a word with him.'

Although he was calm, the tips of his ears had turned red, and he was shuffling uncomfortably. Gemma was sure this was guilt in all its glory.

'And your wife?' Gemma said.

'Well, she and I have been living separate lives for a while now—'

'Oh for God's sake!' Gus threw his hands in the air. 'Surely you don't think we're going to fall for that?'

Edward looked as if he hoped they would.

'That's not going to do it, actually,' Harriet said. 'I don't believe you for a start.'

'Neither do I, you're not wearing socks,' Freddie added. They all looked at his feet; he had brogues on but no socks. 'And I never trust a man who doesn't wear socks.'

Gemma glanced around, but no one seemed fazed by this statement.

'Oh Jesus, of course I don't want you to open a hotel. God, Pippa, it isn't rocket science. You are only a few miles away from my hotel – who would welcome more competition? I'm not mad, but you clearly are,' he said, irritated now, his usual composure slipping.

'So did you get Charles to start the rumours?' Gus asked.

'For goodness' sake, yes, but you have no idea how hard running a hotel is. It's competitive and costly – and you just think you can swan in and open one, just like that. You're all crazy.'

Edward's mask had finally fallen off. His face contorted and not one of them had any doubt about his real feelings. Poor Pippa, Gemma thought.

'And the wife?' Gwen asked. 'Does she know about you dating Pippa?'

'Of course not. Why, Pippa, do you think we always went for dinner early and I couldn't spend the night with you?'

'Because of work, you said, it was because of work and us taking things slowly. And I believed you.'

Gemma's heart went out to her; she sounded so upset.

'What you need to understand about us—' Harriet stood up, her voice threatening '—is that mad or not, if we want to do something we will do whatever it takes to do so. Our father taught us that, and we want to open a hotel. And if you think that you are any match for us, you are very much mistaken.'

Harriet's voice was ice cold. Gemma felt like trembling and they were on the same side.

Edward spread his hands out. 'This house will never be a hotel,' he spat.

'It will,' Harriet said. 'And trust me, if you try anything else, you will regret it. Be careful who you take on, Edward.'

'We will stop at nothing,' Freddie threatened. 'If we so much as hear a whiff of another rumour, we'll step in. Your wife would be a good starting point, don't you think? Maybe your mother as well – we know your parents are here.'

Finally, Edward did look defeated.

'So,' Gwen interjected, 'my advice to you is to quit while you're ahead. You need to remember who you're dealing with and trust me, this family has seen off people far more ruthless than you. So I suggest you go and concentrate on running your hotel and leave us to ours.'

God, she wouldn't mess with Gwen, Gemma thought – she sounded like she meant business.

'Out! Now,' Harriet ordered in a way that made Gemma want to scarper. 'And,' Harriet continued as Edward made to turn away, 'if you so much as breathe the name "Meadowbrook", or do anything to hurt our hotel, I will make you sorry you ever set eyes on us. From now on we'll be watching your every move.'

Harriet ushered Edward out of the door as if she were sweeping him away. He scurried, like a rattled mouse, without looking back once. Gemma couldn't say she blamed him – blimey, the Singers were scary when crossed.

'Sorry, Pip,' Gus said, giving his sister a hug.

'Hey, at least I didn't fall for him properly. I mean I did a bit, but God, why do I have such terrible taste in men?'

'Because you always go for older pompous ones,' Harriet said as she returned. 'Next time choose someone your own age or younger. Preferably one riddled with insecurity and a sensible job.'

'I'm never going to let any man do this to me again. I mean I said that after Mark, but this time I mean it.'

Pippa let herself sob, and Gwen stood up and went over to her, taking her in her arms.

'You listen to me, Philippa Singer. Your dad doted on you, and he tried to protect you because you had such a sweet nature. Not tough like Harry, or sensible like Gus, or super-confident like Fred, but sweet, and he worried that people would take advantage of that. But you know what? He always said he would rather you were you than you lost that lovely sweet nature that we all love. And what's more, you have more than proved you can do this. You would have made your dad so proud, and you'll continue to do so, and you will never stop being you, you hear me?'

Gemma wiped a tear. Pippa nodded.

'But Harry's right, no more older arrogant men – that does have to change.' Gwen's mouth was set in a straight line.

'Thanks, Gwen. Right, that's it. No more men until this hotel opens. The Singers are going to open the best hotel that the Mendips has ever seen, and if The Darnley fails it will be his own arrogant fault.'

'Shall we drink to that?' Freddie suggested.

'It's almost five, I'm sure a small sherry might be acceptable.' Gwen's lips curled.

'Yay!' Freddie hopped like a little boy who'd just been given sweets before dinner. He practically skipped to the drinks trolley and poured sherry for everyone. 'I know no one actually drinks sherry anymore, but this is for Gwen,' he said.

'Let's toast to Pippa, for learning that she is remarkable and that she can do this,' Harriet suggested.

Gemma sipped the sherry, which was sweet and unlike anything she had ever tasted.

'By the way, Harry, how was your weekend away?' Freddie asked. 'I can't believe I haven't seen you properly since then.'

'Bliss! Connor took me to a fabulously fashionable hotel, which I knew he probably hated. In London!'

'Yes, Pip said.' Freddie laughed. 'Not an animal in sight.'

'He enjoyed it, even if he won't admit it. He loved seeing the sights, we were proper tourists, and we ate some lovely food and I enjoyed the city. But, well, he also seemed to have an ulterior motive.'

'What?' Gus asked.

'He wants us to try for a baby,' Harriet said.

Gwen choked on her sherry.

'God, sorry, Gwen, maybe he should have told you.'

'He has done, and I told him I would love to be a grand-mother, of course. But he said you're not sure?'

'I am sure about Connor, although we bicker a lot, but I love him and Hilda. But you know, a baby, a real baby . . . I'd be a crap mother.'

'Don't be ridiculous, you'd make a lovely mum,' Pippa breathed.

'Do you think so? I'm hardly a soft, cuddly person, am I?'

'You have a soft centre. Besides, you've got Connor for that.' Freddie laughed again.

'You were a sort of mother to all of us after Mum died,' Gus said. 'A role you never fully left behind. You still mother us now a bit.'

'God, you're right. I suppose I might be OK. I don't know, but I'm not getting any younger what with my big 4-0 coming up,' she explained.

Gemma couldn't talk. Her mouth had been blocked with envy; her heart was lead. She wasn't proud of herself, but she felt more alone than ever. She felt like an observer to this scene, as if she were watching from behind a pane of glass. Excluded by herself rather than by other people. But she couldn't feel part of it; perhaps she felt she didn't deserve to be. No, she knew she didn't really deserve to be. This was her pattern in life – she didn't feel good enough for other people, so she built a wall between them. And just as she thought it might be on the verge of being torn down, here she was putting it back up again. Why was she so weird? Why couldn't she enjoy being a part of this?

'Is that what brought this on?' Gus asked.

'I think it was the fact that Madonna is pregnant.'

Freddie spat his sherry out. 'Sorry!' He had the grace to blush.

'Madonna, the cow. It seems that David might not be quite as gay as we first thought,' Harriet explained.

Even Gemma managed to smile at this.

'David has impregnated Madonna?' Pippa was incredulous.

'Seems so, and of course that led to Connor thinking he should do the same to me. Sorry, Gwen,' Harriet said again.

Gwen shook her head.

'Freddie, don't you dare tweet that,' Gus said suddenly.

Freddie looked sheepish and put his phone down.

'Give me that phone!' Harriet lunged for it, and after a tussle she grabbed it, threw it to Pippa, who deleted the tweet and then threw it to Gus.

'Spoilsports,' Freddie said, laughing. 'We could have gone viral!'

'So we're getting a baby cow?' Pippa asked.

'Calf, I believe that's what they are called.' Harriet rolled her eyes.

'Pip, should name it, you know, to make up for this whole thing,' Gus suggested.

'Yes, because just when yet another man tries to ruin my life, naming a calf makes it all better,' Pippa said, but her eyes were sparkling with mirth.

'That could be your new motto,' Gemma surprised herself by saying, and they all seemed to remember she was there as they burst out laughing.

'Could we possibly open some champagne to celebrate the cow pregnancy?' Freddie said. 'I really bloody hate sherry.'

*

The knock on the door made her jump. After champagne and dinner, Gemma had cried off as she had some work to catch up on. It seemed the Edward business occupied more of her time than she could spare, and she had a few documents she needed finalising. Although, actually, she'd had a few glasses of champagne, so it wasn't exactly getting done. But she was fretting slightly – her six-month contract date was approaching and there was still so much to do.

'Come in,' she said.

Pippa's face appeared. 'Before you say anything, I know you've got work to do, but . . .' She walked in clutching a bottle of wine and two glasses.

'But you are going to ply me with wine regardless?' Gemma said, closing her laptop lid in defeat.

'Well yes, actually. Firstly, all work and no play and all that, but also I think I really need to thank you for all you've done for me.'

'You mean ruining your love life?'

'Or saving the hotel, you can see it either way. Harriet was really cross with me, actually; she said I didn't appreciate fully all you'd done. I mean you didn't pass the buck onto her, or even Gus, but you came up with a plan, roped Freddie in and sorted it, and that was a lovely thing to do for me.'

'You know, Pippa, I was hoping that Freddie and I would have a fake date and we wouldn't find anything . . . I was just suspicious when I heard his mum in a coffee shop. But I've told you all that. I'm sorry, though, that it turned out like this, but glad we've got to the bottom of it.'

'Yes, me too. I might be upset about Edward for a while, but I mean it now, I am off men – clearly I have the worst

229

taste in them.' Although she wiped a tear away, showing she wasn't as OK as she made out.

'So do I. I mean Chris, well he was just so pompous and not even nice to me. I am only concerned about the hotel. And about you – I want you to be with someone who deserves you, Pippa.'

'Well that makes two of us, so let's drink to that.'

As they settled back on Gemma's bed, with wine and lots of giggles, she felt a sense of fulfilment that had eluded her so far, and it was one of the nicest feelings in the world.

Chapter 25

'But you do realise I have a lot of work to do on the hotel?' Gemma pointed out as Freddie demanded she come with him to the sanctuary.

'I do know, Gemma, as you never tire of reminding me, but it's Saturday and you're not meant to be working, and also Harriet's orders. We've got the open day coming up and she wants all hands on deck.'

'But what I am I supposed to do?'

'She wants both the cat and dog houses to be cleaned, spruced up, you know, made to look good. So I guess you'll be with the cats. Think yourself lucky, we've got to clean up the outdoor barns and make the pigs look presentable.'

Gemma glared at him to see if he was joking. He wasn't.

Harriet had decided to add a sanctuary open day to the Meadowbrook events. She had managed to get it well publicised locally; her motive was to attract people who were looking to adopt a pet. Entrance was free, but there were going to be donations tins everywhere. Thankfully, Harriet had organised this low-key event without a committee. Some of the members were upset that there was no raffle, and of course John was put out about the lack of morris dancers, but Harriet won them round by saying that the spotlight had to be on the animals, and she didn't want to detract with their fabulous entertainment. They grudgingly accepted it.

'You guys do know the hotel will never be open if I have to keep getting involved in everything else, don't you?' Gemma got up from her desk.

'Tell Harry, although if I were you I would just do as you're told.'

'Gemma.' Fleur joined her in the cats' quarters, where Gemma had added cleaner to her job description.

Gemma was sweeping the floor before mopping it. She hadn't protested – she might get on with Harriet quite well now, but Freddie was right. And, actually, it was heartening to see how much this meant to her.

'Aunt Harriet roped you in too?'

'Yes, and Hayley and Amanda. They're on the dogs. I said I'd help you, but it looks OK in here, doesn't it?'

'Not according to your aunt. We need to clean so it sparkles. We also need to groom the cats, but not until next week, which they won't like.' Gemma laughed.

'No, they won't, but I'm happy to help. Maybe one of us could hold and the other brush,' Fleur suggested.

'You look happy,' Gemma said. Fleur seemed more buoyant than she had been lately.

'Well it's a bit thanks to you. I met a girl, Lisa, when I was in the village shop, and I started talking to her. She lives in one of the new houses, at the edge of the village, and she agreed that it's boring here, so we arranged to hang out. I'm seeing her and some of her friends tonight, and she's a bit older than me but so cool!' Her eyes shone.

'Well I'm pleased. Does your dad know?'

'He said I could go out as long as I'm not back too late. It'll make it easier for me having a friend here. I really like Hayley but she likes different stuff to me. She's into sport and I hate sport.'

Harriet arrived, shouting orders at Connor.

'Well it's beginning to look a bit better in here,' Harriet said. 'Connor, when the guys arrive can you get them to hang bunting along one wall?'

'Bunting?' Fleur asked. 'Isn't that going a bit far?'

'No, Fleur. When we open our doors to the public, I want the place looking amazing. Even the animals who aren't up for adoption. Amanda's going to make flower garlands to put round the ponies, and the barns are all going to have flags hung around them – actually, that's being done now. Even the pigs will look smart. I want this to be the best animal sanctuary in Somerset, if not the whole of England.' There was no irony in her voice.

'And re-home a few more of our guys,' Connor said.

'Well that goes without saying. Right, Fleur, I need you to come and help me, I need to get the field looking nice.'

'Auntie Harry, the open day isn't until next week, surely we'll have to do all this again?'

'If we get it looking good now we'll hopefully have less to do last minute. Anyway, the goats – do you think we should get them collars, so they look smart?'

'Yes, and we could also put jewels on their horns,' Connor said sarcastically.

'Not a bad idea,' Harriet said.

The three of them glanced at her but, again, she didn't appear to be joking.

'Right, I think apart from the grooming, this is pretty good,' Gemma said to Connor after they'd gone.

'I know this is nuts, but Harriet doesn't do half measures.'

'Yeah, I'm getting that.' Gemma grinned. She also knew how everything with Harriet was competitive. But her heart was really in this.

'Anyway, next week, if we can get more interest in the place, either homes, volunteers or donations, then that would be great.'

'Understood, but really, bejewelling the goats?'

'I know, don't worry, I'll talk her out of that one.'

Gemma was in her room in her joggers when she heard Freddie's voice screaming up the stairs. She quickly glanced at the clock – it was eleven and she ran downstairs. Pippa was right behind her, still in her day clothes.

'Fire!' Freddie shouted. He was doubled over, winded, trying to breathe.

'Where?' Pippa screamed.

'At the sanctuary! Quick! Get in the buggy, we need to go.'

Pippa ran to the back, grabbed some boots, which she thrust at Gemma, and the three of them ran out of the door and threw themselves into the buggy as Freddie hurtled off. Both Gemma and Pippa were still putting their boots on.

'Is it . . .?' Gemma started, but her voice was lost in the wind as Freddie drove, flooring the buggy.

Pippa's face was ashen as they saw smoke in the distance and as they stopped at the field. The stable where the ponies and Gerald slept was on fire, and it was getting dangerously close to the goats' barn, which was next door, and also Agnes and her lamb, Abigail's quarters, which was next to that.

As the flames grew and shrunk, flying in the air like aggressors, Gemma felt absolute terror; she had never been so close to a real fire before. What about the animals? The smell in the air was of intense heat and Gemma almost froze. This was the most horrible thing ever.

'Shit,' Freddie said, 'shit, come on, quickly!'

They ran to where Harriet was trying to calm down the three small ponies, Clover, Cookie and Brian, as Connor was tending Gerald, who was lying on the ground making an almighty noise.

'What can we do?' Pippa shouted.

'We need to get the goats out.' Connor's voice was full of urgency. 'I can't leave Gerald, he's hurt.' There was panic in his eyes and sweat on his brows as he tried to keep a braying Gerald still.

Gemma and Freddie ran over to the second barn which, thankfully, the fire hadn't quite reached. But the air was thick with swirls of smoke and the warmth, a heat that almost felt fake, enveloped them as they got closer. Freddie unlatched the door, and Gus arrived, puffing his way towards them. Gemma tried not to breathe in the smoke, although it was curling away into the night.

'I came as quickly as I could.' He gasped for breath.

Freddie and Gus went in where the goats, obviously sensing something was wrong, were huddled in the corner. Freddie quickly passed the baby, Kayne, to Gemma, who ran out with him. She handed him to Pippa who was waiting near the door. She then went back inside. The heat was getting worse, as if it were creeping up on them. The goats were bleating and distressed. Romeo wouldn't budge as Freddie and Gus both tried to haul him out. Gemma, driven by pure adrenaline, rugby tackled Romeo, grabbing on tight so he couldn't kick her and then using all her strength, she half pulled, half pushed him out. It took strength she didn't know she had, and her muscles ached at the effort. Once safely in the field, she collapsed and Romeo, looking at her with disgust, gave her a kick as soon as she loosened her grip on him.

'Ow! You ungrateful sod,' she said, but she was trying so hard to breathe the words might have been said in her head.

Pippa managed to lead Agnes, the blind sheep, and Abigail to safety, but the female goats were still resisting.

She felt tears of relief or stress fill her eyes as she saw Gus and Freddie emerge with the other two goats, just as the air filled with the sound of sirens approaching. They were just in time, as the fire had now spread to the barn; the stables were all but destroyed.

Gus and Freddie took charge. For once, Harriet seemed at a loss as she sat, stroking the ponies, tears running down her face. Gemma touched her own cheeks and was surprised to find them wet with tears too. She hadn't realised she'd been crying.

The firemen put the fire out in no time, making it look easy, although the smoke and the mess was a stark reminder that it had been serious. The air burned with an acrid smell. Connor organised them, moving the animals to the other side of the field out of the way of the commotion. They were all making an almighty noise apart from the sheep, who seemed nonplussed.

It transpired that Gerald had injured his leg bashing the stable door – either to escape or draw attention, it was unsure, but either way it made him somewhat of a hero. Connor had called the vet's practice to get someone to come and help him, and Jenni and Amy were on their way. Connor had fetched his vet's bag and with Gus's help, he'd given Gerald an

236

injection to sedate him. Connor seemed calm but his face showed how stricken he was.

'Too close,' he kept saying over and over. 'We could have lost them.'

Gwen arrived with Gerry; they had been at the cinema and saw the fire engine on their way back. Gerry immediately started trying to survey the damage. It was clear the stable and the barns – pretty destroyed, not to mention waterlogged – were out of bounds.

'Oh, love,' Gwen said, giving Connor a hug. 'What happened?'

Connor just shook his head. Gemma went to speak to Freddie, who was with the fire officer.

'Do they know what started it?' she asked.

'Not yet,' Freddie replied. He shook his head.

'Once the place is clear we'll do a survey,' the fire officer, who introduced himself as Joe, said. 'But there's no electrics and so I can only guess at the moment.'

'You don't think it was done on purpose, do you?' Freddie asked as the colour drained from his face.

'Well we'll do a full report in the morning. I promise we'll get to the bottom of it.' Joe gave a reassuring smile.

'Right, well let us know if you need anything,' Freddie said as they made their way over to Connor.

His colleagues had arrived with an animal ambulance which, with the help of Freddie and Gus, they loaded Gerald onto. Apparently, donkeys were heavier than they looked. Gemma didn't know about that. He looked pretty solid to her and she had struggled with Romeo who was less than half his size.

'Will he be OK?' Gus asked.

'Yes, his leg probably needs pinning. We're going to take him to the animal hospital,' Connor explained.

'Where are the animals going to go for now?' Gemma asked.

'There's a barn over that side of the field.' He pointed to the field where the large pigsty also was. 'Thankfully, we had it built not long ago and it's still empty; they'll be OK in there for now. The ponies might be a bit confused by being in with the goats and the sheep, and I'll need you to stay with them all night, if you can do a rota or whatever is best, please,' Connor said. 'Jenni and Amy will be here any minute, so they'll help. I wish I knew what had caused it, though, and if Harry hadn't seen it straight away when letting Hilda out . . .' His voice broke.

'Don't worry, mate,' Freddie said, patting him on the back. 'We'll take care of it.'

As Connor left, it took a while to get the goats into the next barn, even with Jenni and Amy to help. Kayne was fine, he could still be carried, but the others resisted yet again as they tried to use leads to get them in. It took three of them to move each goat, and they were all exhausted by the time they were safely in the barn. Gemma didn't know goats could be so stubborn.

Agnes settled down quickly, Abigail curled up next to her, as if nothing had happened. The sheep were the calmest, and Gemma wished she could be half as tranquil as they seemed. The ponies were still traumatised, but they were being checked over by Katherine, a junior vet from Connor's practice. She gave medicine to those who needed something to calm them – Freddie had asked for something, but she'd assumed he was joking – and declared that it seemed they were all thankfully unscathed.

The Singers were also in a state. Harriet was crying, refusing to let go of Brian as the tears ran down her cheeks. Freddie, although he had shown himself to be very practical when the fire was underway, was now pale-faced and slumped against the shed wall. Gus was mopping sweat from his brow and speaking on the phone to Amanda, and Pippa was sobbing. Gemma's heart was pounding outside her body. The adrenaline that had kept them going was disappearing like the smoke and she felt exhaustion creeping in.

They all stayed there in silence until Amanda broke it by arriving and hugging Gus.

'I'm so sorry, guys. I came as soon as I could; I was at home with the girls.'

'Fleur is there?' Gus asked.

'Yes.'

'She wasn't there when I left. She said she was at a friend's in the village tonight.' He seemed confused.

'I didn't stop to chat, Gus, but she's there now. Do we know what happened?' Amanda asked.

'Nope, not yet, but as there aren't any electrics . . .' Freddie said.

'I can't imagine who would do this, though?' Gus said as he stroked Amanda's back.

'It might not have been on purpose,' Gemma pointed out reasonably. She understood that tempers were frayed but there was no point in jumping to conclusions.

'And the animals?' Amanda asked.

'All fine. The ponies are shaken, the goats cross, and Gerald has gone to the animal hospital,' Harriet explained tearfully. She buried her face in Brian's mane. Brian didn't look thrilled but then ponies generally didn't. 'What about the open day?

It's all ruined.' Tears snaked their way down her cheeks, and Pippa hugged her.

'Right, there's no point in us all being here,' Jenni said, showing her usual efficiency. 'Let's come up with a roster to look after the animals tonight.'

Jenni said she and Amy would do the first few hours, give the Singers a chance to calm down, and then whoever was up to it could come in and relieve them for a few hours. Gemma volunteered, as did Freddie. Harriet said she'd stay close to the phone until Connor was back. Pippa was distraught, and although Gus and Amanda offered to stay, they were told not to worry; there were enough of them to cover.

They all went back to Harriet's cottage, where Gwen poured brandies and they sat largely in silence until Connor phoned to say that Gerald would be all right. He might have a bit of a limp after the damage done to his leg healed, but it could have been a lot worse. Still, despite that, the air was thick with fear.

Gemma not only saw how important the sanctuary was to everyone that night, but she felt it in herself too.

'I'm so tired,' Freddie said at 3 a.m., when he and Gemma took their turn in the barn with the animals who all seemed to be sleeping. 'I could sleep for a year.'

His head lolled against the wall as he sank into the hay, which had been gathered to make it comfortable – for the animals, not the humans. The animals all had blankets over them, and Gemma and Freddie were armed with more blankets, flasks of tea and brandy. Although the animals seemed fine, Connor was insisting they weren't left in case they were in shock – how you could tell a pony, goat or sheep was in shock, Gemma had no clue, but she wasn't going to argue. She was pretty sure Connor was being overprotective, but she understood why. It had been an ordeal for all of them – human and animal.

'I know what you mean; the emotion is the most exhausting. I have never seen Harriet cry like that,' Gemma replied, pouring a cup of coffee from the flask and offering it to him.

He shook his head but took a sip of brandy.

'Showed you her human side? She doesn't like to, but she loves those animals. And she's got the open day coming up. I guess we'll have to cancel it.'

'No, Freddie.' Gemma realised she had learnt more about passion since being at Meadowbrook than ever. All of them were passionate about the place, and she was too. It had crept up on her, but she knew how much it all meant to her now. 'We'll find a way; honestly, this won't stop us. I get it now.'

'Oh, Gemma, you surprise me sometimes.' Freddie moved closer to her and hugged her. 'You really care about this, about us, don't you?'

He looked right into her eyes and she almost faltered. The intensity was terrifying, but she realised as her heart started beating faster that it was also real. She had no idea what any of this meant, but the passion being stirred in her was making her feel alive.

'It was so frightening.'

'My God, wasn't it? Seeing that smoke, those flames, it wasn't real somehow. And typical that it was the bloody goats who wouldn't move. I really would be beyond furious with anyone who did anything to hurt our animals, if anyone did it.'

'I'll be right with you as well.' Gemma shuddered.

'You know, Harriet said it earlier, when you were organising blankets for the barns with Gwen, you're one of us now. You really are. I might tease you, Gemma, but you mean a lot to us, to me.' Freddie had tears in his eyes, and he took her hand and held it.

Gemma was too touched to say anything as she nestled her head into a blanket and felt as if she had found somewhere she belonged. She just hoped that nothing like this ever happened again. Without warning, she found herself crying.

'Sorry,' she sobbed as Freddie held her.

He was so warm and comforting, she wanted to stay in his arms forever. But she couldn't and she disentangled herself. She rested her head on his shoulder and they stayed there for hours, but Gemma would have stayed there forever.

Chapter 26

Gemma felt a hand on her shoulder and she opened her eyes and bolted upright, to find herself looking at a dishevelled Pippa.

'Oh God, sorry.' As she yawned she could see daylight through the window but had no idea of the time.

'It's OK, it's eleven and I thought it best to let you sleep after the night we had. Connor's back now. Gerald will be all right and will come back as soon as he's able to use his leg; it wasn't as bad as Connor first feared. But poor Harry is having kittens, well not literally, about the open day.'

'You must be shattered.' Gemma yawned again. Her body felt as if it were a lead weight and she needed hours more sleep to feel normal again.

'We all are, but I wanted to ask you a favour. I'm going to bed now; I can barely keep my eyes open. Freddie's up and at the sanctuary. Gerry is with him – Gwen's Gerry, not the donkey. They're meeting the fire officers. Connor will be there as well, but he's been rushing around making sure all the animals are OK, so I wondered if you'd go down there. Harry really does need support as well – I doubt she's going to sleep.'

She put on her wellies and a jacket. It wasn't cold but the was weather still unpredictable. She made her way down to the field. There, clustered around the half-destroyed stables and barn, were Freddie, Gerry and Joe, the fire officer from the night before. He had a couple more men with him. They were in uniform, and Gemma couldn't help but think how much more attractive a uniform made a man, which she knew was totally inappropriate but she put it down to the fact she was still tired and emotional.

'I'll bloody kill them,' Freddie was shouting as she got closer.

Gerry put an arm on his shoulder but was shaking his head.

'Who?' Gemma asked, her heart sinking into her boots. Was this deliberate, after all? She wasn't sure she could bear it.

'We don't exactly know,' Joe said, his voice even. 'We've established the cause of the fire – it was cigarettes.'

'Oh God,' Gemma said. 'But who would smoke out here?' She shook her head.

'I am going to see Connor. If it's one of the workers or the volunteers then heads will roll.' Freddie stormed off.

So much for her being there to calm everyone down.

'It was probably teenagers.' Joe turned to Gemma. 'They wouldn't have thought that dropping a few cigarette butts would cause a fire,' he explained.

'It wasn't arson, then?'

'No, no arsonist would just drop some cigarettes. After all, if the wind had been the wrong way or if it had rained then they would have gone out. You were unlucky that it was a dry night and of course hay and fire. And I can't be sure yet, but I think there was some alcohol spilt – not enough for it to be deliberate but it still acts as an accelerant.'

'Didn't they say that Harriet put in CCTV? You know, after what happened last year, Gerry?' Gemma said, remembering Harriet telling her about it.

'She did, and there might be a camera directed here. God, with all the fuss they must have forgotten. Come on, Gemma, let's find her.' Gerry seemed to cheer up. 'And we'd better get Freddie too.'

'We'll finish up here, and then we'll pop into the sanctuary office before we leave,' Joe said, shaking Gerry's hand.

They stood around the desk in the sanctuary office with Martin, who was working the office that day. Connor wasn't there; he'd gone back to see Gerald. Pippa was still sleeping, but she, Freddie and Harriet, along with Gwen and Gerry, crowded round the desk. The dog walking, all the feeding, it all had to carry on regardless and so the sanctuary was business as usual. Gemma even had to go and see her cats after this.

'There we go,' Martin said after what seemed like ages, sitting back in his chair and clicking the screen to enlarge it.

They all peered as close as they could get to the screen.

'Oh hell,' Gemma said.

'I bloody well don't believe it,' Freddie stormed.

'I'll kill her,' Harriet said, her lips clasped together tightly.

On the screen were four people; two looked like boys, two girls, some of their faces lit by cigarettes right next to the barn. There was no sound, but one of the girls was waving her arms and it looked as if she were shouting. She was the only one not smoking and when she turned to the camera, it was unmistakably Fleur. Poor Gus, Gemma thought, this would just about finish him off.

'It doesn't look like she's smoking,' Gwen said, but even her voice was shaking. 'And it does look as if she is trying to get the others to stop,' she added, which in fairness it did.

'Doesn't matter, she says she loves these animals, and she didn't manage to stop them. If you think what the fire could have done,' Harriet gasped and sobs came out. 'Sorry, but I'm tired and angry. Connor will be devastated, not to mention Gus. I'm calling the little madam now; she won't know what hit her.'

'Look,' Gwen said. 'Someone needs to tell Gus first. He'll be upset and I bet Fleur will be too – you know she loves the animals, but being a teenager isn't easy.'

'But the stupidity,' Harriet stormed.

'I remember someone drinking whisky and thinking it was a good idea to go swimming in the lake. Connor thankfully dragged you out,' Gwen said.

'Well yes, but the only one in danger was me.'

'I think we need to be calm about this. It wasn't intentional, and yes, it was stupid and foolhardy and thoughtless, but I think that Gus should be the one to decide how to handle it; after all, she's his daughter,' Gwen continued.

'What about Connor? He loves Fleur, he loves her helping him around here, but I'm not sure . . .' Harriet ran her hands through her hair.

'You need to handle him, don't let him fly off the handle. Gus is going to be angry enough for all of us and Fleur, well, she was stupid but she's not really a bad kid.' Gwen gave Harriet a hug.

'As Gwen said, she looks angry. I can't lip-read but my guess is she's telling them to put the cigarettes out,' Martin said as they all studied the footage again.

'Just a shame the bloody idiot walked off first and let them drop their fags right onto the hay,' Freddie said.

'And they dropped matches,' Martin said; he had clearly watched the footage carefully. 'And there was a bottle of vodka as well.' Very carefully, indeed.

Gemma didn't know what to say but she almost felt sorry for poor Fleur. She was pretty sure the fact that the animals were nearly harmed would be punishment enough, not that she wanted to voice that. Not at the moment.

Gus was understandably beside himself. They decided well, Harriet decided – that they would talk to Gus en masse and for some reason this included Gemma again. It was uncomfortable; she didn't feel confident enough to say much. She was flattered to be included, but she also felt useless. Gwen had to go, because she'd arranged to take Rose to a hospital appointment, which she couldn't really change, so she delegated Gemma to keep everyone as calm as she could. This was not in her job description.

'Gus,' Connor said in his customary light-filled voice, 'I was furious, mate, believe me, and to think it was Fleur who has helped me with the animals almost since the sanctuary opened. But it wasn't deliberate, it was stupid, but then she is fourteen.'

It turned out that after Harriet had calmed Connor down, he was so relieved no one was seriously hurt, and satisfied that Fleur had tried to stop the smoking, that he was far less angry than anyone expected.

'Exactly, she's fourteen and she's hanging out with kids clearly older than her, and they were smoking and drinking,' he fumed.

'How did Fleur react when you told her about the fire, you know last night, or this morning?' Gemma asked.

She felt somewhat responsible. It seemed that Fleur's new friend, the one that Gemma had encouraged her to make, wasn't so great after all.

'We told the girls at breakfast and Fleur burst into tears, refused to eat and wouldn't stop sobbing. I thought it was because she loves the animals, but now I know better. She didn't own up, though.'

'Gus, she must be feeling wretched,' Gemma reasoned, putting her hand on his shoulder. 'She'll know she's done wrong, she's a good girl beneath it, but you know, she's at a difficult age.' Gemma felt as if she were channelling Gwen. 'And it's not my place to say, but I think sometimes when she's here she misses having a social life. She loves being here, that's obvious, but I'm guessing she thought having friends in the village would make it better. Unfortunately, they weren't great choices.'

'I know, I know, and she's been through a lot in the past couple of years. She lost her grandfather, whom she adored, then I met and moved in with Amanda, but that's no excuse.' He scratched his head, but Gemma could see some of his anger ebbing away.

'No fourteen-year-old girl is happy, Gus,' Harriet said. 'I almost remember it.' She tried to laugh.

'What I want,' Connor said, 'is for her to come to me, apologise, and then she can perhaps do more work here, keep her out of trouble.'

'And, about the open day . . .?' Gemma said.

'We'll have to cancel,' Harriet said.

'No.' Gemma felt confidence inflating her. 'No, Roger will

start work on the barns straight away, and I know it won't be ready in time, but maybe . . .' She felt her brain whirring. 'Maybe if we cordon off that bit of the field we can use the rest, the untouched part of the paddock.

'How do we hide three burnt-out barns?' Harriet asked.

'A fence. Like simple garden fencing, and you can use it to partition the field – that won't be hard, and we can all do it,' Gemma suggested.

'Actually, with Gus and Freddie's help, I could get it put up in no time,' Gerry added.

As their faces all stared at her, Gemma thought she had got it wrong. She had overstepped the mark, but then Harriet grabbed her and hugged her.

'You're a bloody genius,' she said.

'Gus, find out who the other kids were,' Gemma suggested when they were alone in the field measuring up for the fencing, with Gerry taking the lead. 'I bet you'll find they put pressure on her.' She felt if she could help Gus build bridges with his daughter, she would feel better about encouraging her to make friends in the first place.

'Do you think?'

'To be honest, I think they looked older than her, didn't you think that?'

'Yes, actually they probably are, and you know what peer pressure's like,' he replied.

'God, I remember, and it didn't end well for me. Although I didn't set anything on fire, thankfully.' She laughed.

Gus actually laughed along with her.

Chapter 27

Gemma had been out early for a run, as was becoming a habit now spring was firmly here, and the mornings were light, chilly but bright. She wanted to make the most of it. She couldn't help but think that her time here was finite, and she couldn't begin to think how much she would miss it. It was already May, time was flying, and she was fully blanketed in the Meadowbrook effect.

She knew for sure that they wouldn't be ready to open the hotel by August when her contract was supposed to be up, and she was trying to gain the courage to have that conversation with the family. The legalities were taking time, as they always did. The builders had been delayed as they were rebuilding the stables and the barn. And as far as marketing was concerned, the actual plan for attracting guests still eluded them all. Thankfully the open day had been a success. The sun had greeted them as they set up, all the volunteers looked smart in their new Meadowbrook Sanctuary T-shirts, rattling their collections boxes like pros. The animals had all been on their best behaviour, apart from the alpacas who were rude to all visitors, and Fleur was instrumental in getting a number of families signed up to adopt dogs and cats. Harriet was proud of everyone for their part, and Gemma had lots of praise heaped on her, but now it was over, it was back to hotel business.

Running through the fields of Meadowbrook, seeing the flowers sprouting, passing the green trees, the lush grass, hearing various animals, stopping to look at the calm water of the lake, it was all so refreshing. Her and her thoughts alone. The smells were changing; she could almost feel summer approaching. It was bittersweet. Summer meant that the six-month contract was nearly at an end, but she longed for summer at Meadowbrook at the same time.

She was just about to head back, when she saw Fleur cleaning out the chicken coop. Fleur had been, as predicted, devastated by the fire, sorrier than she could ever have been, and it had taken her a few days before she could face Connor. She had been grounded as well, had her allowance taken away and also her iPhone. But she had sucked it up, and she was now working at the sanctuary every weekend and in school holidays to try to make amends. She had thrown herself into making sure the open day could go ahead with a work ethic that impressed them all, and Gemma felt that the family were once again back on track.

She explained how the kids were older, the girl was from a new-build housing estate on the edge of Parker's Hollow, and she had persuaded Fleur to take them to Meadowbrook. But Fleur had genuinely tried to stop them smoking around the barn; it just didn't occur to her that the cigarettes weren't put out properly.

Gemma jogged over to her.

'Hello, are you all right?' Gemma smiled.

She and Fleur were pretty close now. For all her confidence and privilege, she knew Fleur suffered from the usual teenage insecurities like everyone else. Gemma, after all, hadn't grown out of hers.

'Yes, I'm getting there. You know those people I was with?' she asked.

Gemma nodded.

'They started attacking me on Snapchat, but then I told Aunt Harry, and she said I was to threaten them with the police, as we had CCTV footage of them smoking by the barn and underage drinking. It seems to have stopped them.'

'But it's not nice to be on the receiving end.' Gemma remembered her school days when a group of girls said nasty things to her daily. Shrugging it off wasn't easy, and she wasn't sure she had done so. She was often thankful that social media wasn't as prevalent in her day.

'You know, I thought Lisa was cool. She seemed sophisticated, but she only cares about drinking, smoking and boys.'

'And you were a bit in awe of her?' Gemma said carefully.

She remembered at one stage she would have done anything to be friends with those horrible girls, even though they treated her so badly. Once, they said they'd be friends with her if she stole some make-up from a shop. Of course she did it, and she didn't get caught, but she still remembered how awful it made her feel, and after that they still didn't let her into their group. That feeling of humiliation still burnt to this day. She didn't want that for Fleur.

'Don't tell anyone, but until Jason I'd never even kissed a boy,' she said.

'Plenty of time for all that,' Gemma said as Fleur leant on the fence and ran her hands through her hair.

'That's what Mum and Dad say, and I know they're right. This guy, Jason, he was fit though, looked a bit like Justin

Bieber, and I really thought I liked him, but he was lame.'

'You know, when you're young you think you need friends, even ones who treat you badly, but you do learn that you don't.'

'Did you?'

'Oh goodness, for most of my school life I was desperate to be friends with this group of girls who basically terrorised me.' Gemma grimaced.

'That sounds awful.' Fleur look horrified. 'I have some great friends at school. And I have Hayley, who is kind of like a younger sister, I guess.'

'Right, well you stay out of trouble.'

'Oh, Gemma, I am definitely going to do that. I mean for a minute I wondered if it was genetic, you know like Uncle Freddie, but then I hated the taste of the vodka and I didn't want to smoke anyway. And when Jason kissed me, it was sloppy and it was quite horrible really.'

'Well yes, I can imagine.' Gemma resisted the urge to laugh.

'And after I told them they had nearly burnt the place down and how much trouble we caused, they said I was a spoilt posh bitch who thought I was better than them because I was rich. I'm not even rich – I don't get the biggest allowance you know, not by a long shot. One of the girls at my school gets four times more than me!'

Gemma contained her grin. For all Fleur's bravado she was still a kid. Straddling that awkward line between childhood and adolescence.

Hurrying into the house, Gemma showered, dressed and went to grab breakfast. Pippa and Freddie were already in the kitchen. Since the Edward debacle, then the fire, everyone had thrown themselves into hotel plans, and there was no time for late mornings, not even for Freddie.

'Morning,' Gemma chirped.

She was feeling happy. Her seesawing emotions, which were a novelty when she arrived at Meadowbrook, were becoming the norm now. She didn't like to think too much about them, and with her mounting workload she didn't have the time.

She was grateful for that. Her work kept her from thinking of how scared she was, of how every time she visited her nan lately she seemed worse, how the bungalow had finally exchanged and they had a completion date of late July, when her childhood home would be well and truly gone. It kept the fears buried, but of course they were still there.

'Hey, Gemma, are you set for today?' Pippa asked.

She was as warm as ever, and they spent more time than ever together; late-night chats were commonplace, and Pippa had opened up about how she felt about Edward's betrayal on a number of occasions. But she was also businesslike, and they were working together as an effective team.

'Sure am. I took an early run knowing the builders will be here this morning.' She was determined to not put a foot wrong.

Freddie yawned loudly. Gemma tried not to look at him. Even bedraggled first thing in the morning he looked hot. Oh God, she was trying, and failing, to keep those thoughts at bay.

'Oh! And Pippa, I think we should look at Gwen's apartment today, see what needs to be done to it, for whoever is going to end up living or staying there.'

This was yet another issue that both Pippa and Freddie had been reluctant to address – where they would be living when the hotel was open. They were so used to living at Meadowbrook that trying to drum into them that the house wasn't going to be their home wasn't proving easy. Although Gemma didn't expect the hotel to be full at all times, because there were only ten bedrooms they would all need to be available for guests. She had spent ages compiling plans for offering late deals, discounts and special weekends for them to push when they needed more people, and she knew it would be important that the rooms were available – it would feel more professional that way.

Also, Freddie needed to stop leaving his socks around and learn that guests would have priority. Pippa, and to a slightly lesser extent Freddie, was so excited about opening the hotel, but the reality, the details, seemed to be something they were in denial about.

The builders were splitting their time between the barn and stables and the house. Today they were starting on the attic rooms, while they waited for some materials they had to order for the barns. It wasn't ideal but they were managing.

'Oh, OK, well Freddie and I haven't spoken about it, but we will. We've got a meeting with Charlotte Stiles, and I'm sure she'll have some ideas.'

'Who's Charlotte Stiles?' Gemma asked.

'Our interior designer. Stiles Design; she's from Bath. Her parents were Dad's designers on this house, would you believe?'

'Her parents?' Gemma was aware of this different world – one of family businesses – and wouldn't she have been lucky to have someone to give her a leg up when she started out? She tried to push the bitterness away – it was so unattractive, yet it was another reminder that she was an alien in this world, this Meadowbrook bubble.

As much as they said she was one of them, she still wasn't. In Meadowbrook, family meant something, and being abandoned by your parents wasn't it. The builders were a firm that Andrew Singer used; nearly everyone who worked at Meadowbrook had some kind of family connection. She guessed she should just thank her lucky stars they had never used a hotel consultant before, or had one in their extended family.

'Yes, they were a team, quite eccentric. I used to think they were so exotic when they came here. Sasha, Charlotte's mum, always wore her hair up in a tall beehive, and I never saw her without a tiara, and her father wore a three-piece suit at all times. They were really something. Anyway, Charlotte has taken over the business and she's a great designer but not as eccentric as her parents. So I've made lists for her, but if you think of anything I've forgotten, then please bring it up in the meeting. She's coming in at two.'

Gemma tried to figure out which pieces of information she needed to retain and which to get rid of, as was often the case when Pippa was excited.

'So you want me there too?' Gemma asked.

Pippa nodded. She and Pippa had discussed plans for the rooms but they hadn't made any decisions, and she felt irrationally put out that the interior designer had been called in without her knowledge. Gemma had to remember that Pippa was her boss. The lines were blurred, they were hazy, they were confusing, but they were still there.

Her thoughts were interrupted by the arrival of the builders, led by Roger, an affable man, about fifty at a guess, with greying hair, a slight paunch and an infectious laugh; Gemma liked dealing with him. He had a team of five at the moment.

Most importantly, he was a professional and knew a lot about houses like Meadowbrook, which he'd worked on for years, taught by his own father, of course. He talked about the house with a reverence and respect that Gemma loved.

She nodded hello to his team: Jake, good-looking, young and confident enough to try and fail to flirt with Pippa; Harry, Roger's son who was an apprentice; Tommy, who looked the same age as Roger; Heather, the only female member, and Don, a man of indistinct age, who was a jack of all trades and also seemed to be Roger's right-hand man.

'Please help yourselves to tea or coffee in the kitchen when you want,' Pippa said. 'There will normally be one of us around if you need anything.'

'Thanks, love, we'll crack on,' Roger said with a chortle as he led his team, as if they were a small army troop, upstairs to the attic rooms.

'Now there is one man who loves his job,' Gemma mused.

'And how fabulous to have a female here as well,' Pippa said. 'Although Heather is Roger's niece, so it really is like a family business.'

And just as Gemma was getting a grip, there it was again: family. Was she the only person in Somerset without one?

Yet again pushing the thoughts that were threatening to topple her aside, she readied the office for the meeting. She still had it to herself a lot of the time. Pippa didn't spend that much time in there – she wasn't a desk kind of girl. But Freddie used it sometimes to revise for his licensee exam, Harriet would come in to do the figures – she kept close control on the money being spent on the hotel – and Gus came in sometimes to bring her a cup of tea and have a chat. He liked to sit on the sofas, and Gemma looked forward to those times. It not only gave her a break, but Gus's calm exterior also gave her confidence. She was beginning to think of it as her office, hers and Andrew's. She was struck with the wish that she had met him. Looking at his portrait every day, she felt she knew him, maybe because she saw him in all his children and the house.

Pippa pushed open the door, balancing some huge books.

'Let me help,' Gemma said, taking them from her. 'What have you got here?'

'Sample books, carpets, wallpaper, that sort of thing. I've been collecting them. I know it's silly, but I worked so hard on our townhouse when I was married to Mark that I feel that interiors is something I'm not too bad at. Do you mind?'

'It's your hotel,' Gemma pointed out. Although, ridiculously, she did mind a bit.

Gemma knew she shouldn't, but she liked it when Pippa confided in her, asked her advice, made her feel as if her views were important. She was a child craving praise. It was time to grow up.

'Thanks, I'm not pushing you out, but I know you've got a lot on. So although I think you should sit in on the meetings, and actually I'd be glad of the help with Gwen's apartment, I'll do the brunt of the work with Charlotte.'

'That makes perfect sense to me.'

And it should have done; after all, Gemma was getting to grips with the practicalities rather than the cosmetic, which was definitely where her strength lay. She was thinking about storage and housekeeping, and who would launder all the linen – an outside service. She had drawn up plans for that, and she was proud of her attention to detail. The way she was working had taken her by surprise; she was growing in confidence every day. She actually was beginning to believe that she was capable of the job she'd been doing for months now.

Gemma heard the doorbell go, and Pippa rushed to get it. Gemma saved the spreadsheet she'd been working on as Pippa returned with Charlotte.

'Gemma, this is Charlotte,' Pippa introduced. 'Gemma's our hotel consultant, in charge of getting us open really.'

'Pleased to meet you,' Charlotte said, extending a hand.

Gemma took it and tried to smile. Charlotte was nothing like she expected. For some reason, Pippa's description of her eccentric parents had led Gemma to expect someone a little wild, but she wasn't. Well-spoken, tall, blonde and wearing an amazing floral jumpsuit that showed off her slightly curvy figure to perfection. Her nails were painted a fashionable grey, her hair highlighted. She was attractive and held herself with a confidence that Gemma could only envy.

'Sit down,' Pippa said as Charlotte sat on the sofa, Pippa next to her.

Gemma, unsure of her place, stayed behind the desk.

'So, did you look at the list I gave you?' Pippa asked.

'I did, and I've got loads of ideas. I remember when Mum and Dad worked here, and boy I loved this house so much. I used to pretend I lived here. Sorry, Pippa, don't think I'm a mad stalker who'll move in when your back is turned.'

They both laughed.

'Were you a child then?' Gemma asked.

'No, goodness, I'm forty-two now, so the last time I was here, let me think . . .' She pursed her lips. 'Oh! I know, I was twenty and at uni, but I did some work experience with Mum and Dad. Remember, Pippa, we did some of the rooms and the summer house?'

'Yes, I do. You and your parents seemed so glamorous to me, and you worked on my bedroom I think later on.'

'Goodness, yes, I was so jealous of that room!' Charlotte laughed. She was posh, yes, she was confident, yes, but she was also warm and friendly. 'So, Gemma, tell me where you are with the hotel at the moment.'

'I'd love to,' Gemma said, meaning it. It gave her a chance to talk about it and the more she did, the more it seemed it was becoming a reality.

The afternoon passed quickly as Charlotte looked at the apartment, had a tour of the rooms and spoke extensively to Roger. She was efficient, and Gemma couldn't fault her.

'Right, I'm just about done.' Charlotte came to find them in the office. 'It's still amazing but I have to go and put my hotel head on. I know you want to keep it with the feel of a home, and I love that, but we also need to be practical. God, I hate that word.'

'I know, it's so dull,' Pippa agreed.

If only you knew that that was all I am, Gemma thought.

'So, I'll go away, do a proposal, and we'll take it from there.'

'Yes, but, Charlotte, time is of the essence,' Pippa said.

'Of course, and you'll be my priority. I can't wait to get started.'

Freddie appeared. 'Oh, hi, I remember you – you came here years ago.' Freddie beamed as if greeting an old friend.

'Yes, well remembered. You kept offering me wine, if my memory serves right.'

'God, I was a terror even then. I had a massive crush on you.' Freddie laughed.

Gemma felt her insides burn.

'Oh! If only I'd known. Well actually, the age difference might have caused a bit of an issue.'

'I was just a teenager then. But well, anyway, nice to see you again.'

'I'm just leaving, actually.'

'Can't I offer you some wine again?' Freddie smiled. 'Come on, I'll show you out.'

The irrational jealousy that Gemma felt refused to go away; it burned away in the pit of her stomach. Especially as Freddie didn't come back in for ages. When he did, he was whistling tunelessly.

'God, Fred, what's is up with you?' Pippa said as she noticed his red cheeks.

'Oh, you know, I've got a date with Charlotte,' he said proudly.

'Bloody hell, Fred, fast work.' Pippa's eyes were wide.

'Is that a good idea?' Gemma said, sounding like a prig. 'I mean she's about to start working here – what if things go wrong?'

'Gem has a point. What if you go on a date with her, scare her so much she refuses to work here, and then I've lost the best interior designer I've ever had,' Pippa pointed out.

'The only interior designer you've ever had, even.' Freddie laughed. 'She did bring up that objection, but I promised that we would remain professional even if it was the worst date ever. And besides, I'm hard to hate.'

'Isn't she a bit old for you?' Pippa asked.

Gemma wanted to hug her. She was too old, too successful, too confident, too not Gemma.

'Oh she mentioned that too, but you know, age is nothing,

it's not even ten years. She's divorced, she's lovely and I am taking her out. I didn't realise I needed to ask your permission.' With that, he flounced out of the room.

Pippa raised her eyebrows. 'That told us then.'

And Gemma sadly thought that it really did.

Chapter 28

'So, as you can see, with the documents I have carefully put together, my contract is up in August, and we've still got a way to go. May is already speeding past and thanks to Roger and his team, and Charlotte of course, I do believe the hotel may be there, or almost there cosmetically, although I think that's cutting it fine. And the marketing plan is still not set, nor are the plans for attracting visitors or, in fact, for characterising the hotel.' Gemma felt her cheeks flame, but she had done it and the words gushed out. She had taken control, and it felt amazing. Unless they didn't agree with her, of course.

Gemma was so nervous, it reminded her of the time when she had been asked to present at the end of her probationary period. Although she felt she was doing a good job, and she certainly felt part of Meadowbrook, she took nothing for granted. They could easily get rid of her and the thought terrified her.

She had gathered all the Singers together, having put together a bundle of documents, which covered every aspect of the hotel, from the staffing needs, to the building work, to the legal permits, to details of getting from physically being a hotel to being a hotel with paying guests. She was feeling quite proud of herself, as she was pretty sure she had left no stone unturned.

'So, do you want us to extend your contract?' Harriet asked, but she didn't sound as if she hated the idea.

'If you so wish. I accept you might want someone else, or to do it yourselves, but I feel we've come so far, and what I would like to do is to lock down an opening date. A date when we open the doors to the Meadowbrook Hotel and start having paying guests as something to aim for. I've been realistic, I believe, in saying February next year. It will be a year since I arrived, yes, but of course these things do take time. If we're ready before then that's great, but at least we have something to aim for.'

'I have to say,' Gus started, 'that I know I keep my counsel on most things hotel-related, but I do think, and this isn't just Gemma's job, that we need to sit down and try to come up with a marketing vision. Gemma can help, but we are the owners of Meadowbrook – it's important to each of us, and we've sort of ignored that part of it. Mainly because I'm not sure we agree.' He scratched his head.

Gemma shot him a grateful glance. Trust Gus to take the awkward away.

'Gus is right,' Harriet said. 'No one opens a business not knowing the market, or where we are going to get our clients or guests from. I've been trying to get you guys to talk about this for ages.'

'But it's so hard. Meadowbrook is transforming, and we know what we're doing, but I'm still a little lost to see how we're going to attract guests, and what type of guests they are,' Pippa added.

'Let's hope rich ones who like cocktails,' Freddie quipped.

'Can I make a suggestion?' Gemma asked. She was surprised by how easy she was finding it to take control when it came

264

to the hotel. And possibly because she had proved herself, they all listened to her now. They nodded. 'You guys put your heads together and write a mission statement for the hotel – who would want to stay here, why they should stay here, what they will get from staying here – and when you've done that I'll look at it. Then we need to decide if we should hire an outside marketing consultant to put together a strategy. I think we can take care of social media – after all, Freddie's a whizz at that – but advertising and PR are tricky, so I believe that we'll need some help with that.'

'Gemma, that sounds perfectly reasonable,' Harriet said, which made Gemma feel not only relieved, but also a little bit proud of herself. 'I for one am happy for you to continue for another six months, and I'll draw up the contract. You've done a great job so far, the budgets have been kept to, thanks largely to you, and the fact you won't let Freddie order the most ridiculously expensive alcohol is a big bonus.'

'Oi!' Freddie objected with a grin.

'I would love you to continue,' Pippa agreed. 'It wouldn't feel the same here without you.' Pippa came over and gave Gemma a hug.

'We definitely need Gemma – that's one thing I think we all agree on,' Gus finished.

'Right, it's decided. You're stuck with us for a bit longer.' Harriet smiled.

Gemma had never felt needed before, or wanted, and for a moment she felt both. Look how far she had come in a few short months? She believed she could do the job – hell, she was actually doing the job – and she wasn't even scared of Harriet anymore. OK, she was, but only a tiny bit.

'Actually, it's good timing – we're about to start planning

the summer fête,' Pippa announced. 'And I know the hotel is a priority, but you're doing such a good job, and Freddie and I are a bit preoccupied for a couple of months, so if we're not quite as present as you'd like you'll know why.'

'Is there a lot to organise?' Gemma asked.

'You'd be surprised,' Harriet replied. 'You've met the committee, right? We have the traditional stalls we have every year, but as it's grown in the last couple, we get requests from outside traders wanting to sell, which if they're suitable we let them. Then we have our annual baking competition, which now attracts people from quite far away, as well as the dog show, the pig racing, which Gus runs, and all manner of activities. Oh! And we also need to find a celebrity to open it. It's a lot of work, but not only do the villagers love it, it raises a lot of money for the sanctuary as well.'

Gemma nodded.

'Now we've resolved that—'Gus appeared bashful '—I would like to tell you all something.'

'What?' Harriet swung round to face him.

'I've proposed to Amanda, and she accepted.'

'Oh Gus, that's wonderful,' cried Pippa.

Pippa was the first to launch herself at her brother, followed by Harriet, as they bundled him.

Freddie slapped him on the back. 'Nice work,' he said.

Gemma hung back. 'Congratulations, you are such a lovely couple,' Gemma said when everyone calmed down.

'Thank you.' Gus grinned. 'I am so happy.'

'Oh! I can't wait to see Amanda,' Pippa said.

'How did my lovely niece take it?' Harriet asked.

'Fine, as long as she didn't have to wear a "bloody flouncy dress" then she was happy for us.'

'Chip off the old block,' Freddie added.

'Don't say that, Fred – we've only just started talking again after the fire business. And she has been on her best behaviour ever since, so I really think she might have turned a corner.'

'Right, family dinner, this Friday, is in your honour,' Harriet announced. 'We all love Amanda, and I want her to know how excited we are to welcome her into our family.'

'That would be lovely, and hopefully I'll get both Fleur and Hayley to come.'

'That would be lovely. Gemma, I hope you'll join us,' Harriet said.

'Me, but I'm not—'

'Yes you are,' Pippa interjected. 'You've been part of Meadowbrook for months now and it feels like years. Of course you're invited.'

'I agree,' Gus said.

Gemma inflated with happiness.

'In that case, can I invite Charlotte?' Freddie said.

Her happiness got a puncture.

'Charlotte?' Gus asked.

'Our interior designer,' Harriet said. 'Why would you invite her? Next you'll want Roger there as well.' She laughed.

'Actually, we've been on a date,' Freddie explained.

'She is lovely,' Pippa added. 'But she's almost ten years older than him.'

'An older woman, wow.' Harriet arched an eyebrow. 'If you think Gus's engagement dinner is the place to introduce her to us all, then fair enough.'

'The more the merrier, I say, but perhaps not Roger,' Gus added.

'Oh Gus, will you be having the wedding here?' Pippa asked.

'Well, Amanda and I have spoken about it, and I think it's for her to decide. If John is happy to marry us, what with us both being divorced, we'd love to get married in the church, in honour of Dad and the village, and I can't speak for Amanda, but I would love to have the reception here.'

'Oh how marvellous. Freddie and I can organise it.' Pippa clapped her hands together.

'As long as it doesn't get in the way of the hotel.' Harriet's lips twitched.

'I've got an idea,' Gemma said. Everyone looked at her. 'Why don't we make this the hotel opening? I mean, I'm not sure how many people you'd invite, but if we did a buffet rather than a sit-down, we could accommodate quite a few, especially as the bar will be open, and some of the guests could use the rooms. Like a sort of test run.'

They all stared at Gemma, and she had no idea what they were thinking.

'And we could stay here after the reception, and Amanda the night before the wedding with her family.' Gus's eyes lit up.

'What a brilliant idea,' Pippa gushed.

'So, you'll have to get married in February,' Freddie said.

'Let's have a Valentine's Day wedding!' Pippa sounded as if she would explode with excitement.

'Hang on a minute, don't you think we should ask the bride?' Harriet interjected.

'Oh I will, on Friday at dinner. But I'm sure she'll love the idea.' Pippa brushed away her objections.

By the look of them all, Gemma realised that Amanda didn't stand a chance.

Chapter 29

Gemma put her wine glass down and told herself to steady on – she felt the alcohol coursing through her; she'd already drunk too much. She was struggling with the evening, as was becoming her usual contradictory state. It was a lovely dinner – Gwen had cooked up a mouthwatering feast, as always, and there was a festive air at Meadowbrook. The evening had begun with champagne in the drawing room, and now they were enjoying wine, which was so delicious that Gemma couldn't stop drinking it. The dining room looked beautiful – Pippa and Harriet had spent hours not only getting the table right, but also hanging "congratulations" banners, which somehow managed to look tasteful rather than tacky.

Everyone had made an effort, including Gemma herself, although she couldn't help but feel she didn't quite measure up. Not to perfect Charlotte, she thought bitterly.

Charlotte had arrived in a cloud of expensive perfume. She wore skintight leather jeans and a top that gave just a small hint of cleavage – Gemma was sure those breasts weren't real, as they seemed far too upright. But she greeted everyone warmly, and had brought the hugest bouquet of flowers for Gus and Amanda, and a bottle of vintage champagne.

Charlotte's confidence seemed to diminish Gemma's. The worst thing was that she was lovely.

When the spotlight was on Charlotte, she didn't hog it but tried to turn the attention back to Gus and Amanda. She was great with the girls – it turned out she had two children, which made Freddie pale slightly, but only slightly, when she spoke about them. It was as if there were no bad side to the woman. Gemma desperately wanted to hate her – no, not hate, that was horrible, but dislike her – but she couldn't. She could only feel the knot of envy twisting inside her.

Charlotte was everything Gemma wanted to be: beautiful, stylish and confident. She was kind, and interesting, and she was funny. She was almost perfect, Gemma thought. Despite how far Gemma had come, Charlotte was a stark reminder of how ordinary she actually was.

She could hardly bear to see how attentive Freddie was to her. Gemma felt so foolish. Yes, she had a crush on Freddie, probably from when she met him, but it didn't matter. Because Freddie wouldn't look at her twice, not in that way. It was the bloody fake date and the kiss that cemented it. It made her feel things she had no idea a person could feel. Then the night in the barn after the fire, when emotion stripped away and she felt she really knew him. When he asked her to help him study for his licence and she could see how nervous he was, how important it was for him to succeed, which just endeared him to her more. And now she was ruined. Freddie was oblivious, but her feelings for him made her feel alive for the first time in ages. Really alive.

Now, though, she had to hold it together. She needed to seem as if she were having a wonderful time, rather than wanting to stab herself with a fork. Amanda had never looked prettier. Even the girls, especially Fleur, were on their best behaviour. Gemma, feeling a loss of control unlike anything she had ever felt before, needed to pull herself back. She needed to be sensible, boring Gemma again, because that was far safer. Although, she couldn't help but think that even the confusion and the envy, the anger and the pain was good for her in some way.

'So,' Gwen said, 'Gus, Amanda, are you going to have a Valentine's wedding?'

Gwen was taking on the role of mother of the groom. She had been talking about buying a hat and offering advice about catering. She did keep sneaking looks at Connor and Harriet, but Harriet obviously cottoned on to this and avoided all eye contact with her.

'You know when Gus first mentioned it, I thought gosh no. I mean I'm so not a romantic, although Gus surprised me with a very romantic proposal.' She reached across and kissed his cheek.

'Yuk,' Fleur said, not quite quietly enough.

'Fleur, when you get a boyfriend and snog him all over the place I'll remind you of this,' Harriet chastised.

'Sorry,' she mumbled. 'I am actually happy for you.'

'Thanks, love.' Amanda was her usual unruffled self. 'When Gus explained that the wedding would be the test for the hotel, I thought great. I've always liked the idea of a winter wedding. The snowdrops will be out and I love snowdrops. Meadowbrook is the perfect venue, it means a lot to both of us, and after all we met here, so why not? Also, it means that Valentine's Day will be our wedding anniversary, not just Valentine's Day, which makes it so much better. I can buy Gus an anniversary card rather than a Valentine's one.'

'You've never given me a Valentine's card,' Gus said.

'Exactly.'

'It gives us a great opening date.' Gemma spoke – she needed to say something before they all thought she'd become mute again.

'And we want a small wedding,' Gus said. 'Although we really do have to invite the gardening club and the committee members, so it might not be that small.'

'We can use the bar area for drinks,' Gemma said, forgetting to feel miserable. 'Then if we clear the drawing room, that could be the reception room, and have all the food laid out in the dining room. It'll mean a buffet, but I reckon we could get a hundred in here easily.'

'Gemma, you are so on top of things,' Pippa said proudly.

'And it won't be a hundred.' Gus paled at the idea. 'Hopefully.'

'It's all decided,' Harriet said. 'Valentine's Day, here. And now Pippa and Freddie as the organisers will plan the wedding for you, and all you have to do is approve them.'

'God, that is my idea of wedding bliss.' Amanda laughed. 'The last thing I wanted was to have to turn into bridezilla.'

'I can't imagine that.' Harriet laughed. 'Gus would be more likely than you.'

'What about the stag do?' Freddie asked. 'I mean, assuming I'm your best man.'

'Of course you are. I mean I meant to ask you, but I forgot,' Gus said. 'But saying that, Connor, would you organise the stag do?' He grinned.

'Yes, whisky and poker at mine OK?' Connor replied.

'Perfect.' Both their lips twitched as Freddie looked horrified.

'No way, we're going away, for the weekend, Amsterdam maybe.'

'No drugs or whores, Freddie,' Harriet stated.

'God, Auntie Harry, should you be saying that in front of me and Hayley?' Fleur asked.

'You've heard worse. I mean it, Freddie.'

'What about a golfing weekend in Portugal?' Gus suggested.

'God, it's a stag do, not a retirement do. OK look, Gus, whatever you want, but can we have one stripper?'

The phone woke her. She looked at the time and it was only 5 a.m. Her head was thick as she looked and saw the number for the nursing home on the display. Her heart started beating faster as she answered.

'Gemma Matthews,' she said, her voice shaking.

'It's Marian from the home, Gemma,' a kind voice said. 'I'm so sorry to call you so early, but your nan's had a stroke, and she's been taken to hospital, Southmead. I can't tell you any more. I called you as soon as I could, love.'

'I'm on my way,' Gemma said and hung up.

She dressed, not noticing what she was putting on. She somehow made it downstairs and grabbed the keys to Pippa's car from the console table and quietly left the house, which was so silent it was almost eerie.

She put the hospital address into the sat nav and started driving there, furiously wiping the tears from her cheeks as she did so, to ensure that she could actually see where she was going. She said fervent prayers as she drove; she knew her nan was unwell – no, more than unwell, she was becoming enslaved to a cruel master: dementia – but she was alive and, selfishly, Gemma wanted her to stay that way. Because without her she would have no family at all and that terrified her. More so now she had experienced Meadowbrook and the Singers.

She bashed the steering wheel as she sat at traffic lights, which seemed to take an interminable time to turn green; emotions weren't what they were cracked up to be, after all.

She found a space in the hospital car park, which was shrouded in darkness, and only a scattering of cars occupied it at this early hour. Gemma's legs shook as she let herself out of the car, remembering to grab her bag, which at least had a purse and her phone inside, then made her way to the main entrance.

'I'm looking for my nan, Sue Matthews,' she said as the tears returned and her voice choked.

She was directed to the stroke unit.

'Please let her live,' Gemma said, silently. 'Please, just for a while longer. I'm not ready to let her go.'

The beeping of her phone woke her. She must have fallen asleep in the chair. She shifted uncomfortably; her body seemed to have seized up. She looked at her nan. Lying in bed, she was sleeping now, but there were wires and tubes monitoring her. The stroke hadn't been a major one, but they were keeping her in for observation and tests.

She had woken briefly but hadn't seemed to be aware of anything around her as she went back to sleep. Her arm was slack as Gemma clutched her bony hand, and she was struck again by how selfish she was being, because her nan looked so shrunken in that bed, and it seemed almost worse to Gemma to want to keep her alive like this.

The young female doctor had said to her that it was too

early to tell but her mobility might be affected, and also her speech, which wasn't great at the moment anyway. Was Gemma trying to condemn her nan to an existence, a not very nice existence, rather than a life? But she still couldn't bear to say goodbye. She just couldn't bear it.

She finally remembered the phone. It was nearly lunchtime. She'd been here hours but hadn't left the bedside, and her phone, as she pulled it from her bag, informed her that she had missed calls, voicemails and texts. All from Pippa. Damn! She hadn't thought to let her know, and now she probably thought she'd stolen her car. She wasn't sure about the rules of using phones in hospital, but she took the risk and dialled.

'Oh, Gemma, are you all right? We've been so worried,' Pippa breathed as she answered her phone almost immediately.

'It's my nan,' Gemma said and then she burst into tears.

She heard their voices before she saw them.

'Bloody hell, how are you meant to find anything in this place?' Freddie said.

'Shush, Fred, there are ill people here,' she heard Pippa reply.

'I'm ill, my hangover is a killer.'

'Really, really inappropriate.'

Both heads appeared.

'Oh, Gemma, I'm so sorry.' Pippa rushed to hug her.

Freddie shifted uncomfortably from foot to foot.

'You didn't need to come,' Gemma said, but her tears were now flowing intently, so it came out like hiccups.

'Nonsense, I wasn't having you alone here and as you had my car, Fred offered to drive. He wanted to check you were all right as well.'

'Yes, how is your nan?' he asked, running his hands through his hair and looking slightly horrified at the scene in front of him.

'She's going to be OK, they think. Well, you know, as OK as she can be with dementia and having just had a stroke,' Gemma said more calmly. 'But it's just, well, we don't know much yet, and she could have another stroke any minute.'

'Right, have you eaten?' Pippa asked.

Gemma shook her head.

'Fred, go and get some coffees and some sandwiches.'

'Great.' Freddie sounded relieved.

'I'm staying right here with you,' Pippa said and took Gemma's hand.

'No one, apart from my nan, has ever done anything like this for me,' Gemma said, touched to her core.

'Well that's just wrong, no one should go through this alone. Freddie, go – and remember, I hate egg mayonnaise,' Pippa said.

'Right, see you in a minute.' Freddie scurried off.

'I'm not sure that you're supposed to be here,' a nurse, with the name badge "Helen", said as she came into the room to check the charts.

'I'm her granddaughter,' Gemma said, terrified she would be asked to leave.

'Of course, I meant the other two.'

'I'm her best friend,' Pippa said loyally.

'And I'm, well, I'm her best friend's brother.' Freddie grinned.

'It is meant to be family only, you know; visiting hours haven't started yet.'

'But surely you would be so kind as to make an exception in this case?' Freddie asked, looking at Helen through his long eyelashes. 'It's just that Gemma really shouldn't be alone at such a traumatic time.'

'Yes, of course, I'll let you carry on.' She seemed mesmerised by Freddie, as she turned and walked out of the room backwards, banging into the sink next to the door.

As she hurried out, red-faced, Pippa laughed.

'Poor Helen, she's probably mortified now,' she said.

'I can't help it if I have that effect on women,' Freddie said. 'Right, ladies, as we're in for the long haul, do you want to do a crossword, a word search or to play cards?'

'What on earth?' Pippa asked.

'Well it was the only entertainment the hospital shop offered, but I thought it might help pass the time.'

They opted for a crossword, and Gemma was glad of the distraction. She realised that sitting, fretting on her own, was so painful, and even though they weren't much good at the crossword, she felt so much better having company.

The afternoon passed into evening. Nurses came and went, all flirting with Freddie, who seemed to be an excuse for the whole female nursing staff to come into the room; they even offered them refreshments – albeit weak tea and biscuits. Her nan was definitely getting the best care.

A different doctor came in, shooing the nurses out impatiently, along with Freddie and Pippa, before explaining that her nan was stable now, and although the long-term effects weren't apparent yet, she was out of immediate danger. They were monitoring her closely, and he advised that Gemma go home, have a good night's sleep and then return the following day.

'If Freddie drives his car, I'll take you in the mini,' Pippa offered when she relayed this to them.

Gemma nodded. Her nan's eyelids fluttered and she opened them. Gemma grasped her moment.

'Nan, this is Pippa and Freddie, my colleagues and my friends,' she said proudly, wishing that she could have met them before she got ill.

Her nan seemed to take them in, and Gemma could have sworn she saw a smile at her lips as Freddie went to shake her hand, and Pippa kissed her cheek.

'We'll wait for you outside,' Pippa said.

'I'm going now, but I'll be back tomorrow morning, Nan. And I need you to know I love you so, so much,' she added.

'I love you,' she thought she heard her nan whisper. She leant in close, as close as she could without squishing her. 'And I like your young man very much too,' she whispered, so quietly that, again, Gemma wondered if she'd imagined it.

Gemma kissed her cheek, tears welling. She wanted to tell her that he wasn't her "young man", not her man at all, but that she wished he was, but as she saw the content look on her nan's face, she knew she wouldn't. She wasn't sure she had even spoken at all.

'See you in the morning. Sleep tight,' she said instead, kissing her cheek again, but her nan's eyes had already closed.

Chapter 30

Gemma opened the front door. She could hear voices coming from the dining room, but she paused for a moment. She'd returned from a meeting with a couple of design firms about the brochures. They were a long way off from that, but she was drawing up a shortlist of companies for when they were ready.

She looked around the entrance hall, which she and Charlotte were due to discuss transforming into a reception area. She could hear the distant sound of builders, who were working in the attic rooms at such an efficient pace they were on schedule. It was beginning to feel more of a reality by the day, and although it was only June, and they still had months until their February deadline, she knew that time was fleeing like a burglar.

Her nan was back in the nursing home. She'd mainly recovered from the stroke, as much as she was going to, but now she was even less mobile than before, even less aware. And although the staff were kind and caring towards her, they all knew that quality of life wasn't something that she would see again. Gemma prayed every night for a miracle, because as long as her nan was still breathing, Gemma would keep hoping.

And she felt closer than ever to Pippa now, and Freddie

even. Now they'd met her nan, they talked about her with Gemma a lot, which was comforting. For someone who never confided thoughts or feelings, she realised how sometimes just sharing details helped, and when they explained that they felt the same about their parents, she understood. It was very late in life for Gemma to join the normal human race, but she felt as if she were doing so. And she hadn't perfected being human yet, but she was learning.

She entered the dining room, where around the table, the summer fête committee, who were the same as every other committee as far as she could tell, were all chattering at once.

'Oh, Gemma, how nice to see you,' Edie shouted.

Gemma and Edie were properly bonded now. She had given her a crash course in rose care, which Gemma loved, and she always sneaked out to the gardens when the gardening club was there to help her. She could see the attraction of gardening – it was creative, it was calming, it helped her gather her thoughts. It helped her relax.

'We're trying to decide on a few things about the fête this year,' John interrupted.

Although it was Pippa and Freddie's event, they often let John act as chairman; it kept him happy and from throwing his "bells out of the pram", as Freddie liked to say.

'Right,' Gemma said, finding a spare seat next to Harriet. 'Hi,' she said.

'Thank goodness you're here – we need to wind this up. It's been going on for hours,' Harriet hissed in her ear.

'Where's Connor?'

'New arrival at the sanctuary – he needed to be there, lucky him.'

'Right, so as we were saying, we need a celebrity to open the fête,' John boomed.

'What about Simon Cowell?' Edie suggested. 'I really fancy him.'

'Not sure we can get Simon Cowell,' Freddie said.

'Look,' Gus interjected, 'I think we need to be realistic. If we get anyone, we probably have to pay them, and that eats into our profits. Do we really need a celebrity, or can we agree on someone local? You know, from Radio Bristol, or maybe a Bath rugby player.'

'Oh now rugby, that might be nice.' Edie's eyes lit up.

'But not the radio,' Margaret said. 'No one even knows what they look like.'

'Who did you get last time?' Gemma asked.

'Ah! That's the thing. We had Hector Barber the last two years, because I know his agent and he's become a friend of Meadowbrook, but three years in a row is a bit much. People want new blood.'

'Yes, we love Hector, but there's no excitement in having him anymore,' Hilary said.

'Who is he?' Gemma asked, feeling as if she should know.

'He was on that *Singles Holiday* TV show, and then he was on every other reality TV show going – the dancing one, the roller skating one, the one where you had to pretend to be a fugitive, baking, flower arranging . . . you name it, he's been on it,' Rose explained with authority.

'I don't watch much TV,' Gemma admitted.

'Well, basically he was a reality TV whore, but he's like part of the family,' Harriet explained, sounding as if she wanted to put an end to the conversation. 'And he'll probably come to the fête to support us, but the guys here—'she gestured to those around the table '—want a celebrity to open the fête as well.'

'What about Noel Edmunds?' Gemma suggested, immediately regretting it.

'Do you know him?' Edie asked, wide-eyed. 'I mean he's no Simon Cowell but he's quite tasty.'

'No, I don't.' Gemma felt a bit foolish. 'But he doesn't seem to be doing much at the moment, and I'm sure I read somewhere that he lives in the West Country.'

'Right,' Harriet said. 'Thanks, Gemma, but we might need to try to find someone we actually know, or know how to get hold of.'

'Let's leave that for us all to think about and bring it up at the next meeting,' Pippa suggested.

'Good plan.' Freddie breathed a sigh of relief.

As usual – this was becoming so familiar to Gemma – it took ages for everyone to gather themselves up to leave. Edie was putting uneaten biscuits in her bag. Samuel took ages to be woken up. John was trying to find someone who wanted to hear about his latest morris-dancing exploits – they entered a local competition and came third – only three entrants but still, it was like a bronze medal – and the others were lingering, which Gemma realised they liked to do.

When they had all been loaded onto the minibus and John drove away, the smiles plastered to the siblings' faces finally dropped.

'Kitchen?' Harriet said as they headed back into the house.

'Drink?' Freddie suggested.

'It *is* six o'clock,' Pippa pointed out.

'And that was one long meeting,' Gus finished.

They sat around the kitchen table, with gin and tonics in

front of them. Freddie mixed them, saying he needed to perfect the making of every drink.

'How can you go wrong with a gin and tonic?' Gus asked.

'You need to get the amounts right, and also the right level of ice, and just enough cucumber, or lemon or whatever other fruit you're using,' he answered with authority.

'Right.' Gus sipped his drink, his eyes widening – they were strong.

Gemma winced as she did the same.

'How did you get on today?' Harriet asked her.

'Possibly better than you guys,' Gemma joked. 'And I know that this is a delicate subject, but when this is a hotel, you know you can't really hold your committee meetings here, not if you've got guests. I know it's a way off, but I thought perhaps you might want to think about that.'

'Good point,' Harriet replied.

'The committee won't like it,' Gus said, shaking his head.

'I know, but Gemma's right – imagine if the guests are here for peace and quiet and well, Edie basically tries to molest them all,' Freddie quipped.

'We'll have to think of somewhere else,' Pippa added.

'There is something else I thought of, but not to do with the committee,' Gemma said.

It had come to her when she visited her nan. Her nan was sitting up in her bed, staring at the television as if she were watching but with no visible response. Sitting with her nan was heartbreaking, more so since the stroke, so the only way she could cope was to focus on something else. The worse her nan got, the more she threw herself into the hotel plans, in order to stop herself from falling apart. Her mind drifted to the hotel and the rooms, which Charlotte was about to start planning the interiors of. The rooms in her nan's care home all had names – they were, for some reason, named after birds – but it gave Gemma an idea.

'I was thinking how in hotels the rooms are normally numbered, but here, as we want everything about it to reflect the personality of Meadowbrook, I was thinking we should name the rooms.'

'Name them? What like – Henry?' Freddie asked.

'If you want. For instance, Freddie, I thought that your room could be called "The Prince Regent". It reminds me of you.' Gemma sounded bold as she spoke.

'Oh God, how fabulous, and then perhaps Charlotte can design the room accordingly. I mean it doesn't have to look like the Brighton Pavilion,' Gus clearly liked the idea, as his voice reflected excitement, 'but we can put something in, a nod to it.'

'Gem, that's fantastic. Daddy's room can be named after a king or a president.'

'Or we can call it The Oval suite – not only does that allude to the president's office, but also how much he loved cricket,' Harriet suggested.

'Oh this is fantastic.' Pippa clapped her hands with glee. 'I like the idea of having rooms named after classic books as well, like *The Princess and the Pea*. We could have a high bed,' she suggested.

'You have all got the idea perfectly.' Gemma grinned, she was so happy. 'And what I thought was, if you agree, that once you've decided on the names, Gus can paint something for each of the doors.'

'Really? You'd want me to do that?'

'What would be more perfect?' Gemma said as Gus flushed

with happiness. 'This is a family hotel, and I want everyone's personalities here, especially your father's.'

'Oh, Gemma, I am so glad we found you.' Pippa leant over and hugged her.

Gemma felt like a million pounds. Not only did it seem she could actually help them to open a hotel, but she had also found her creative side, one she never knew she had.

'I have to admit, you are really pulling this together,' Harriet beamed.

'Stop it or I'll get really bigheaded,' Gemma protested, but only half-heartedly. She was basking in the praise and wanted the feeling to continue, as she was loving every minute of it.

Although she'd had two gin and tonics, Gemma went to the sanctuary to see the cats and especially Albert. She had missed the cats today, having been so busy with her meetings. It was late, but Connor was in the office, and Harriet had asked her to get him to call her when he was finished. She left them all debating the perfect gin and tonic, and she was happy to have a bit of time with her cats, and her thoughts.

'Hi, Connor,' she said as she popped her head around the sanctuary office door.

'Hey. Here to say goodnight to the cats?'

'Is that OK?'

'Course, I'll get the key. I'll walk you over, I'm pretty much done here.'

'Harriet said to call her when you're done.'

'Right.' Connor led her out.

'Are you all right?' she asked. He looked sad.

'I'm just worried about Harry. Or me and Harry. I think we've cruised through the honeymoon period and now reality is setting in and I seemed crippled with insecurity.'

Gemma looked at him in surprise. It seemed she was the Meadowbrook confidante again. But she was hardly a relationship expert.

'Why is that?'

'My last serious relationship broke down pretty badly. We both wanted different things; she met someone else. I love Harry, I think I have for most of my life actually, but I'm scared of losing her. Now we've settled into a routine, I think she'll get bored of me.'

'I would hardly say you're boring,' Gemma said. Connor was one of the nicest men she'd ever met – he was funny, and dedicated to animals, she admired his passion and he had an enormous heart. 'And Harriet doesn't think so.'

'I'm worried about pushing her into doing something she doesn't want.'

'What do you mean?'

'Well, we had the marriage conversation, and we both agreed that it wasn't something we really felt strongly about. She doesn't like marriage, and I've never been that much of a fan. Don't know why; but I'd love to be a parent, and I'm not sure she feels the same.'

'You need to talk to her and tell her that you won't push her into anything until she's ready. And also, you probably have to convince her that you didn't decide you wanted a baby because your cow got pregnant.' Gemma's lips curled.

'Ha, you are so right. God, that must have sounded so odd. "Madonna's pregnant, how about we have a calf too!" What was I thinking?'

'I think, deep down, Harriet would love a baby, but I also think she's scared.'

'Of what?'

'I'm not sure – not being good at it, probably. Not all women feel that natural maternal thing. I'm not sure I do, either. And you know how Harriet can only be the best at everything.'

'That makes sense. Harriet is an overachiever, so she only does things she's brilliant at.'

'Then convince her she'll be brilliant, and let her know that you love her whatever she decides.'

'God, Gemma, you're right. Since when did you become the Meadowbrook agony aunt?'

'Well it's quite a recent appointment.' She laughed.

'Thank you so much for listening to a boring vet go on – no wonder the cats like you so much. When you've finished, just put the key through the office letter box and I'll go and get Harry.'

'See you.'

Gemma went to see Albert straight away. He swished his tail angrily, clearly wanting to punish her for her neglect today. But in the end, he let her cuddle him and purred into her shoulder. She thought about Connor and Harriet and hoped they'd be all right. Because she knew Harriet was just scared, and she also knew because when she'd seen the fear in her eyes, it was just like looking in a mirror at the fear in her own.

Despite the victories that she was winning with work, despite the closeness to the Meadowbrook family she was experiencing, the fear never left her, and she wasn't sure it ever would.

Chapter 31

'Harriet, will you come for a walk with me?' Gemma asked.

Hilda was wagging her tail next to her; they had called in at the house just as she and Pippa were finishing their breakfast. July was well underway, summer was in full swing at Meadowbrook, and Gemma had an agenda. She had been running around the estate and spotted something, and she knew that Harriet would be the person to speak to. As much as Gemma adored Pippa and had conceded that they were friends now, good ones, she had also learnt that Harriet was the person to go to for anything practical. She marvelled at how confident she was, how ideas she never thought she would have were flowing, and she was determined to embrace rather than shy away from them.

'OK, but can I finish my coffee?' Harriet asked, rubbing her eyes as if she were sleepy.

'Sure, I'll just go and grab my trainers,' Gemma said.

As she left, she bumped into Freddie, who was wearing a short dressing gown and not much else. She blushed and averted her eyes at the same time.

'It's OK, I've got pants on,' he said. She blushed even deeper. 'Just getting some brekkie for Charlotte and me. She needs to go to work, but as she's working here I've given her an hour off, hope that's OK with you.'

She felt like a silly schoolgirl.

'I'm not the boss,' Gemma mumbled as she fled to get her shoes.

She needed to stop being such an idiot and get used to seeing Freddie with Charlotte. They'd been spending a fair bit of time together, and although she wasn't sure it was true love – she certainly hoped it wasn't – they seemed to be a couple. The upside of this was that she was even more ensconced in work. It was the only thing that stopped her from thinking about Freddie, Charlotte and her nan, and she was getting loads done.

She pushed the thoughts aside as she went back to where Harriet was sitting with Pippa, finishing her coffee.

'Good to go?' Harriet asked.

'Yes.'

Gemma needed to refocus and stamp out her bad mood. But she had to admit she was jealous. She had never felt this type of jealousy before, over a man. It made her insides burn and twist, and her thoughts dark and unpleasant. This was yet another side to her that she'd never known existed. When she was young and she saw the girls at school with their mothers, she vaguely remembered she had experienced something similar. She told her nan, who explained that although the feelings were natural, the only person jealousy hurt was yourself. So she had pushed them away. And how true that was. She was the only one hurt by these feelings now.

'Are you all right?' Harriet asked as they settled into a brisk pace, Hilda trotting ahead of them.

'I'm fine, why?' Gemma replied tetchily. She worried that

the others noticed her awkwardness, and she was doing her best to hide them.

'Your nan, you've been through an ordeal, but you've thrown yourself into work, which I understand, but I just wanted to check that you're OK. I mean you've been working so hard, I barely see you. Maybe you need to lighten up a bit?'

'Not if you want a hotel. But seriously, I mean, it's hard. I feel like I'm saying goodbye to Nan every time I see her. And it's like she's there but she's not there, so maybe I said goodbye a long time ago. It's so confusing,' Gemma replied honestly. 'Work keeps me distracted.'

'I know. With Dad I was so angry he didn't tell us he was ill, but then I realised we probably would have just been waiting for him to die, and he would have hated that. But you're never ready to say goodbye, whether you have any warning or not.'

'No, I'm definitely not ready.'

'But you're doing a great job.' Harriet was sincere and Gemma smiled.

They had built quite a nice kind of friendship, not like Pippa's enthusiastic one, but she felt as if she might have earned Harriet's respect.

'Thank you. You know I love it, and I'm so happy, but at the same time I have all these confusing feelings,' she admitted.

'About your nan?' Harriet asked.

'Of course,' Gemma mumbled, beginning to feel uncomfortable. She didn't need to confide in Harriet right now. She didn't quite know how.

'Sorry, I really am. Remember when you started, and I said I couldn't figure you out? Well I still can't fully, but you work hard, you are lovely, you put up with us, and you're a great friend to Pippa, well to all of us actually, so it doesn't matter. And also, it does feel as if you're becoming part of the family. I mean that, and I wanted you to know.'

'Thank you.' Gemma tried and failed to feel emotional.

'You will tell me if there's a problem?' Harriet asked.

Gemma nodded. She wondered, fleetingly, if she would prefer scary Harriet back.

'This is what I wanted to talk to you about,' she said, leading Harriet to a field with two slightly crumbling old barns in it. 'Harriet, are these part of Meadowbrook?'

The crumbling barns were old, made of stone, and enormous. Gemma had run past them a number of times, and she always wondered why nothing had been done with them. Then she'd had a brainwave.

'Oh, yes! I always forget they're here. I believe Dad was going to do something with them at one point, but then the sanctuary was built nearer the cottages, and he must have forgotten about them,' Harriet said as they stopped.

'What I wanted to know is do you think you could do anything with them?' she asked.

'What are you thinking?'

'Making them both into homes. Or one into a home and the other could be a sort of conference space. You could hold your committee meetings here, and either Pippa or Freddie could live in the other. I know Gwen's apartments are being readied for someone to be on site at the hotel, but that does leave one sibling sort of homeless . . . I just wondered if you could convert them.' Gemma thought that they could easily get road access, and they wouldn't be disturbing anyone else, as there were no other houses around. It was all Meadowbrook land.

'They're not too far from the hotel but also just out of sight,' Harriet mused. 'And there is access to the main road at the bottom of the field.' She pointed and Gemma nodded.

'Exactly, and it would be good to put them to use.' Gemma always used to think she would love to live in a barn conversion. Her nan loved watching those home shows about building projects, and Gemma watched many with her. 'And well, also, if you could convert them then it will add to the estate. You could have workers staying there if you needed to, you could have Freddie or Pippa or both of them in one. I mean, it's just an idea.'

'A bloody good one, potentially. I'll get Roger out here as soon as we get back to the house. Gemma, you are a star.'

Gemma was going to thank Harriet, but she had already turned and started running, quite fast, back to the house. Gemma sprinted after her, trying to keep up.

The house was a hive of activity by the time Gemma showered and changed, then went to the office. She was feeling pleased about the outcome of the meeting with Harriet and how far she had come. A few months ago, she would have been far too scared to bring that up with her, but now, well now she had barely given it a second thought. Gemma was growing into herself, the good, the bad and the ugly, and although she was finding it hard, deep down she felt it was necessary. She was evolving. A bit late but better late than never.

Pippa, Freddie and Charlotte were designing the bar, and the three of them were in the newly cleared and cleaned garden room, heads together, discussing plans. Gemma didn't feel that she was needed. Harriet hauled Roger out to look at the barns, not stopping for a minute; the rest of the builders were all in the top rooms, and Meadowbrook felt alive with all the activity.

She was going to try her best to focus on the good, the now, work, friendship and her nan. She was going to see her nan more often. She had a feeling she was slipping away, and even though more often than not she didn't know Gemma was there, and she slept through most of her visits, she was going to be in her presence as much as she could. But she had to brush those thoughts away now, she had work to do, so she clicked on her to-do list and began ticking things off.

She wasn't sure what time it was when Pippa and Charlotte came into the office.

'I wondered if you had any time to talk about the reception area,' Charlotte said, sitting down on the sofa.

Gemma both marvelled and felt annoyed by her confidence. She walked into any room and commanded it, Gemma normally tripped over or walked into something; they were so different.

'Sure,' Gemma replied, trying to breathe.

'I've told Charlotte that you're in charge,' Pippa explained.

'Thank you. Right, well . . .' Gemma needed to take control. 'I did have a thought, which was instead of having a traditional hotel reception, we have a sort of lounge area. And when people arrive – as it's a small hotel, it's easy to keep track of when guests are due – they are greeted with a welcome drink, and then a member of staff checks them in using an iPad, so there won't be a need for a desk, or a big computer.'

'I love that idea,' Charlotte said. 'I can make the reception area inviting, with perhaps two sofas, an upright chair and a large coffee table.'

'That's exactly it.' Gemma grinned. 'I mean that was how I saw it in my mind.'

'Can I just ask, you know when people want to come and go, they usually go to reception to ask for things, or to hand their key in . . . so what do we do about that?' Pippa said sensibly.

'What about finding a high-tech answer?' Charlotte suggested.

'What do you mean?'

'Well this is a lovely traditional house, and in decorating we're mixing the modern with the traditional, so how about finding a communication system within the hotel using the latest technology?'

'I'm rubbish at technology,' Gemma said. 'But perhaps we could give everyone an iPad or something like that while they stay here, so they can ping the hotel reception when they need something?'

'That's such a good idea, but we'd have to look into it a bit more,' Pippa said.

'It should be easy enough, we just need to find someone who is a bit of a technology expert,' Gemma said.

'Perfect, what a team,' Pippa said. 'And speaking of that, are you both excited for the summer fête?' Pippa asked.

'I can't wait,' Charlotte said.

'Well now you've saved the day with the celebrity guest, you are going to be guest of honour yourself.' Pippa laughed.

'My children are really looking forward to it. How about you, Gemma?' Charlotte asked.

Gemma had stopped listening, so she just caught the last sentence.

'Oh I don't have any children,' she replied, to be rewarded with two puzzled glances.

As she burned with embarrassment at her mistake, she

realised she needed to pull herself together. She'd made great progress with Harriet and now she was back to feeling like an idiot in front of Charlotte and Pippa One step forwards and a mile back.

Chapter 32

Gemma was thankful that the day was finally upon them. The last few weeks had been unbelievably hectic, with all the Singers preoccupied with preparations for the summer fête, and the last couple had been filled with hysteria over every little detail. Gemma tried to lie low, as Harriet had spent most of her time outside with a clipboard as she ticked things off a very long list, barking at people. Pippa and Freddie were checking all the stalls had been allocated the right space, the marquees were going up, the ring for the dog show set, and a main stage, which Gerry took charge of and hoodwinked all the builders to make, meaning the work on the hotel had ground to a halt.

The stage wasn't just for the fête opening, announcements and prize-giving. They had also organised for an up-and-coming boy band to perform – Freddie knew someone – which had attracted quite a buzz. Edie said it was going to be just like Glastonbury; although, she admitted, she'd never been. Fleur was so excited, but she got in trouble for selling "meet and greet" tickets to girls from school, which didn't exist. In the end, Freddie had persuaded Gus to let her honour them if she donated the money to the sanctuary, and Harriet quietly told her that she was proud of the initiative she'd shown.

John, the vicar, was miffed about the stage, because although the morris dancers were due to perform on it, they hadn't built the stage for them, and they weren't headlining the event. It had caused quite a stir, as he almost refused to dance, but then as Pippa said, he never would pass up a chance to get his bells out. And Freddie, feeling guilty, and showing his softer side, had told John that their dance was always his personal highlight of the day.

After a row about the theme for the baking competition – someone wanted to let only traditional English recipes enter, which was a little bit racist according to Hilary – in the end Hilary had her way and it was open to anyone who wanted to bake anything. There was never a dull moment at Meadowbrook – that much was true.

The celebrity guest problem had been solved by the perfect Charlotte, who knew Philip Dunster-Blythe, one of the judges on *Inventors*, the popular TV show where everyone showed their new ideas and one idea from every week was chosen for a grand final. Philip had invented a special kind of duster years ago and made a fortune with a cleaning goods empire. Apparently he owed Charlotte a favour, because she did up his last four houses – after each of his divorces.

'Oh I love a rich older man,' Edie had said.

'Edie, you know he's younger than you, right?' Harriet pointed out.

'Whatever.' She shrugged like a teenager.

But the presence of a TV personality meant that local TV and papers were covering it, and Freddie had spent hours on social media. The event was promising to be one of Meadowbrook's most successful.

Gemma had dipped in and out of the arrangements, but

she was snowed under with hotel work, which had mostly landed firmly on her shoulders while the others concentrated on the village fête. She didn't mind – she realised that she loved working, loved her job, and she felt ambitious for the first time in her life. God, maybe she was turning into Harriet . . .

'Are you ready for this?' Pippa asked with a grin.

'I'm not sure. I mean I've never been to a village fête before.' Gemma smiled back.

'Really?'

'No, I mean we had school fairs, but they were always in village hall, so I've never been to a proper one.'

'Not sure this will change that.' Freddie laughed as the doorbell went.

He came back with a man who was so good-looking, Gemma had to blink to see if he were real. He walked in, dropped a weekend bag on the floor and made straight for Pippa.

'Hector, how lovely to see you,' Pippa said, giving him a hug. 'Gemma, this is Hector Barber. Hector, this is our friend, Gemma. She's also our hotel consultant.'

'Pleasure.' He was well-spoken yet affable as he shook her hand. 'Pippa, you look more beautiful every time I see you.'

Pippa blushed. 'Come on, let's get this show on the road.'

Despite being August, it was a bit chilly and drizzly as rain threatened, so they all wore wellies and raincoats as they made their way to the main field. The field they used for the fête didn't have any animals in it, but it was near the field belonging to the ponies, as well as Gerald – who was watching it all, his leg now fully recovered – and the goats and sheep. Their noises could be heard drifting over. The pig's field adjoined on the other side, but they ignored the proceedings – Gus had set up a track for pig races, but Geoffrey was the only one who even moved, so Freddie was trying to put his money on him, although of course there was no gambling. The alpacas were further away – they weren't keen on the fête or people – and of course the cows were safely the furthest away. If David was aggressive before, he was even more so since Madonna had become pregnant. Even Connor had to tread carefully.

'Wow! It looks great,' Hector exclaimed.

The place was abuzz with activity and excited chatter as stalls were being set up. The refreshment tent was gearing up for a busy day, the bake tent was accepting competition entries, people were bustling around, and you could almost feel the community spirit in the air. Gerald was being spoilt by Fleur who, still feeling guilty about the fire, was undoubtedly feeding him something she shouldn't. Harriet was running around, Connor by her side, checking the last-minute details and telling people where to go. They were all frazzled, Gemma noticed, which was not a state she saw the Singers in often.

'I know I'm not your star guest anymore, but you know, if you want me to do anything?' Hector asked.

'I've put you down for judging the dog competition,' Freddie said. 'I mean I know you're not an expert, but just choose whichever you like.'

'Great.' Hector looked thrilled. 'Will you help me, Pippa?' he asked with a flirtatious smile.

'No, sorry, I'm tied up, but I'm sure Connor will.'

'Um, but Connor isn't my biggest fan.' His face paled.

'Why not?' Gemma couldn't imagine Connor not liking anyone.

'He doesn't approve of the fact I got famous for having sex on telly. But I've changed now, I'm not that womaniser anymore.'

'Well, I'm sure he'll be fine today.' Pippa rolled her eyes and for a moment reminded Gemma of Harriet. 'I'll have a word.'

'I really think you guys have done an amazing job.' Gemma decided to change the subject.

'Tell us that when it's over,' Freddie said.

'Right, come on, Gemma, time to get stuck in.' Pippa led her to the main stage, where Gerry was testing the microphone.

Philip Dunster-Blythe arrived with Charlotte. He was inappropriately dressed in a pinstriped suit – Gemma later found out it was his signature style – and shoes that were clearly expensive and would be ruined by the mud that was already churning in the field. He seemed confident as he strutted up on stage and introduced the fête. Gemma noted how his hair didn't seem to move, despite the wind, and wondered if it was a hairpiece or just really strong hairspray.

'Thank you all for coming. This promises to be the best fête Meadowbrook and Parker's Hollow have ever seen. I hope you've got your programme of events but if not, go and see one of the stewards. They are the old people in yellow T-shirts,' he explained as if he did this all the time.

Gemma was glad Edie didn't seem to hear him.

'So, if you want a photo with me or an autograph, can't imagine why, ha ha . . .' He paused for laughter and the crowd obliged. 'But if you do then please queue up here. Oh! And if any of you have any great inventions, then I'll give you the email address of the production company – we're always looking for new entrants for our TV show.'

'He'll regret saying that,' Hector said as people surged forwards to queue for him. 'I love these guys, but they don't half like to talk. He'll never get away. And they will all want to go on TV, believe me.'

'So, are you glad you're not opening the fête this year?' Gemma asked.

She liked him, she decided. He might have been a Lothario, but he seemed sweet and clearly had a crush on Pippa. And, of course, he was incredibly good-looking.

'Nah, I'm happy to take a step back. I've stopped all this reality TV stuff now, and I'm going to prove myself.'

'How so?' Gemma was interested.

'If I'm honest, I did the TV thing because I was lazy. I saw an opportunity to make some cash with no discernible talent, which I've done, but now I want to do something I care about, so I'm going to write book.'

Connor, who had approached, coughed.

'Can you write?' Connor asked, clearly not convinced.

'I've always been good at English, and so I got my agent to find me a literary agent. They thought I'd need a ghostwriter when I told them my idea for a novel, but then I wrote the beginning bit and they loved it. So now I've actually got to write it.'

'Wow! That's incredible.' Gemma was impressed.

'Well, it's time to do something I can be proud of.'

'Good luck, mate,' Connor said, sounding as if he meant it.

'Thanks, Connor. It's about a family, four siblings. All of them live in a big old mansion, and then someone starts killing the others' partners, and finally, when they're all dead, they start killing the siblings. And the pets, because there are a lot of animals. It's a bit gruesome. You don't know if it's one of the siblings or an outsider.'

Gemma choked back a laugh. Connor had turned incredibly pale.

'It's a joke, Connor,' Gemma said, glad for once not to be the one without a sense of humour.

'Come on, I'll show you the ropes for the dog show,' he said, still not laughing.

Hector winked at Gemma before following him.

'Gemma, can you get me a drink?' Edie asked.

She, along with Margaret, was in charge of the bric-a-brac stall, which seemed to have almost sold out. They were both taking their job very seriously; they wouldn't leave the table unattended. Actually, they liked people running around after them while they sat and gossiped in between selling things. Most of the time people queued while they finished talking.

'What can I get you, ladies?' Gemma asked fondly.

'Tea and a nice bit of cake, please,' Edie said. 'Gemma is such a great girl, like the daughter I never had,' she boasted.

Gemma flushed with happiness.

'Same for me, love,' Margaret said.

'OK, see you in a bit.'

Gemma ran into Freddie in the refreshment tent.

'I've been sent to fetch tea,' she told him.

'The band are here, and we've got them in the summer house, which we've said is the changing area. The problem is, as you know, it's got a lot of glass and not enough blinds, so Fleur and her friends are just staring at them. I told them it's good practice for the groupies they'll inevitably have soon, but . . .'

'Oh to be a teenager again,' Gemma said, thinking she didn't even know how to be a teenager when she was one. 'Do you want me to round up the girls?'

'How?'

'I'll tell them Hector is about to judge the dog show; they all love him as well, don't they?'

'They do. Good thinking. Maybe Fleur should have sold tickets for them to see him too. You are a genius, Gemma Matthews.' He leant over to kiss her cheek, and she felt herself turn red. 'Oh! There's Charlotte. I promised that I'd help her children win a coconut.'

He wandered off and Gemma shook her head. He really had no idea the effect he had on her as, still blushing, she went to deliver the tea and cake.

'I have to go and sort out Fleur. She and her friends are trying to watch the boy band change,' she explained.

'Where are they?' Edie asked.

'Summer house. They need to come and see the dog show,' Gemma replied, turning to go, but Edie grabbed her hand.

'We'll go,' Edie said. 'I need to stretch my legs. Come on, Margaret, Gemma can watch the stall.'

As they practically ran off – the new hip was obviously working – Gemma didn't know if the boy band were more a threat from Fleur and her friends, or Edie and Margaret.

'How much is this?' Steve from the pub asked, picking up a pottery chicken.

'Oh gosh, I don't know, no one told me about prices,' Gemma said, realising that she'd been left in charge of a load of tat she knew nothing about.

'Here, have a fiver.'

'I don't think it's worth that,' Gemma started.

'You probably don't want to let Edie hear you say that and anyway, it's for a good cause.' Steve laughed, pressing a note into her hand.

Gemma could now add terrible saleswoman to the list of jobs she'd had to do since she'd been here.

Gemma couldn't believe it was over. The last visitors left the field, and those left behind started the long job of packing up. The afternoon had flown past, and it had been so much fun. The drizzle had eventually stopped and although the sun wasn't exactly putting in an appearance, it had at least been dry as Philip gave the prizes out before he left. He looked quite relieved to go. Hector was right: he had been bombarded, and nearly everyone seemed to have invented something. Gerry insisted on showing him a new tool. It was a bizarre cross between a saw and a spanner, and seemed to baffle everyone. Gwen had to tell him he was needed elsewhere before he took anyone's ear off, or worse.

The dog show was a huge success, and Connor was even being nice to Hector, as more families lined up to enquire about adopting a dog, and Hector charmed them all. The bake-off competition didn't end in a fight, as everyone agreed that Margaret's traditional scones with a twist (rosemary) were worthy winners, as was a pudding thing that Celia, a younger member of the village, had baked. It was from the olden days, and no one had ever heard of it, but it was delicious and took second prize. Hilary got a special commendation for her quiches, but they had already decided it would be unfair for her to win a prize, as she had won for the last two years. It seemed the bake-off was the most political event at the fête, and everyone had to tread carefully so as not to upset any of the bakers. But they managed it, as the local paper photographed all the entrants together. No one had thrown cake, and it was most civilised.

The boy band was pretty dire, Gemma thought. The rapper was trying to sound as if he were from LA, but he had an unmistakeable Somerset twang, they were all wearing tracksuits and baseball caps, and they looked a bit like the Ali G character from back in the day. Gemma couldn't believe it – they were acting as if they were from the "hood" rather than the middle-class suburb in Bath. But the girls, led by Fleur and Hayley, screamed the whole time as if they were the best thing ever.

They finally finished the meet-and-greets – which they hadn't actually agreed to, but were persuaded by their manager to do with the promise that next time they might actually get paid – and in the end they got out in one piece; although Fleur declared herself to be in love with all of them. Gus loomed threatening when any of them went near his daughter, and Amanda had to try to assure him that she was quite safe – they were eighteen, they weren't going to be interested in Fleur. She might only be fourteen, but she looked older, so Gemma agreed with Gus.

It was quite late before they headed back to the house, exhausted, where they shed coats and boots in the boot room then collapsed in the kitchen, as if they didn't have the energy to go any further.

There was only Pippa, Freddie, Harriet, Hector and Gemma left. Gus and Amanda had gone with the girls, because Fleur had to go back to her mum, Gwen and Gerry had retired to her cottage, and Connor was checking the animals. Freddie opened a bottle of wine and poured them all a glass.

'A toast to a very successful day,' he announced.

He looked pleased and Gemma could see how much pride he took in today.

'You guys did a great job,' Gemma said. 'It was such a brilliant day!'

She could feel her eyes shining with happiness; she really had enjoyed every minute. From the opening, to when she won a bottle of Malibu on the tombola, to watching the dogs refuse to do anything they were told, to the pig race, where Geoffrey won by default as he made it halfway down the track. Even John and the morris-dancing performance had been entertaining.

'I think I was a natural, judging the dogs,' Hector said with a laugh.

'Yes but still, you could have given Hilda a prize,' Harriet replied with a smile. 'And you might want to learn some breeds next time. Calling out "the one with the curly hair" wasn't very technical.'

'Hilda sat on my foot and refused to move,' Hector pointed out. 'Then she wagged her tail so hard against my leg that I'm sure she's bruised me. And as for the other dogs, they don't need to know what breed they are.'

'Potential adoptees might, though,' Pippa pointed out. 'But I can't believe it's over for another year,' she said, sipping her wine. 'And we'll have a lot to do to beat it next year. Although perhaps we shouldn't think about that just yet.'

'You know, the hotel will be open then,' Gemma pointed out.

But, of course, the fête was far enough away from the main house that the guests could either enjoy it or happily ignore it. Gemma could see that they would never cancel the fête

– it was far too important to everyone. It felt important to her now.

'My God, it will be, won't it!' Pippa's eyes shone.

'Well I've got a feeling we did well with money,' Harriet said. 'I reckon we've beaten last year easily.'

'Oh yes,' Freddie said. 'And not only did Philip not charge us for appearing, but he also gave me a big cheque.' He pulled it out of his pocket, and they all looked at it.

'Ten grand, wow!' Gemma said.

'He's got gazillions,' Hector said. 'It's spare change to him.'

'Besides, he said that he felt guilty. His latest girlfriend wanted this particular kind of dog, and it cost him thousands, so when he saw the sanctuary, he actually realised how awful that was.'

'Good, it's disgusting,' Harriet said. 'Pets aren't status symbols.'

Gemma grinned. She loved Harriet's conviction when it came to the animals; it went against the character who Gemma first met.

'Well, I think Philip might have seen that now. He was talking about there being a vacancy for a new one soon.'

'What a new dog?' Harriet asked.

'No, girlfriend. I think he's got a bit of a crush on Charlotte, actually.' Freddie said this without a hint of jealousy.

'Does she like him?' Hector asked.

'No idea,' Freddie replied. 'But with his money, if I were her, I'd jump at it.'

'What about you two?' Pippa asked. 'I mean you and her?'

'Oh, I forgot about that. More wine anyone?'

Chapter 33

Time was running away from her. Autumn was upon them. The hotel opening was everyone's focus, apart from the sanctuary, and it was all hands on deck. Harriet had come up with pages and pages of figures, which Gemma had to comprehend fully. Freddie was in panic mode about his upcoming exam, and Gemma had spent time testing him, impressed again by how seriously he was taking it. The interior was taking shape and Gus had come up with a blueprint for workshops, both for painting and for gardening.

What she didn't tell them was that although they still had about four months until opening, the amount of work that needed doing seemed insurmountable. She was spending hours and hours in the office, late into the night, with early mornings, because the idea they wouldn't be ready to open for Gus and Amanda's wedding wasn't an option. But she was working herself into a tizzy, because the work wasn't being ticked off as quickly as she needed. In fact, it seemed to grow rather than shrink. As much as Gemma loved this job, she was still unsure if she could do it at times, and at the moment that was definitely her overwhelming thought. Failure wasn't an option, but then there were times when she didn't think success was, either. It almost made her want to hyperventilate.

'Why have you got your head between your knees?' Harriet asked as she and Pippa appeared in the office.

'Oh I was thinking,' Gemma mumbled, red-faced.

'I think it's because she's working too hard,' Pippa stated.

'I'm not, there's just so much to do, and if we don't—'

'Yes, we know, Gemma.' Harriet put her hand up in front of her face. 'If we don't, then the hotel will never open, and Gus will never get married, and Meadowbrook will be a failure.'

'Exactly.'

'No, Gemma, it won't. None of those things is going to happen. You might not think it, but we know you're on top of things, and we are all on top of our jobs thanks to you,' Harriet said firmly.

'Which is why you're going to leave that now, go and get glammed up and come out with us.'

'I can't go out.' Gemma's eyes widened.

'Actually, you can and you will, even if we have to kidnap you,' Harriet said. 'Girls' night. Either you come with us looking glam, or we drag you out as you are. The choice is yours.'

It didn't exactly sound like a choice.

Gemma looked around at the packed, hot club and wondered why she never went out. At first she panicked about work, then she felt as if she were a fish out of water, but now it was a new world and she liked it. People were laughing, drinking, dancing, kissing in corners. She was having fun unlike any she'd had before. Although up until now, she didn't really have anyone to go out with.

At college she had a couple of girlfriends, but they weren't into going to clubs, and she didn't think she was either – probably because she'd never been. Chris hated clubs; in fact, Chris hated going out full stop, as he thought it was a waste of money. And she had heard that so many times, she thought he must be right.

They went to the cinema if he was feeling daring, but most of the time they stayed at home – where his mum cooked for them before, like teenagers, they went into his room, or to the bungalow, where they would watch TV with her nan. God, she thought, really, what kind of relationship was that? The odd fumble while they tried to keep quiet lest their family heard. Although Chris's parents went away a lot, so they did get the place to themselves . . . She pushed thoughts of him away and returned her focus to the dance floor.

'My God, this is so much fun,' Pippa squealed, twirling around.

Gemma smiled – it really was. Harriet had organised the girls' night for the three of them plus Charlotte. Amanda was going to join them, but then she'd come down with a sore throat at the last minute, so it was just the four of them.

They'd been dancing for hours – after a few cocktails, which gave Gemma Dutch courage. Pippa seemed to be lost in the music, while Gemma was just happy to be jigging around – she was no dancer, but at least she hadn't fallen over so far. Harriet and Charlotte bonded over their new favourite sport of getting men to leave them alone. Gemma felt like an alien who had just landed on Earth.

'I can't believe that men come up to me,' she said, shouting above the music to be heard, after Harriet swatted away a man with a beard and a man bun, who tried to dance with Gemma.

'What are you talking about?' Pippa asked.

'I mean, I've never been chatted up before really.' She felt stupid saying it. She was pretty sure that even Chris never actually chatted her up. But she didn't want to think about him now.

'Whyever not? You're gorgeous.' And she twirled around again before Gemma could respond.

'God, the bar is awful,' Harriet complained as she and Charlotte handed over two drinks.

Gemma wasn't drunk – she had been dancing so much – but they'd finally taken a breather, mainly because the dance floor was suddenly so packed they kept getting jostled and also, her feet were killing her.

'OK, so sad status alert, but how do people wear heels all the time?' Gemma asked. 'My feet are literally crying.'

'I've worn them all my adult life,' Charlotte replied. 'You get used to them. Well, sometimes, but they play havoc with your feet; my bunions could give Victoria Beckham's a run for their money.'

'At Meadowbrook we don't often get a chance to wear heels,' Pippa pointed out.

'I found it hard when I first moved back,' Harriet admitted. 'I was very much a corporate high-heels sort of person, so to go to trainers and wellies was a bit of a shock.'

'But I bet your feet were glad.' Gemma pointed her cocktail umbrella at her.

'They actually were.' Harriet smiled.

'So, what are you intentions with our brother?' Pippa asked Charlotte.

Pippa was tipsy, at the giggly stage of drunk, and Gemma tried not to look too interested in the answer.

'Oh well, you know,' Charlotte said.

'No we don't, which is why we're asking,' Harriet stated.

'I'm not sure. I mean Freddie is divine, and so funny, but he's also younger than me, and the fact I have kids terrifies him, so it's just a bit of fun really.' She smiled as if it didn't really bother her.

Gemma felt relieved. She wanted to lean over and hug her, which would have looked suspicious, so instead she concentrated very hard on her drink.

'But if you break up . . .' Pippa's face was stricken.

'Yes, you still need to work for us,' Harriet cut in.

'Oh God, of course, there won't be any animosity. Besides, I love working at Meadowbrook. Even if you fired me, I'd still insist on working for you.' She laughed.

'Come and dance with me,' Pippa begged, and Charlotte held out her hand and let herself be dragged up.

'OK, but last time, I am almost dead.'

'She's nice,' Gemma said when the other two were safely on the dance floor.

'I know,' Harriet replied. 'But things aren't always straightforward. When I first came home, we hired this PR consultant, a friend of Pippa's, and she started dating Connor. She was lovely, sweet, warm and actually good at PR, but I couldn't stand her. I was so jealous.'

'What's that got to do with me?' Gemma asked. How could Harriet see how she was feeling more than she even admitted to herself? 'I like being on my own.' It was a lie, but she said it as forcefully as she dared.

'No, of course not. Oh, but good news, it looks as if the barn conversions might be a go, after all.'

'Wow.' Gemma was grateful that Harriet managed to

change the subject so totally, despite the fact they were talking shop in a nightclub.

'I know. Roger's got an architect coming over to look at options, but you were so right. If we could have another house on the land for the family, that would be great. And if we could have two, well who knows? I mean Gus and Amanda are buying a new house together, but maybe Freddie can have one and Pippa the other . . .' She shrugged. 'Dad would have liked the idea, I think.'

'They'll have amazing views, as well,' Gemma said. 'They'd overlook the lake on one side and the house, or hotel, on the other.'

'OK, this is bad; we shouldn't be talking about work. I always used to and, I think, Gemma, you bring out the worst in me. Oh God, I'm just about ready to go home. I think I'm a bit drunk as well, and Pippa is one Sea Breeze away from being a nightmare.' Harriet laughed.

'Me too—' Gemma froze. She found herself staring into the coldest eyes she had seen in a long time. Her heart started to race, and the colour drained from her face.

'Why, if it isn't Gemma Matthews.' Clarissa, her ex-boss, approached.

Gemma closed her eyes and then opened them. No, unfortunately, she wasn't dreaming, as in front of her the woman who made her life a misery stood by their table. The woman who . . . Oh God, she felt as if she were going to be sick.

'We were just leaving,' Gemma stuttered and grabbed hold of a shocked Harriet. 'Go and get the others,' she begged as she shoved her away from Clarissa.

Harriet blinked in surprise but did as she was asked.

'What the hell are you doing here?' Clarissa hissed.

'I'm just on a night out,' Gemma stammered. One sighting of Clarissa, and all her new confidence completely fled.

'Really? Don't tell me that boring old Gemma Matthews actually has friends,' she slurred, and Gemma was glad Clarissa was clearly quite drunk.

Gemma started to walk away. Clarissa's hand shot out and grabbed her arm. Pippa was almost level with her.

'Well I've got to go,' she squeaked, trying to pull away quickly.

Clarissa tightened her grip, but somehow Gemma broke free.

'Oh,' Pippa said innocently. 'Are you a friend of Gemma's? How nice to meet you—'

'Who are *you?*' Clarissa narrowed her eyes.

'We have to run.' Gemma cut her off and literally pushed Pippa out of the club.

Gemma didn't look back, and it was only when they were outside, with Harriet and Charlotte, that she checked Clarissa hadn't followed them. She hadn't. They were safe for now. But her breath quickened and her head started spinning. She put her arm on the wall to steady herself.

'Oh God, are you all right, Gemma? Is she having a panic attack?' Charlotte asked.

Gemma couldn't respond – her breathing was fast and loud, her heart beating out of her chest, and she didn't know what was going on.

'Here, sit down.' Charlotte propped her against the wall.

'I'll get a cab,' Harriet said, and went to the taxi rank opposite.

After a few minutes, she called them over. Gemma walked, flanked by Charlotte and Pippa, across the road.

'I had to convince him you weren't drunk and also, promise him my first born if you're sick,' she said as she climbed in the back next to Gemma.

Pippa was on the other side of her, and Charlotte hopped in the front and immediately started charming the anxious taxi driver.

'Who was that woman?' Harriet asked when Gemma finally calmed down.

She had never been good at lying, she hated lying, but now, she needed something, she needed to think and fast.

'She's a girl I knew at school,' Gemma answered breathlessly. 'She was in the year above and hated me, a total bully, made my life a misery.' Tears sprung into her eyes as all the pent-up misery, frustration and hatred flooded back, and she couldn't stop them. The story might not be exactly genuine, but her tears were.

'Oh no, you poor thing. I guess seeing her must have brought up bad memories?' Pippa asked, putting her arm around her.

Gemma nodded. 'I hated school, dreaded going in, and it seems that she still manages to have that effect on me.' That was true, but it was work, not school.

'I can't stand bullies. If I'd known, I would have squared up to her,' Harriet said aggressively, and Gemma felt thankful that she had managed to get them all out in time.

The tears continued to fall as she let Harriet, Pippa and Charlotte rant about what they would like to do to Clarissa, and she stayed silent all the way home.

She went straight to bed. She didn't bother to take her make-up off, but she did put on an old T-shirt before sobbing into her pillow. Her nan would be ashamed of her; she was ashamed of herself. Gemma had been a good girl all her life, but she had taken a chance, a risk, and tonight had reminded her how fragile her life was. Why did Clarissa have to be there? Why did they have to choose that club? She might have lied about who Clarissa was, but she didn't lie about the bullying, about how making Gemma's life miserable was her favourite pastime, and Gemma just took it. Never stood up to her, couldn't stand up to her. Until she did by leaving and walking into Meadowbrook. And even then, she only stood up to her in her own mind.

She let the sobs overtake her. She wasn't having a panic attack now, but she was panicking. The anxiety levels rose to a peak, and she realised tonight what she'd done. She knew why she'd done it but still, seeing Clarissa she'd been reminded of the magnitude of her deception. She'd almost forgotten it. She loved her job, she loved Meadowbrook, and she adored the Singers. And she was beginning to think she deserved it, but now, after tonight, huge, horrible doubts had returned and were threatening to eat her alive. It was a close call, far too close. And a stark reminder of all she had to lose.

Chapter 34

She managed to put the thought of Clarissa to the far recess of her mind over the next couple of weeks; after the initial way she haunted her, when she was awake or asleep, she reasoned that she had been unlucky to see her and wouldn't again. If another night out were suggested, she would insist on Bath rather than Bristol. She didn't have the time to dwell on her, though; there was always so much to do. She was deep into the paperwork, which she was only managing to keep on top of. Her days were longer, and although she and Pippa always enjoyed their chats in one of their bedrooms before they went to sleep, increasingly now the chats centred on work. Her life was work, and she loved it. It was all coming together, slowly and surely, and she could almost see the light at the end of the tunnel.

Although she had until February, it was already October, and there was still a way to go. But overshadowing the work, the excitement, the thrill of the job, was guilt. Like a tormentor, it had settled in, and she couldn't get away from it. It followed her everywhere, it inhabited her, and it would never leave her alone. Guilt and fear. Fear and guilt. They ran around her mind like tap dancers. All because of bloody Clarissa.

She poured it out at her nan's bedside at the home. Tears,

like unwanted guests, kept coming back, her voice cracking as she explained everything from start to finish. Her nan didn't even flinch as Gemma, holding on to her hand, confessed everything. Her eyes stayed resolutely closed. She didn't even know if she heard her – she was pretty sure that she didn't. Her nan was a shell now, an uninhabited body. That was how it felt, and on top of everything else, her heart was breaking daily. Thank goodness for work and Meadowbrook and the Singers – she dreaded to think where she would be without them.

She wished that her nan could give her some advice. She would give literally everything to have her tell her off, tell her she'd done a bad thing and tell her what to do about it. Should she confess everything? Risk it all? Was bumping into her old boss a sign that she should come clean? But then if she did, she would lose everything, and for once in her life she felt as if she had a lot to lose.

Her nan wasn't going to tell her what to do – her conscience wasn't exactly forthcoming either – so she decided that she would work her socks off, make sure she did the best job ever, and that would hopefully atone for what she had done.

It was getting dark as Gemma left her nan and drove back to Meadowbrook. She parked the car, grabbed her bag off the front passenger seat and started to go inside. As soon as she pushed open the back door, she felt it. Something had shifted; something had changed.

She went into the house and saw them all sat round the kitchen table: Pippa, Harriet, Freddie, Gus, Connor and Gwen. She could immediately see that something was very wrong. Pippa was crying. She hovered by the door – what was going on?

'Gemma, I had an interesting phone call from Clarissa,' Harriet said, staring at her and not beating about the bush.

Gemma's heart sunk.

'How?' she asked, quietly, her voice unsure.

'She said she thought she recognised Pippa in the club that night, did some digging. Gemma, we put you on the Meadowbrook social media, remember, as our hotel consultant, and she contacted me through the sanctuary.'

Gemma felt herself deflate. Why had she thought Clarissa would let it go? She must have seen Pippa before Gemma managed to push her away. She could kick herself for being so stupid.

'Clarissa said she was your boss, and you were her secretary,' Harriet continued. 'She wondered how a mere secretary managed to get this job.'

'Yes but . . .' She was at a loss.

'Why did you lie to me?' Pippa asked through her tears.

Gwen was holding Pippa's hand. Gemma felt herself being sliced open. The game was up. They had found out after all, and it was all about to turn to dust.

'And why the hell did you steal Clarissa's CV?' Harriet demanded.

'You know?'

'After a bit of a chat, she emailed her CV over to me, and it seems it was identical to yours, apart from the name and contact details.' Harriet looked grave.

'I'm sorry,' she stuttered, and she turned and ran.

She had no idea where she was going as she made her way across the garden, but Freddie caught up to her and almost rugby tackled her to the ground.

'Ow,' she said as he seemed to squeeze the air out of her.

'Hey, Gemma, don't run. Surely you owe us that much?' He sounded more serious than she had ever heard him.

As she looked at him, she saw his features etched with confusion and hurt.

'Sorry, I got scared,' she replied. 'Oh God, I'm so scared.'

'Gemma, you need to sort this out.' He frog-marched her back inside, not letting her go for a moment. 'You need to explain.' His voice betrayed the fact that he didn't think she could have an explanation.

'Sorry I ran,' she said as she stumbled back to the kitchen, trying to calm her voice.

She had no defence. The game was up, and it was time for her, little mousy Gemma Matthews, who had never done anything bad or interesting or daring in her life, to come clean. She'd stolen a CV, and she'd pretended to be someone who could do a job she had never done in her life.

'Who are you?' Pippa spat.

Gemma had never seen her this angry. Not even over Edward.

'I'm Gemma Matthews, I'm me.'

'But you stole someone else's identity,' Pippa continued.

'I stole their CV – it's not quite the same,' Gemma replied quietly.

She looked at her hands, which were shaking. Could she justify this? She wasn't sure, but she knew she had to try. She had taken a ridiculous chance and for a while it paid off. She could cower as the old Gemma would undoubtedly do, or she could try to fight for what she wanted.

'Everyone lies on their CV,' Connor said, and immediately Gemma felt she might have an ally.

'Yes, but they don't lie about everything.' Pippa shut him down.

'Look, Gemma, what part of your CV is true?' Harriet asked. 'Let's try to speak about this rationally.'

'My name.'

'Are you telling me that you took Clarissa's CV and literally just changed your name?' Harriet's eyes were on stalks.

'Pretty much,' Gemma breathed. 'And my contact details.'

'Can you just tell us why you did it?' Harriet asked.

'Can I tell you the whole story?' Gemma asked, and Harriet nodded.

Gemma sat down at the end of the table. She knew that she had to try to explain everything to them; this was her one and only chance at survival.

'I left school at eighteen. I had A levels, but the idea of the future terrified me. I wasn't good at thinking about the future, and I didn't want to go away to college, because I worried about leaving my nan. I told you the truth – I don't remember my dad, he left as soon as I was born, and my mum, well she left when I was four. I haven't seen or heard from any of them since, and I'm not trying to use them as an excuse, but I think it explains why I was always so scared.'

'That must have been hard,' Gus said, his voice sincere.

'I only had my nan, and I was terrified of losing her. Without knowing what I wanted, career-wise, to tide me over, I got a job in the local bakery, met Chris, my ex, and six years and a lot of sausage rolls later I was still there.'

'I can't imagine you in a bakery,' Freddie stated. 'Did you have to wear one of those horrible hair nets?'

'Unhelpful,' Pippa snapped. 'So how did you get from there to here?'

Gemma saw her hands were still shaking, but she tried to keep her voice together.

'One day, my nan sat me down and said that she knew I was capable of more and that she had some money saved, which she wanted me to use for my education. We talked about what I thought I'd be interested in and came up with hotel management. I'd always liked the idea of hospitality, and I also thought it would be a secure profession to follow. I found a three-year course at a college that was quite local – by this time, not only did I want to stay with nan, but I also had Chris, you see, and I applied. Six months later I started.'

'And how old are you?' Harriet asked, eyes narrowed as if she were trying to figure it out.

'I'm twenty-eight.' Her voice was calm, but she felt full of shame.

'Your birthday?' Freddie said as the penny dropped. 'Oh, I get it. It wasn't your birthday, or your age.'

She shook her head miserably.

'Carry on,' Pippa said. Her voice was almost venomous. 'I do like a good story.'

Gemma couldn't blame her for her anger, but it was shocking coming from the sweetest person she'd ever known. She wished, fervently wished, she could turn the clocks back.

'Chris wasn't happy, probably the loss of sausage rolls, but I loved college. I found something I was good at, and my confidence started to grow. I even made a couple of friends. I'd never really had friends before. But after the first year, Nan started getting confused. It was little things at first, but well, it got worse, and she went to the doctor, had tests done and was diagnosed with dementia.' Gemma wriggled in her seat; it was difficult. This was the worst bit. This was the bit that still broke her heart.

'So, you left college?' Gus prompted.

'Yes, after a while, I gave it up to look after nan, but after a few years she was in a bad way, and I wasn't coping. The GP was helpful, and I had help from a part-time carer, but it soon became too much for me. I didn't want to do it . . .' She wiped angry tears from her cheeks. 'But I had to get her proper care and that meant a residential home. So I looked around and found the one she's in now. But it wasn't cheap. So I got a job, which was with Clarissa.

'She was the manager of the hotel, not me. I was just a secretary. I didn't lie about her, though – she was a bully, she terrorised me, which what with my nan being so ill, and then the panic about money, really stamped any life out of me. Chris dumped me because I told him I had to sell the bungalow so nan could stay in the home. He thought he'd move in, and we'd live unhappily ever after in a free house.'

'Sounds like a charmer,' Freddie said.

'He only wanted me for my baked goods at first, then my nan's bungalow.' She tried to laugh, but it sounded more like a gurgle.

'Gemma,' Gwen said gently. 'I understand it's been hard, and you were in a terrible position, but I still don't understand why you lied to get this job.'

'After my nan went into the home, my doctor diagnosed me with depression. Dementia, well it's evil. She would be passive one minute, then angry the next. I didn't know who I would get if I visited her, and I didn't know if she would remember me or not.'

'I do see how awful that must have been,' Harriet said.

At least she sounded sympathetic, unlike Pippa.

'My life was a mess. Clarissa, my boss, sharpened her nails on me every morning by flinging insults before I'd even had a cup of coffee. She made me do all her work while she swanned around, charming the guests and doing very little else. Then she would go berserk if I made even the tiniest mistake. I basically did manage her hotel, but I'd never been unhappier in my life. I was being paid a pittance, but I worked all the hours, I really did. I missed my nan, I was worried about money – it all felt so insurmountable.' She wiped away tears as she remembered how exhausted she was, how down-trodden she felt, as if life were too much for her, and misery was her only friend.

'OK, I get the Cinderella story.' Pippa glared at her, bringing her back to the present. 'But how did you end up stealing you boss's CV?'

'One day, Clarissa flung her CV at me. She told me to tidy it up and then write a covering letter to apply for the job here. I couldn't believe how brazen she was. She threatened me to keep my mouth shut, and said she expected the immaculate CV and letter for the following day. So I looked up the job advertisement you'd put out there, and I started to do as Clarissa asked, but I ran out of time, so I took it all home. That night, alone in the bungalow, feeling wretched, I couldn't stop looking at Meadowbrook. And I read the ad over and over, and I don't even know how or why, but I felt drawn to it. So, without really knowing what I was doing, I retyped Clarissa's CV, putting in my name and address, then I wrote a covering letter and sent it to you, posting it off before I even had the chance to change my mind.'

'Clarissa's application?' Gus asked.

'I showed her so she could sign the covering letter, offered to post it for her, and then I shredded it.' Gemma couldn't believe the words coming out of her mouth. None of this sounded like her. Even now, she found it hard to believe she had done it.

A loud sob escaped Pippa, and Gemma felt wretched.

'Right, so what exactly was your hotel experience?' Harriet asked.

'Just over a year of my hotel management course, where I was top of the class, by the way, and nearly three working for Clarissa,' she admitted.

'So that's the only experience you've got of working in a hotel?' Connor was aghast.

Gemma nodded at him.

'So you really were secretary to the manager?' Harriet clarified.

Gemma nodded again.

'Hold on.' Gus scratched his head. 'Can I point out that you've done a good job, so you must have known a bit about what you were doing, surely?'

'The course taught me a lot, and I have a stack of books upstairs that I read every night. The rest was instinct, and yes, I did feel as if I was capable of doing this job, was *doing* the job.' She did believe that. She got the job on false pretences, but she kept it because she was good.

'You lied to us,' Pippa said simply.

She saw in Pippa's face that there was no hope.

'I did.' A calm enveloped her. It was all over now; she'd lost everything, she had nothing left to lose. 'And I never lie, not even as a child. I was so scared that if I did I'd lose my nan, who was the only person I had left. I did this on impulse. I was desperate. I was about to lose my childhood home, I was going to have to rent a room in a house or, if I was lucky, a bedsit, and I had the job from hell. I also needed to pay for my nan's care. I was near rock bottom, and then when I saw Meadowbrook, I just took a risk.

'It was reckless, and I've never been reckless in my life, but I never expected you to interview me. And when you did, I certainly didn't expect you to offer me the job. And when you did, for the first time in my life I took a giant chance, and you know what? I'm glad I did, because I got to meet you all, and especially you, Pippa, and I got to be a part of Meadowbrook, which is the most special place. And I even got to spend time with animals, especially the cats and Albert, who I adore. So, I know I was wrong to lie, but I did it for the right reasons, and I really hope that one day you'll believe that.'

'You are good with the cats,' Connor said, but quickly shut up, as Pippa scowled at him.

'Look, love, you've had a tough time,' Gwen added. 'And I almost understand why you'd do it, but you know, this is going to take a bit of thinking time.'

'Although, I do think that you've proved yourself to be loyal,' Gus added. He was championing her, and she wanted to hug him with gratitude. 'I mean, I know it was wrong, but hell, we've all been in bad places. And well, Gwen's right, it might take a bit of time for us to get our heads around it all.'

'I almost admire you,' Harriet put in. 'I really didn't think you had it in you.'

'Or me,' Freddie agreed. 'God, it makes you so much more interesting.'

Gemma didn't know what to say. She decided that she'd probably said enough.

'Guys,' Pippa chastised, 'you are all missing the point. Everyone I trust apart from my family manipulates me. Mark,

326

Edward and now you, Gemma. I thought you were my friend, and you lied. This was everything to me, my chance to prove I could do it, and you've made me look a fool.' She stood up, and Gemma's heart started pounding again. She should have realised how tenuous Pippa's grip on trust was, and she should have told her the truth before. Pippa started over, her eyes hard and devoid of emotion. 'I hired you without the others' approval, and now I'm firing you, and I never want to see you again.'

Leaving everyone open-mouthed, Pippa stood up and walked out.

'So what now?' Gus asked.

'Let me go to her,' Gwen said. 'She needs a hug and some space.' She got up. 'Gemma, I don't agree with what you've done, I can't condone lying, but I also understand, love. And Pippa will see that, but she needs time.' Gwen patted Gemma's hand before she left the kitchen.

'I should go and pack,' Gemma said.

Now she had made her big speech and felt calm, she was about to fall apart again. It was all over, and she had nothing left.

'Look, just take what you need for a few nights,' Harriet suggested. 'I'm sure that Pippa will calm down, but she can be stubborn, so you'll need to give us some time to try to talk to her. We will try to talk her round. So, can you do that, give us time?' She reached her arms around Gemma and enveloped her in a hug.

'Why are you being nice to me?' Gemma let herself enjoy the warmth of Harriet's arms.

'You lied, yes, bloody hell, you stole someone else's CV, for goodness' sake, and I'm probably in the minority, but I can see you've had a really shitty time, and also I think it shows you have balls.'

'I think so too,' Freddie concurred.

'And, I also feel that we know you. You've been living here and working here for over six months. You're a good person, we're all fond of you, and you've been great here, not only with the hotel, but also with the family. We're a slightly crazy bunch, and you handled us all perfectly. As well as actually making me think that this house might become a hotel in reality, you've also become a friend to us all. Oh, Gemma, I honestly believe you can do this job, CV or no CV.'

Harriet sounded so genuine that Gemma felt her heart lift a tiny bit.

'Harriet, thank you so much.' She stepped out of the hug and gave Harriet's hand a squeeze. She couldn't believe she was losing all this.

'But you need to give Pippa some space and us some time. She's angry; she's probably taking some residual anger she has about Mark and Edward out on you too, so it'll take some work.'

'Where will you go?' Gus asked, brows furrowed.

'The bungalow,' she replied; there was nowhere else. 'But I don't have a car, so I'll need a taxi.'

'No, I'll take you,' Freddie offered. 'Go and pack a few bits and we'll be off.'

'You really all forgive me?' Gemma couldn't believe it.

'Look, we were a bit miffed at Pippa for hiring you in the first place without telling us, but then it seemed she'd made the right decision. I still believe that. And you didn't lie about anything important. Well, apart from your age, your birthday and your experience,' Connor pointed out.

328

'I really did love working here,' Gemma said, furiously wiping away even more tears.

'Honestly, Gemma, we'll do all we can to bring Pippa round, OK?' Gus sounded so tender that Gemma knew she would have to leave the room before she fell apart.

Chapter 35

'Is this it?' Freddie asked, pulling up in front of the bungalow.
'Mmm,' Gemma replied.

She hadn't been able to stop crying the entire journey. Despite Freddie trying to make jokes: 'my driving isn't that bad,' and 'you're the worst sat nav I've ever had'.

The "Sold" sign greeted her with the realisation that it was no longer her home. Technically it was – the sale wasn't completing for another month – but it already belonged to someone else, in her heart especially.

'Shall we go in?' Freddie asked, raising his eyebrows.

Gemma had made no attempt to move; she wasn't sure she could.

'You can leave me here. Thanks for the lift,' she said lifelessly.

'Oh no, I've had my orders. I'm to stay with you, until I think you're OK, which at the moment means I might have to move in.' He grinned. 'Let's hope my little sister comes round quickly, huh?' He laughed.

Poor Freddie was trying so hard to cheer her up, but she couldn't, just couldn't.

Gemma found her legs and got out of the car. Freddie grabbed the weekend bag she'd hastily packed, and they walked up the path. The house was shrouded in darkness as she unlocked the door, and feeling Freddie's presence behind her, she went inside, shivering. It wasn't cold but it was hostile, as if the house were now a stranger. It held none of the warmth of Meadowbrook.

'Christ, Gemma, there's literally nothing here!' Freddie exclaimed as she flicked on the hall light. He peered into the empty living room. 'Have you been burgled?'

'No, I didn't know when they'd want to move in, so I kind of got rid of everything already,' she sniffed.

'Right. Do you have a bed?' he asked.

She shook her head.

'Any bedding?'

She shook her head again.

'So you're planning on staying in a house with no furniture, no blanket and nothing to sleep on?' He eyeballed her as if she were crazy.

She nodded.

'For God's sake, you can't stay here. Look at you, you're in a state, and whatever you've done, I am not going to leave you alone in this place.'

'I've got nowhere else to go,' Gemma said quietly.

'Listen to me.' He looked directly at her. 'The fact that Harry's OK with this whole crazy situation means that it'll probably be all right. If she'd been angry like Pippa, well you would have run off again, and we'd probably have all come with you, but she's in your corner, we're in your corner. I think it's because she admires what you've done for us. And, after all, you didn't kill anyone, or break the law, and this ex-boss of yours sounds like a horror, so she probably deserved you ruining her career.'

'I don't think I ruined her career.'

'Well, whatever, so, where are you going to stay?' He scratched his head and looked around. 'Right, give me a minute.' He left her standing in the empty hallway.

She didn't have the energy to move.

'Right, so this is definitely not the hotel you worked in?' Freddie said when half an hour later they pulled into the car park of a hotel on the outskirts of Bristol.

Gemma nodded.

'And Gus has booked a room, so we're all good. OK?' He spoke to her as if she were a small child.

He led her inside and marched straight up to reception, while Gemma, feeling as if the floor had been swept from under her, tried to take in her surroundings. It was nice enough, she thought, nicer than she deserved, bright, modern.

Freddie led her to the lift and they went to the second floor. When they got out, he found the room quickly. Using the keycard, after a couple of tries, he opened the door and stood aside to let her into the room. It was large, bigger than she expected, with a king-size bed, white linen and white walls. It was a bit soulless as the trouser press glared at her from the corner, but it was clean and comfortable. There were splashes of colour around, red mainly, and she collapsed on the bed. She was just glad she had something to sleep on and something to sleep under. She thought she might sleep for years. It would be easier than being awake.

'What now?' he asked as he gently sat on the bed beside her.

He flicked the TV on, which was showing the hotel welcome message, with awful music piped into the background.

'Aren't you going to leave?' Her head pounded from recent events, but she also felt fearful of being alone.

'I told you, I'm not leaving you in this state. I'll stay as long as necessary.'

She saw he meant it, and she nodded again. She looked around the room; it was suddenly a small space with the two of them in it. What was she going to do now?

'There's only one thing for it,' she said, hardly believing the words were going to come out of her mouth. 'Let's empty the minibar.'

'Gemma Matthews, bloody hell, since when did you turn into me?' Freddie laughed.

Gemma managed to giggle. 'Maybe I've gone from sad to mad.'

'I'll take anything as an improvement on the crying,' Freddie said as they both dove for the minibar.

'The problem is that these tiny bottles are, well, quite tiny,' Freddie said as they finished the gin, then the vodka, and were thinking about starting on the whisky.

Gemma had already opened the M&M's, and Freddie had bagged the mini Toblerone.

'Room service?' Gemma asked.

For once, she didn't care about money, or the fact she was now unemployed, or that someone would have to pay for the room, or that she was practically homeless. Actually, she did think about all that, which was why she reached for the tiny whisky and downed it quickly.

Freddie's face kept changing from surprised to worried to grudgingly impressed.

'Let's get wine,' she decided.

'Are you sure?' Freddie glanced at her through those long eyelashes of his.

No, she wasn't, but she also wasn't yet drunk enough to stop thinking.

'God, Gem, really? I mean I know I like a drink, but even I know that it's not the answer.'

'No, it's not the answer, but it's all I can think of right now, and if I don't get wine, then I think I'm going to cry again.'

'It'll be quicker for me to nip to the bar,' Freddie said quickly, his brow raised in what could be fear or dismay. 'And also, I need to check in at home, well you know . . .' He took the room card and left her alone.

She missed him the second he was gone. She was suddenly scared of being on her own, left with her thoughts and her tears. She grabbed the last bottle of whisky, wincing as she took a sip, but then she took another one. She was determined to kill off all thoughts with alcohol.

It seemed like ages before Freddie returned laden with wine and bags of crisps. He threw one to her.

'Dinner,' he announced.

'Oh, lovely, I am honoured. Dinner with you in a hotel room – who would have thought this would ever happen?' she said, opening the packet and stuffing crisps into her mouth. She realised she was hungry and couldn't remember the last time she'd eaten.

'Not me, that's for sure,' he replied.

'Will Charlotte mind?' Gemma said.

'What, me babysitting you?'

'Is that what this is? You're babysitting me?' She tried to sound angry, but it was a bit half-hearted.

'I meant looking after you, it just, you know, came out wrong.'

'I am not a baby,' she stormed, stamping her foot and then crying again just as a baby would.

Freddie shook his head. 'Gemma, Charlotte won't mind, we're . . . Well, we're not really . . . Anyway, everyone likes you and more than that, we all care about you. At the moment, we're worried. Now, please, can you try to be a bit sane?'

'Give me some wine and I might.'

'You know, when we first met I thought you were far too uptight,' he said.

'I am, or I was.' Now she was tipsy.

'But now I know what an enormous secret you were hiding, it almost makes sense. Because as I got to know you more, I thought you needed to be more like me. And I could do with being a bit more like you.' Freddie sounded confused. 'Does that make sense?'

'It makes perfect sense,' Gemma slurred, because that was exactly how she felt about Freddie.

'And, Gemma, you know?'

She rested her head on his shoulder and snuggled down. Her eyes felt heavy, but she loved being this close to him.

'Um?' she mumbled and fell asleep.

She woke up and for a moment forgot where she was – that moment was blissful, until the events of the previous day started playing in her head. Which was thick with a hangover, she realised, getting worse by the minute. John and his morris-dancing troupe were doing a routine in her head.

She became aware that she was lying fully clothed on the bed, a tiny bottle of brandy in her hand – empty. Oh God, she must have passed out. But she couldn't remember much about the evening, not past crisps. She moved, slowly, gently easing her body into an upright position. Freddie, also fully dressed and looking faintly amused, was sitting up next to her with a cup of hotel room coffee in his hands.

'Uggh,' she said.

'Yes, well it was a bit. Are you all right?'

Gemma shook her head, which made it rattle and then feel as if it would explode. Freddie looked normal, his normal gorgeous self. How had that happened?

'Here, paracetamol and water.' He picked them up from the bedside table and handed them over. 'Take those straight away.'

'Thank you.' She managed to get them down her. 'Was I, did I, what did I?' She could barely get the words out.

It was beyond strange, both of them in the bed. Even though it was clear nothing happened, it still felt intimate, uncomfortably so.

'You, my dear Gemma, were plastered. We were having a really good conversation, and you passed out. It was quite impressive, but you know, I don't normally have that effect on women, so perhaps I should be offended. A smile curled at his lips.

'Oh God.' She rubbed her temples.

'Listen, I have to go in a bit. I need to change my clothes. I have bit of work to do, but I've ordered you breakfast, so please try to eat. Two packets of crisps and the M&M's aren't going to sustain you. Then take a shower and go back to sleep. I'll call you later this afternoon and see how you are.' He was speaking to her quite slowly, for which she was grateful, because words weren't easy to follow.

'OK. But, Freddie, when you see Pippa, please tell her again how devastated I am.' She felt her eyes fill with tears again.

'I will. Have faith, it'll be OK.' His brows furrowed. 'I'm almost sure that it will be, anyway.' He hugged her before leaving the room.

Breakfast arrived. Gemma tried to eat it but as soon as she did, she threw up. She actually felt marginally better afterwards, so she showered and then took herself back to the big bed, where she promptly fell asleep.

Chapter 36

The insistent ringing of the phone woke her with a start. She sat up, groping for it on the bedside table, and thinking it would be Freddie or one of the Singers, she snatched it up.

'Hello,' she said, her voice drowsy from sleep.

'Is that Gemma Matthews?' a voice asked.

'Yes,' she said.

'Hello, it's Marian, from the home. I'm sorry, but I have some bad news.'

How could everything implode at once? She had lost her job, her home, her best friend and now her nan. Her life had literally been swept from under her feet. She now could say, hand on heart, she had nothing left that mattered. When she took the job at Meadowbrook, when she'd lied, she did it for her nan as well as for herself. To help with the care home fees, to put a roof over her head. Was the irony that she now had neither? Not her nan, nor her job. Was this punishment?

Her nan had had a massive stroke and slipped away in her sleep. The woman who brought her up, who sacrificed every-thing for her, the only person in her life who truly loved her, was gone. Gemma knew that she had lost her, piece by piece, over the last couple of years, and her death was only the final, physical detachment, but that didn't make her feel any better. She took a breath. She needed to get to the home straight away.

'We can help you organise everything,' Marian said kindly.

She was clearly used to dealing with this; Gemma was not. She was going to the home for the last time, where her nan was, but she wasn't, because she wasn't anywhere anymore.

'Right, yes.' Gemma was confused for a moment, but she realised she meant the funeral. 'Do I need to call an undertaker?' she asked.

'Not if you're happy for us to use the one we normally use. Brown's, they're local and very good.'

'That's fine,' Gemma said, wondering how you could be good at dead people. Or worse, how you might not be . . .

'Will you be ready if I get them to meet you at the home today?' Marian asked.

'Sure.' Really, she knew she would never be ready.

She pulled on a pair of clean jeans and a light sweater. She had brought the one Harriet and Connor gave her for her fake birthday with her, but she couldn't bring herself to wear it. Her hangover was gone, but her head was reeling. Marian had asked her if there was anyone to help her, but she had said, honestly, that no, it was all down to her. She was about to go to reception to ask for a taxi, when the phone rang again. Harriet's name flashed on the display.

'Gemma, I'm checking in. Freddie and Gus are here. Pippa's still angry and now she's angry with us too, for supporting you. But never mind; she'll come round.' Harriet sounded almost cheerful.

Gemma sobbed loudly.

'Gemma? What is it?' Harriet asked.

'My nan died.' And the floodgates opened yet again.

Gus and Freddie appeared at her door, or the hotel room's door, within about forty minutes as Harriet had said they would on the phone.

'You poor thing,' Gus said, hugging her, only slightly awkwardly.

'Harry would have come – she would be much better in this situation – but Pippa had gone out in a huff earlier, so she thought it best she wait for her to come back. So you're stuck with us.'

'You didn't need to come; I was going to get a cab,' she said numbly.

'Don't be ridiculous, Gus and I wouldn't dream of letting you be alone. Right, give me the address, and we'll head out,' Freddie said, giving her shoulder a squeeze.

'I don't know what I'm going to do,' she said, her voice seemingly small as she sat in the back of Gus's Audi.

The two men glanced at each other. They clearly weren't equipped to deal with this, but then who would be?

'When Dad died, we had to do all the practical things first,' Gus said, almost proving her wrong. 'So, we go and sort out the funeral, we collect her belongings, and we'll have to register the death. You need to book an appointment—'

'Gus, is this really necessary?' Freddie asked. 'She's only just had the news.'

'But, Fred, it's best to focus on the things that need doing – it helps.'

'He's right,' Gemma said. 'It means I have to pull myself together, which can only be a good thing.'

'Phew!' Gus sounded relieved he'd got something right. 'And also there's the newspaper; you should put an announcement in the local paper, so people who knew your nan can pay their respects.'

'Bloody hell,' Freddie said, but then he shut up.

Gemma pulled her notebook out of her bag. She started writing everything down. It made it easier to have something to focus on. It was a slight relief, and it kept her mind occupied until they pulled up in at the home.

Marian, a matronly woman with tight curled hair, hugged her warmly. Gus and Freddie hung back.

'Your nan is still in her bed. You can see her if you want, but it's up to you,' Marian said; she hadn't yet let go of her.

'Please,' Gemma said. 'My friends will wait here.'

Gus and Freddie looked relieved.

The tears flowed the minute she saw her nan lying there. She looked so peaceful yet so pale. Gemma touched her face, which was cold, and she broke down sobbing.

'Oh, Nan, what am I going to do without you?' she asked. 'You're all I've got, and I can't do it, I can't do it without you.' She laid her head down on the bed and cried until she felt as if she had no tears left. There was a knock on the door. Marian put her head round.

'Oh, love, I know it's hard.' She walked over to Gemma and gave her a tissue. Gemma blew her nose noisily.

'Thank you,' she managed.

'Right, can I help you choose what you want your nan to wear for the funeral home? They'll be here any minute.'

'Please.' Gemma nodded.

They chose her nan's favourite summer dress. It was floral and she loved it, because she wore it when Gemma and she

341

went on holiday to the caravan in Wales, and it reminded Gemma of their happiest times. Because they were happy.

Yes, they both carried so much grief. Her nan never stopped missing her granddad or her daughter, and Gemma never stopped wishing her mum would come back for her, but they loved each other and that carried them through. Gemma packed up the rest of her nan's clothes.

'I'm not going to make you clear out right now,' Marian said.

'It's best done quickly,' Gemma said. She didn't want to come back here, she was sure about that. 'I'm going to give all her clothes to charity; she only needs the dress.'

Marian nodded. 'If you want I can arrange that for you,' she offered.

'Thank you.'

Gemma took the personal belongings, the photograph of the two of them that was on her nan's bedside table, her small amount of jewellery, apart from the wedding ring, which seemed only right to be cremated with her.

'Gemma, I found this,' Marian said as she finished emptying a drawer.

'What is it?'

Marian handed her an envelope. Her name was written in her nan's spidery writing on the front. She could tell there was a letter in there. She felt sick, but she couldn't open it now. She put it in her handbag and turned her attention to checking the room for anything she might have missed. She really didn't want to have to come back here.

Just as Gemma began to pull herself together, the door opened and a short man, wearing a black suit, with thinning grey hair and kind eyes, entered and introduced himself as Peter Brown, the funeral director.

'I'm sorry for your loss,' he said, and Gemma wondered how many times a day he had to say that.

Thank goodness for Marian from the home; she organised everything. Gemma was uncertain, but Marian was with her every step of the way.

'What kind of funeral do you want?' he asked.

Gemma hadn't thought about it.

'Do you want a cremation?' Marian asked.

Gemma nodded. She knew her nan wouldn't want to be buried, but they hadn't discussed details – I mean who did that? Most people, she guessed, as Peter asked about what type of coffin she wanted, and as she was at a loss, he advised her. She tried not to balk when he told her the rough cost of the funeral – she had money from her wages saved and she could pay for it, thankfully. She only had to choose the coffin, then they would prepare her body at the funeral parlour. When she was ready, she could go in to finalise all the details.

By the time she rejoined Gus and Freddie, she was exhausted. She didn't know what to do, but suddenly she craved sleep and her bed.

'Can you take me back to the hotel?' she asked.

'Do you want to go and get something to eat?' Gus asked.

'No, if I want anything I'll call room service, but really I think I need to sleep.'

'Look, I know Pip might still be mad, but in light of what's happened I'd rather you came back to the house.'

Gemma shook her head. 'No, nothing's changed. My nan's died, but I don't want Pippa to forgive me because she feels sorry for me. No, I want to go back, and you've been great, but I need to be alone.'

She saw Gus and Freddie exchange a glance but, thankfully, they didn't argue with her.

'Is this gentleman your husband?' Peter Brown asked the following day as Freddie took her to the funeral home.

'Good God, no,' Freddie said.

Gemma gave him a sharp stare.

'Sorry, no, I mean we're very good friends,' he corrected quickly. 'Not that I wouldn't . . . well you know. And we're not friends with benefits, either.'

Gemma shook her head.

'Right, would you like to see Mrs Matthews?' he asked.

'Hell no,' Freddie replied. 'Oh, sorry, you meant Gemma.' He had the grace to look a little ashamed.

'She's in one of our remembrance rooms. You can visit her as many times as you want. I'll leave you and when you're ready, come out and we can discuss the rest of the funeral arrangements.' He gave her shoulder a squeeze and took her to see her nan.

The previous day, Gemma had slept fitfully. She woke frequently, but forced herself back because she wasn't ready to face any kind of reality. She fielded a couple of calls from Harriet, who tried to persuade her to come back to Meadowbrook. It seemed that Pippa had come home, still angry and upset, but when she'd heard about her nan, she immediately said that Gemma should come back.

But Gemma told Harriet that she couldn't come back because of sympathy. Either Pippa could forgive her or she couldn't. But Gemma wasn't going near Meadowbrook until she did. Harriet said she respected her for that, but she also tried to change her mind. Then Harriet, exasperatedly, said that both Gemma and Pippa were ridiculously stubborn.

Gemma knew it was time to grow up. She was alone now, properly, and whatever she was going to do with the rest of her life, she needed to take control, and she wasn't going to be anyone's sympathy project. But at the moment she needed to wallow in her grief, and she could do that perfectly well on her own.

The Singers had other ideas. Harriet had called her again this morning, to check on her, and when she said she was going to the funeral parlour, Harriet immediately said she would send Freddie.

'No, honestly, I'll get a cab,' Gemma protested.

'Nonsense. Besides, he's the most dispensable of us at the moment. Look, Gemma, Pippa is feeling awful about your nan, and she wants to speak to you, but I don't think she knows how to go about it. Won't you come here after and see her?'

'No, Harriet, sorry. I just can't, not with things as they are.'

'I honestly think she's missing you, Gem, really.'

'Look, Harriet, one thing at a time, please. I have to arrange a funeral, I have to say a final goodbye to my nan, and I'm not sure I have the capacity for anything else right now.'

'Fair enough. Fred will be with you soon.'

Gemma tidied the room. She still felt embarrassed about the fact she'd emptied the minibar the other night. What must housekeeping have thought? She was sure they'd seen worse, but still, she was trying to redeem herself by keeping the room neat.

She put on her smartest black trousers and a black top, which seemed appropriate for visiting a funeral parlour, but then she was new at this. She had emailed an announcement the previous night to the local paper, and she'd called the post office where her nan had worked for years, and a few of her friends, to tell them. It was hard, so hard saying it out loud, but she promised to let them know when the funeral was and felt better for being proactive. Gus was right about that.

In the small room, her nan looked even more serene than she did in the home, but she also had a bit more colour – probably dead people's make-up. She was wearing the dress and for a moment, the years slipped away as Gemma remembered them paddling in the cold Welsh sea and eating ice creams, before having fish and chips back at the caravan. Simple pleasures, but they really were happy memories.

She often felt sorry for herself growing up; she was the odd one out at school from day one. Mums picked up the kids, even dads occasionally, but nans came to visit, they spoilt their grandchildren, they didn't bring them up. She loved her nan, but at the time she wished she were like the other children – oh, how she had wished for that.

There were a lot of good times. Her nan did her best for Gemma, and it was more than good enough. Enough love, enough food, enough. It was enough. The dark clouds of her upbringing were nothing to do with her nan; after all, she was the only one who kept them at bay. She was the best, and Gemma was lucky to have had her.

'I love you so much, Nan.'

Gemma kissed her cheek, which was strange, a sensation she didn't quite know how to describe, then she glanced at her nan for the last time, before she left the room. She wouldn't see her again, but she would have to be stronger than she ever had been from now on. That was all there was to it. She thought of the letter, still unopened in her bag. Maybe it was time she read it. On her final visit to her nan . . .

My dear Gemma, she read, hearing her nan's voice so clearly.

I'm not much of a writer, as you know, but when the doctor diagnosed me, I thought I ought to do this before I forgot who I was or, God forbid, who you were. I am sorry if I've done that, but as you know – you were holding my hand when the nice doctor explained – it's a very mean illness and just my bloody luck to get it!

I know we don't joke enough, or didn't, but you were always such a serious child. I know I could never really mend the scars your parents left, but I hope you think I did my best by you, which is all I could do. I felt so guilty, my lovely granddaughter. You see, I thought it was my fault in a way. I brought Sandra up, and she walked out because she couldn't cope, and that seemed to be more of a failing in me than her. I am sure when you are a mum yourself – and, by the way, I think you would make a wonderful mum – then you'll understand. Your children are your joy, but in my case also pain and guilt.

I hope I told you how much I loved you enough times, because I always will, Gemma. And, more importantly, I always have. I will always be so proud of you. You had a tough time, but you are a fighter – more than you know. You might not always get it right, but none of us do. But you are special, clever, lovely. You are quite simply the best granddaughter I ever could have had, and I was lucky to get to bring you up.

If I die, it's not because I want to leave you. I don't know why your parents did what they did, but believe me when I say they missed out on the most wonderful girl in the world. And I am just thankful, so thankful, that I did not. I love you, but always be true to yourself and always know you deserve only the best. Believe in yourself the way I do, live your life the way you want and, above all, enjoy yourself, my lovely girl.

Lots of love,

Nan.

Freddie jumped up as soon as she returned.

'Are you all right?' he asked.

She nodded, not trusting herself to speak as tears streamed from her eyes.

'When would you like the funeral?' Peter Brown asked, all business as he had a massive diary laid out in front of him.

'As soon as possible,' Gemma replied.

She wasn't ready to say goodbye, she never would be, but she had to and therefore she didn't want to prolong the agony. She couldn't wait to read the letter again, actually. It was as if her nan were still with her.

'Don't people need notice?' Freddie asked.

'There aren't many people. I've not got any other family, and Nan's friends, well some of them are still around and they'll probably come.'

She hated the idea that the church, or rather the crematorium, would be empty, but she hoped that people who knew her nan would show up.

'We've had a cancellation for Monday. It's only a few days, but—'

'I'll take it.'

'God, how do you get a funeral cancellation? Did someone get undead?' Freddie asked.

Peter gave him a quizzical look and shook his head.

'God, that's a relief. I mean my biggest fear is not really being dead and then being burnt or buried alive. Gemma, promise me if I die you'll double triple-check?'

'Freddie, not exactly appropriate. But if I'm around I will.' Gemma arched an eyebrow; she was somehow glad for his utter madness. It was making her feel better or if not better, distracted.

'So Monday it is. Midday?' He wrote in the diary.

'Thank you. Now how do I pay? I guess you take cards?'

'Bloody hell,' Freddie said as she took the invoice from Peter. 'Dying is a seriously expensive business.'

Gemma shook her head again.

'When did you last eat?' Freddie asked as they got into the car.

He'd brought the Range Rover that the family seemed to share; apparently, the Porsche wasn't appropriate for a funeral parlour. That made her smile.

'I don't know,' she admitted. She hadn't last night, but this morning, maybe?

'Right, I'm taking you to lunch, no arguments. I saw a pub on the way, which looked as if it might be OK.'

They drove in silence, Gemma trying to order her thoughts, and Freddie pulled into a space outside the pub then got out. She followed him, her stomach rumbling at the idea of food. Freddie was efficient as he read the menu, and when Gemma shook her head, he ordered for them both, at the same time directing her to a table.

'Here you go,' he said, putting a brandy in front of her.

'I can't drink that!' She was horrified.

'You need it, for shock.'

He went back to the bar and returned with a large bottle of mineral water and two glasses. She downed the brandy and then gulped some water. She'd never get used to the taste.

'Do you need to phone people about Monday?' he asked.

'Yes, I've got a list back at the hotel. Speaking of which, I can't stay there forever. I know it's a bit silly as the bungalow is empty, so I was thinking I'd buy an airbed and some bedding and go back there for now.'

'No way. You'll be on your own. At least in a hotel we know you can call room service, or there are people there if you need anything. Please, at least until after the funeral.'

She nodded.

'And Pippa is feeling terrible,' he said. 'I know you think it's just sympathy, but actually she misses you. Harriet keeps reminding her of what a good friend you were. Not just what you did for the hotel, but also what you did for her and the family. How you mucked in with the animals, how you got on well with the locals, the gardening club, how you got us to church and made John, the vicar, happy, how you listened to all of us drone on as well, not to mention what a hero you were in the fire.'

'I didn't—'

'You did so much. You went out with me to catch Edward out – I mean it wasn't your finest moment, but you still did it. And that speech to the village – you stood up in front of everyone and you won them round. You were really quite impressive. Everything you've done since being with us has showed how much you cared. You are amazing, and if Meadowbrook is ever going to be a hotel, we need you.'

'But—'

'No, Gemma. In these past months, you've become part of Meadowbrook, and this hotel, when it opens, will only open because of you. You rallied us, organised us, focused us. For goodness' sake, I am even taking an exam because of you. If it wasn't for you we would still be talking about it, trust me.'

'I'm so touched you think that.' She really was.

'It's not just me – Harry, Gus, Gwen, Connor, Amanda, even Charlotte said you were doing a great job and you'd helped her a lot. And of course the cats miss you too.'

'I miss them.' She felt so emotional about them, how she hadn't seen them. Would Albert think she'd abandoned him?

'Even Pippa sees it now, but not only is she stubborn, she's also a bit embarrassed about her behaviour.'

'But only because my nan died.'

'She might have realised sooner because your nan died, but it's not that. She knows deep down that you're nothing like Mark or Edward. You might have lied to get the job, but you were helping us, not trying to rip us off, and when Gwen sensibly pointed that out to her, she realised how right we all were. Pip's never been great at admitting she was wrong. She's sweet, but not when she digs her heels in, trust me.'

'Look, Freddie, that's all great, and you know you are making me feel better. But I need to focus on the funeral right now. After that, maybe I'll feel strong enough to see Pippa, but don't you see, it's not just her forgiveness I need, but I need to forgive myself? I feel so horrible for upsetting her after all she did for me. All of you, actually.'

'I know, but you need to, because we need you back at Meadowbrook.' He took her hand. '*I* miss you.'

She felt herself heating up. She knew he didn't mean it in that way, but God, being around him, her feelings, her nan, it was all too much. She snatched her hand away.

'And I want nothing more than to be there, but at the moment, please let me focus on my nan.' She couldn't bring herself to look at him.

'But, I would be happier if—'

'Look, Freddie, if I promise to stay at the hotel until after the funeral, will you stop trying to get me to come to the house?'

'Deal.' He sighed and shook his head.

Chapter 37

She got out of the limo, which felt ridiculous for one, but it was part of the "funeral package". Which made her giggle irrationally and think of a meal deal. You get a coffin, a funeral and a car, all in one. Since the last visit to the funeral home, Gemma had been experiencing weird and unwelcome moments of euphoria, in which she just found everything funny as if she were drunk. She googled it, because Gemma didn't like being out of control, but apparently it was a normal part of grief, which fascinated and horrified her in equal measure. The old Gemma couldn't bear feeling out of control of her feelings, but the new one was more accepting of it. Actually, the new one had no bloody choice.

She still couldn't quite believe that nan was gone – it didn't seem real. She had said it out loud on the phone to countless people, she had registered the death officially, she had told the bank, the estate agent, anyone else who she needed to inform – she had been given power of attorney when her nan got sick, so she had to tell the solicitor – and all these details kept her busy.

She had tried to keep all the Singers at arm's-length. They seemed to check on her on a rota. First Harriet, then Freddie, and Gus or Amanda. She knew they meant well, but . . .

353

She shouted at Harriet – look how far she'd come – and told her she didn't need her feeling sorry for her. When Harriet laughed and said she didn't, she simply wanted her to 'come back to work so she could stop playing at hotels.' Gemma apologised and said she would like nothing more. She missed Meadowbrook more than she thought possible. Freddie kept checking she was eating, and she told him to bugger off, which, irritatingly, he said he liked. Gus and Amanda she was nicer to – she cried when Amanda spoke to her, and said that she was fine but just very, very sad.

There was still no word from Pippa.

The hotel room was beginning to close in on her; although, weirdly, it felt a bit like home now. She'd had deliveries of flowers (Charlotte), cakes (Gwen) and cards from the gardening club, which had made her so emotional. There was no getting away from Meadowbrook. She didn't realise what a part of it she was, or what a part of her it had become. It was her community, she realised, and it was so important to her, but it had taken her losing it to see all that.

Harriet had visited the previous night to bring her a black dress, her heels and a jacket in case it was cold. She'd insisted they eat dinner together in the hotel restaurant, and although Gemma had struggled to eat, she had been glad of the company. Harriet had reluctantly left her, after making her eat at least half her meal, and then she'd gone to bed, feeling alone again.

Gemma was so grateful that they cared about her, surprised and grateful, but she wanted Pippa. She missed her friend so much. Her smile, her kind words, her gushing chatter about everything and nothing. She would have given anything for that right now. It was funny how reluctant she had been to let Pippa get close to her, yet now life felt wrong without her in it. She had never had a friend like that before – actually, she'd never had friends like Harriet, Freddie and Gus either – but it was Pippa she wanted to see. She needed her forgiveness; she needed her friendship.

Now, standing alone under an umbrella on a rainy September day, she looked at the hearse that carried her nan's body, and loneliness enveloped her. People started arriving, giving her no time for despair – this was for her nan, not her. The staff of the post office, both past and present, arrived, as well as Marian, Sarah and a few others from the residential home. Mr and Mrs Glover from next door stopped on the way in to reassure her the bungalow hadn't been burgled, not that there was anything left there to take. There were volunteers from the local charity shop, where her nan worked before she got sick, and even the owner of the fish and chip shop where they got their takeaway from on Fridays. A few more of her nan's old friends arrived, and Gemma felt her heart swell. These people were all here for her nan, but she still couldn't help but think that no one was here for her.

Peter Brown glanced at his watch. 'A few minutes, now,' he said.

Gemma nodded and thought about the fact she would walk in behind the coffin on her own, as tears stung her eyes and her legs began to feel like jelly. A cacophony of car engines interrupted her self-indulgence and then she heard shouting.

'I told you we'd be late, Fred,' Harriet shouted.

'I couldn't find my shoes,' he shouted back.

'Who loses their shoes? Apart from a child,' Gus replied.

'For goodness' sake, shush, it's a funeral,' Gwen snapped.

355

Wondering if she could trust her ears, the Meadowbrook minibus appeared, and Gemma was startled as John, the vicar, got out of the driver's seat, and various members of the gardening club and the fête committees emerged. Gemma blinked, but they seemed real as John helped Samuel out.

'Oh, my dear Gemma,' Edie said, rushing up to her and hugging her warmly. 'We're so sorry, and we had to come and pay our respects. Well we did, but I think Samuel thinks it's a day trip to the seaside.'

'This doesn't look very much like the seaside,' Samuel shouted from under a straw hat.

John and Hilary shushed him.

'Gemma, we are very sorry for your loss. I would have been happy to do the service, but I appreciate your nan didn't know me, so I shan't take offence.'

'Um, thank you?' Gemma replied uncertainly.

One by one, they hugged her and went inside. She felt choked; she couldn't believe they had come to support her. Well, apart from Samuel, who was asking when he'd get an ice cream.

'Gemma, are you holding up?' Harriet asked, giving her a brisk hug. 'You look lovely, by the way.'

'Just about,' her voice cracked.

Gwen squeezed her, and she felt the tears burst forth. Then Connor kissed her wet cheek, as did Gus and Amanda. Finally, Freddie appeared, dishevelled, tucking his shirt in as he walked.

'Sorry, I couldn't find my good shoes,' he said, giving her a quick kiss. 'Charlotte is sorry not to be here, but one of those children things of hers is ill,' he explained. 'Not that we're together anymore, did you know that—'

Peter Brown coughed.

'Oh God, we'd better go in,' Harriet said. 'Can I say God?'

'It's not a church,' Gus pointed out.

'Hurry up, Pip,' Harriet shouted and to Gemma's amazement, Pippa appeared from behind the Range Rover.

'Oh, Gem, I am so sorry,' Pippa said, grabbing Gemma and hugging her in the warmest hug ever.

'No, I'm sorry.' Gemma's tears continued to fall.

'This isn't the time,' Pippa said. 'You did what you did for the right reasons. I sort of understand that, but today is about you and your nan. And I'm here to support you. As your friend.'

'Thank you.' Gemma felt herself shaking. Relief, sadness, fear, guilt and a sparkle of hope.

'And we miss you, and we need you at Meadowbrook. I'm sorry I didn't contact you, but I'm stubborn, and I hate admitting I was wrong, but I was wrong, and I'm ashamed of how I behaved. Oh, Gem, can you forgive me?'

'No, I was wrong,' Gemma said. 'I've never had a friend like you before.'

'Well you still have a best friend if you want her, although that does make us sound about six years old!' Pippa laughed, but Gemma saw the tears in her eyes.

Gemma nodded, too full of emotion to speak.

'There's so much I want to know, but anyway, that can come later. The main thing is will you come back?'

'Yes, please.' Gemma laughed through the tears.

'Fantastic, and also, as your friend, would you like me to walk with you? Behind the coffin. You know, just in case you keel over or something?' Her lips curled in a smile.

'I really would like that very much,' she replied.

She got through the funeral with Pippa by her side and the Singers all around her. The songs Gemma had chosen were all sung loudly, especially by John. She decided that she would speak, and of course after the village meeting at Meadowbrook, it didn't feel so daunting – the only thing she was worried about was whether or not she would do justice to her nan.

'Thank you all so much for coming,' she said, clearing her voice and wiping away a stray tear.

'Speak up!' Samuel shouted.

Gemma almost laughed.

'Nan, Sue, would have been touched to see you all here. She was a special woman with an unusual life. She lost her husband young, to cancer, and I hope she's with him now. And then my mother left, so she had to bring me up on her own, probably at a time in her life when she was ready to enjoy more freedom. But never once did she ever complain, or at least not to me.'

Gemma paused, and she heard the audience laugh. She looked at Freddie who was giving her a thumbs-up.

'And she was the best mother/nan I could have asked for. She was sensible, practical even, and she loved me very much. She did everything to make me feel secure, and if I didn't, which I often didn't, it wasn't her, it was me. She tried so hard to get me to believe in myself, and I realise now that it was only fear that stopped me from doing so.

'She really was a special, wonderful woman, taken by a cruel illness, long before now, and I hope that she is now at peace. I want to say that she goes with love, and gratitude, and she will never, ever be forgotten.'

As Gemma almost collapsed in tears, Pippa rushed up.

'She'll always be in your heart,' she said as she led her back to the seat.

When the coffin disappeared behind the curtain to the furnace, Gemma thought that her heart would explode. It was the worst thing she had ever seen, but she breathed and she clutched Pippa's hand so tight she was sure she bruised her. But Pippa didn't complain – she sat there next to her, holding her up.

When she had to walk back outside, Freddie stood on the other side of her, and he and Pippa supported her. Somehow, she made it and somehow, she managed to stop the tears, which felt as if they had been flowing forever.

The mourners who knew her nan gave her their best wishes and left. She had explained, in the funeral notice and on her numerous phone calls, that there would be no wake because the bungalow was empty, and she felt bad, but she didn't know what else to do. She had nowhere to host it for anyone, and she just hoped that her nan wouldn't feel let down by that. Although she was never one for a party, so she probably wouldn't.

'I'd better get back to the hotel,' she said after bidding Peter Brown and the rest of the funeral guys a goodbye.

'Ah, about that . . .' Harriet said.

'You can't,' Gus added.

'Why not?'

'Well, we kind of checked you out,' Amanda said with a smile.

'Which is why we were late; I did know where my shoes were really,' Freddie replied, looking pleased with himself.

'But how, you aren't me?'

'Oh, Fred kept the keycard from the other day. We rushed

359

in, packed up your stuff, paid the bill, you know – no one argues with Fred, anyway,' Pippa explained.

'But why?' Gemma asked, genuinely flummoxed but ridiculously relieved.

'Because we want you to come home with us,' Pippa said.

'I know you said there wasn't a wake, but was that true?' Edie asked. 'I really could murder a glass of wine, and a funeral isn't a funeral without a paste sandwich, I always say.'

'No, there isn't, I'm sorry,' Gemma said, overwhelmed. 'I don't have anywhere to hold one.'

'Course you do,' Gwen said. 'John, bring everyone back to Meadowbrook, we'll have a drink to toast Gemma's nan, and I'll rustle up some sandwiches. Not sure we have any paste though, Edie.'

'But—' Gemma started.

'No buts. It's time for you to come home,' Harriet said.

'So, what do you say?' Pippa asked.

'I hope when the Meadowbrook Hotel opens, we'll have better security than the hotel I was in,' Gemma quipped.

Pippa laughed.

'Did she just make a joke?' Freddie teased.

'When do I get my ice cream?' Samuel shouted as John tried to get him on the minibus.

Gemma, wondering if now her nan was at peace she could be too, went up to him and kissed his cheek.

'Samuel, you can have anything you want,' she said.

No one seemed more shocked than her, apart from Samuel.

'Oh, now I'm far too old for any of that how's your father.'

She had never seen him move so quickly as he practically ran onto the bus.

Gemma waited patiently as the Singers bickered about the

cars the way they bickered about most things. Harriet tried to organise the Range Rover, and she said Connor, Gwen, Pippa and Gemma should go in it, and Freddie should go with Gus. But he objected on the grounds that Gus drove like an old man, which of course Gus took offence to, and it was down to Amanda and Gwen to reason with them both.

Gerry was on the minibus to help with the older ones, and in the end, so they didn't stay in the grounds of the crematorium all afternoon, Gwen went with Gus, and Freddie with them. None of it bothered Gemma – she had a warmth inside her that she believed her nan had sent her. It was so terrible saying goodbye, but she didn't feel alone anymore. With Pippa holding tightly to her hand, and Freddie sitting the other side of her, with Harriet, next to Connor, who was driving back to Meadowbrook, and Gus, the others and the minibus following, she felt wanted. She actually felt as if she had people who cared about her. More people than she ever had before. Yes, she had to say goodbye to her nan, but it was as if she had given her a new family as a parting gift: the Meadowbrook family.

And it was all the strangest sensation – a mixture of sadness, happiness, calm and acceptance. For the first time in her life, the one thing she didn't feel was fear.

'You know, after Dad's funeral we all got hammered in the summer house,' Freddie said as the last of the "guests" departed.

Gwen and Gerry insisted on clearing up, leaving them all collapsed in the drawing room.

'The summer house is Gus's studio now, though,' Pippa pointed out.

'And the last time I went in there, I knocked over his easel,' Gemma said.

'Oh God, yes, you are so clumsy.' Freddie laughed.

'It was fine, though,' Gus said kindly. 'No harm done.'

'It's OK, I know I'm a klutz, always walking into things or falling over.' She smiled.

'But you're our klutz.' Harriet giggled. 'Seriously, it does feel as if you belong here, and I'm sorry I was suspicious of you.'

'To be fair, you should have been,' Freddie said, pointing at Gemma.

'Oh yes, but Harry let me hire you, and actually, if it hadn't been for my need to prove myself, I bet she'd have uncovered the truth about you ages ago,' Pippa said.

'I'll admit that I was sure she would. God, I was so scared of you, Harriet.'

'We all are,' Freddie quipped as his sister threw a cushion at his head.

'I didn't try to find out about you because I didn't want Pippa upset, and OK, so it was a bit of a roller coaster, but we're on track now, aren't we? Despite everything, Pippa was right to hire you, so well done, Pip.'

'I can do this,' Gemma said determinedly. 'I can help you to open this hotel.'

'I know you can,' Pippa replied. 'You've already proved it.'

She looked around. Pippa was sat next to Freddie; they were both relaxed, smiling. Gus and Amanda were holding hands, looking every inch the perfect couple, as were Connor and Harriet, who couldn't have been sitting any closer without her actually sitting on him. It was lovely, and she felt content.

She took a sip of her wine; she wasn't drunk, because she

wanted to savour the evening as she gave a silent toast to her nan. She said goodbye, she told her she loved her, she always would, she thanked her for all she did for her and was pretty sure still was, because her nan had somehow led her here, and now she felt as if she belonged somewhere.

She didn't even mind admitting her shortcomings, because they didn't scare her anymore. She could be herself, it was all out in the open, and besides, she had proved herself. Seeing them all believe in her, and Pippa too, she knew it was time to believe in herself. Her future, whatever that may be, was full of promise. She would help them open Meadowbrook, and when they no longer needed her, she had options. She might even go back and finish her studies.

She had thought it was too late, but it wasn't. While she was breathing, it was never too late. And she knew now that when she did leave Meadowbrook, she would always have the Singers in her life. Pippa, her best friend, Harriet, who no longer scared her, Gus, who was the kindest person she knew, Freddie, who was, well, Freddie. Amanda, Connor and Gwen, who had all helped her adjust to life at Meadowbrook, in their own way. And of course the villagers, especially Edie, who told her, after a few too many drinks, that she would love Gemma to see her as her surrogate family, which Gemma gratefully leapt on.

It felt nice. No, that didn't do any of it justice – she felt her heart swollen with love and gratitude; she felt as if she could conquer the world now she had all these people, kind, loving, warm, crazy people around her. And she knew full well that they had all saved her.

Meadowbrook had saved her.

Epilogue

Freddie rushed in through the back door, wearing a pair of baggy joggers and a hoodie, and even in that he was impossibly handsome.

'God, it's a nightmare being kicked out of my own house,' he said as he grabbed the cup of coffee that Pippa was holding and greedily drank from it. 'Yuk, I hate sugar,' he pronounced.

'It was my coffee.' Pippa shook her head. 'And, Fred, it's not your house, well it is, but it's a hotel now,' she said proudly.

It was. As of yesterday, The Meadowbrook Hotel was a reality.

'And aren't you supposed to be with Gus?' Gemma asked.

'Oh, he's fine, he's down chatting to his pigs. Honestly, I'm amazed he didn't insist on them coming to the wedding. I think he would rather Geoffrey be his best man than me.'

'Hilda's coming,' Pippa pointed out.

'That dog goes everywhere,' Freddie replied with an eye roll.

It was the day of Gus and Amanda's wedding. The rooms at Meadowbrook had been ready since the beginning of February and were now filled with guests. Pippa and Gemma were staying in Gwen's old quarters, which the genius of Charlotte and Roger had managed to make into a

364

two-bedroom apartment. It was small but it was liveable, for now. As well as the two bedrooms, there was a bathroom. They had commandeered the snug in the main house as their living room; after all, it was too small for hotel use, so they would watch TV in there in the evenings, and of course it meant they were on hand for when any guests needed them. Which they could let them know via the iPad system they had set up. Anyone working in the hotel had one, and guests were given a mini iPad to use on arrival for the duration of their stay.

It had certainly been put to the test when Freddie had insisted on playing the guest, and his demands had kept both Gemma and Pippa on their toes for hours. They conceded if they could deal with him asking for things every five minutes, any other guest would be easy.

They hadn't yet had any paying guests. The Valentine's Day wedding was the real test. Gus and Amanda had filled the rooms with Amanda's family and some of Gus's friends; they were also staying after the wedding. Gus had requested his old room, which had been named The Gloucester Old Spot in honour of Geoffrey, the pig, and he'd painted a beautiful picture of him on the door. Amanda had spent the night before the wedding there, and observing tradition, Gus had stayed at home, with Freddie and Connor to try to calm his nerves. Hayley and Fleur were sharing one of the attic rooms so they could get bridesmaid ready.

This morning, they had all had the first ever hotel breakfast in the dining room, cooked by Vicky, who had been trained by Gwen, and served by the three members of staff: Robin, who was a waiter, as well as a barman; Chantelle, who was both helping with the kitchen and serving; and Mickey, who was hired as sort of an assistant to Gemma and Pippa. The job titles were vague because the hotel was far from traditional, but they were managing to fill roles easily and with an impressive calibre of people. Although Harriet insisted on full background checks for all staff.

After the wedding, when the real work began, they had some journalists staying to try to get publicity, and they had managed to procure their first actual paying guest. It was Hector Barber though, and Gemma was convinced he had booked himself in to try to win over Pippa. She didn't care, as long as he was paying, and also, the publicity he was going to generate for the hotel wouldn't hurt. And actually, he was coming to the wedding, due to arrive any minute.

Freddie, the proud licensee, had shown himself to be hard-working and dedicated as he set up the bar, which looked amazing. Gemma was incredibly proud of what he'd done. The garden room had turned out gorgeously opulent, and they'd hosted a preopening reception for the villagers, to see how it would work. The brass-and-marble tables and rich velvet furnishings might have been a little wasted on some of them, especially as they said they preferred floral and complained that it was very dark – which is was, but then it was February and pitch-black outside, and inside Freddie and Charlotte had gone for a sort of seductive look. But, Freddie's cocktails went down well. Gemma had to practically carry Edie to the front door.

No one had broached the subject of Gemma leaving, but she knew she would have to soon. Not only was the apartment too small, but she also didn't feel she'd be needed for much longer. She was sure, although it hadn't been said, that Pippa and Freddie would share the general manager role between them, which made sense. Harriet took charge of all the finances, and as all the systems had been set up, once they were up and running and had ironed out any teething trouble, it would be time to move on. To where, she had no idea. But it didn't scare her like it would have done a short while ago.

The bungalow had been sold, and although she had lost her nan, for the first time in her life she had some money. She wasn't rich, but she had enough to buy a small flat somewhere and think about returning to her studies. She was no longer terrified about leaving Meadowbrook, sure she'd miss it, but she would be here a lot. They weren't going to get rid of her that easily.

For now, Freddie had moved in with Harriet and Connor, which didn't suit any of them. But until the barn conversions were finished – which would be a while – he was technically homeless, as he liked to remind everyone. Gus and Amanda had just exchanged on a bigger house in Parker's Hollow, and they had offered Freddie the temporary use of their old house when they moved, until the barn was ready. Freddie jumped at it. Even though it meant driving to Meadowbrook every day, he said anything was better than Harriet's bossiness. He declared that Connor deserved a medal for putting up with her. Harriet said it was like living with three children. Although Hilda was the least problematic.

Everything was almost in place, Gemma thought with a huge feeling of joy as she inspected the hotel. She'd hired a marketing consultancy, and they'd come up with a strap line: Meadowbrook, the hotel with a beating heart. Which Pippa loved, and their proposals for local advertising, social media and corporate targeting with regard to the painting, animals, gardening and baking breaks was all ready to go. It was exciting, seeing it come to fruition, and Gemma couldn't have been prouder. Of everyone, but also of herself. A new but wonderful feeling.

'Hey, what do you want me to do?' Hector Barber appeared, wearing a smart grey suit and a cravat.

As the hotel was full, he was staying with Freddie at Gus and Amanda's house.

'You're dressed already? The wedding isn't until three,' Pippa replied, straitening his cravat.

He did look good in his suit, Gemma thought, and she had even told Pippa what a gorgeous couple the two of them would make, but Pippa dismissed it – apparently he was too young. Gemma secretly thought it was time she went for someone younger, rather than her usual middle-aged type, but she held her thoughts – for now.

Their friendship was stronger than ever. She had opened up to Pippa in a way she hadn't done with anyone ever and they had talked about abandonment, losing parents, feeling as if they didn't fit in, and she was amazed to know that Pippa – beautiful, sweet, confident Pippa – had felt a bit like she did growing up. She struggled at school, and felt that her siblings were so talented and she came up short. Pippa had even broached the subject of looking for Gemma's mother, but Gemma said she wasn't ready, and she wasn't sure she ever would be. She was terrified of more rejection.

'But I thought if I was ready, I could make myself useful,' Hector protested, interrupting her thoughts.

He had booked to stay at the hotel for at least a month to write this book of his. And to win over Pippa as well, hopefully.

'Come with me; I'm checking all the flowers,' Pippa said, and like a puppy, Hector bounded off after her.

The house/hotel was a flurry of activity as everyone got ready for the wedding. The cars lined up on the drive, to take them down to the church, where Gus would be waiting, nervously. After Freddie made more coffee and stole some toast, he left to do his best man bit. Harriet arrived with Hilda, who had a big bow around her neck, which she was trying to eat; Connor had gone with Freddie to Gus. Fleur and Hayley were giggling and excited. The day was cold but bright, and excitement buzzed around Meadowbrook. Its walls were full of happiness.

Gemma had bought a new outfit for the day; she and Pippa had gone shopping together. It was another first for her, shopping with a friend, and Gemma was finding a life where she wasn't isolated suited her. She was coming out of her shell, and her tongue-tied clumsiness seemed to be lessening as well. She hadn't fallen over or knocked into anything for ages.

Gemma spoke to her nan regularly, and going to church comforted her. She wasn't sure she had found religion, but it was a good place to think about her nan, and John's sermons were priceless. The last one was about how Jesus was obviously a morris dancer. Freddie had been with her, and he could barely hold himself together.

She also sat with Edie, who Gemma told Freddie was her surrogate gran now.

'Surrogate mum,' Edie snapped at her. 'I'm nowhere near old enough to be your gran.'

They were silent as they waited for the bride to come down the Meadowbrook staircase. Pippa was wearing an emerald green dress, with a fake fur jacket – a vintage look – and she was stunning as per usual. Hector hovered next to her, lining up compliment after compliment. They had all had their hair and make-up done professionally, and Gemma felt that she looked better than she thought possible, her hair swept up and her blue velvet suit fitting perfectly. Fleur and Hayley stood with them clutching their bridesmaids' bouquets and wearing simple dresses and stoles – they both looked lovely, neither children nor women yet. Gwen, in her huge hat, twitched nervously as Gerry held on to her. Amanda's family and friends were all chattering excitedly.

When Amanda emerged in a beautiful satin gown, her hair flowing around her shoulders, she looked like The Lady of the Lake, which one of the attic rooms had been named, as it overlooked the lake. She smiled as she clutched a beautiful bouquet of snowdrops, and made her way down the stairs, with her father proudly by her side.

Gemma choked up. She doubted she would ever have this, but she was happy for Amanda rather than sad for herself. She had come a long way. But then, she thought, it was lucky it wasn't her – she would definitely trip on her dress and probably tumble down the stairs, not even making the church. She smiled at Fleur, who smiled back.

'I know I said weddings were lame, but it's kind of nice,' she whispered to Gemma.

'People being happy is nice, remember that,' she said. 'I didn't for a long time, but I will do now.'

'You know, I like having you around, Gemma,' Fleur said and gave her hand a squeeze.

The day passed in a blur. The church service was beautiful. Edie ate a whole bag of sherbet lemons, Gwen cried, Harriet did a lovely reading, Pippa cried, and even Gemma felt tearful when they were declared "man and wife". John, the vicar, didn't mention morris dancing once.

The reception at Meadowbrook was a bit of a squeeze, as most of the village was there, as well as friends and family, and they all crammed in, but it worked. Gemma helped the catering staff that they'd hired in for the day, and they were all kept on their feet. The food was a success, as was the special cocktail that Freddie had designed for the happy couple.

The speeches were touching; even Freddie's was unusually sentimental. Amanda's dad said that he felt his daughter had got it right this time, and he hoped that it was the same for Gus. Fleur choked loudly on a posh cocktail sausage as he said he would like some more grandchildren, and she had to have her back slapped.

'No bloody babies,' Fleur said.

'You don't fancy a little brother or sister?' Gemma asked.

'God no, they'd probably get me to change nappies or babysit for free. And all that crying and puke. Yuk.'

'Charming,' Connor said.

'Anyway, my dad's past all that,' Fleur said.

Harriet's mouth gaped open. Gemma resisted the urge to laugh.

'You do know your dad's younger than Harry, don't you?' Pippa said.

'Oh well, you know, I mean . . .' She grimaced.

'So if you don't want a brother or sister, how about a cousin?' Harriet asked.

'What?' Pippa asked.

'Connor's done it, he's got me up the duff,' Harriet

announced with a smile, which almost stretched across her whole face.

'Oh my God! I'm going to be an auntie again.' Pippa launched herself at Harriet. 'Harry, Connor, that's wonderful.'

'Shush, I didn't want to say anything today. You know, it's Gus and Amanda's day.'

'Yeah, but that wouldn't work, would it?' Fleur pointed out. 'I mean even I was beginning to notice that you've had that same glass of champagne for hours, Aunt Harry.'

'I'm not like Freddie,' Harriet retorted. 'Anyway, we're having the twelve-week scan next week. I should have waited until then, but I'm actually really excited.'

Connor hugged her.

'Congratulations,' Gemma said, hugging them both.

'Well, hopefully, if I manage to look after the new baby as well as I did the calf, I should be a good father,' Connor said.

Harriet shook her head.

'As long as we don't let Fleur name the offspring.' Pippa grinned.

'What's wrong with the calf being called Ed Sheeran?' Fleur asked. 'And we could call yours Beyoncé, if it's a girl, and Calvin if it's a boy, after Calvin Harris.' Her eyes lit up.

'No and no. No baby of mine is being named after a pop star,' Connor stated. 'I let you name some of our animals, Fleur, but I do have a line.'

'Whatever. Anyway, I am happy for you,' Fleur said. 'But don't think I'm going to be a free babysitter.'

'Course you will,' Harriet replied. 'And you're going to change nappies.' She grabbed her niece and hugged her tight.

*

As day turned to evening, Gemma took a glass of champagne – she had barely drunk so far, as she was too busy ensuring it was all running smoothly – and went to get some air. It was a cold, clear night as she sat on a bench, and made a toast to her nan. She thanked her again for everything, and said she hoped that she was proud of her. And happy – most importantly, she hoped her nan was happy now. Because Gemma was happy – she was happier than she'd ever been, anyway.

She felt his presence before she saw him and, as usual, her heart started beating that little bit faster.

'Can I join you?' he asked.

'Sure.'

'Aren't you cold?'

Gemma shivered. 'A bit, but it's such a lovely night. The sky is so clear, the stars bright, I just thought it would be nice to get away from the throng.'

'Well you are missing Edie dancing. She keeps asking the poor DJ for the "Birdie Song", and he's far too young to know what she's talking about.'

'Oh boy, do I need to go and take my surrogate gran, I mean mum, in hand?'

'No, I'm sure she'll wear herself out soon enough. She is a character, though.'

'Everyone around Meadowbrook is.'

'As are you.'

'What?' She turned to face Freddie. 'You used to think I was dull.'

'I never said that.' He took a sip of his drink, which looked like whisky.

'You pretty much did, you know, and you said that I had

no sense of humour, I was clumsy and what was it? Like a little mouse. In fact, when you found out that I stole my boss's CV you said it made me more interesting.' She took a sip of her drink.

'Ah, well, in my defence, you were pretty much like that when you first came here. Not anymore though, not for a long while, actually. Now you are sometimes funny, you're interesting, you're quite attractive now you've lost that permanent scowl, and you have a bit of a sense of humour.' He grinned.

She saw his face lit up by the moon and tried to stop herself from feeling so silly. Yes, he was the most beautiful man she had ever met, but she wasn't a child anymore.

'I guess that's enough of an improvement. I'll take it.' She giggled. 'Although as compliments go, it might not really be up there with the best.'

'OK, so how about this?' He turned to face her. She felt his eyes boring into her very essence. 'You're incredibly special, Gemma, you need to know that. It took me a while to realise it, but your strength and courage, your heart, well it's impressive.'

'Gosh, thank you.' She looked down at her lap.

'And what you've done with this place, it means so much to us; we all want it to be a success, but more than that, we need it to be. Our dad was a hard taskmaster, and he didn't really do failure. We are all ingrained with that, so we need this to work, for him, or his memory, for Meadowbrook, but also for all of us.'

She had never seen him look or sound so serious.

'When Pip first came up with the idea, and I agreed, I'm not sure either of us believed we could pull it off, or Gus and

374

Harry actually, but now, with all the work you've done, I know it's going to be a great hotel. It's different from anything around, and that is down to you, but it is also Meadowbrook. The heart of the house is still there, and that was what we all wanted, yet didn't know how to achieve. You did, though – somehow, you did.'

'I was chasing that all along, you know, trying to make sure the essence of Meadowbrook was reflected in the hotel, but I wasn't sure.' She felt herself floating at his praise.

'But you did, and you did it marvellously.'

'OK, now you are giving me too many compliments. Stop, or I'll start blushing or fall off the bench.'

'See, a bit funny, I told you.' He lapsed into silence.

Gemma saw a bright star and impulsively made a silent wish.

'You know, I'm really fond of you,' he said, suddenly sounding like something from a Jane Austen novel.

'Yeah, and I am of you,' she replied. 'Fond, I mean.'

She felt hot all over and her stomach was churning as he moved in closer.

'OK, not fond of you. Oh, for God's sake.' He drained the rest of the liquid in his glass. 'I think I might have fallen for you,' he said, almost sounding surprised at his words. 'I mean I didn't expect to feel this – you were right. When you first came you were awkward, and quiet, and you didn't seem to know fun if it came up and bit you on the arse.'

'What?' She didn't think she could trust her ears. Was he saying he liked her, or that he didn't?

'Oh, for goodness' sake. The woman who first came to Meadowbrook isn't the one sitting next to me now – I know that. And knowing what you went through, I understand now.

But you are not that quiet, awkward woman anymore; in fact, you're amazing.'

'I am?' She didn't dare look at him.

'And beautiful, but you don't know it. I mean you really are – even Hector asked me why I hadn't hit on you, and he's got very high standards.'

'He has?'

'Well not normally, but recently he does; there was a time he'd go for anything with a weak pulse. Anyway, where was I?'

He had that Freddie look of confusion in his blue eyes, and Gemma felt as if she might drown in them.

'Um, you might like me?' She was still unsure, or perhaps she couldn't believe what she was hearing.

'For God's sake, Gemma Matthews, I have been trying to flirt with you for weeks now.'

'Really? I didn't notice any difference.'

Had she? Or had she just been too scared to see it? Too scared to hope, or perhaps because no one ever flirted with her, she just didn't know when it was happening.

'No shit. You are hard work. And I can flirt with anyone – it's one of my skills – but not you. You're infuriating. You don't know what's right in front of you. You make me want to be a better person, less self-centred, kinder. You make me think, and I don't like thinking. I even spoke to Harriet about you, and when she stopped laughing she said she could see it, she said we brought out the best in each other – you my serious side, me your fun side. But she also said that I should wait because you were grieving.'

'I'm sorry?' Harriet really said that?

'No, you don't need to be sorry. God, you are so bloody

infuriating. I'm telling you I like you, and asking if you feel the same.'

'No, I mean yes. But, Freddie, I can't do this if you don't mean it.'

Did those words actually come out of her mouth? As her heart hammered in her chest, she was sure that the whole of Meadowbrook could hear it.

'I mean it. That night, when your nan died, I realised how much I wanted to be with you. Sleeping next to you in that hotel bed but not touching you, well it wasn't easy. Then I thought I'd drop a few hints, and when I moved out I thought it would be easier, but you seemed to remain oblivious to my charms.'

Had he been dropping hints? How had she missed that? Since her nan's funeral, they had all grown closer, but she still felt that Freddie saw her as a clumsy, slightly dull woman, and she had pushed all her feelings for him right to the dark recesses of her mind, hiding behind work to ignore how she really felt. Although it hadn't been that simple – her heart skipped every time she saw him, and of course she had never forgotten that kiss . . .

'I'm not oblivious. Not since that kiss outside The Darnley.' She didn't dare look at him.

'You remember that?' Freddie asked.

Gemma nodded.

'Me too. I was a bit shocked, as the kiss was amazing, but I didn't see us together then. I mean, you got pissed after one glass of wine for a start, and you also seemed scared of your shadow. You really were a contradiction. When you worked you became someone else, but when you were not hiding behind the hotel you were so different.'

'And now?'

'Now you are all I think about, you bloody crazy woman. Charlotte was my usual type, I'll admit, but I didn't have proper feelings for her – not that she did for me either – and as you know that just fizzled out. But you're different from any woman I've ever been with, in a good way. You make me want to be a better person. I want to be with you, and I promise you that I will never let you down. Well not on purpose, anyway.'

'I feel the same.' She drained the last of her champagne. Was this even happening, or was she dreaming, hallucinating, or had she finally gone mad? 'You bring out the fun in me, Harriet was right with that.'

'I know that we're not supposed to mix work and romance – Charlotte and I are fine even after we broke up. But you have to know that I'm not planning on us splitting up. I'm thinking that we're going to go the distance. But bloody hell, Gemma, I've never had to work this hard with any woman, that's how serious I am.'

'Really?'

She turned to him, searching his face for any hint of a joke, but he started staring at her in a way that no one had ever looked at her before. She thought she might faint.

'Well apart from anything else, I've never seen anyone drink a minibar in the way you did.' He laughed.

She gulped. 'I need you to mean it, Freddie,' she said again. 'I can't play at this. I've never . . .' The words choked her, hope strangled her, fear engulfed her.

'I'm not playing now, and nor will I ever be. For a start, if anything bad happens both Pippa and Harriet will skin me alive.'

'That's true,' she admitted, and she had seen first hand how scary both of them could be.

'You are part of the family, so we can't enter into this lightly, but I know, it just feels right in the way no one has done for me.'

'But really, Freddie? I mean me? I mean—'

'Will you shut up so I can kiss you?'

'God, I hope so,' Gemma replied and as she let his lips find hers, she knew that this was the best Valentine's Day ever.

Freddie was right: she wasn't the woman who had turned up at Meadowbrook a year ago. For the first time in her life, she was who she was supposed to be. And where she was supposed to be.

They broke away, and she didn't know if she would ever stop smiling.

'I want to be the man who puts that smile on your face every single day,' Freddie said, his arms still wrapped around her.

'You are,' she replied. 'You absolutely are.'

Acknowledgements

It has been a real treat to be able to return to Meadowbrook and the Singer family, so I hope everyone enjoys the book. I certainly loved writing it.

Thanks go to my fabulous editor, Victoria, who has made this book even more of a joy than it already was. I will definitely miss you. And also to all the team at Avon, I feel very lucky to work with you all.

For continued support I am forever grateful to my agents, Northbank Talent, especially Kate, Diane and Chloe. As always, it's a pleasure working with you.

I have the usual guilt of being a working mum, but my son Xavier has always been forgiving of me, even when I'm typing and trying to cook his tea at the same time – rarely works. But he is the light of my life, and one day I hope he might even be pleased his mum is a writer! There is a lot of behind the scenes support that I am so lucky to have: my family, Mum and Thom, The Langmeads, Becky, Helen, Martin, Jak, Megan and Rory. I am forever grateful to have you in our lives.

My friends who help me hang on to a semblance of sanity: Jo, Tammy, Jessica, Jas, Tam and Tyne. Also thanks to Kate and Dany, two wonderful authors who always show me such support and kindness as well as friendship. Big, huge, thanks to Sue who kindly took my author photos, and I actually love them!

I want to give a big thanks to all those who read my books. Book bloggers who help spread the word, thanks for the wonderful job you do. And of course to all my readers. Those who have left such kind reviews, especially. I so appreciate each and every one of you.

Follow me on Twitter: @faithbleasdale, or visit my Faith Bleasdale – author Facebook page.

Loved your time at Meadowbrook Manor? Why not head
back to where it all began . . .

One divided family, one life-changing year...

If you love Faith Bleasdale, why not try Tracy Corbett next?

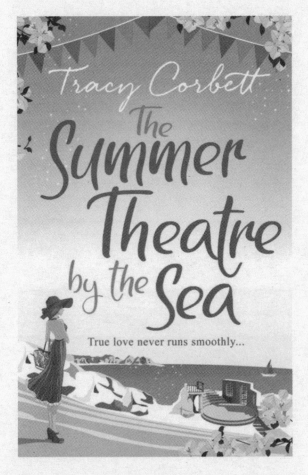

The Saunders sisters need a bit of Cornish magic
this summer...

If you enjoyed *Secrets at Meadowbrook Manor*, then you'll love the Little Cornish Isles series.

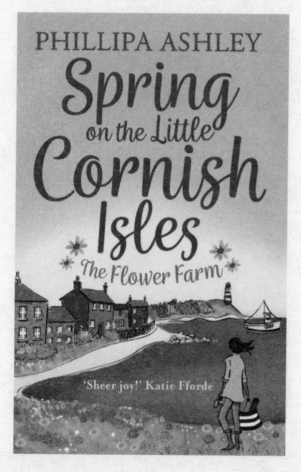

Escape to the Little Cornish Isles with Phillipa Ashley.

Why not sail away with Maddie Please this year?

It's time for Alexa to discover that sometimes romance can surprise you!